Royal Seductions: Diamonds

MICHELLE CELMER

All rights reserved including the right of reproduction in whole or in part in any form. This edition is published by arrangement with Harlequin Books S.A.

This is a work of fiction. Names, characters, places, locations and incidents are purely fictional and bear no relationship to any real life individuals, living or dead, or to any actual places, business establishments, locations, events or incidents. Any resemblance is entirely coincidental.

This book is sold subject to the condition that it shall not, by way of trade or otherwise, be lent, resold, hired out or otherwise circulated without the prior consent of the publisher in any form of binding or cover other than that in which it is published and without a similar condition including this condition being imposed on the subsequent purchaser.

® and ™ are trademarks owned and used by the trademark owner and/or its licensee. Trademarks marked with ® are registered with the United Kingdom Patent Office and/or the Office for Harmonisation in the Internal Market and in other countries.

Published in Great Britain 2014
by Mills & Boon, an imprint of Harlequin (UK) Limited,
Eton House, 18-24 Paradise Road, Richmond, Surrey, TW9 1SR

ROYAL SEDUCTIONS: DIAMONDS © 2014 Harlequin Books S.A.

The King's Convenient Bride, The Illegitimate Prince's Baby and An Affair with the Princess were first published in Great Britain by Harlequin (UK) Limited.

The King's Convenient Bride © 2008 Michelle Celmer
The Illegitimate Prince's Baby © 2008 Michelle Celmer
An Affair with the Princess © 2008 Michelle Celmer

ISBN: 978-0-263-91189-3
eBook ISBN: 978-1-472-04484-6

05-0614

Harlequin (UK) Limited's policy is to use papers that are natural, renewable and recyclable products and made from wood grown in sustainable forests. The logging and manufacturing processes conform to the legal environmental regulations of the country of origin.

Printed and bound in Spain
by Blackprint CPI, Barcelona

Bestselling author **Michelle Celmer** lives in southeastern Michigan with her husband, their three children, two dogs and two cats. When she's not writing or busy being a mum, you can find her in the garden or curled up with a romance novel. And if you twist her arm really hard you can usually persuade her into a day of power shopping.

Michelle loves to hear from readers. Visit her website at: www.michellecelmer.com, or write to her at PO Box 300, Clawson, MI 48017, USA.

THE KING'S
CONVENIENT BRIDE

BY
MICHELLE CELMER

To my mum, Karen,
who is hands down my most devoted fan.

One

Though she had been preparing for this day for eight years, as the limo pulled up to the palace steps and Hannah Renault caught her first glimpse of the prince—make that the *king*—waiting to welcome her, she trembled in her ecru Gucci pumps.

Wearing his royal dress uniform, King Phillip Lindall Augustus Mead stood at the top of the stairs flanked by what had to be the entire palace staff. A collection of medals and commendations on his jacket glittered in the sun and a gilded sword hung at his hip.

Outside the gates, residents of Morgan Isle crowded to get their first glimpse of their soon-to-be queen.

Aka: *Her.*

The limo stopped at the base of a gold-rimmed red carpet. The door swung open and a gloved hand appeared to help her out.

She smoothed the skirt of her dark blue linen suit. *This is it,* she told herself. This is the day you've been dreaming of. The time to make a good impression on your husband-to-be and, from the looks of it, half the country. So, whatever you do, as you're climbing those stairs, *don't trip.*

With all the grace and dignity a woman could manage while climbing out of a vehicle, her heart fluttering madly in her chest, Hannah stepped into the balmy sunshine. Beyond the gates a cheer broke out among the onlookers.

Warring with the sudden, intense urge to turn around and dive back into the limo, she took a deep breath, straightened her spine and lifted her chin high. As per the instructions she received from the royal social secretary, she stood her ground and waited for the king's formal greeting. She held her breath as he descended the steps and a deafening hush fell over the crowd, as though they were holding their breath with her. *Don't be nervous,* she told herself, but nervous didn't even come close to what she was actually feeling. She bordered more along the lines of *terrified.*

Just breathe, Hannah. In and out. You can do this.

It had been two long years since she had seen her fiancé face-to-face, and he was more handsome, more heart-stoppingly beautiful than she remembered.

As instructed, the instant the king's foot hit the bottom step, Hannah stepped forward and dipped into a routinely practiced curtsy. With a bow of her head, and in a wobbly voice, she said, "Your Highness."

"My lady," he returned in a deep, rich voice, with proper British inflection, then offered his hand. A small burst of energy arced between their fingers an instant before they actually touched. When she met his eyes, something warm and inviting swam in their smoky-gray depths. Taking her hand gently in his own, he bent at the waist and brushed his lips across her skin. "Welcome home."

Her stomach bottomed out and her legs went weak while thunderous applause rattled her eardrums.

You must appear regal and confident, but never *cold,* she had been told a million times from her royal-appointed etiquette coach.

But under the circumstances, it was all she could do to stay upright and conscious.

This was really happening. In two weeks she would marry this handsome, powerful man. In two weeks, she would be a *queen.*

Shaking with excitement and fear, from her toes all the way to the ends of her hair, she allowed him to lead her up the steps, chanting to herself: *please don't trip, please don't trip.*

Picking up on her abject terror, and in a serious break of royal tradition, he slipped his arm around her waist and drew her close to his side. Then he dipped his head and said in a low whisper, so only she could hear, "Relax. The worst is over."

She was so grateful she nearly dissolved into tears right there on the steps. He felt so solid and sturdy and he radiated self-assurance. If there were only a way she could absorb a bit of that confidence for herself.

They reached the top step, where they would stop and she would formally greet the staff and country. But in another breech of ceremony, the king swept past the receiving lines and led her directly to the enormous, gilded double doors that, seemingly on their own, swung open to welcome her inside.

He led her through the cavernous foyer. Two royal attendants were close behind them, the soles of their shoes clicking against the polished marble floor. He stopped in front of a pair of ceiling-high, carved mahogany doors.

"Give us a minute," he told the two attendants, which Hannah took to mean they were not to be disturbed. Then he ushered her inside and closed the door behind them.

She found herself surrounded on three sides by bookshelves that climbed high to kiss the outer rim of an ornately painted cathedral ceiling. She'd never seen so many books in one room. Not even in the university library back home. Furniture upholstered in a rich, deep red leather formed a sitting area in the center of the room. He led her to a chair and ordered, "Sit."

Her legs were so shaky it was that or fall over, so she sat, and took what was probably her first full breath since the limo pulled up to the wrought iron gates.

"Shall I get the smelling salts?" he asked.

For an instant, she thought he might be angry, and she couldn't really blame him, considering how seriously she had blown it, but, when she looked up, he wore the shadow of an amused grin.

She shook her head. "I think I'm okay now."

He crossed the room to the wet bar, chose a decanter and poured a splash of amber liquid into a glass. She thought it was for him, but then he carried it over and pressed it into her hand. "Sip. *Slowly.*"

She sipped and it burned a path of liquid fire down her throat all the way to her belly, temporarily stealing the air from her lungs. When she could breath again, she wheezed, "I'm sorry."

He crouched down beside her chair, leaning on the arm. "For what?"

"I really blew it out there."

"How's that?"

"I was supposed to greet the staff."

He shrugged. "So, you'll greet them later."

"And we were supposed to turn and wave to the people outside the gates."

Again with the shrug. "What they don't know won't hurt them."

She worried her lower lip with her teeth. "But I don't want people to think I'm a snob."

"Are you?"

His question threw her. "Well…no. Of course not. But—"

"Then don't worry about it."

"Isn't it kind of important that the people of the country like me?"

"They will," he assured her, as if he had no doubt.

"What about the press?" Reporters in the States were sometimes brutal, but she'd been warned the media in Europe could be downright vicious.

Phillip didn't look the least bit concerned. "See this?" he asked, indicating his left jacket pocket. "This is where I keep the press. In other words, you have nothing to worry about."

Oh, well, that was good to know. It seemed as

though he had all his bases covered. And why wouldn't he? He was the richest, most powerful man in the country.

She took another sip of her drink, felt the knots in her belly begin to unravel. "My coach insisted I was prepared for this. You can bet she's going to hear from me."

"You did fine. You will grow accustomed to it."

She sure hoped so.

A moment of awkward silence followed and she racked her brain for something to say. Since turning sixteen, everything she had done, all that she had learned, had been in preparation for this day. Now that she was finally here, she was at a total loss.

It wasn't helping that, technically, she was supposed to be marrying a prince. She should have had an indeterminate number of years as a princess, time to adjust to the lifestyle. But the queen's death had unexpectedly moved plans forward.

Phillip, now as king, needed a queen to stand by his side. Even more important, he needed an heir. So, instead of a courtship, in which they would have six months to get to know one another before they took the plunge, they had two very short weeks before they said their *I do's*.

Two weeks.

She downed the contents of her glass, the sting of

the alcohol sucking the air from her lungs and making her eyes well up.

His expression somewhere between amusement and curiosity, he took the glass from her and set it on a nearby table. "Feeling better?"

She nodded, but it was pretty obvious from the crooked, wry smile he wore that he didn't believe her. And it dawned on her, as she glanced around the quiet, empty room, that for the first time since this marriage had been arranged, she and Phillip were alone.

Totally alone.

In the past, to keep things proper and by the book, on the rare occasions they visited each other, there had always been a chaperone present. Though Hannah's experience with the queen had been limited to a few obligatory and brief meetings, she'd heard the rumors. She'd heard that the queen was cold, heartless and ruthlessly demanding.

It was her way or the highway.

But the queen was gone now, and right here, in this empty room, there was no one to stop them from…whatever.

Suddenly she felt ultra aware of his presence. The clean, crisp scent of his aftershave. The weight of his gaze as he studied her. He was just so…*there*.

And so close.

It would take little more than a fraction of movement and she could touch his sleeve. With a lift of her hand she could brush her fingertip across his smooth cheek. And the idea of touching him made her legs feel all wobbly again.

"If you keep chewing your lip that way, there'll be nothing left for me," he teased, and something playfully wicked flashed behind his eyes.

Oh, boy.

In all of the years she'd studied in preparation for this marriage, she had learned about things like etiquette and social graces, bloodlines and royal custom, but no one ever taught her about this kind of stuff. Sure, it had been drilled in her head that she would be expected to produce at least one heir, preferably more, but all advice stopped *outside* the bedroom door.

And to say she was a novice was a gross understatement.

Though her high school girlfriends and college sorority sisters often questioned her sanity, she had made the decision a long time ago, even before the arranged marriage, that she would save herself for her husband on their wedding night.

She and Phillip had never kissed. Never so much as held hands. Not that she hadn't wanted to. But it wouldn't have been *proper.* Right now, here in this room, there wasn't a single thing to stop them.

The idea made her both excited and terrified at the same time. The truth of the matter was, she barely knew him, and that had never been more evident to her than at this very moment.

He leaned forward a fraction and she just about jumped out of her skin. With an amused grin, he asked, "Do I make you nervous, Hannah?"

She took a deep breath, fighting the urge to gnaw her lip. "You're a king. It is a tad intimidating."

"I'm just a man."

Yeah, kind of like The Beatles were *just* a rock-and-roll band or the Mona Lisa is *just* a painting.

"I've been anticipating this day for a really long time," she said, hoping her voice didn't sound as wobbly to his ears as it did to her own.

"Well then, I'll do my best not to disappoint you." His eyes searched her face and she wondered what he was looking for. What did he see when he looked at her? Did he know deep in his heart, just as she did, that they were perfectly suited? Was he as excited about the future as she was?

Though her parents insisted she wait until she was eighteen before making the decision to marry Phillip, from the day she met him, she knew that she would someday be his wife. Had he felt it, too?

With all of her dedication and careful planning, how could their life together not be storybook perfect?

"You are beautiful." He lifted one hand to her face, brushed the backs of his fingers across the curve of her jaw. Her skin warmed and tingled and a funny tickle rippled through her belly. "Does it strike you odd that we'll be married in two weeks, and yet I've never even kissed you?"

"It would have been difficult with the chaperone watching our every move. Of course, that was the point of the chaperone, I guess."

He leaned in the tiniest bit and her heart went berserk. "There's no chaperone here."

"Well," she said, with a confidence she'd dredged up from God only knew where. "I guess now is your big chance."

A grin curled his mouth. He slipped his fingers across her cheek, cupped her face with one large but gentle hand, and goose bumps broke out across her skin. "I guess it is."

Two

Maybe it wasn't proper, but as he leaned in she felt herself tipping forward to meet him halfway. Since she was sixteen years old, she had imagined kissing him, so sue her if she was more than a little enthusiastic.

Her eyes slipped closed and she felt the whisper of his breath, then his lips brushed hers…

Across the room the doors flew open and Hannah was so startled, she shot to her feet.

Phillip sighed and sat back on his heels. Leave it to his sister, Sophie, to kill a moment.

Sophie merely smiled.

He rose to his feet to stand beside his fiancée. She was red-faced with embarrassment, or maybe arousal. Or perhaps a bit of both. "Hannah, you remember my sister, Princess Sophie?"

"Of course," Hannah said, executing a flawless curtsy. "It's so nice to see you again, Your Highness."

"As I'm sure my brother will tell you, I don't care much for titles." She offered Hannah her hand for a firm, very unroyal shake. "From now on, it's just plain old Sophie, okay?"

Hannah nodded, her lip clamped between her teeth. A habit he found rather charming. If it weren't for his sister and her most inconvenient timing, he might be the one chewing that plump, tender flesh.

"I wanted to let you know that the receiving line has been moved to the foyer," Sophie told him. And added with a wry grin, "If you're *ready,* of course."

He turned to his bride-to-be. "Hannah?"

"Is there a powder room I could use first? I have the feeling I gnawed off the last of my lipstick."

"Of course." He gestured to the door. "Right through there."

"I'll try to hurry."

"Take all the time you need."

He watched her cross the room, noting that in

spite of her apprehension, she carried herself with the utmost grace and dignity. It was hard to believe it had been two years since their last meeting. And the fault was entirely his own. Since his father's death he had been too busy to give his impending marriage much attention. There wasn't even supposed to be a marriage for at least another year. Not that he would be any less opposed to the idea then, as he was now.

If it were up to him, he would *never* tie the knot. The idea of being chained to a single woman for the rest of his life sounded so…claustrophobic. But he had a duty to his country. One that he did not take lightly.

And unlike his father, from whom Phillip had inherited his restless nature, he intended to be faithful to his wife.

"You certainly don't waste any time," his sister said. "Although, in the future, you might want to lock the door."

He shot her a warning look.

"It's a good thing the powder room has only one exit," she said. "Or I fear your betrothed might just make a run for it."

He wouldn't even justify that with a response. "Surely you have something better to do."

Sophie grinned. There was nothing she loved more than ruffling his feathers. From the time she was old enough to form words, she had been the consummate, bratty younger sister.

"Your intended is quite lovely," she said.

"Yes, quite," he agreed. Everything a king could want or expect in a wife.

Though at first the idea of an arranged marriage had been archaic even to him, at the insistence of his mother—who had rejected the concept of the word *no*, unless, of course, she was the one speaking it—he had flown to the States to meet the young woman.

It had been clear to him immediately that at the age of sixteen Hannah already possessed great potential. Despite the eight-year age difference, he found her undeniably attractive. And he could see that the feeling was mutual. And even better, were he to acquiesce, it would keep his parents off his back. At his own request, future meetings were arranged, and plans for a courtship were set in motion.

By eighteen she had blossomed into a woman of exceptional beauty and poise, and their feelings had matured from ones of sexual curiosity to intense physical attraction.

She was everything a king could want in a mate, and right now her innocence, her eagerness to please, appealed to him. Sadly, he was easily bored and quite sure that the novelty would soon wear off.

"Do you think she has the slightest clue what she's getting herself into?" Sophie asked.

"The slightest." There was only so much she could learn from a book or a tutor. The rest would come through experience.

"While I have you here, I was hoping to have a word with you."

He felt an argument coming on. "If this is about what I think it's about—"

"He's our *brother*. You could at least hear him out."

"Half brother," he said firmly. A product of their father's infidelity. "I owe him nothing."

"What he is proposing would ensure the stability of our empire for *generations*."

"And his own, no doubt."

She looked at him as though he were loony. "You say that like it's a *bad* thing."

"I don't trust him."

"If it's the crown that concerns you, he wants no part of it."

Not unlike Sophie, he thought, who had spent the better part of her twenty-five years expressing her dislike of the monarchy's rules. But in the case of their half brother, Ethan Rafferty, their father's blood ran through his veins. As a result, he did have a claim to the crown. If something were to happen to Phillip, he would be next in line.

For Phillip, that was unacceptable.

"I won't discuss this," Phillip told her. "Period."

Her cheeks flushed with frustration. "Bloody hell, you're stubborn!"

She was one to talk. "That distinction, dear Sophie, is not limited to me."

The door to the powder room opened, and Hannah emerged. Grateful for the interruption, he crossed the room to meet her. "Feeling better?"

Hannah nodded. "I think I'm ready to do this. And I'm sorry again for getting so freaked out."

"Were you?" Sophie asked from behind him. "I'm quite sure no one noticed."

Hannah cracked an appreciative smile. The first one he had seen since she arrived.

He offered his arm to her. "Shall I escort you?"

She looked from his arm to the door, then took a deep breath. "I appreciate the offer, but I think that after what happened outside, it's important that I stand on my own two feet."

"As you wish." He opened the door for her and watched, feeling an unexpected surge of pride as she swept out into the foyer.

Sophie stepped up beside him and, in a quiet voice, said, "Impressive."

"Indeed."

"You think she's ready for this?"

He nodded, and said with genuine honesty, "I do."

"I agree," she said. "The real question, Your Highness, is are *you* ready for *her?*"

This day turned out to be, by far, the most demanding, frightening and exciting in Hannah's life. After the receiving line, which in itself took the better part of an hour, they attended a luncheon in her honor. Following a meal she had been too self-conscious to do more than pick at, she and the king mingled with dozens of state officials and their spouses. So many, in fact, that remembering all of their names would take nothing short of a miracle.

After lunch there was a photo shoot in the garden, followed by a short press conference in which she and the king were bombarded by the reporters with questions of her background and education, how she felt about becoming queen, their upcoming nuptials and the plans for the gala to celebrate the country's 500th anniversary.

To stand beside the king, to feel the air of confidence and supremacy all but spilling from his pores, was as fascinating as it was intimidating. He was the most powerful man in the country and he embraced the designation. And for what wasn't the first time that day, she couldn't help but wonder if she'd gotten in way over her head. Years of training and preparation and still she felt overwhelmed. She knew though, had her father been there, he would have been so proud of her, and that was all that mattered.

She endured another exhausting evening meal shared with a new blur of names and faces she barely had a hope of remembering, although there was one woman she recognized from earlier in the day. And only because of the way she watched Hannah so intently. She was dark and very beautiful, close to Hannah's age, if not a year or two older. She had the kind of voluptuous figure that turned men's heads. Hannah considered going to talk to her, but that would require leaving Phillip's side, and she wasn't ready to do that yet. But every time Hannah looked her way, the woman was watching. Shamelessly and blatantly. But just as Hannah began to feel uncomfortable, the woman vanished. She craned her neck, checking every corner of the room, but didn't see her.

That was odd. And she couldn't shake the feeling she had imagined her.

After another hour of small talk and chatter, the king finally bid the guests good-night and offered to escort Hannah to her suite.

She was so exhausted, the thought of collapsing into bed made her want to weep with relief.

Offering his arm, Phillip led her to the private residence at the north end of the palace. Though it may have been used only by the family and limited staff, it was no less luxurious than the common areas. More modern, and not nearly so formal, but dripping in extravagance and style. Her parents' estate in Seattle was by no means small, but wealth of this magnitude was foreign to her.

It would take some getting used to.

The instant they were inside with the door closed, he unfastened the button at the collar of his jacket and, just like that, transformed back into the less intimidating version of himself—the compassionate man who had whisked her up the palace steps and inside to the sanctuary of the library.

"You did well today," he told her.

"To be honest, it's all a bit of a blur." And all she could comprehend at the present moment was the pain in her feet. The desperate need to kick out of the pumps the salesgirl had assured her would spare her any discomfort. *Like walking on a cloud, my foot.*

"Would it be possible to get a photo and bio of the government officials?" she asked.

He regarded her curiously. "What for?"

"So I can learn their names. I met so many people tonight, I have no hope of remembering them all and I don't want to appear rude. That should include information of their spouses and families as well. I'm assuming you can do that."

The king looked surprised and impressed. "Of course. You'll have it first thing tomorrow."

They stopped outside what she assumed was her suite. "I have to apologize for the temporary accommodations," he said. "This suite is somewhat small."

She didn't care about the size. So long as it had a tub to soak in and a bed to melt into, he wasn't going to hear her complaining. "I'm sure it will be fine."

He opened the door. "You'll stay here while the permanent suite is being renovated. In fact, I believe you have an appointment with the decorator tomorrow afternoon."

She didn't want to think any further ahead than a hot bubble bath, but as he led her inside, she found herself facing three more new faces. Two were dressed in formal black-and-white maid's uniforms and the other in a modest, navy-blue pinstripe business suit.

"Hannah, I'd like to introduce you to your staff. Miss Cross and Miss Swan, your personal maids, and your personal assistant, Miss Pryce."

All three curtsied and said in unison, "My lady."

She smiled and said, "It's a pleasure to meet you."

Miss Pryce stepped forward, a leather-bound folder tucked under one arm. "I have your schedule, my lady, and your agenda for tomorrow."

"My fiancée is quite exhausted," Phillip said. "I think this can wait until morning."

She nodded and retreated a step. "My apologies, sir."

With little more than a flick of his wrist and tilt of his head, he dismissed her staff. "Your suite includes a sitting room, sleeping chamber and office."

"And a bathroom, I hope."

He smiled. "Of course. With all the amenities you could possibly need. In your office you'll see that you've been supplied with all the computer equipment you asked for."

"Thanks." She turned in a circle, taking in the decor. The room was decorated in neutral shades of brown and beige and the furniture looked comfortable and inviting. It was more than large enough to suit her. Larger even than her residence on her parents' estate. She wasn't sure why they would go through the trouble of decorating a suite especially for her since, after the wedding, she would be sharing a suite with her husband.

Or maybe they would be moving into the new suite together. In which case it was nice of him to let her do the decorating. To extend that sort of trust to a woman he barely knew. "It's lovely, and more than adequate."

"Excellent." He removed his jacket and tossed it over the arm of a chair. Underneath he wore a plain, white long-sleeved knit shirt, similar to a mock tur-tleneck. It clung to the contours of his chest and arms, accentuating what appeared to be toned, defined muscle underneath. Even without the bulk of his jacket, the expansive width of his shoulders was impressive to say the least.

She wondered how it would feel to put her hands on him. How would his arms feel around her?

The thought of him touching her, and their almost-kiss in the library, had her blushing from her toes to the ends of her hair.

Once again they were alone together. Just the two of them, but this time in her suite. Mere steps away from the bedroom. And Hannah seriously doubted that Princess Sophie, who she had seen sneaking off with one of the guests shortly after dinner, would be around to interrupt them this time.

Is that why he'd sent the staff away? Did he have…*plans* for them?

He walked across the room to a cabinet that held a dozen or so decanters of alcohol, chose one and poured them each a drink. He turned to her, looking surprised to see that she was still rooted firmly to the same spot.

"It's been a long day," he said, walking toward her. "Sit down. Relax."

Her feet were throbbing, but the idea of taking off

her shoes while he was in the room made her feel so...*vulnerable.* "You're staying?"

"Would you prefer I leave?"

"No, of course not. I just... Is this okay?"

He set both drinks on the table beside the couch. "Is what okay?"

"You being in my suite. You know...before the wedding."

He shrugged. "Why wouldn't it be?"

"It's not against the rules?"

"Is there a reason it should be?"

Why did she get the feeling he was making this up as he went along? "Next you'll be telling me it's all right for you to tuck me into bed."

His mouth tipped up in a feral smile. "If that's what you wish."

He was teasing her again, and she was a little stunned to realize that she was teasing him right back. It was...empowering. And a little scary.

"As you pointed out earlier, I'm a king. I make the rules." He gestured to the couch. "Join me?"

Her feet were killing her, and God knows it would feel absolutely wonderful to sit down. Maybe just for a little while.

She took a step forward, then hesitated.

"Don't worry. I don't bite." A grin split his face. "Unless, of course, you would *like* me to."

She bit her lip.

"You can trust me," he assured her.

Maybe that wasn't the problem. Maybe it wasn't Phillip's behavior that she questioned.

Maybe it was herself she didn't trust.

Three

Phillip sighed.

He had things to do tonight. A long-awaited task to accomplish, but she wasn't making this easy. Of course, he probably wasn't helping matters. But he did so very much enjoy teasing her. "I promise to be on my best behavior."

She surprised him again by folding her arms across her chest and saying, "With no frame of reference, how can I begin to know what your best behavior is?"

He liked Hannah, and was saddened by the thought that it wouldn't last. That someday soon he would grow bored with her. But he might as well enjoy it while it lasted. "How about I promise to keep my hands to myself? All right?"

She considered that, and he wasn't sure if she looked relieved or disappointed. Finally, she nodded. "All right."

She walked to the couch and sat primly on the edge of the cushion—knees pressed firmly together and tipped to one side—smoothing the creases from her skirt and jacket. He sat beside her, far enough away that it would be considered proper by anyone's standards.

"Feel free to remove the torture devices from your feet," he said, and at her look of confusion, added, "Your shoes. They look uncomfortable."

She glanced down, a pained look on her face, then blatantly lied to him by saying, "They feel fine."

Why did she have to be so…difficult? He wasn't exactly looking forward to what he had to do, but it would go much more smoothly if she would just relax.

He handed her a drink, watched as she took a sip, then he took a healthy swallow of his own. Hopefully the alcohol would loosen her up a bit. Make this less painful for both of them. Not that he thought she would voice an objection once he got started.

He had considered the garden as a more suitable location. More romantic, he supposed, but more than likely someone would have seen. In a life so very public, he felt he deserved a few private moments. Especially for an act as intimate as the one he was about to perform.

Maybe it was like taking off a bandage. The faster he did it, the less it would sting.

He downed the last of his brandy then took Hannah's barely touched glass from her and set them both on the table.

Well, here goes.

With Hannah watching him curiously, he lowered himself to the floor beside the couch on one knee and produced the small velvet box from his pants pocket.

Hannah's eyes went wide and her mouth fell open in surprise before she caught herself and snapped it shut again.

He flipped the box open to reveal the fourteen-carat diamond ring that had been passed down through his family for the past twelve generations. Hannah gasped softly.

Breaking his promise not to touch her, he took her hand in his. "Hannah Renault, would you do me the honor of becoming my wife?"

In a soft, breathy voice, she said, "Of course I will."

He lifted the ring from the satin pillow that was inside the velvet box and slipped it on her ring finger, feeling the sickening sensation of his freedom slithering from his grasp.

He let go of her hand and she stared in wonder at the enormous rock on her finger. When she looked back up at him, a pool of tears welled in her eyes.

Bloody hell, did she have to go and do that? As if this wasn't awkward enough. But for her sake, he did his best to hide his discomfort. Besides, what woman wouldn't get a little misty-eyed to have such a fine piece of jewelry in her possession?

"I've never seen anything so beautiful," she said wistfully.

Or so big, he imagined. If there was one constant with women, it was a love of things that sparkled. "It's been in my family for generations."

"It's amazing."

The moisture building in her eyes hovered precariously at the edge of lids, threatening to spill over at any second. A good reason for him to—as the Americans liked to say—get the hell out of Dodge.

He shifted his weight, preparing to pull himself to his feet, but before he got the chance, she vaulted off the couch, threw her arms around his neck and hugged him.

In all of her preparations for this marriage, not even in the instructions that had been sent to her, breaking down the events of her first day in the palace, had one word been mentioned about a formal proposal. Which, in her mind, could mean only one thing.

He had gotten down on one knee before her not out of duty, but simply because he *wanted* to.

It was the sweetest, most romantic thing anyone had ever done for her. Like her fairy-tale dream coming true. And it was the only logical way to explain how, one minute she was sitting across from him, and the next she was pressed up against him, her arms linked tightly around his neck.

She felt his arms circle her, his large palms settle on and cover the entire width of her hips. He smelled masculine and inviting. And she liked the way their bodies fit together just right. The warm, solid feel of him. He made her feel…safe.

But was she really? His hands were mere inches from parts of her that had never been touched by a man. Parts that shouldn't be touched for at least another two weeks. Then his grip on her tightened almost imperceptibly.

A warm shiver of awareness coursed through her from her head all the way to her toes and she was suddenly hyperconscious of not only his body, but of her own. The slight quickening of her breath. The tingle in her breasts where they crushed the solid wall of muscle in his chest. She could even feel the heat of his skin seeping through the layers of their clothing.

A hot curl of desire started in her belly and spiraled outward in a thrilling rush. Into her arms and legs, her fingers and toes, and some very interesting and wicked places in between.

Every scent and sound and sensation seemed to jumble together, making her feel dizzy and confused. There was an incredible energy building between them. She could feel his breath deepen, his pulse quicken to keep time with her own frantically beating heart.

It was frightening and exciting and arousing all at the same time. And though she knew it was wrong, it felt too good to stop.

Phillip moved his head and Hannah felt the scrape of his beard stubble against her cheek. The warm rush of his breath on her ear. *Pull away,* her conscience warned. *You do not want to do this.*

Oh yes, I do, answered back the part of her that had been looking forward to this for the past eight years.

His lips were so close. So near she could almost taste them. He moved his head, nuzzled her cheek lightly, and everything inside her melted to hot liquid. If she hadn't already been sitting, her legs surely would have buckled out from under her.

Anticipation buzzed between them like an electric, live wire. He turned just a little and she felt his lips…on her cheek, at the corner of her mouth….

His mouth brushed hers and though she was expecting it, longing for it even, it still surprised her. And scared her half to death. It felt too wonderful, and she had come too far, saved herself for too long, to turn back now.

Gathering up the absolute last shred of restraint left in her, she turned and rested her head on his shoulder. "You promised me that you would keep your hands to yourself."

His voice sounded rough when he spoke. "That's not exactly fair, considering you started it."

She couldn't argue with that. She had literally thrown herself at him. The only person to blame here was herself. "You're right. But we have to stop."

"No, we don't." His hands slid from her hips to the indent of her waist. He nuzzled the tender spot just below her ear and she shivered. "You can't tell me that you don't want this as much as I do."

Of course she did, maybe even more, but that wasn't the point. She dropped her arms from around his neck and flattened her palms on his chest. "As you get to know me, you'll find I have this annoying habit of doing things by the book. And we're not married yet."

"No one will know."

"*I'll* know."

He sighed, a long, tired sound tinged with frustration. Then lifted her up, as though she weighed nothing, and deposited her back on the couch.

Since she didn't trust herself and she clearly couldn't rely on him to apply the brakes, from now on there would be no more temptation. That meant no kissing or touching of any kind until after the wedding. "We've waited this long. Two more weeks aren't going to kill us."

He pulled himself to his feet. "Speak for yourself."

She diverted her gaze, finding that it both embarrassed her and gave her a depraved thrill to know that touching her had aroused him. "Are you angry with me?"

The hard lines of his face softened. "Of course not. If more people honored their values the way you do, the world would be a much better place."

Of all the things he could have possibly said to her, that had to have been the sweetest. And he said it so honestly, as though he really meant it. Maybe he wasn't so tough as he liked people to think.

"I should go," he said. "You've had a long day."

"I am exhausted," she admitted. With the time change and the long trip, she had been up for more than twenty-four hours straight.

"There's a directory by the phone if you should need anything." He grabbed his jacket from the chair and walked to the door.

She followed, several steps behind. "Thank you."

He stopped, hand on the doorknob, and turned to her. "For what?"

She shrugged, suddenly feeling embarrassed. She was twenty-four years old and still so terribly naive about certain things. But anxious to learn. "I don't know. *Everything,* I guess."

"You're welcome." He pulled the door open, then hesitated. "By the way, where do you keep your lipstick?"

"Lipstick?"

"You carried no handbag, yet you've freshened your lipstick numerous times throughout the course of the day. I was just wondering where you were hiding it."

It was funny that he had even noticed. Although, she had the sneaking suspicion there wasn't much that the king missed.

She smiled. "A proper lady, Your Highness, never tells."

"I had a feeling you would say that." With a shake of his head, he stepped into the hall, then turned back one last time. "I should warn you, *my lady,* that I am used to getting what I want when I want it. Though we may not officially consummate this relationship until after the wedding." His mouth curled into a hungry, feral smile. "I can't promise that in the meantime there won't be a bit of fooling around."

At first she thought he was only teasing her again, but she could see, by the look in his eyes, that he was dead serious.

She opened her mouth to respond, but nothing came out. What could she possibly say? It occurred to her, not for the first time that day, that she was *way* out of her league.

He flashed her the smile of a man who knew he had just hit his mark. "Good night, Hannah. Sleep well."

The door snapped shut quietly behind him, and she didn't doubt for an instant that he would make good on his threat.

And damned if she barely slept a wink all night.

Four

Hannah was awake, showered and dressed when Miss Pryce knocked on the door to her suite the next morning at 9:00 a.m. on the dot. Beating down a monster case of jet lag, Hannah opened the door and invited her in.

"Good morning, my lady." She curtsied, quite an impressive feat considering her arms were stacked with file folders and binders. "I have the information you requested."

"My gosh, someone must have been up all night compiling this." She shuddered to think of all the reading she had ahead of her. She would have to call down for a second pot of coffee. But with any luck, the mystery woman from yesterday would be among the pages and Hannah might learn her identity. And maybe have some clue as to why she'd watched Hannah so intently.

"Would you like it in your office?" Miss Pryce asked.

She hated being cooped up in an office. "Why don't you set it down on the table by the sofa."

She did as requested then stood stiffly, clutching the leather binder she'd had with her last night. The dreaded schedule.

"Would you care for a cup of coffee, Miss Pryce?"

"No, thank you."

"I could call down for tea."

She didn't even crack a smile. "I'm fine, thank you."

How about a valium, or shot of whiskey? Hannah thought. She wondered if everyone around here was always this formal. If so, it was going to take some serious getting used to. For them, that is. Hannah's staff at home had always been more like an extension of the family than actual employees.

Being royalty didn't mean she had to be a cold fish.

"Do you have a first name, Miss Pryce?"

She looked confused. "Of course."

"What is it?"

She hesitated for an instant, as though she wasn't quite sure why Hannah would even ask. "Elizabeth."

"May I address you by your first name?"

Miss Pryce looked utterly confused.

Hannah sighed. Something this simple shouldn't be so difficult. "Miss Pryce, I'm not sure how things are done here in the palace, but as my personal secretary, I can only assume we'll be spending quite some time together."

Miss Pryce nodded.

"In that case, it would be nice if I could address you by your first name."

"Of course, my lady. I would be honored."

This *my lady* stuff was going to get old fast. "And I don't suppose there would be any chance you could call me Hannah?"

Miss Pryce lowered her eyes and shook her head. "That wouldn't be proper. I would lose my job."

She would push the issue, but Hannah could see that she was making her uncomfortable. After she and Phillip were married, at least her title would change to a less pretentious, *Ma'am.*

"Before we get started, I was hoping to have a word with my fiancé." Since he left her suite last night, she had been anticipating seeing him again. She had a million questions to ask him. Things about him she was dying to know.

"He's not here."

"Oh. Do you know when he'll be back?"

"Friday, I think."

"Friday?" *Five* days?

"If the weather holds," she added.

"Weather?"

"He and his cousin, Sir Charles, don't care to hunt in the rain."

Hunt? He went *hunting?*

She willed herself to remain calm, to ignore the deep spear of disappointment that lodged in her heart. She'd been here less than twenty-four hours and he'd left to go on a *hunting* trip? That would leave them barely a week to get to know one another before the wedding. Didn't he care about her?

Calm down, Hannah. Of course he did. His actions yesterday proved his affection for her. There had to be a logical reason. A hunting trip to disguise business, maybe? Some secret trip no one could know the truth about?

There was no way he would just *leave* her.

Her distress must have shown, because Miss Pryce looked suddenly alarmed. "If it's an emergency—"

"*No.* No emergency." She forced a smile. The last thing she wanted was for her assistant to know how deeply her feelings had been hurt. "It can wait until he returns." Hannah gestured to the sofa. "Shall we get started?"

Hannah sat, and Elizabeth lowered herself stiffly

beside her. Apparently it was going to take time for her to relax in Hannah's presence. Baby steps.

"So, what's on the schedule for today?"

"You meet with the decorator at eleven o'clock, followed by a luncheon at one with the wives of the heads of state."

"That sounds nice." She would be sure to skim the files Elizabeth brought so she could pluck at least a few of their names from memory. "What next?"

She went on, but Hannah was only half listening. Her mind was still stuck on Phillip's abrupt disappearance. Was it possible that he wasn't hunting at all? That he might be with another woman? And what if it was the mystery woman who wouldn't stop staring at her?

She dismissed the thought almost as quickly as it formed. Now she was being paranoid and silly.

She wasn't so naive as to believe that Phillip had saved himself for her. But he'd had the decency to keep that aspect of his life quite discreet. Which told her that he was a man of integrity. And men of integrity were faithful to their significant others.

Finding suspicion with his every action would only make her life miserable.

She was sure that if he had to leave, it was for a good reason. Though Phillip was her fiancé, and would later be her husband, he was a king first and foremost. A servant to his country. That was a fact she would have to accept.

This brief absence would just make them appreciate each other that much more when he returned.

This is just a hiccup, she assured herself. Everything would work out just the way she'd planned.

Phillip stood on the steps leading to the garden, an unseasonably warm breeze ruffling the collar of his shirt, his attention on his future wife.

She sat on a blanket in the shade of a tree whose leaves had just begun to change, legs folded underneath her, hair tumbling in silky chestnut waves down her back. She wore a simple slip dress the exact shade of amber as the turning leaves.

He stepped down onto the grass and walked toward her, finding himself mesmerized by her beauty, intrigued by the intense desire to be near her. To touch her again. In profile, her features looked finely boned and elegant. Regal and confident, with a hint of softness that he found undeniably appealing.

Fine breeding stock, his mother had assured him when the pairing had been suggested and he had yet to meet Hannah, or even see a photo of her. He recalled thinking at the time that his mother could have been describing a head of cattle, not a future member of the family.

Beside her on the blanket sat a pile of binders, and one lay open across her lap. She was so engrossed in whatever it was she was reading, she didn't hear him approach.

"Good afternoon."

She let out a squeak of surprise and the folder tumbled from her lap onto the ground. When she looked up and saw it was him standing there, she scrambled to her feet, which he noticed were bare.

"I'm sorry," she said and executed a slightly wobbly curtsy. "You startled me."

As she straightened, her hair slipped across her shoulders, thick and shiny, resting in loose spirals atop the swell of her breasts. It all but begged to be touched and his fingers itched to tangle in the silky ribbons. From that day forward he would insist that she never wear it up again.

"If I startled you, perhaps *I* should be the one apologizing," he said.

She clasped her hands in front of her, her lip clamped between her teeth, but behind it he could see the shadow of a smile. "You're back sooner than I expected."

Despite that, he would have anticipated her to be angry with him. Seeing as how he had left so abruptly. Instead, she seemed genuinely happy to see him.

It had been selfish and insensitive of him to leave her alone, but a lesson she needed to learn. It was best she understand that he had no intention of changing his habits simply because he had a wife. This was an arrangement, a business deal of sorts. The sooner she realized and accepted that, the better off they would both be.

Which did little to explain why, as she'd pointed out, he was home three days early.

"I had to cut my trip short," he told her.

"Bad weather?" she asked. And, to his look of confusion, added, "Miss Pryce said you don't like to hunt in bad weather."

The weather on the opposite end of the island where the hunting cabin was located had been much like it was here. Idyllic. Clear skies and temperatures ten degrees above the usual for late September. And though the company had been equally adequate—he looked forward to trips with his cousin, when he could relax and just be Phillip—this time he'd felt restless and bored.

"Stop acting like an ass and go home to your fiancée," Charles had urged after having his head all but snapped off for the umpteenth time in two days.

Indignant at first, Phillip was now glad that he'd listened. Best he enjoy the novelty of this relationship while it lasted.

And just for fun, he planned to test the values to which she clung so firmly.

"If you prefer," he said, "I could go back."

"N-no, of course not, I just…" She noticed his wry grin, and flashed a somewhat shy smile of her own. "You're teasing me."

He nodded.

"I'm glad you're home."

Oddly enough, so was he.

He gestured to the work she'd abandoned on the blanket. "Sorry if I disturbed you."

"Not at all. I had some spare time and thought I would catch up on my reading. And take advantage of the mild weather."

"They're keeping you busy?"

"Swamped. It seems as though I've had more meetings in the past three days than in the last two years. And I've met so many new people, their faces and names all blur together. Every time I get a free minute or two, I try to study the profiles."

"I was thinking, since it is such a beautiful day, that you might like to take a walk around the grounds with me."

"I would love to, but…" She glanced from him, to the palace, then to the delicate gold watch on her left wrist.

"Is there a problem?"

"I have a meeting with the decorator in fifteen minutes, then the wedding coordinator after that."

"Not anymore."

She blinked with confusion. "Pardon?"

"I told Miss Pryce to clear your schedule for the rest of the afternoon."

"You did?"

He nodded. "You're free for the remainder of the day."

"Is that okay?" she asked. But before he could answer, she held up a hand and said, "I know, you're the king. You make the rules."

He smiled and held out his hand, found himself eager to touch her again. "Shall we?"

She hesitated, probably remembering her no-fooling-around-until-after-the-wedding rule. But he had no intention of waiting until their wedding night to take her to his bed.

And he would seduce her so cleverly, she would believe it had been her idea in the first place.

"Something wrong?" he asked.

She shook her head, gazing at his hand as though it were a poisonous creature poised to attack.

"Surely you don't find holding hands with your fiancé inappropriate."

"Not exactly."

"Do I frighten you, then?"

"Not in the way you might think. It's more a matter of trust."

"You don't trust me?"

"I don't trust *me*. Women have desires, too, Your Highness."

Her candor both surprised and impressed him, and told him that, despite her resolve, she was as good as him. He'd yet to find a woman able to resist his charms. He doubted that Hannah would be any different.

She finally slipped her hand in his, and he could swear he felt her shiver.

This was going to be *too* easy.

Five

Though Phillip's leaving had been a blip in her carefully laid plans, the instant his hand slipped around her own, the second his fingers threaded loosely through hers, as far as Hannah was concerned, things were back on track.

Dressed in slacks, a plain white button-down shirt and a caramel cashmere sport coat, he looked casual, but carried himself with an air of supremacy that was almost intoxicating. A woman could feed endlessly off the energy he exuded.

They took a long, leisurely stroll through the gardens and, for the first time since she'd arrived, she felt as though she could finally relax. She had begun to feel as though she were being pulled in ten directions at once. Then Phillip appeared, snapped his fingers and made it all go away. Somehow she knew deep down that, no matter what, he would take care of her.

They walked across the pristinely maintained lawn—she'd seen golf courses that didn't look this good—in the general direction of the woods bordering the estate.

"Did you have a successful trip?" she asked.

"You mean, did I kill anything?" he replied, and she nodded. "Not this time."

"What's in season here this time of year? No, wait, let me guess. You're king, so *you* make the rules. You can kill whatever you want, whenever you want."

He grinned and she felt an honest-to-goodness flutter in her heart. She would call his smile beautiful, had he not been so utterly male.

"I have to follow the laws of the land like everyone else," he said. "Right now we're hunting small game and birds."

"Could I go with you sometime?"

"Hunting?"

She nodded, and he looked genuinely surprised.

"My father and I went every year up until his death." A knot of emotion rose up and clogged her throat, the way it always did when she talked about him. Losing him so unnecessarily had left a laceration on her heart that, a year later, was still raw and bleeding.

Everyone kept telling her that it would get easier, but the truth was, each day it seemed to hurt a little bit more. For her anyway. Her mother, it would seem, had little trouble moving on.

"You were close with your father," Phillip said. A statement more than a question.

She nodded, and he gave her hand a squeeze. It was a simple gesture, but it meant everything to her. "He was my hero."

"It was a car accident?"

"His car was hit by a drunk driver. He was killed instantly. Of course, the other driver walked away with barely a scratch. The worst part was that it wasn't the first time. He had three prior convictions for DUI and was driving on a revoked license."

"The laws here are much tougher on repeat offenders than in the U.S."

"It's tough enough losing someone you love, but for it to be so…senseless. It's just not fair."

"No, it isn't," he agreed.

She realized that recently losing a parent was one thing they had in common. "Reports of your mother's death said she was sick, but they never really specified what she died of."

"She had cancer of the liver."

"It must have been quick."

"She was given six months when she was diagnosed. She only lived three."

"There was nothing they could do?"

He shook his head. "It was too far advanced."

She searched his face for a sign of remorse or loss, but there was none. When he spoke of her, he sounded almost…cold. "Do you miss her?"

"I barely knew her." He glanced over at her. "She was cold, overbearing and heartless."

Her parents certainly hadn't been perfect, but she never once doubted their love for her. "That's sad."

He shrugged, as though it didn't bother him in the least. They stopped at the edge of the woods, near the base of a barely perceptible and frightfully narrow path cut through the trees flanked with thick underbrush. "I'd like to show you something."

"Okay."

"It's untended, so watch your step."

He tugged her along after him, the woods swallowing them up, transporting them instantly into a world that was quiet and serene, and rich with the scent of earth and vegetation. Even the sun couldn't penetrate the dense canopy of leaves overhead.

"I'm going to assume there are no dangerous wild animals out here," she said, ducking under a low-hanging branch.

"I assure you, we're perfectly safe."

She followed him for several hundred feet, and could swear she heard the sound of running water. The deeper they descended, the louder it became. Finally they reached a clearing and bisecting the forest was a quaint, bubbling brook. It was like something out of a storybook.

"It's lovely!" she told him.

"My sister and I used to play here when we were children," he said, releasing her hand so she could investigate. "It was forbidden, which made it all the more appealing. We would sneak away from our nanny and spend hours investigating."

And so would her and Phillip's children.

She made her way to the water's edge, and though it probably wasn't *proper,* she couldn't resist toeing off her sandal and dipping into the chilly water. "You were close? You and Sophie?"

"When we were small. But now Sophie and I are very…different."

"How is that?"

"You'll find that my sister is something of a free spirit."

"She's independent?"

"That's putting it mildly."

She might have been imagining it, but she could swear he sounded sad. Maybe he missed the relationship they'd had. If his mother was as cold as he'd described, maybe they were all the other had.

"I always wanted a brother or sister," she told him.

"And ironically, I always wished I were an only child. Siblings are highly overrated."

Somehow she doubted that. "You have a brother, too."

"Half brother." His response was so full of venom, his eyes so icy, it gave her a cold chill. Maybe this was a subject best left alone for the time being. She was sure that once they got to know each other, he would open up more.

One step at a time, she reminded herself.

She slipped back into her sandal, a sudden chill making her shiver. Goose bumps broke out across her arms and she rubbed to warm them.

"You're cold," he said. He shrugged out of his sport coat and slipped it around her. It was warm and soft and smelled like him.

He arranged it on her shoulders, using both hands to ease her hair from underneath it, his fingers brushing the back of her neck. She shivered again, but this time it had nothing to do with the temperature. At least, not the air. Her inner thermostat on the other hand had begun a steady climb.

It was the way he looked at her, so…thoroughly. As though he wanted to devour her with his eyes.

"I like your hair down," he said, brushing it gently back from her face. "Promise me you'll wear it like this all the time."

"I have so much natural curl that when I wear it down, it tends to look kind of…untamed."

His mouth pulled into one of those sexy, simmering smiles. "I know. I like you that way."

Oh, boy, here we go again.

"It wouldn't be proper."

"*Proper* is also highly overrated. Besides, I make the rules. And I hereby decree that, from this day forward, you are to wear your hair down."

She might have been offended if she thought for a second that he was serious about the royal decree thing. Besides, he was standing so close that the testosterone he was giving off was beginning to short-circuit her brain.

He cupped the side of her face, traced her features with his thumb. Her cheek, her brow, the corner of her mouth. Her internal thermometer shot up another ten degrees and her knees started to feel soft and squishy. She knew it would be best to stop him, but they had connected emotionally today. Physical affection just seemed like the natural next step.

Maybe a bit *too* natural.

His eyes searched her face. "You're beautiful, you know."

She took in a deep breath. "Your Highness, I suspect you're trying to seduce me."

"If I am, it seems to be working." His thumb brushed her cheek. "You're blushing."

She didn't have a snappy comeback for that one. And, oh, how she wanted to touch him. To put her hands on his chest and feel his heart beating, feel the warmth of his skin through his shirt. She wanted to run her fingers through his hair, across his face, feel the faint shadow of stubble on his cheeks.

He brushed his fingers across her cheek. "Your skin feels warm here."

Probably because her blood was hovering just below the boiling point.

He stroked lower, down her chin and throat, his eyes following the path of his hand. Then lower still, just above the swell of her breasts. It was a move so intimate and sexually charged, and *wonderful,* that she went weak all over. With desire and fear and curiosity.

He lifted his eyes to hers. "And here."

"Phillip—"

"I know, I'm breaking the no-touching rule." He caressed the uppermost swell of her breasts with the tips of his fingers and her knees nearly buckled with the new, erotic sensation. "But as king, I make my own rules." He leaned in closer, until his mouth was only inches from hers. "And nothing is going to stop me from kissing you."

Well then, there wasn't much point in telling him no, was there? Besides, what harm could one kiss do? A *real* kiss this time. How far could it go, out here in the woods?

"Just one kiss," she told him, as though his demand even required a response.

He cupped her cheek and mini explosions of sensation detonated under her skin.

She was getting that weak, dizzy feeling again. "Then we stop."

His other hand slipped through her hair to cradle the back of her head. He lowered his head and she lifted hers to meet him, her eyes slipping closed. Then their lips touched, barely more than a brush, and time seemed to stand still. It was just her lips and his lips, their breath mingling.

It was unbelievably wonderful. So sweet and gentle, as though she were a delicate piece of china he thought he might break. And while her head was telling her it was time to pull away, time to stop, her heart was telling her just a little longer. Because sweet and gentle wasn't enough for her this time. She wanted more.

Which was why, when Phillip deepened the kiss, when she felt his tongue tease the seam of her lips, she didn't do or say a thing to stop him. And when she gave in, opened up to him, the kiss went from sweet to simmering in the span of a heartbeat.

He tunneled his fingers through her hair, drew her against the length of his long, solid frame. She couldn't help but put her arms around him, flatten her hands against the ropes of muscle in his back. It seemed as though her entire body, from the tips of her toes to the crown of her scalp, came alive with brand-new and intense sensations. And there was an ache, real and intense, building deep within her. A clawing need to be touched, in a way that no man had ever touched her before.

It was exhilarating and terrifying, and more wonderful than she could have ever imagined.

As though reading her mind, Phillip let one hand slide down her back to cup her behind. He drew her against him, and she could feel that he was just as aroused as she was. And instead of feeling wary or afraid, she felt a need for more. And she longed for the day when she didn't have to tell him no.

Unfortunately, that was not today.

She broke the kiss and pressed her forehead against his shirt, felt that his heart was thumping as hard and fast as her own. And said the only thing she could think to say. "Wow."

A chuckle rumbled through his chest. "Thank you."

She looked up at him, saw that he was smiling. "It's not completely obvious that I have zero experience when it comes to this sort of thing?"

"A little, maybe. But I think that's what I like about you."

"That I'm inexperienced?" She thought men liked women who knew how to please them.

"That you're not afraid to admit it. That you embrace your values, not lean on them. You have no idea how rare that is." He touched her cheek. "Although, I fear your honesty might get you into trouble one of these days."

"My father always told me, nothing bad can come from telling the truth."

"In that case, he would have been very proud of you."

She felt the beginnings of tears prickle in her eyes and laid her head back against his chest, so he wouldn't see. "You think so?"

"I do."

He could really be quite sweet. When he wanted to.

"They're bound to be wondering where we've disappeared to," he said. "We should get back before they dispatch a search party."

Though she would be content to stand here all day, wrapped up in his strong arms, just the two of them, she knew he was right. And as she backed away, she took heart in the fact that today had brought them one step closer to the ideal future that she knew they would have together. Things were falling right into place.

"Let's go," she said.

He reached out and took her hand, laced his fingers through hers and led her out of the woods.

"By the way, I wanted to ask you about something." She told him about the woman who had been staring at her Monday. "She wasn't in any of the profiles. I thought maybe you'd know who she was."

He shrugged. "There were so many people there."

"She would be hard to miss. Long, dark hair, very beautiful. And she never took her eyes off us."

He shook his head. "I'm sorry."

She couldn't shake the feeling that he wasn't being honest with her. He'd been by her side the entire day. Surely he would have noticed someone staring. Wouldn't he? Or maybe, people stared at him all the time.

Besides, what reason did he have to lie? She was probably just being paranoid again.

The walk back to the palace went far too quickly, and when they reached the steps, Phillip's valet was waiting for them.

"An urgent call from the prime minister, sir."

"I'll take it in my office," Phillip told him, then turned to Hannah. "I enjoyed our walk."

He was wearing one of those secret, just-between-us smiles, and it made her feel warm all over.

"Me, too."

"We should do it again soon."

She had a feeling he wasn't talking about the walking part. "I'd like that."

As he started to walk away, Hannah called after him.

"Phillip."

He stopped and turned to her.

"Would you have dinner with me tonight?"

There was a slight hesitation before he said, "I can't."

No explanation, no excuses. No apology.

The sting of disappointment was quick and sharp. Can't, or *won't?* she couldn't help but wonder as he turned and walked away. Why, after they'd had such a good time together, would he not want to be with her? It didn't make sense.

You are not going to let this bother you, she told herself as he disappeared inside, then she walked back over to the blanket where she'd left her things. Only then did she realize that his jacket still hung on her shoulders. But even that couldn't shelter her from the chill that seemed to settle deep in her bones.

They'd taken a huge step forward today. She felt as if they really connected.

Why then, did it feel as though, for every step they took forward, they took two back?

Six

Phillip had just hung up the phone with the prime minister when the door to his office flew open and his sister barged in unannounced.

His secretary stood in the doorway behind her, looking both pained and apologetic. "Princess Sophie to see you, sir."

Even the most loyal of servants were no match against Sophie. Phillip dismissed her with a wave of his hand, and she backed out of the room, closing the door behind her.

"I see you're back," he said.

In lieu of a civilized greeting, she said, "You're an idiot."

Obviously she was in a snit over something. He sighed and leaned back in his chair, curious as to what he had done to provoke her this time, and sure he was about to find out.

"Your fiancée was barely here a day and you took off? To go *hunting?* That was harsh, even for you."

He wasn't even sure why she cared. And because he didn't owe anyone an explanation, least of all her, he didn't give her one.

"She must scare the hell out of you," she said.

Instantly his hackles went up, and before he could stop himself, he warned her, "Don't even go there."

Leave it to Sophie to know exactly which of his buttons to push. From the moment she was born, she had made it her mission in life to torment him, as sisters often did.

"She's the real deal. But you already know that, don't you? That's why you're so determined to keep her at arm's length."

She couldn't be more wrong. He was doing Hannah a favor. But Sophie would never understand that. "You're in no position to give me relationship advice. Who did you run off with the other night, Sophie?"

Her smug smile was all the answer he needed.

"You're coming to a family dinner tomorrow night," she told him. "You and Hannah, at my residence."

"Is that so?"

"It is."

Though he was inclined to refuse, for no reason other than the fact that she demanded it, he realized it was probably a good idea. Were Hannah to befriend Sophie, she might be less unsettled in his absence. She had looked utterly crushed when he refused her dinner invitation. He liked Hannah, and he didn't want her to be unhappy. But he couldn't change the person he was.

"All right," he told Sophie.

She looked surprised. "Really? And here I was all prepared to pull out the brass knuckles."

He would have guessed as much. But, after the heated disagreement he'd just had with the prime minister, he simply wasn't in the mood for another fight. "What time would you like us?"

"Seven o'clock. And bring a bottle of wine. In fact, bring a red and a white. I'm making roast leg of lamb."

"*You're* making it? Well, I'll be sure to bring a bottle of antacid, too. And perhaps I should put the palace physician on high alert as well. Just in case."

Pleased that she had gotten her way, she ignored the jab. Besides, she knew as well as he did that the insult was unfounded. She had trained at one of the most prestigious culinary academies in all of Europe, and was an accomplished, gifted chef. It was a passion that had been vehemently discouraged by their parents. But Sophie somehow always managed to get what she wanted.

It both annoyed and impressed him.

"I'll see you both tomorrow then," she said.

He kept his face bland. "I can hardly contain my excitement."

She only smiled.

"Is that it?" he asked.

"I suppose you noticed Madeline on Monday."

The mystery woman Hannah had asked him about. Of course he'd noticed her. She would have been hard to miss, staring at them the way she had been. "What about her?"

"It would seem she's back to her old tricks."

"Forgive me if I don't shudder with fear." Madeline was of no consequence to him or Hannah, which was why he hadn't felt the need to explain who she was. She was nobody.

"You know how she can be. Anything to get attention."

"And confronting her would only feed that need. She'll get bored and find someone else to antagonize."

"She could do some damage in the meantime."

He seriously doubted that. "Is there anything else you needed?"

Sophie shook her head, obviously exasperated with him. "Does your fiancée have the slightest clue how difficult you can be?"

He didn't respond.

"So, I'll see you both tomorrow evening?"

"We'll be there."

She flashed him one of those cryptic, I-know-something-you-don't smiles. One that made him uneasy. Then she was gone.

Forget Madeline. Sophie was the one he should be worried about. This whole dinner scenario seemed a bit too...*domestic* for her taste. Why did he suspect that there was more to this than she was letting on?

Hannah had just finished a quiet dinner alone in her suite, a meal she'd had little appetite for, when Elizabeth knocked on the door.

"You should have left hours ago," Hannah scolded her. She may have been a palace employee, but for heaven's sake, she needed a life of her own outside of work. It seemed as though she was *always* there.

"I was just finishing up a few things," Elizabeth told her. "I was on my way out when a call came in for you."

"Who is it?" She was hoping maybe a friend from back home. God knows she could use a friendly voice right now.

"It's your mother," Elizabeth said, then added, "Again."

This was the fourth call since Hannah left Seattle. Hadn't her mother gotten the message that Hannah wasn't ready to talk to her? She was still too bitter and angry. It was very possible, if Hannah talked to her in her current state of mind, she might say something she would later regret. Like she had the last time they spoke.

"Tell her I'll call her back."

"She said it was urgent."

She would say just about anything to get Hannah's attention. To get her to come to the phone.

"She sounded upset," Elizabeth added.

Hannah felt a slight jerk of alarm. She remembered the last urgent call from her mother. She had been in the university library studying for exams, so engrossed she almost didn't answer her phone, when it buzzed in her pocket. And when she heard her mother's distraught voice, her heart sank.

Sweetheart, you need to come home. Daddy was in an accident….

But he was gone now, and she couldn't imagine anything urgent enough to warrant a return call. "I'll call her tomorrow."

Elizabeth didn't say a word, but she had this look. Not quite disapproval, because a palace employee would never be so bold as to disapprove of anything a royal did or said. It was more the lack of emotion that was giving her away. It was obvious she was trying very hard not to react. Or maybe it was Hannah's own guilty conscience nagging at her. Either way, Hannah knew exactly what she was thinking.

And she was right, of course. "I know, that's what I said yesterday. So technically, today is tomorrow. Right?"

"That is true," Elizabeth agreed.

"You think I should call her, don't you?"

"It's not my place to pass judgment."

Maybe not, but Hannah was pretty sure that's what she was thinking. And the truth was, her mother wasn't likely to stop calling. Not until Hannah gave her the opportunity to apologize for her inappropriate behavior these past few months.

Maybe it would be best, to ease her mother's guilt and Hannah's, if they cleared the air. And besides, it was what Daddy would have wanted. Hannah had always been more like him than her mother. So many times her father had told her, "Your mother isn't like us, Hannah. She's fragile. You just have to be patient."

But sometimes her mother could be so insecure and vulnerable it had been difficult even for her. Not that she was a bad person. She needed constant reassurance that she was loved and appreciated. At times her neediness was utterly exhausting.

"My lady?" Elizabeth was watching her expectantly.

Hannah sighed, knowing what she had to do. Knowing that, for her father's sake, she had to settle this. "I'll talk to her."

"She's on line two," Elizabeth said. Then, ever the proper assistant, nodded and slipped quietly from the room, shutting the door behind her.

Hannah walked over to the phone, hesitating a minute before she finally lifted it off the cradle and pressed the button for line two. "Hello, Mother."

"Oh, Hannah, honey! It's so good to hear your voice!"

Hannah wished she could say the same, but right now the sound of her mother's voice, that syrupy sweetness, was just irritating. "How have you been?"

"Oh, fine. But I've missed you *so* much. I was afraid you wouldn't come to the phone again."

"You said it was urgent."

"How have you been? How do you like it there?"

"Everything is fine here." If she discounted the fact that her fiancé had taken off the minute she arrived. Or that he refused to share dinner with her.

"I've been very busy," she told her mother.

"Is the palace beautiful? And is Phillip as gorgeous as I remember?"

She was stalling. Hannah wished she would just say what she had to say and get it over with. "The palace and Phillip are exactly the same as the last time you saw them. Now, I'd like you to tell me what was so urgent."

"Can't I have a pleasant conversation with my daughter?"

Sadly, no. She had shot any chance of that all to hell with her selfishness. "It's late, and I'm tired."

"Okay, okay." She bubbled with phony laughter. "I'll get to the point."

Thank goodness. Just apologize and get it over with already.

"Now, Hannah, I don't want you to get upset…"

Oh, this was not a good sign. That didn't sound anything like an apology. "Upset about what?"

"I called because I have some good news."

"Okay." Spit it out already.

"Keep December thirtieth open on your calendar."

Oh, no.

"Why?" she forced herself to ask, even though she already suspected what was coming next.

Dreaded it, in fact.

"Because I'm getting married!"

"Married?"

"Now, honey, I know what you're thinking—"

"Daddy has been gone barely a year!"

"Hannah, please, you're not being fair."

"Fair?"

"A year is a long time when you're alone."

It was the same song and dance she'd fed Hannah three months after his death, when she'd gone out on her first date. *I'm lonely,* she'd told Hannah. What she didn't seem to get is that she had just lost her husband, therefore she was *supposed* to be lonely. She was supposed to mourn his death, not take the first opportunity to run out and find a replacement.

"Please don't be angry, Hannah."

"Who is he?"

"No one you know. He owns a small law firm outside of Seattle. But you'll love him, honey."

No, she wouldn't. No one could replace her father. *Ever.* And if her mother honestly believed someone could, she was more oblivious than Hannah could have imagined.

"I was thinking, I could bring him to your wedding. So you could meet him."

She didn't want to meet him. "For security reasons, that won't be possible."

"Please give him a chance. He's such a sweet, generous man. And he loves me."

Hannah was sure that what he probably loved was the substantial estate her father had left behind. "You say that like Daddy *didn't* love you. Or is it that you didn't love him?"

"That's unfair. You know that I loved your father very much." There was a quiver in her voice that said she was on the verge of tears. No big surprise there. She often used tears to win sympathy. But Hannah wasn't buying it this time.

"Then why are you so eager to replace him?"

"You've gone on with your life. I should be allowed to go on with my life, too."

It wasn't the same thing and she knew it. Besides, Hannah wasn't out trying to find a new father, was she? "And so you have, Mom. You don't need my permission."

"No, but I would like your blessing."

"I really need to go now."

"Hannah, please—"

"We'll talk about this when you're here next week," she said.

"I love you, honey."

"Goodbye, Mom." She could hear her mother still talking as she set the phone back in the cradle. But if she stayed on the line any longer, she would have wound up saying something she regretted.

There was nothing she could do or say to change her mother's mind. She had obviously made her decision. And since Hannah had no control over the situation, there was no point in wasting her time worrying about it.

She had other things to keep her occupied. Wedding plans and redecorating, and hours of reading to do. She didn't need her mother anymore.

She sat on the sofa, surrounded with binders full of information to read, color swatches and wallpaper samples to choose from, last-minute wedding plans to tie up. But she couldn't seem to work up the enthusiasm for any of it.

She felt too…*edgy.*

Hannah decided a long, hot bath with her lavender bath gel might relax her. Afterward she towel-dried her hair and changed into her most comfortable cotton pajamas. She curled up in bed to watch television, browsing past the gazillion channels available, but there wasn't a thing on that held her interest.

She snapped the television off and tossed the remote on the coverlet. She was bored silly, yet she didn't feel like doing anything.

Hannah glanced over at the closet door, where Phillip's jacket hung. She had planned to give it back to him tomorrow. But what if he'd forgotten he'd lent it to her, and was wondering where he'd left it.

Yeah right. She just wanted an excuse to see him. Which in itself was silly because he was her fiancé. She shouldn't *need* an excuse to see him. Right? If she wanted to see him, she should just…*see him.* Shouldn't she?

Yes, she decided. She should.

Before she lost her nerve, she rolled out of bed and grabbed her robe, shoving her arms in the sleeves and belting it securely at her waist. She stuck her feet in her slippers, grabbed Phillip's jacket, and headed out into the hall.

His suite was all the way down the main hall at the opposite end of the east wing. She had never actually been there, but it had been part of the tour Elizabeth took her on earlier in the week.

When she reached his door, she lifted her hand to knock, then hesitated, drawing it back.

What was she *doing?* Begging for his attention? Was she really so pathetic? Had she so little pride? Wasn't she stronger than that?

She turned to walk back the way she came from, but hesitated again.

On second thought, why shouldn't she stop by to give him his jacket? He was her fiancé, wasn't he? And damn it, she had worked hard to prepare herself for her role as his wife. Didn't she deserve a little something in return? Was a little bit of his time really all that much to ask for?

No, she decided, it definitely was not.

She turned back, and before she could talk herself out of it again, rapped hard on the door.

Seven

Get a grip, Hannah, she told herself, since her heart was about to pound clear through her chest. It's not like he's naked.

But darn close.

A pair of Egyptian cotton pajama bottoms rode low on Phillip's hips as he opened the door. Other than that, all she was able to comprehend, to process, was the ridiculous amount of muscle she was seeing.

Wide, ripped shoulders and bulging biceps. Lean hips and toned, defined abs. And she could only imagine what was under the pajamas. In fact, she *was* imagining it.

She was so stunned silly by his perfect physique, it took a moment to register that he was speaking to her.

She peeled her eyes from his flawless pecks, located his face, and uttered a very eloquent, "Huh?"

Amusement danced in the depth of his eyes. "I said, is there something wrong?"

"Wrong?"

"Why are you here?"

Think, Hannah. Why did you come all the way down here? Then she remembered the jacket still hanging from her left hand. "No. Nothing is wrong. I just wanted to give this back to you."

She held the jacket out to him, and he took it.

"Is that it?" he asked.

"Yes." She shook her head. "No."

He leaned in the door frame, arms folded across his chest, waiting patiently for her to elaborate. And, boy, were his biceps *huge*. So thick and strong looking, like he could probably bench-press a compact car and not break a sweat.

Did it suddenly get a lot hotter in here? Her cheeks were on fire and she was feeling just a little light-headed.

What was wrong with her? It wasn't as if she had never seen a half-naked man before.

The biggest problem here wasn't that she was wary of what she was seeing. Instead, she felt a very real and intense desire—no, not desire, *need*—to put her hands all over him.

She locked them together behind her back. Just to be safe.

"Are you all right?" he asked, though he looked more amused than concerned.

"Yes. I just…" She shook her head again. "No. I'm not."

"Maybe you should come in." He opened the door wider and stepped aside.

You know you shouldn't be doing this, she told herself. Their wedding was still more than a week away. It was one thing to flirt and steal a kiss here and there, but going into his suite, at this late hour. In her *pajamas*. And Phillip almost naked.

She was really pushing it.

So you just won't let anything happen, she decided. It's not as though she was a slave to her libido.

She had waited this long. She could wait a little while longer.

But the question was, could Phillip? And if he took matters into his own hands, would she find the strength to stop him?

Bad idea or not, she followed him inside. His sitting room was much larger than her own, and closer to the size of the one they would be moving into after the wedding. And it was undeniably masculine. Dark polished wood and dark patterned fabric in rich hues. But not so dark that it was dreary or threatening. In contrast, the effect was warm and welcoming.

"This is nice," she said, ideas popping into her head of how she might incorporate both his and her individual styles to create a decor they could both be comfortable in.

See, she told herself, coming here was a good thing.

"So, what's up?" he asked.

She turned to him, with every intention of meeting his eyes, but her gaze kept snagging slightly lower.

"Hannah?"

She pried her eyes from his torso and met his gaze. He was grinning again.

"If it would help get the conversation rolling, I could put on a shirt."

Though she knew he was only teasing, her cheeks flamed with embarrassment. "Sorry."

"No apology necessary. I'm flattered. But maybe you should tell me what's wrong."

"Wrong?"

"I asked if you were okay, and you said no."

Had she? My goodness, he must have thought she was a total ditz. Now that she was here, she had no idea what to say to him. So she blurted out the first thing that came to mind. "My mother called."

He didn't seem to get the significance. "Is *she* okay?"

"She's fine, she just…" Her voice cracked, and she realized, with horror, that tears burned the corners of her eyes. What was *wrong* with her? She was not a crier. She was tougher than that. Besides, she wasn't that upset. More angry than sad.

"She just what?" he asked.

"She's—" A half hiccup, half sob, worked its way up her throat and she battled to swallow it back down. "She's getting married."

Despite her resolve, the instant the words left her lips, the tears welled up over the edges of her lids and rolled down her cheeks. Mortified, she covered her face with her hands.

What was wrong with her? She should be spitting mad, not blubbering like a baby.

Then she felt Phillip's arms go around her, draw her against him, and something inside her seemed to snap. Every bit of tension and anger that had built inside her let go in a limb-weakening rush and she all but melted against him.

"You think it's too soon?" he asked. "For your mother to remarry, I mean."

Because she wasn't sure her voice was steady enough for a verbal reply, she nodded.

"Do you want to talk about it?"

She shook her head. Just knowing he was there for her if she needed him was enough right now.

He didn't say anything else. He just held her and stroked her hair. She held on tight, her face pressed to his warm, bare skin, and concentrated on taking slow, deep breaths, until she felt the tears begin to work their way back down. Apparently, this was exactly what she'd needed. How did he always seem to know exactly what to do and say to make her feel better?

"You okay?" he asked.

She nodded. "I'm sorry."

"Sorry for what?"

"For barging in on you like this. And getting all wishy-washy and emotional."

"It's okay."

"I don't usually do this. I'm not a crier. It…it's just been a really stressful couple of days."

"I can imagine."

"Bringing the jacket back was just an excuse," she admitted, and could swear she felt him smile.

"I know."

She looked up at him. Of all the women in the world that he could have had, why did he pick her?

"I guess I just… I guess I was lonely."

He touched her cheek, brushing away the last remnants of the tears with his thumb.

"All day I have appointments and meetings, and sometimes I just can't wait to be alone, to have a minute to myself. But then, when I'm finally alone, I feel so…isolated. Does that make sense?"

"Trust me, I know exactly what you mean. And you get used to it. I promise."

Maybe she didn't want to get used to it. She wanted them to be a regular family. She wanted it so bad she ached deep in her heart.

"I was going to wait until tomorrow to tell you this," he said. "My sister invited us to dinner at her residence tomorrow evening."

"Really?"

"I hope you don't mind, but I told her we would be there."

Mind? She was absolutely ecstatic. They would *finally* share a meal together. Like a *real* family. Not to mention that she had been eager to get to know her future sister-in-law. "I would love to."

She was so happy, she nearly burst into tears again. Instead, she rose up on her toes and kissed him. Just a quick, sweet kind of kiss, so he would know how much it meant to her.

But it felt so nice, so…*perfect,* she kissed him again. This one lasting just a little longer than the first. She felt his arms tighten around her, the flex of his back where her hands rested.

And because the second one was even better than the first, she kissed him again.

And *again*.

And then she couldn't stop.

Phillip had Hannah exactly where he wanted her. Her body pressed against him, her arms circling his neck, hands tangled in his hair. And her mouth— damn, what she could do with her mouth. He had never been with a woman who kissed so…earnestly.

He could have her tonight if he wanted, *before* the wedding, just as he'd planned. So, why did it feel wrong? As if he were somehow betraying her trust?

Since when did he care about anyone but himself?

He wouldn't be having this problem, this case of an overactive conscience, if she wasn't so damned honest all the time. If she didn't walk around with her heart on her sleeve.

He'd told her, just this afternoon, that her honesty would get her into trouble, and she insisted that honesty was a good thing. Well, it was looking like maybe she was right.

Yet here he was, kissing her, touching her, when what he should be doing was telling her no. But, damn, she felt good.

Maybe she didn't understand the consequences of her actions. Maybe if he pushed just a little further, tempted her just a little bit more, she would realize what she was doing and put on the brakes.

Maybe he could *make* her tell him no.

He let his hand slide down her back, slowly. Over the dip of her waist, the curve of her hip. Then he went lower, cupping the soft swell of her behind. She whimpered softly, but didn't attempt to pull away. He took it one step further, pulling her against him, so she would feel exactly what all of this fooling around was doing to him. And, hell, she felt amazing. All soft and warm and sweet smelling. And rather than deter her, his actions seemed only to fuel her determination.

She drew her nails across his skin, arched and rubbed herself against him, and he couldn't stop the husky sound of need that welled up from his chest.

She had given every indication that she was a virgin, but now he wasn't so sure. And he didn't know how he felt about that. He liked the idea that she would be his alone.

Her hands were on his shoulders, his chest, traveling slowly downward, in the direction of his waistband. A few more inches, and he wouldn't be able to stop.

Virgin or not, how could he, in good conscience, deny Hannah what she told him she wanted—the privilege of waiting for her wedding day?

The truth of the matter was, as good as this felt, as much as she seemed to want this, he couldn't.

He broke the kiss and backed away, leaving her flush and out of breath. And honestly, he wasn't faring much better. "We have to stop."

Her cheeks were red, her voice husky with desire. "Why?"

"Because you don't want this."

"Yes, I do. I want us to make love."

She tried to kiss him again, to touch him, but he manacled her wrists in his hands. "No, you don't. You're upset, and it's affecting your judgment."

"I'm not upset. Honestly."

"Hannah, if we let this happen, you'll regret it."

"I won't."

"It's only a week." He could hardly believe what he was saying. That he was the one talking *her* out of sex. He must have been completely out of his mind.

Her expression said she was thinking the same thing. "Today, next week. What's the difference?"

"You don't mean that."

"Phillip, I want this. Tonight. Right now."

She tugged against his grip, but he didn't let go. She could beg and cajole until she was blue, and he still wouldn't change his mind. And the worst part was that this was all his fault. He had driven her to this by shutting her out of his life.

He'd thought that, by keeping her at a distance, he was doing her a favor. So she wouldn't get too attached. He could see now that he was only making her miserable. She had left everything familiar to move to a strange country with people she didn't know, and he'd welcomed her by shutting her out. It's a wonder she hadn't packed up and headed back to America.

Sophie was right. He was an idiot.

At the risk of hurting her feelings yet again, he said the only thing he could to get his point across. "Maybe you want it, but I *don't*."

Phillip's words splashed over her like a bucket of ice water. Was he actually telling her *no?* He was a man, and didn't all men inherently want sex? She thought he would jump at the chance.

He let go of her wrists and she took an unsteady step backward. "You're serious?"

"Believe me when I say, I'm just as surprised as you are."

This didn't make sense. He was turned on. All she had to do was look at the front of his pajamas and she could *see* how aroused he was. Why didn't he want her? "Did I do something wrong?"

"Oh, no. You did everything right."

"Then, why?"

He shook his head, dragged a hand through his hair. "I respect you too much to let you do this."

She was so stunned, it took a second for the meaning of his words to sink in.

It was probably one of the sweetest, most wonderful things anyone had ever said to her.

And he was right. If they had made love tonight, she would have regretted it. She was feeling emotional and upset, and she was letting it cloud her judgment.

She wanted to feel close to someone. And she just naturally assumed that, by sleeping with him, she would bring them closer together. But as important as sex was in a relationship, it was still just sex. The other stuff mattered a whole lot more.

Like the fact that he cared enough about her to stop her from making the biggest mistake of her life. What more could she possibly ask for?

"Waiting one more week isn't going to kill us," he said. "Is it?"

She bit her lip and shook her head. Not after waiting twenty-six years. And she didn't miss the irony that it had been her saying the exact same thing to him less than a week ago. "I'm sorry. I don't know what I was thinking."

"You have nothing to be sorry about. I should be more attentive."

"You're busy. I understand that."

"But not so busy that I can't have dinner with my fiancée occasionally."

He touched her hair, brushing it back from her face. "So much has been expected of you, but you've received little in return."

The last thing she wanted was for him to think she was ungrateful. "I'm well aware of the fact that my position will require a certain amount of sacrifice."

"I'm just not used to sharing my time," he admitted.

Or his feelings, she was guessing. And considering the environment he was raised in, it's no wonder. With a mother that cold, and a father whose mistresses were common knowledge, who wouldn't grow up learning to hide their emotions?

But she knew with time she would be able to draw him out of his shell. She would make him see that it was okay to trust his feelings, to let his guard down. It would just take time.

"I'll try not to be overly demanding," she said. Like her mother could often be. "I'll try to give you the space you need." Phillip nodded, although she couldn't help noticing he made no promises in return.

She could see that making this marriage work was going to be a lot harder than she anticipated.

Eight

Phillip knocked on the door to her suite at exactly 6:45 p.m., just as he'd promised last night before she left his room.

When she opened the door and he stepped into her sitting room, she breathed a soft sigh of appreciation. As always, he looked perfect. Dark wool slacks that fit him just right, a long-sleeved, cashmere pullover sweater the same rich, smoky gray as his eyes, topped with a stately jacket.

"I'm just about ready," she told him.

He eyed her with obvious appreciation. "You look beautiful."

The compliment, the way his eyes swept so leisurely over her, left her feeling warm and fuzzy. The extra time she'd taken to blow her hair out smooth and straight, the care she had taken on her makeup, and her choice of dress—a red, clingy number that was sexy, without being too flashy or risqué—had been worth the effort.

"I'd have been ready sooner," she told him, "but my meeting with the wedding planner ran longer than I anticipated."

"No rush," he said. "I doubt she'll start without us."

Still, she hated to be late for anything. "I just have to grab my shoes and a sweater."

She scurried into her room to her closet. She yanked her cardigan from the hanger and grabbed a pair of sling-back, marginally sexy heels from the top shelf. Her totally impractical, just-for-fun shoes.

"How are the wedding plans going?" he called from the sitting room. And because she was sure he was only asking to be polite, she didn't embellish. The important thing was that he was making an effort.

"Very well," she called back, tugging the shoes on her feet. "Did you have a productive day?"

"Not really."

His voice was close. She turned and saw that he was leaning in the bedroom doorway, watching her.

"Did I mention how beautiful you look?"

"I believe you did."

He was wearing that hungry, I'm-going-to-eat-you-alive expression. Like the one he wore last night. And when she remembered what it felt like to touch him, to put her hands on his bare skin, she started to get a funny tickle in the pit of her stomach.

Exactly one more week until the wedding. This time next Friday, they would be legally married and probably at their reception. And after that, either his or her bedroom….

This week couldn't go by fast enough.

"I'm ready," she said.

"There's a car waiting." He stepped aside so she could exit the bedroom, but as she was walking past, he curled a hand around her upper arm, tugged her to him and kissed her. A deep, toe-curling, out-of-this-world kiss that she felt from her toes to her scalp and everywhere along the way. And it was over way too fast.

"What was that for?"

He grinned down at her. "Do I need a reason?"

Heck no.

But if he kept doing stuff like that, looking at her like a hungry wolf, this was going to be the longest week of her life.

The car dropped Hannah and Phillip at Sophie's residence. When they knocked, a butler answered the door. He nodded and motioned them inside, just as Sophie swept into the foyer.

She wore a flowing, gauzy dress that complimented her long, willowy figure. She wore her long, dark hair up and off her face. She looked utterly elegant, if you overlooked the fact that she was barefoot.

"You're right on time!" She pulled Hannah into a warm embrace and kissed her cheek. She smelled of honeysuckle and faintly of apples. Then she stepped back and looked them both up and down. "Aren't you two the handsome couple."

Phillip handed her the bottles of wine. "I hope these will do."

She read the labels, then flashed him a bright smile. "Perfect."

She passed them along to the butler. "Would either of you like a drink before dinner?"

Hannah shook her head. "No, thank you."

"Me neither," Phillip said. "Unless you think I might *need* a drink."

She smiled sweetly, but with just a hint of sass. "Why would I think that?"

There was something going on, Hannah could feel it. Sophie was up to something. Or at least, Phillip suspected she was.

"Dinner will be a few minutes yet. Why don't we wait in the study?"

Her residence was as richly decorated and furnished as the palace. More modern, but just as warm and inviting. And the scents coming from the kitchen were mouthwatering.

"Your house is beautiful," Hannah told her.

"Thank you, Hannah. After dinner I can give you the full tour."

"I'd like that."

As they entered the study, Hannah was so busy taking in the interior that, only when she felt Phillip go board stiff beside her, did she realize something was wrong.

She followed his line of sight and realized there was someone else in the room with them. For a second she was confused, then she recognized the man sitting in the winged leather chair across the room.

The family resemblance was undeniable.

"What's the meaning of this?" Philip demanded. Hannah actually took a step aside, so she wouldn't get caught in the crosshairs. "You never said *he* would be coming."

Sophie shrugged. "You never asked."

Phillip's half brother rose from his seat and shot Sophie a stern look. "I'm a bit surprised myself."

"I knew you were up to something," Phillip told his sister. "But I never imagined you would pull something like this."

He looked seconds from blowing his top. Hannah wouldn't have been at all surprised if steam shot from his ears. She had never seen Phillip this way and, frankly, it intimidated as much as fascinated her. She was just happy that the animosity he shot like laser beams from his charcoal eyes wasn't directed her way.

Sophie, on the other hand, didn't look the least bit rattled. The glare Phillip shot her would have crushed the average person, but she didn't even flinch.

She had probably seen it so many times, she was immune.

"I invited you over for a family dinner. And we're all family, aren't we?" She turned to Hannah. "I don't believe you've met our brother."

Hannah didn't miss the fact that she said *brother*, not *half brother*. "No, I haven't."

"Hannah, this is Ethan Rafferty. Ethan, this is Phillip's fiancée, Hannah Renault."

Hannah stepped forward and shook his hand. His grip was firm and unashamed.

"It's a pleasure, Hannah." He spoke with a very distinct American accent, and though it was silly, she couldn't help liking him instantly.

She had seen photos of him in the paper and always thought he bore a resemblance to Phillip, but in person, the similarities were striking. They were built similarly, even though Ethan wasn't as tall, and their coloring was the same. Intense smoky-gray eyes and dark hair, although, while Phillip's was short and wavy, Ethan's hung long and straight to his shoulders.

They also wore identical angry expressions.

Hannah had the distinct impression that this was not going to be the pleasant family dinner she had been hoping for.

"We're leaving," Phillip said.

"Great idea," Ethan replied.

Sophie rolled her eyes. "Oh, for heaven's sake, you two are acting like spoiled children. *Grow up,* already."

They refocused their glare from each other to their sister. They looked so much alike, it gave Hannah chills. If only they could see themselves. But Hannah was sure neither would be able to see past their preconceived notions of one another.

And though Hannah was inclined to agree with Sophie, and would have happily backed her, she was still an outsider. It wasn't her place to interfere with family issues. Besides, she didn't have siblings, much less illegitimate ones, so how could she begin to understand the complicated relationship they must have?

"Glare at me all you like," Sophie told them. "Whether you like it or not, you two are related. So just deal with it." With a frustrated huff, she turned to the door. "What is it, Wilson?"

Hannah turned to see that the butler was standing in the doorway.

"Dinner is served, miss."

Sophie turned back to her brothers. "Is one civilized meal together really too much to ask for? Can't we put aside our differences, forget the past for one night and *try* to get along like mature adults?"

Hannah could see, by both men's expressions, that she had hit a nerve. After a moment, they both grumbled an agreement.

"Thank you." Sophie led them all to the dining room, and had the good sense to seat the men on opposite sides of the table.

The food was beyond fantastic, each course more delectable than the next. The conversation however was pathetically lacking. Though Sophie tried to start a dialogue, extracting more than a one-word answer from either of them was like pulling wisdom teeth with a pair of tweezers. Despite what Phillip had told Hannah about Sophie being a free spirit, it was clear that she cared very deeply for both her brothers, and wanted to see them acting like a family.

"Everything was delicious," Hannah told Sophie as the dessert dishes were being cleared.

Sophie smiled. "Thank you, Hannah. I don't get in the kitchen nearly as much as I'd like these days. It's nice to know that I haven't lost my touch."

Sophie made dinner? "I didn't know you cook."

"Sophie is an amazing chef," Ethan said, an undeniable note of pride in his voice. "She studied in France. I offered her a position as head chef in the resort of her choosing, but she turned me down."

Phillip shot him a look, one that said he'd heard nothing of the job offer, and didn't like being left out of the loop. "Sophie's place is here, with her family."

At first, Hannah thought he was just being stubborn, then she realized he was jealous. After all, she was the only immediate family he had left. If she moved away, he would be alone.

But if he could care so deeply for one sibling, surely he could find room in his heart for one more. Did it really matter so much that he and Ethan shared only one parent?

"Until he agreed that opening one here on Morgan Isle would be the perfect compromise," Sophie said. "Speaking of that, Phillip, did you read the proposal I left on your desk?"

"I may have skimmed it," he said.

Phillip hadn't mentioned a business proposal to Hannah. Of course, he wasn't exactly chatty when it came to the professional aspects of his life. Or any part of his life, for that matter.

Picking up on Hannah's confusion, Sophie said,

"I've proposed a business partnership between Ethan and the rest of the family."

"And why is it he needs a new business partner?" Phillip asked.

Ethan shot daggers with his eyes, so Hannah was guessing the reason was an unpleasant one.

Sophie only smiled. "If that's the way you want to play this, I'd be happy to quote a list of each and every one of your mistakes and transgressions, Phillip."

Phillip glared silently at her, and Ethan actually smiled. No doubt about it, Sophie was the driving force in this family. She pulled the strings.

"Here's the thing," Sophie told Phillip, leaning toward him to emphasize her point. "I want this. But I can't do it without you."

"So, what's in it for me?" Phillip asked.

"Besides the money? You've complained incessantly, for as long as I can remember, that I need to embrace my position in this family. Well, if you agree to this partnership, you'll never hear a complaint from me again."

She definitely had Phillip's attention. "How do I know you'll live up to that?"

"Have I ever lied to you?"

Hannah could see by his expression that she hadn't.

"Well?" she asked. "Are you in or out?"

"I need time to think about it."

"No. You've had months to think about it. I want an answer tonight." She turned to Hannah. "I think the boys need a few minutes to talk. How about that tour I promised you?"

Sophie led Hannah to the study, where she poured herself a tumbler of scotch. She offered Hannah a glass, but she shook her head.

Sophie took a long sip. Then she took a deep breath and asked, "So, how did I do in there?"

Hannah realized that, although Sophie seemed to be in complete control, the experience had really taken a toll on her. "You were great. It was impressive how you kept them both in line."

"Years of practice, believe me. I've never known two more stubborn men in my life. Though they would die before acknowledging it, they're so much alike."

"I noticed that."

"And I love them both to death, even though they don't always make it easy."

"Tell me if I'm overstepping my bounds, but what did Phillip mean when he asked why Ethan needs a new partner?"

"Ethan's former business partner recently embezzled several million then disappeared. He risks losing everything. And it's not like any of that money was handed to him either. He started with nothing and built his empire from the ground up, one brick at a time."

Hannah shook her head. "How awful."

"I was the one who suggested the partnership. At first he wouldn't hear about it. He was too proud to accept what he considered a handout. But as it stands now, he doesn't have much choice. When our lawyers came up with a business proposal, and it was clear that it was a partnership and not charity, he finally gave in." She took another sip of her drink. "Phillip, I wasn't so sure about. We've been going back and forth with this for months."

"I think he'll go for it."

Sophie smiled. "I like you, Hannah. I think you'll be good for Phillip. I just hope you realize what you're getting yourself into, marrying my brother."

"I've been preparing for this for eight years."

Her eyes widened. "Seriously?"

She nodded. "I had tutors and coaches and advisors."

Sophie shook her head in disbelief. "Wow. And you think you're ready?"

She sure hope so. "I guess we'll see."

"The 'rents tried to handpick a spouse for me, too. He was a duke. Not bad looking, but he had the personality of a brick."

"I take it that didn't go over well."

She shook her head. "If I ever get married, it will be to someone I love. Not that I'm knocking what you and Phillip are doing," she quickly added.

"You wouldn't be the first. My friends thought it was really cool at first. I mean, who wouldn't want to marry a prince and live in a palace? It's every girl's fantasy. Then they saw me spending my weekends in the dorm studying while they went out and had fun. They all had boyfriends, and I was always alone. When they realized how much work it really was, they all thought I was crazy."

"It's kind of ironic. You spent years training for a life that I couldn't get far enough away from."

"Yes, but I wasn't forced into this life. It was my choice."

"Was it?"

She nodded. Though raised in the U.S., her father was born on Morgan Isle. A cousin to a cousin of the royal family. It was the only reason she was chosen to be Phillip's wife. Something about maintaining the royal bloodlines.

"There is one thing I never learned," she told Sophie. "Cooking."

"You don't cook at all?"

"The most complicated thing I've ever made was boxed macaroni and cheese."

Sophie made a sour face. "That sounds dreadful."

"But I've always wanted to learn."

"I could teach you," Sophie said.

"Would you really?"

"Of course! I would love to."

"Okay," Hannah said, feeling suddenly and inexplicably happy. Not only would she have a sister, something she had yearned for as long as she could remember, but it looked as though she had made a friend.

"Now, how about that tour I promised?" Sophie said.

Though Hannah's life here started out a bit rocky, it seemed that things were taking a turn for the better.

Nine

It was after eleven o'clock when Phillip and Hannah returned to the palace. And most of that time he and Ethan spent holed up in the dining room discussing the proposed partnership. On the ride back, Hannah asked how it had gone and got a noncommittal shrug, but *something* must have gone right. When all was said and done, Phillip agreed to the proposal. Already plans were being made for him to tour several of the resort sites.

In fact, he would leave Sunday morning and wouldn't return until Thursday evening, less than twenty-four hours before their nuptials.

"Does that upset you?" Phillip had asked her as they walked up to her suite.

She shook her head. It was business. And important. Besides, it was bad luck for the bride and groom to see each other right before the wedding. This would remove any temptation.

"It will make seeing each other on our wedding day that much more special," she said. And that made him smile.

They reached her door, and though she'd planned to tell him good-night, kiss him and go inside alone, he asked, "Are you going to invite me in for a nightcap?"

It would probably be better if she didn't, but it had turned out to be such a nice night, she hated to see it end just yet. "Can you promise to behave?"

He grinned. "Can you?"

God, she loved it when he teased her.

She opened the door. "Phillip, would you like to come in for a nightcap?"

"I would love to." He followed her inside, shutting the door behind them.

Alone again. Five days ago she would have been a nervous wreck. Now she looked forward to the times they spent, just the two of them.

The room was dim, the only light from a small lamp in one corner of the room. She reached for the light switch by the door, but he intercepted her hand.

"I prefer it darker, if you don't mind." When she shot him a questioning look, he grinned and added, "Didn't I tell you, I'm part vampire?"

If that was true, he could bite her neck anytime.

He crossed to the wet bar. "Brandy?"

"That sounds good."

He poured two brandies while she took off her shoes and sweater.

Phillip sat on the sofa and when she sat down beside him, he looped an arm around her shoulder, drawing her close. For several minutes they just sat there, sipping their drinks in companionable silence. He was a warm, solid presence beside her, the stubble on his chin rough against her forehead. And he smelled so good. So…familiar.

Yet there was still so much about him she didn't know. And that was okay, she realized. At first, she thought they should know one another completely before the wedding. Now she liked the idea of getting to know him gradually.

She set her drink down and curled closer, drawing her knees up and resting them over the tops of his thighs. She closed her eyes and laid her head on his chest, taking it all in. The way he felt, the way he smelled, the thump of his pulse against her cheek. The way his arms felt around her, the sensation that she was and would always be safe there.

She stored every second of it in her memory, so that when he was gone, she wouldn't miss him as much. Or, who knows, maybe it would make her miss him even more.

After a while he gave her a little nudge. "Are you falling asleep on me?"

"Just thinking."

"About what?"

"How many times I imagined us like this. What it would feel like."

"How does it feel?"

She wrapped both arms around him and squeezed, feeling sleepy and content. "Wonderful. Perfect."

He set his glass down beside hers. "Is that all you imagined?"

She grinned up at him, knowing exactly what he was suggesting. "Usually we were kissing."

He cupped her chin and raised her face to his, brushed his lips across hers, and a purr of pleasure curled in her throat.

He lifted his head and looked down at her. "Like that?"

"Hmmm, just like that."

He lowered his head and kissed her again, deeper this time. And longer. And she could feel herself beginning to melt. But something was different this time. As much as she wanted him, wanted to be close, she didn't feel the urgency that was usually there. That soul-deep ache that seemed to push them too far, too fast.

Phillip must have felt the same way, because he took it slow. Kissing, touching. And she couldn't get over how right it felt. The way they seemed to fit, to be completely in sync.

She wasn't sure how much time had passed, but after a while he whispered against her lips, "It's late. I should go."

She pressed her cheek against his chest, felt his arms tighten around her. "I wish you could stay."

"It won't be long before I can."

Reluctantly she uncurled herself from around him and climbed from his lap. He rose to his feet and offered a hand to help her up. At the door, he kissed her again, but what was meant to be a quick goodbye peck progressed to another ten minutes of kissing and touching.

When he finally pulled away, they were both a bit breathless.

"I really have to go," he said. "I have a busy day tomorrow. And I'm sure you do, too."

He was right. She let her arms fall from around his neck and backed away from the temptation. "Is there any way you could spare a few minutes tomorrow afternoon? The decorator will be here and I could show you the plans for the suite. I want to know what you think."

"You're free to do whatever you'd like."

She appreciated his trust in her, but what she would appreciate more was his input. "I want to be sure you like it, too."

He shrugged. "If it's that important to you."

"It is."

"All right. I suppose, if the designer is adequate, it might be time that I redecorate my own suite."

It took a second for his words to sink in, and a few more for their meaning to register. Then it made sense. She suddenly knew exactly why he didn't care what she did with the suite. And it had nothing to do with trusting her taste.

It was of no consequence to him, because he wasn't going to be living there.

There was something wrong.

Phillip could feel it. He could see it written clearly on Hannah's face. Although for the life of him, he had no idea what it could be.

He had done everything right tonight. And, with the exception of the stunt Sophie pulled at dinner, it hadn't been nearly as trying as he'd anticipated. In fact, being with Hannah wasn't a hardship at all. He enjoyed her company.

Yet, as hard as he'd tried, she was *still* unhappy.

"What did I do?" he asked.

She blinked rapidly, as though surprised by his question. "Wh-what do you mean?"

Did she honestly think him so daft or self-centered that he wouldn't notice when she was upset? "You have that look," he said. "And I have the distinct impression I did or said something wrong."

She shook her head, too emphatically to be believable, and plastered a smile on her face. "No. Of course not."

He sighed. "Hannah, you're a terrible liar."

She bit her lip and lowered her eyes.

She wasn't going to make this easy. She was going to make him drag it out of her. As long as he lived, he would never understand the inner workings of the female mind.

Fine then, if that was what she wanted. "Just tell me why you're upset."

"It's really late, and I'm exhausted," she said, but she wouldn't look him in the eye.

He folded his arms across his chest. "I'm not leaving until you tell me what's wrong."

She glanced up at him, saw that he was serious. That he really wasn't going anywhere. "It's stupid."

"Go on."

"I thought... I just assumed..."

He waited patiently for her to continue.

She looked down at her hands, clenched in front of her, and said softly, "I thought that, after the wedding, we would be sharing a suite."

He wasn't sure what surprised him more, that she would want to share a suite, or that it upset her that they wouldn't. Honestly, it had never crossed his mind. His parents had been married, yet they never shared living quarters. Maybe in her world, that was what married couples did.

But this was not going to be a typical marriage. She knew that going in and he wasn't about to change his ways. "Hannah—"

"It's okay. Really."

Obviously it was not okay. He could see that she was trying to be tough, but her voice had that wobbly sound she got just before she cried. He was sorry she was hurt, but this was not negotiable. "This is the way things are. My parents conducted their marriage the same way and I intend to follow those rules."

"I understand," she said. But he could see that she didn't. She was hurt and confused.

"I thought you knew coming into this that it was an arrangement. I'm sorry if this upsets you or you were misled about my intentions." Hadn't they determined, on more than one occasion, that he was the king, and he made the rules?

But that had been in jest. There was nothing funny about this.

She sniffled softly and swiped at her cheek. "I'm well aware of our arrangements. Just forget I said anything."

It pained him to see her so distraught, and trying so hard to hide it. He wanted to say something, anything, to make her feel better, but the words escaped him. How did she manage, without even trying, to make him feel so helpless?

So…inadequate?

She took a deep breath and blew it out. "I'm sorry. I'm just tired." She flashed him a smile that almost looked genuine. "I'm up way past my bedtime. Not to mention that it's been a really crazy week."

That it had. Both of their lives had been changed dramatically, but he had to remind himself that hers bore the brunt of it. It was just going to take time for them to adjust. And would it kill him to spare her just a little bit more of his time? At least until she settled in.

"Do you have plans for lunch tomorrow?" he asked.

"Nothing I can't change."

He had a ridiculously busy schedule, but he could spare some time if it kept the peace. "We could eat, then take a walk in the garden."

Her smile grew. "I would love to."

Though he felt ridiculous for it, the happiness that filled her eyes warmed his heart. "One o'clock?"

She nodded vigorously.

"It's a date then." He pressed one last lingering kiss to her lips, then opened the door. "I'll see you tomorrow."

"See you tomorrow," she said, before she closed the door behind him.

And as he walked to his own suite, he considered the events of the past week, since the minute she stepped out of that car and into his life. He knew she had prepared for her position as his wife, and it was clear she took it very seriously. It was her motivation that had him puzzled. Until she moved to Morgan Isle, he had been sure she'd done it for the title. For the security of her family. Yet she seemed to have every intention of making this marriage work.

She seemed to want the real thing.

But that was more than he was willing, or *capable,* of giving.

Friday came faster than Hannah could have imagined. Faster than she was ready for. She'd spent the past eight years preparing for this, and suddenly everything was happening so fast, she barely had time to catch her breath. And though she vowed not to let the living arrangements upset her, it had been in the back of her mind.

She was beginning to suspect that her ideas about her perfect life with Phillip, all her carefully mapped plans, were silly and immature. And for the most part, totally unrealistic.

She of all people should understand that life didn't follow a plan. If it did, she never would have lost her father, and her mother wouldn't be trying to replace him. She couldn't expect Phillip to fall into line and live his life, one she knew virtually nothing about, by her preconceived notion of what a marriage was *supposed* to be.

But even if things didn't go exactly as she planned, that didn't mean she and Phillip wouldn't be happy. It was just going to take time to figure things out, to get them running smoothly, and a lot of compromise. She would have to be patient with him.

Honestly, what did it say about his childhood that he'd never considered sharing a living space with his own wife? A person didn't grow up like that without collecting scars along the way. She would have to be pretty coldhearted not to cut him some slack.

The more she thought about it over the course of the week, when she took the time to consider his feelings, more than being hurt, she felt sad. For him, because of the loving environment he deserved, and obviously never had. She would show him how unconditional love and dedication felt. No matter what it took.

Everything was going to work out all right.

She kept telling herself that all week as last-minute preparations were being made, and when her bridesmaids and mother arrived for the rehearsal luncheon Thursday afternoon.

She chanted it over and over during the final dress fittings, and later at the impromptu bridal dinner Sophie hosted at her residence. While everyone sipped champagne and shared stories of love and relationships, Hannah pasted on a smile to hide the fact that, for the first time since she made the decision to do this, she was questioning herself.

She even pretended, when her mother mentioned her own impending wedding, that she wasn't horrified by the idea. And when everyone gushed over the palace and asked her if royal life was everything she had dreamed of, she told them yes. Because it was, or, it *would* be. At least she hoped so.

It was after midnight when everyone retired to their rooms, and Hannah was finally alone, with nothing but time to think about what she was doing. It wasn't as if she could back out at this point. Not that she would even want to. She was just confused and scared.

What if she was making a mistake?

What she needed was a sign. She needed something to happen that would assure her she was doing the right thing.

She'd barely completed the thought when someone knocked on her door. Then she heard Phillip's voice.

"Hannah, it's me."

She rushed to the door before he could open it. As desperately as she wanted to see him, with the wedding less than twenty-four hours away, she couldn't. It would be bad luck and, honestly, she didn't need another black cloud hanging over her head.

She opened the door a crack, and stood behind it, so she wouldn't be tempted to look. "We can't see each other."

"I know," he said, his tone hushed. "I just wanted to let you know that I'm back from the States. I didn't want you to worry that I might be late for our wedding."

"How was your trip?"

"Exhausting. I toured ten resorts in five days. I'm glad to be home."

And she was glad he came home.

"I ran into Sophie downstairs. She said there was a bridal party tonight."

"It was fun," Hannah said. "It was nice to see all of my friends again. You'll meet them tomorrow."

"Sophie also said that she thought you might be upset about something."

How could Sophie have known? Hannah had been so careful not to let it show. "Why would she think that?"

"I don't know. But I wanted to make sure you're okay."

He was worried about her.

Though it was a small thing, for her, it meant so much. "I'm okay."

"I'm glad," he said. And she could hear that he was honestly relieved. "I worried you might be having second thoughts."

Was he seriously thinking that she wouldn't marry him? The idea that he could be even the slightest bit unsure made her feel a million times better. It made her realize that she wasn't in this alone. "Are you?"

There was a pause, then an emphatic, "No. I'm not."

She smiled. Neither was she any longer. "I'm not either."

"I missed you," he said. He sounded a little surprised. Like he hadn't expected to miss her, but it just…happened.

This was it. This was her sign.

"I missed you, too," she told him.

"I'm going to get to bed. I'll see you tomorrow. Sleep well."

"You, too."

She heard his footsteps as he walked away, then she closed the door and leaned against it.

The sense of dread she had been feeling all week was suddenly gone. The gush of relief that replaced it was so swift and intense her knees nearly buckled. Tomorrow she'd be Queen Hannah Augustus Mead.

Ten

The next day rushed by in a blur. Hannah was so busy, she barely had a moment to be nervous. And only when the time came to walk down the aisle, did she feel a twinge of sadness. Her father should have been here to give her away. But because there was no one in the world who could ever take his place, she insisted walking it alone.

When she saw Phillip standing at the end of the white runner, stoic and regal in his dress uniform, she felt a dizzying mix of excitement and nerves. And as she walked toward him and their eyes connected—when she saw a smile tug at the corners of his mouth and a dance in the depths of his eyes—a deep feeling of peace washed over her.

The ceremony itself was over quickly, and when the priest introduced them as husband and wife, the guests cheered.

Photographs seemed to take forever, and by the time they were escorted to the ballroom, the reception was already in full swing. Dinner was served shortly after, then they covered all of the formalities like the cutting of the cake and the first dance.

Her mother was her usual clingy self, and beginning to get on Hannah's nerves, until Sophie swooped in and whisked her away to meet some foreign dignitary.

As lovely as the party was, as much as she enjoyed seeing her friends and family, not to mention hobnobbing with the worlds elite, she couldn't seem to stop thinking about after the party. When she and Phillip would finally be alone, and free to do whatever they wanted.

She realized that Phillip was thinking the exact same thing when he stepped up beside her and asked, "How soon before we can leave?"

"At eleven o'clock we're to bid everyone farewell, so we can prepare to leave for our honeymoon." Even though there wasn't all that much preparing to do. Her maids had already packed her bags, and she was sure Phillip's had done the same.

She couldn't help but think that the instant they left, every single guest was going to know exactly what they were planning to do.

He pulled a pocket watch from his jacket and flipped it open. "It's ten-fifteen."

"So we should make the rounds one last time, say our goodbyes and thank-yous."

He took her arm. "That sounds like an excellent idea."

They went from group to group, thanking everyone for sharing their special day, hearing more congratulations and good wishes than she could count. There were even a few inquiries of how she felt now that she was officially queen.

"Honored," was her stock answer. Also terrified and unsure, but she didn't tell anyone that.

It was five minutes to eleven o'clock and they were saying good-night to the prime minister and his wife, when Hannah had a familiar and unsettling sensation she was being watched. She scanned the room briefly and when she reached the dessert table, her eyes caught on the source.

The dark-haired mystery woman.

She was staring intently at Hannah, this time with open hostility.

What could Hannah have done to a woman she had never even met, to earn such a look?

She wanted to point her out to Phillip, but he was in the middle of a conversation and she didn't want to appear rude by interrupting him. When she turned to look at the woman again, she was gone.

Hannah looked around frantically, trying to locate her, but it was as if she'd vanished. Like the last time, she even entertained the notion that she'd imagined her.

"Is something wrong?" Phillip asked.

She looked up to see that he was watching her with concern. She considered telling him about the woman, but what good would it do, now that she was gone? She smiled instead and said, "I'm fine. Just looking for my mother so I can say goodbye."

"Let's go find her so we can get out of here."

Hannah was sure the woman was no one, and she had nothing to be concerned about. So far her wedding day had been perfect, and she wasn't going to let anything ruin it.

Still, somewhere deep down, she couldn't help feeling the slightest twinge of something unpleasant. A foreshadow of something to come.

It was 11:15 p.m. by the time Phillip walked Hannah to her suite. He left to change out of his uniform while she went inside where her maids were waiting to help her out of her gown. To unfasten the row of miniscule buttons up the back.

It seemed to take forever, but finally she was free. She dismissed them immediately, so she'd have time to see to all the preparations she had been planning.

She took the box down from her closet, the one she had been saving for this day, and from inside of it pulled out the pure-white, silk-and-lace nightgown. She slipped it on and it dripped over her body like liquid, conforming to every curve.

Since Phillip liked her hair down, she fished out the pins then brushed out all the gel and hairspray until it lay shiny and soft against her shoulders. She dabbed a touch of perfume behind her ears and along her collarbone.

As Hannah asked, Elizabeth had decorated the bedroom with white candles. Dozens of them on every possible flat surface, all lit. When she turned out the lights, the effect was exactly what she had hoped for. Soft, flickering light.

The maids had turned the bed down and left two perfect red rosebuds, one on each pillow. A bottle of champagne chilled in a stand by the dresser.

It was exactly as she'd imagined.

"You've been busy," Phillip said.

She jolted with surprise and spun around. He stood, leaning in the bedroom doorway, watching her. He wore slacks and a long-sleeved silk shirt that was untucked and lay open. His skin looked warm and golden in the candlelight.

She felt absolutely naked in the scant gown, but she resisted the urge to cover herself. She didn't want him to know how nervous she was. "I didn't hear you knock."

"That's because I didn't. I thought you wouldn't mind, now that we're married." He walked toward her, a hungry look in his eyes as they raked over her. "It would seem that I'm overdressed."

The shirt slipped off his shoulders, down his arms and landed on the floor. The candles were supposed to make her look good, but, oh my goodness, he was beautiful.

He didn't stop until he was standing right in front of her. She just hoped he didn't notice the thud of her heart, the way her hands trembled. She didn't want him to know how nervous she felt.

He reached up and touched the lacey edge of the gown where it rested on the swell of her breast. "This is nice."

She swallowed hard, willing herself to relax.

"Nervous?" he asked.

"No," she said, but it came out as more of a squeak than an actual word. She cleared her throat and amended her answer to, "Maybe a little. Are you?"

He grinned and shook his head.

Of course he wasn't. Unlike her, he had done this before.

He leaned down, kissed her bare shoulder, his lips soft, his breath warm on her skin. "You smell good," he said.

So did he. She loved the way he smelled, the way he felt, yet she couldn't seem to make herself touch him.

Why was she so afraid? It wasn't as though she had never touched him before. But for some reason this time was different. Maybe because she knew what the end result would be.

His hands settled on her hips, large and steady, and she couldn't help it when she tensed.

"Relax, Hannah."

She took a deep breath and blew it out.

"I'm not sure what I'm supposed to do. This is my first time."

Rather than act disappointed, he smiled. Not condescending either. This was a smile of pure affection. "Just do what comes naturally. Act on your instincts."

That was the problem. Her instincts seemed to have lost their voice.

"You could start by touching me." He took her hand in his and pressed it flat against his chest. It felt so solid under her palm, his skin hot to the touch.

He tugged her closer, nuzzling the hollow behind her ear. It felt amazing, *better* than amazing.

He nipped the curve where her neck met her shoulder, making her skin shiver with awareness. "Honestly, I wasn't sure you were a virgin."

"You weren't?" How could he not tell?

"Not after that night in my suite. You seemed to have a pretty good grasp on what you were doing."

He kissed her throat, the line of her jaw. "This is no different."

His hands slid up her sides, his thumbs brushing the outermost edge of her breasts. She felt them tingle, the tips tighten into painful points.

"So, no man has touched you like this?" he asked.

"Nope."

"Never?"

She shook her head. She could see by his smile that he liked knowing she was his, and his only. She liked it, too.

"No one ever did this?" He cupped her breasts in his hands and a whimper slipped from her lips. His thumbs grazed back and forth, teasing her, and her skin went hot.

Then he picked her up and placed her on the bed. He unfastened his pants and slid them off.

Hannah couldn't help but be drawn to the front of his boxers. To the impressive-looking ridge underneath. She was no expert, but he looked…*generous*.

He settled beside her, propped up on his elbow,

smiling down at her. A sleepy, sexy grin. "Here we are."

"Here we are," she agreed. Finally. She had been beginning to feel as if this day would never come.

He brushed her breast with his lips. Once, then twice, then he took her in his mouth, silk and all, and the sensation was so shockingly intense that she gasped and arched her back.

She couldn't help wondering what other places he could use his mouth.

He hooked his index finger around one strap of her gown and eased it down her arm until her entire breast was exposed. And when he took her in his mouth this time, there was no fabric barrier. This time she felt *everything*. His tongue, his teeth. The wet heat.

A sound came out of her, like a moan, but more desperate, and she realized her fingers were tunneling through his hair. She was arching against his mouth, urging him to take more.

Phillip seemed to be fascinated by her. He kissed her breasts, her mouth, touched her in ways that made her shudder and quake. And her own hands seemed to have taken on a life of their own, exploring the secrets of his body, touching him like she had only imagined in her most intimate fantasies.

It wasn't long before the gown that was meant to arouse him was only getting in the way.

"This has to go," he ordered, helping her tug it up over her head, until the only thing left was a pair of scant thong panties made of the same fragile lace. Then he just looked at her, his eyes dark with arousal. "You're beautiful."

She felt beautiful, and not the least bit afraid. In fact, she couldn't imagine why she had been so nervous. This was so absolutely and completely right. She had never felt so close to him. To *anyone*.

He touched the minuscule triangle of lace between her thighs and it felt so amazing she nearly vaulted off the bed.

He eased her thong down her legs so slowly that she got impatient and kicked it the rest of the way off. Then she did something that surprised them both. She reached for the waistband of his boxers and tugged at them. She wanted them both to be naked.

He captured her mouth with his and kissed the last of her sense completely away. She didn't think she could be any more aroused, but somehow Phillip managed. Kissing her, touching her, until she could hardly stand it.

What felt like hours later, he eased himself over her, between her thighs. "I'll take it slow."

But she didn't want slow. She wanted to feel all of him now. She reached for his hips and pushed them hard against her.

She shuddered a moment, and then the pain was gone. What she felt instead was indescribable. She felt…complete. The ultimate in closeness.

He thrust into her, slowly at first, then faster.

She wound her legs around his, dug her nails into his shoulders. "Phillip," she begged, even though she had no idea what she was begging for.

He thrust himself inside her again, harder this time, and she was so stunned by the sensation she cried out.

He eased back and thrust again. Phillip could feel her inner walls flex and contract around him. Her eyes looked bleary and unfocused and her skin was blushed and hot.

He had never seen anything more arousing or sexy. Had never been with a woman so easy to please. And though it was taking every bit of concentration he could muster to maintain control, he didn't want to rush this.

But he could feel her losing it, feel her body clenching down on him. Then she tensed and bucked up against him. Her eyes went wide and sightless, with shock and pleasure and wonder. That was all it took. He lost it. His body coiled then released, letting go in a hot rush that seemed to wring the last trace of energy from his very cells. And for a minute, he couldn't find the strength to do more than breathe.

* * *

Hannah was gazing up at him, looking just as physically spent as he felt. Her cheeks and chest were deep red and her breath was coming in short, sharp bursts.

"Are you okay?"

She nodded, but when he shifted his weight, she grimaced.

"Hurt?"

"A little," she admitted.

He eased off her slowly, then he rolled onto his back and pulled her along with him. She curled up against his side in the crook of his arm, soft and warm and boneless, her head resting on his shoulder. The covers had somehow wound up in a bunch at their feet, but it didn't matter. He was so relaxed he felt as if he were melting into the mattress.

Oddly, it was perfect.

Getting married, saying the vows, hadn't been the disconcerting experience he had expected. When Sophie came to him the night before to say that Hannah was upset, the idea of her changing her mind, of her backing out and moving back to America, made him realize just how fond of her he'd become.

He just hoped that would be enough.

They were quiet for several minutes while their breathing evened out and pulses returned to normal.

"Is it always like that?" she asked.

"Like what?"

"It just felt so…so…*good.* I thought that wasn't supposed to happen. Not my first time."

He shrugged. "I guess you're a natural."

That made her smile. "Do we have to wait long?"

"For what?"

"To do it again?"

Already? "I thought you were sore."

"Not anymore." She put her hand on his stomach, a little shyly, but insatiably curious, and that was all it took for him.

He rolled her onto her back and smiled down at her. "Who says we have to wait?"

It was her innocence and her honesty, her complete trust, that was such a turn-on. But what did that mean for their future?

She would only be innocent for so long. Then what?

Eventually the novelty was going to wear off. It would become a duty instead of a pleasure, until the day came when they didn't bother at all.

She wrapped her arms around his neck and pulled him down for a kiss, and he decided not to worry about that now.

He would just enjoy it while it lasted.

Eleven

They left early the next morning for the private yacht off the coast of Monaco where they would be spending their honeymoon. In a way Phillip was dreading it. Two weeks, stuck in close quarters with the same woman. It was bound to get monotonous.

He spent most of the flight devising excuses to get them back to the palace early, and trying to determine how soon he could suggest going back without upsetting her too much. At least a week, he decided. By then he should be crawling out of his skin.

The first day, all they managed, on so little sleep, was to lie around and sun themselves, occasionally dipping in the water to cool off. They snacked on caviar and sipped champagne. And every so often Hannah would get this look, and next thing he knew, they would be tumbling into bed.

The second day was much of the same, and because it was rare that he allowed himself the privilege of just laying around and doing nothing, he let himself enjoy it.

Monday, Phillip and Hannah went ashore. They spent the day sightseeing and shopping, where he expected to put his credit card to good use, but Hannah surprised him again by showing little interest in spending his money. She only purchased a few modest souvenirs for family and friends, and she used her own money.

When he noticed her admiring a sapphire teardrop pendant necklace in a shop window, and saw the way her eyes lit, he suggested they go in and buy it.

She shook her head and said, "It's too much."

"You like it?"

She shrugged, but he could see that she was holding back.

"Do you *like* it?"

She bit her lip and nodded.

"Then let's get it." He took her hand and reached for the door handle but she resisted.

"I don't *need* it, Phillip."

"Consider it a wedding gift."

"But—"

"Let's at least look at it."

It took several more minutes of cajoling, and he still had to practically drag her into the shop. But when the salesclerk took the necklace from the case and handed it to Hannah, he knew he had her. With little argument, she allowed him to purchase it for her, and it surprised him how much her happiness pleased him.

Rather than let the bodyguard stow it with the rest of their packages, she insisted on wearing it. And as they walked, she kept one hand in his, and the other at her throat, smiling and fingering the gem as though it were the most precious thing she had ever owned. And she must have thanked him a dozen times.

"You act as if no one ever bought you a present," he said. "I thought your father was very wealthy."

"He was. But he also believed it was important to teach me the value of a dollar. I received gifts for the usual occasions. Holidays and birthdays and graduations. But nothing too extravagant. If I wanted something, I had to earn it."

"Like what, for example?"

"My first car. Daddy said owning a car is a privilege I had to earn. I worked in his office for a year before getting my license. Weekends during the school year so it wouldn't interrupt my studies, and five days a week during the summer. When I finally did get a car, all that hard work made me appreciate it. I took such good care of it that I drove it through the rest of high school and all through college."

"Even though you could have afforded a new car?"

She shrugged. "There was nothing wrong with the one I had."

Hannah never ceased to fascinate him. Just when he thought he had her figured out, she would do or say something to completely skew his impression of her.

"Does it bother you to always have someone watching you?" Hannah asked, referring to the bodyguards who shadowed their every step.

He shrugged. "It's always been that way."

"But don't you ever get tired of it? Do you ever wish you could be completely alone?"

"Sometimes, but I have a duty to my country to stay alive," he joked, and she laughed.

She seemed to find him genuinely entertaining, and he could recognize counterfeit laughter a mile away. He liked that he could make her happy so effortlessly. He'd dated women in the past who needed constant attention and ego stroking. He was beginning to believe that Hannah was one of the most low-maintenance women he'd ever known.

And what he liked even more was that she had a

mind of her own. He was accustomed to everyone doing exactly as he asked. Especially women. But Hannah wasn't afraid to question his motives. And often it took nothing more than a look. He might have suspected her to be manipulative, but he honestly didn't believe she had a deceitful bone in her body. She was too sweet and honest. Yet still managed to possess the resolve and character of ten men.

He liked her. Probably too much for either of their best interests.

Tuesday morning they docked in *Port De Fontvieille* where they would spend the day as guests of the Grimaldi family, with whom he'd been friends with since childhood. Yet, all he could think about over the course of the day was getting back to the ship so he and Hannah could be alone.

He'd never met a woman so curious or honest in bed. So responsive to his touch, or willing to experiment. And she was a quick study. Every day she became more and more adventurous.

Phillip kept waiting to get restless. For the familiar edgy feeling that would signal it was time to cut their vacation short and get back to the palace. He even had the perfect excuse. This was an arrangement. He was fulfilling his duty and shouldn't be having a problem controlling his urges. But, well into their second week, he began to realize that he wasn't growing restless. Spending time with her wasn't the burden he'd imagined. He liked her. She was witty and smart. And fun. He could talk to her. Intelligent conversations. He would even find himself telling her things that he'd never told anyone. Personal things. Even more odd, he felt as though he could trust her. Though it went against everything he had learned.

As the last day of their vacation drew closer, he found himself wishing it were longer. Which meant nothing, he told himself, other than the fact that she had preoccupied him longer than most. They would return to the palace, get back to *normal* life. He would go his way and she hers, meeting in the middle every so often. Often enough to placate her.

And as tempted as he might be to let things slide for just a while, he would be treading on dangerous ground. It was more important now than ever to draw the line. To make it clear exactly where she stood.

She wouldn't be happy about that. Not at first, but she would become used to the way things were. And maybe she wouldn't be happy, but she would adjust. She would adopt a cause, or find some purpose in her life that would keep her occupied. Then, when the children began to come along, she would immerse herself in being a mother.

And he was confident that she would be an excep-

tional one. Their children would know what it felt
liked to be loved. And even if he wasn't capable,
Hannah would love them enough for the both of them.

Though he couldn't help thinking that Hannah
deserved so much better than that.

Twelve

They returned late Saturday night from their honey-moon to find that Hannah's new suite was finished and all of her things already moved in. But she was so exhausted, she didn't have the energy to investigate.

She stood in her sitting room Sunday morning, as her maids unpacked her things, taking in each and every detail. It was gorgeous, and exactly as she'd planned, but her excitement fell flat. As close as she and Phillip had become over their honeymoon, she half expected him to say he'd changed his mind, that he wanted to share a suite with her. When that didn't happen, when he chose to sleep in his own suite last

night—*alone*—she felt a deep sting of disappointment. Apparently things would go back to the way
they had been before the wedding.

But what had she expected? That in two weeks,
everything would change? That he would come home
a new man?

Okay, maybe she *had* expected it. Or, at the very
least, wished for it. But these things took time. It
would take a lot longer than fourteen days to over-
come years of abuse and dysfunction. Which is
exactly what Phillip had endured, though it had been
kept well hidden behind the royal crest. His parents'
treatment of him was reprehensible.

And a little voice in the back of her mind whispered, *Like father like son?* Would he do the same to
his children? But she would never let that happen. Her
and Phillip's children would know they were loved.

"Welcome home."

She sighed and turned to see Elizabeth standing
in the doorway.

Elizabeth smiled. "You asked me to remind you
about the gifts in the study."

Wedding gifts from all over the world had begun
arriving the Monday before the wedding. And since
her regular schedule didn't resume until tomorrow,
she figured it would be best to get everything taken
care of this afternoon. "Why don't we go take a look?"

They stepped out into the hall together and headed toward the stairs.

"Did you have a nice vacation?" Elizabeth asked. "I hear Monaco is lovely this time of year."

"The weather was perfect. We had a wonderful time together. How about you? Did you take any time off while I was gone?"

She was being nosy, but after learning Elizabeth didn't even have a boyfriend, Hannah insisted that she worked too hard. She was too young to be alone. She needed to live a little. But Hannah could see from her expression that Elizabeth hadn't taken her advice.

"I've been so busy with plans for the gala, I haven't really had time."

"Maybe I could help you," Hannah said. "I don't know a lot about planning parties, but I'd like to learn. Since this is my home now, I should get more involved."

"I would be honored." They reached the study door and Elizabeth asked ominously, "Are you ready?"

Ready? How bad could it be?

She opened the door, and when Hannah saw the state of the room, she gasped. Then she blinked several times, to be sure it wasn't an optical illusion. "Oh my God."

"Most of them came the past two weeks while you were gone."

What had started out as a few dozen gifts was now hundreds—heck, maybe even a *thousand*. Ornately wrapped packages in every conceivable size and shape were stacked nearly waist high in one corner of the study. "Who are they all from?"

"Government representatives, friends and relatives, business executives. They came in from all over the world."

No way she could open all these in one afternoon. It could take weeks to sort through it all, and she dreaded the nightmare of writing all the thank-you cards.

"It's something, isn't it?"

Hannah turned to find Sophie standing behind them. "I can't believe it. Is this normal?"

Sophie shrugged. "The last time anyone around here got married, it was my parents, and I wasn't around for that."

"It's going to take forever to open them all."

"Not if you have help," Sophie said. "I'm free today."

"Me, too," Elizabeth said. "I'm sure your maids would be happy to help as well. And we could probably round up a few other people."

"And what about Phillip?" Sophie asked.

Hannah could ask, or insist even, since they were his gifts as well as hers, but she had the very distinct feeling he needed some space. Though he never once, in the entire two weeks of their vacation, seemed restless or claustrophobic, the minute they returned home he immediately retreated to his suite. But not before mentioning a golf outing he had planned with his cousin today. Even though they were technically still on their honeymoon until tonight.

"He's spending the day with Charles," Hannah told her, and she could swear she saw disapproval in her sister-in-law's eyes. But for whom? Phillip for leaving, or Hannah for allowing it?

She wasn't sure she wanted to know. It disturbed her to think that Sophie might be disappointed in her, though she wasn't sure why. Maybe because Sophie was so strong. She seemed to know exactly what she wanted and wasn't afraid to fight for it.

Hannah hoped that someday she could be like that.

"The most efficient way to handle this would be two people per gift," Hannah reasoned. "One to open, the other to write down the sender and what the gift is."

"Sounds like a good idea," Sophie agreed. "Elizabeth, why don't you gather everything we need, and everyone you can find to help. I'll call over to the house and see what my housekeeper is up to."

"And I'll start sorting," Hannah said.

After Elizabeth left to round up more help, Sophie asked, "How was your honeymoon?"

"It was wonderful. Perfect."

"And now he's pulling a disappearing act?"

"It's not like that," Hannah told her, even though she suspected it was. "After two weeks solid together, who wouldn't need a break?"

"You, I suspect."

She hated that Sophie could read her so well.

"You didn't even sleep in the same room last night," Sophie added.

How could she possibly know that? "What, do you have spies in the palace watching us?"

"Who needs spies? Your rooms face my residence and I know every window in this place. The lights were on in both your suites last night."

Hannah didn't know what to say, what she *could* say, to convince Sophie that everything was okay. So she didn't even try. "It's just going to take time."

"You really believe that?"

"Yes, as a matter of fact I do. I'm committed to make this work."

Sophie smiled. "You'll be okay, then."

Hannah must have looked confused, because Sophie chuckled. "I like you, Hannah. I think you're good for my brother. He needs someone to give him a swift kick in the ass every now and then. Remind him that he's worthy."

"Worthy?"

"Of love. Of happiness."

"Why would he think that? I know your parents were cold, but that certainly wasn't any fault of yours and Phillip's."

"Try telling that to a young child. When your parents don't show you love and affection, you feel as if there's something wrong with you. You think that, for whatever reason, you're not lovable."

Hannah couldn't even imagine how that would feel. The idea of her parents not loving her was so far out of her range of comprehension.

"Add to that all of the women showering him with false affection. For the money, or the crown, or whatever their particular agenda might be. You never know who to trust."

"You seem to get it."

"*Getting it* doesn't mean anything. I've never been in a relationship that lasted more than four months, Hannah. Why do you think that is?" She shrugged. "It's like telling an alcoholic they have to stop drinking and expecting them to go cold turkey."

That was just so…*sad*.

Sophie must have read her expression. "I'm not telling you this so you'll feel sorry for me. I just want you to know what you're up against. He really cares for you. I can tell. Even if he's not so great at showing it. It's going to take time."

"I'm not in a rush. I'm determined to make this work. No matter what or how long it takes."

Sophie smiled. "I'm glad. Now, enough of this. I'm going to call home and see if I can wrangle up a bit more help."

"I'll start sorting this mess."

"Back in a few," Sophie said, then she was gone.

Until just then, Hannah hadn't realized how lucky she was, how good her parents had been to her. And she felt bad for the way she'd been treating her mother.

Her mother was right when she said Hannah wasn't being fair. Maybe she just didn't like that she wasn't the center of her mother's world any longer. She was in limbo. Not a part of her old life any longer, but not quite into her new one yet.

She felt unsure of what she was supposed to be. In the past she would go to her father for advice, to help her sort things through, since he knew her better than anyone in the world. He understood her.

With him gone, for the first time in her life, she was entirely on her own.

It was past 10:00 p.m. when Phillip returned to the palace. He noticed the light on in the study and walked over to investigate. There he found Hannah, sitting on the floor, opening wedding gifts.

He realized he was happy to see her. He'd thought of little else all day but her smile. Which is why he'd made it a point to stay away. He didn't want her getting the wrong idea. He didn't want to delude her into believing that anything had changed.

The mountain of packages that had been there last night when he stepped in to get a book had been reduced by at least half. What was left of the wrapped gifts was on one side of the room, sorted by size, and the opened ones still in boxes on the opposite side.

"Did you do all this on your own?" he asked.

She looked up at him, but her smile wasn't as bright as usual. "I had help. I hope you don't mind that we started without you."

He stepped farther into the room. "I don't mind."

"That's what I figured."

She was still wearing the necklace he gave her. As far as he knew, she hadn't taken it off yet. "Did we get anything good?"

"Lots of crystal and silver. Kitchen and bed linen. I can't begin to imagine where we'll put it all."

"Storage?" he suggested.

"But doesn't that seem like a waste? I'm flattered by everyone's generosity, but I can't help feeling that it's too much."

She looked genuinely distressed, and it occurred to him that her chilly greeting had nothing to do with his behavior. She was upset over the gifts. It was her conscience distressing her, not his apparent relationship phobia. And despite telling himself otherwise, he was relieved. Seeing her unhappy was unpleasant enough. Knowing it was his fault made him feel unfit.

He was royalty, the leader of his country, yet somehow she managed to make him feel…inferior. And she did it without even trying, because Hannah wouldn't have the first clue how to be vindictive. The word wasn't even in her vocabulary.

He sat down beside her on the floor and she leaned against him, letting her head drop against his shoulder.

"It feels wrong that we've received all these lavish and, to be honest, *excessive* gifts when so many people around the world lack the basic necessities."

"So what do you want to do?"

"I did have an idea. Maybe we could sponsor an auction and the proceeds could be donated to charity."

"Auction off our wedding gifts? You don't think people would be offended?"

"We can release a statement. Something about how grateful we are, but we want to share it with the rest of the world. I'm sure your press people can put just the right spin on it."

If so, it would make the royal family look good,

not that he suspected for a second that image was her concern. She was just a generous, caring person.

"Because there's so much," she said, "we would probably have to do a live auction for the more valuable pieces and a silent auction for the smaller stuff."

He looked down at her and smiled. "I think it's an excellent idea."

Her face lit up. "Really?"

"I do. First thing tomorrow, I'll look into it."

"Thank you!" She threw her arms around his neck and hugged him, and he scooped her up and sat her in his lap.

Ah, yes. This was what he needed, what he had been craving since last night when he went to bed alone. Not that he'd slept much. In two weeks' time, sleeping alone had lost its appeal. But like everything else, eventually the novelty would wear off.

"Why don't we go to bed?" he suggested.

"We, as in, both of us together? In the same bed?"

"That was the idea." Although, after last night, he couldn't really blame her for being unsure. "If that's okay with you."

She smiled, happy once again. "Your bed or mine?"

"Yours."

"I need to take a shower first."

He rose to his feet and pulled her along with him. "Perhaps I should join you."

She gave him that wicked smile. "You know I love you all soapy and slippery."

And that feeling, he decided, was most definitely mutual.

Thirteen

The weeks that followed their honeymoon flew by for Hannah. Between organizing the auction, which would take place just before the holiday season, and planning the gala, which would happen in the spring—not to mention her regular royal duties and cooking lessons with Sophie—she barely had a free moment.

Phillip's schedule was no less hectic. Though they didn't always manage dinner together, their nights—when he wasn't traveling—were reserved for each other. They alternated between his and her suite. They made love often, although there were times when they were both too exhausted to do more than lie in bed and watch the evening news, fighting to keep their eyes open.

Somehow, since she had moved to Morgan Isle, she and Phillip had become a couple. And while it wasn't exactly the way she had planned on and dreamed about, different was all right. It kept things interesting. It was more work than she had imagined, but she was happy, and Phillip was, too.

At least, that was what she thought.

The afternoon of the auction, she was a nervous wreck, hoping everything went well. What if no one showed? What if people really were insulted that she and Phillip would cast off their gifts?

"You're worrying for nothing," Phillip assured her. "It's going to be a huge success."

And as with most situations like this, he was right. The moment the doors opened, the room flooded with people. Two hours later, just before the bidding for the live auction was to begin, it was standing room only.

She and Phillip were making the rounds, socializing and drumming up business, when she felt that disturbing, familiar sensation of being watched. Sure enough, when she scanned the room, her eyes connected with those of the mystery woman.

She nudged Phillip to get his attention. When he saw her face, he frowned. "What's the matter?"

"That woman is here."

"What woman?"

"The one who was staring at me the afternoon I arrived. I saw her at our wedding, too."

"Where?" he asked.

She gestured in her general direction. "Long dark hair. Really attractive."

She could tell the instant Phillip saw her, the way recognition lit his eyes, that he knew her. And rather than look away, the woman smiled and waved to him. Then she started walking toward them and Hannah's heart bottomed out.

Finally, she would meet face-to-face with the woman who so openly resented her. Though she was relieved to be getting it over with, her hands still trembled. She was so beautiful, and she practically oozed sensuality. In contrast, Hannah looked almost plain and dowdy.

"Phillip!" she said, her voice low and sultry. "So good to see you again!"

Phillip didn't look as if he shared the sentiment, but he was polite. "Madeline, hello."

She accepted his outstretched hand, then took it a step further by kissing his cheek. No one would be so bold, unless they had a somewhat intimate relationship with the king. And it was more than obvious these two did. And to do it right in front of Hannah? No doubt this woman had some kind of agenda.

"Hannah, this is Madeline Grenaugh," Phillip said. "Madeline, this is my wife."

"Your Highness," she said, but the words dripped with barely masked distaste, then she dipped into the most pathetic excuse for a curtsy Hannah had ever seen. The tension was so thick it seemed to cling to her skin and clothes, fill the chambers of her lungs until it was difficult to breathe.

"Well, the auction will be starting soon," Phillip said, and Hannah could see that he was antsy to move on.

"Yes, I should decide which pieces I plan to bid on. It was a pleasure to finally meet you, Hannah."

Not addressing Hannah by her title was a direct and blatant insult, nor did she bother to curtsy. Phillip didn't seem to notice, or didn't care.

"I'll see you again very soon," she told Phillip, and gave him a smile, as though they shared some sort of secret. And as she walked away, she leaned close to Hannah and said under her breath, "You may be his wife, but I'll always be the one he loves."

Hannah was so stunned she didn't know what to say. She stood there frozen, dumbfounded.

"What did she say to you?" Phillip asked.

Hannah shook her head. Phillip looked as though he might push the issue, but then someone else approached them and he seemed to forget about it altogether.

Hannah couldn't though.

She wasn't foolish enough to believe that Phillip had no women in his life before her, but to have one thrown in her face was more disturbing than she could have dreamed. Especially one who looked like that. And what if Madeline had been telling the truth? What if Phillip *did* love her?

No, that was ridiculous.

Phillip loved Hannah. He may not have been able to say the words, but he expressed his feelings in so many different ways. She could even live her entire life without actually hearing him say the words, just as long as his actions spoke for him.

Couldn't she?

By the time they got home late that evening, Hannah felt as if she'd been in a knock-down, drag-out fight with every one of her fears and insecurities. And she was losing.

She followed Phillip to his suite, sat on the edge of the bed while he undressed.

"Long night," he said.

"Yes, it was," she agreed.

He unlooped his tie, slipped it off and draped it over the chair by the closet. "I'm exhausted."

"Me, too."

He shrugged out of his jacket, and tossed it on top

of the tie, then he turned to her, unsnapping his cuff links. "So, are you going to tell me?"

"Tell you what?"

He dropped his cuff links on the bureau. "What's wrong."

For a second she considered denying it was anything other than fatigue. But it had been nagging her all night and she couldn't hold it in any longer. "Madeline Grenaugh."

"What about her?"

"Who is she?"

"She's a family friend."

"I get the feeling she was a lot more than a friend."

He sighed, looking resigned, as if he'd been expecting this. "What did she say to you?"

"She insinuated that you and she had a relationship."

"We saw each other on and off for a while, yes."

"Was it serious?"

"She seemed to think so. She had herself convinced we would get married, even though I never said a word to give her that impression. When the engagement was announced, she was quite…upset."

"Did you sleep with her?" The question was out before she even realized she wanted to ask it.

"Don't do this, Hannah."

"I want to know."

"Do you really?"

She could tell by his reaction that the answer was yes. She knew she was being unreasonable, but for reasons that made no sense to her, she needed to hear it from him. She needed to hear him say the words. "Did you sleep with her, Phillip?"

He paused, searching her face. At least he had the guts to meet her eye. Finally, he said, "Yes. I did."

She knew it, but it still hurt.

"It was a long time ago, and I refuse to apologize for something I did before we were married."

Nor should he have to. "Are you in love with her?"

He cursed under his breath. "No, Hannah. I am not now, nor was I *ever* in love with her. Or anyone else for that matter."

"Including me. Is that what you mean?"

He only stared at her.

And then she couldn't hold back any longer. "I love you, Phillip."

His expression didn't change, didn't soften with affection. He didn't look sad, or regretful. Just…cold. "Your love is wasted on me."

That stung more than she could have imagined. To offer him her love and have it thrown back in her face. "How can you say that?"

"Because I can't love you back. I'm not capable."

"You have feelings for me, Phillip. I *know* you do.

You've shown it in a million little ways. Why can't you just trust them?"

He shook his head. "I knew this was a bad idea."

"What?"

"This." He gestured to the bed, around the room. "Us being in such close quarters. I've given you the wrong idea, led you to think this is something it isn't."

"What *isn't* it?"

"A marriage. Not the kind you expect. I've already told you this."

But it was. Why couldn't he see that? "So why did you?"

He didn't seem to know how to answer that, but finally he said, "It's important we give the impression that we have a good marriage."

"And here I thought it would be more important that we actually *have* a good marriage. Not to mention that what we do in private has nothing to do with public image."

"And that's my fault. I'm sorry. But I told you how this was going to be."

"You're *sorry?*" She wanted to grab him by the front of his shirt and shake some sense into him, convince him that it was okay to feel. To love her.

"I will never be unfaithful to you, Hannah."

"Wow, *thanks.*"

Her sarcasm seemed to surprise him. And she

couldn't resist twisting the knife. "Although, honestly, I can't see the point in either of us remaining faithful in a marriage that isn't real."

His expression darkened. "What is that supposed to mean?"

She could see he was interpreting her words to mean that she wouldn't be faithful. As he should. But she couldn't imagine, if he had no feelings for her, why he would care.

"Nothing, Phillip. It doesn't mean anything." She got up and grabbed her purse.

"Where are you going?"

"To bed. You know, you have your suite, I have mine."

Phillip's mouth pulled into a stubborn, straight line. He nodded. "Fine."

All he had to do was ask her to stay, and she probably would, but he couldn't even manage that. And she could only assume it was because he didn't care. And she was too angry to stay and try to talk some sense into him. She would only wind up saying something she regretted.

She stopped at the door and turned to him. "Out of curiosity, what about children?"

"What about them?"

"You say you're not capable of love. Does that apply to your children, too?"

She could swear he paled a shade. And for the first time since she had known him, he looked genuinely uneasy. Finally, he said, "You'll love them enough for the both of us."

"You know, I feel sorry for you, Phillip. You'll be miserable your whole life." She turned and left him there, drained and disappointed. And deep down she knew it was the beginning of the end.

"How does roast duck sound?" Sophie asked Hannah.

They sat together in Hannah's suite, discussing the menu for the gala.

Hannah shrugged. She honestly couldn't care less. She didn't care about much of anything these days. She and Phillip barely spoke more than a word or two in the weeks following the auction. And Hannah had never felt so isolated or lonely in her life. On top of that, she'd been feeling under the weather for the last few days. If it weren't for Sophie and the friendship they had formed, Hannah might not have been able to stand it.

They spent many evenings together, the time Hannah used to spend with her husband. They had even begun the cooking lessons Sophie had promised, but Hannah had given up after the first few. Every time she even looked at food she felt sick to her stomach.

In fact, she felt sick almost all the time. Sick in her heart and in her soul. She knew what she had to do, she just hadn't managed to work up the courage yet.

She kept telling herself that maybe he would come around. And every day that he didn't, she could feel her hope deflating. She thought she could do this. She thought she could make this work, but she just wasn't strong enough.

"I have a new recipe I wanted to try," Sophie said. "I was hoping you and Phillip would be my guinea pigs. How about dinner, Friday, at my place?"

Why? So she and Phillip could go through the motions? Pretend that everything was okay? That she wasn't miserable?

She knew Sophie was trying to help, but Hannah was past believing there *was* hope for them.

"Hannah?"

"I don't think…" Her voice broke.

"I know you guys have been going through a rough patch."

"Rough patch?" Tears welled up in her eyes.

Sophie touched her arm, her eyes so full of sympathy, Hannah could barely stand it. She tried to swallow the tears down, but it was no use. They spilled over onto her cheeks.

She swiped at her face with the corner of her

sleeve, embarrassed and disgusted with herself for being so weak. "What the heck is wrong with me?"

"You're upset. It's understandable."

"But I'm not like this. I can't seem to stop crying."

"PMS?" Sophie suggested.

"Maybe." It was as good an excuse as any.

She handed Hannah a tissue. "When is your period due?"

Hannah shrugged and dabbed away the tears. "Probably soon. I haven't really been keeping track."

"How long has it been?"

"I'm not sure. Why?"

"Is it possible you could be late?"

"*Late?* No, of course not." Surely it couldn't have been that long.

"Maybe you should check. Just in case."

It was a waste of time, but to appease Sophie, she crossed the room to her desk and rifled around the top drawer for her personal planner. Flipping through, she was stunned to see that the last red check, indicating the first day of her cycle, was nearly five weeks ago.

Her heart sank. Had it really been that long?

No, that couldn't be right. It had to be a mistake.

"Well?" Sophie asked.

"According to this, I should have started a week ago," she told her, feeling a wave of nausea so intense she nearly gagged. "You don't think…"

"Have you been taking precautions?"

"No, but…it's only been a few months. It took my parents years to get pregnant. I just assumed…"

"It only takes one time, on just the right day."

Well, in that case, they certainly had their bases covered. Up until a couple of weeks ago, there hadn't been very many days when they *didn't* make love. "Do you really think…?"

Sophie took her hand and squeezed it. "What I think, is that we need to go see the family doctor."

Hannah sat on pins and needles, convincing herself it had to be a mistake—a glitch in her cycle from all the stress lately, despite the fact she'd always been regular as clockwork. Not to mention that she'd been feeling physically ill for two weeks now, but that could be easily explained. A touch of the flu, or even depression.

"You are not pregnant," she told herself, and had repeated the phrase at least a hundred times when the doctor came in to see her. He handed her a pregnancy test and showed her to the bathroom.

"I'll be right here if you need me," Sophie said.

Hannah had never so much as held a pregnancy test, much less had to use one. She flipped it over to read the directions.

It seemed odd that such a life-altering result could

come from such a simple procedure. Although, the result was going to be the same, no matter how long she waited. Negative. In fact, she would probably go in the bathroom to find that her period had already started. And miraculously without any of the cramping or bloating that typically preceded it.

It was as easy and quick as the box boasted. And when the result formed in the indicator window, she felt numb.

She opened the bathroom door. Sophie stood there waiting anxiously. "Well?"

"I'm not pregnant," Hannah said, then dissolved into tears.

Fourteen

After dismissing the physician, Sophie took Hannah in her arms and hugged her. "Don't be unhappy. It'll happen."

She wasn't unhappy. It was worse than that. She was *relieved*. And, at the same time, she was completely and utterly sad. Because she knew that this meant her marriage was over.

"He doesn't love me. He says he's not capable."

Sophie held her at arm's length. "Hannah—"

"And when I asked him about our children, if he could love them, he said I would love them enough for the both of us."

"He didn't mean it."

"Yes, he did. And I won't do that to a child."

"What are you saying?"

"I'm saying that I made a mistake, and maybe it's a mistake I need to fix."

Sophie clutched her hands. "Just give him time."

"How much time? Months? Years? I've wasted eight years already, grooming myself to be the perfect royal wife. What has he done for me, Sophie?"

She didn't seem to know how to answer that.

"I can't do this anymore. I *won't*." She wouldn't waste another minute on him.

"Please, Hannah, give him a chance to make things right."

"He's had chances." She shook her head, determined now. "Life is too short, and I deserve better. I've stayed too long already. I'm through compromising."

Sophie seemed to recognize that it was a losing battle, and Hannah wasn't going to budge. "What will you do?"

She had been thinking about that a lot lately. What she would do if she ever worked up the courage to leave him. "Go back home, to Seattle."

"And you really think he's just going to let you go?"

"He doesn't have a choice. This is still a free country. He doesn't own me."

Sophie didn't say anything, but Hannah could see that she was upset.

Then tears filled her eyes. Tough Sophie, who Hannah suspected didn't even possess tear ducts. "But I don't want you to go."

She hugged Sophie, and they cried together. Even though they wouldn't technically be sisters after she left Phillip, they could still be good friends.

Sophie barged into Phillip's office without knocking. "You're an idiot!"

He sighed and put down his pen. He tried to work up the will to be annoyed, but he couldn't manage it. It's not as if he'd been doing anything important. Just staring blindly at the document he was supposed to be reading.

Besides, Sophie had been giving him the silent treatment lately, and he was surprised to find he actually missed her. Although he had no doubt the tirade that was surely to follow had more to do with his marriage.

"Lovely to see you, too," he said.

"You're going to lose her. You realize that, right?"

Of course he did. In fact, he was counting on it. "It's for the best."

She looked absolutely appalled. "Are you kidding me? She's the best thing that ever happened to you.

Up until a couple of weeks ago, I've never seen you so happy."

His happiness wasn't the issue. "I can't give her what she needs."

"She's not asking for much. Just for you to let down the wall. She just wants you to love her. Which I suspect you already do. You're just too afraid, or too bloody stubborn to admit it."

"You couldn't possibly understand."

"Look who you're talking to, Phillip. They were my parents, too."

"It has nothing to do with them."

"It has *everything* to do with them. They did a lousy job raising us. But how much longer are we going to let it ruin our lives? Why can't we let ourselves be happy?"

They were who they were and nothing was going to change that. "It's over, Sophie."

"Talk to her, Phillip."

"There's nothing left to say."

For a moment she just stared, then she shook her head. "You're a coward." She stormed out, slamming the door behind her.

Maybe she was right. But since Hannah arrived, she had managed, single-handedly, to turn his entire life upside down.

He just wanted things back to the way they used

to be. And he hated to admit that the days of not communicating with her made him feel empty.

Hannah was unhappy and he had no one to blame but himself. How could he have been so careless, let this spin so far out of control?

He didn't want to hurt Hannah. He wished he could be everything she wanted and needed him to be, but he couldn't change who he was.

She had every right to be angry with him. And she deserved so much more than he was capable of giving. She deserved to be happy, to be with a man who could return all the love she had to offer. One who appreciated her in a way Phillip never could.

And he needed to find someone who would accept him for his limitations. One who was more concerned with the title than building a long-lasting love affair. Who would be content to raise his children, living a lavish lifestyle. That, at least, he could provide with a clear conscience.

Maybe it was time to face the truth. That this marriage didn't stand a chance.

But he realized that he wanted this marriage to work. He wanted Hannah in his life. But could he do that? Did he even know how?

He got up and walked to his bedroom, needing space to think.

He switched on the bedroom light, and something

on the covers caught his eye. He walked over to the bed and saw that it was the sapphire necklace he bought Hannah on their honeymoon.

At first he thought maybe she had dropped it there by accident the last time she was in his room, but that had been weeks ago. Besides, Phillip had seen it around her neck since then.

No, she put it here.

He might have thought it was her way of hurting him, rubbing it in. But that wasn't Hannah's style. If she was giving it back, there was a reason.

He thought about Sophie, the urgency in her pleas when she insisted he talk to Hannah, and his heart actually sank. He hated to admit it, but Sophie was right. He did love Hannah. He was not too scared and stubborn to admit it. He knew what he had to do now. He needed to get his wife back. He grabbed the necklace and walked to Hannah's suite.

Phillip found Hannah in the bedroom with several open, half-filled suitcases on the bed.

"What's going on here?" he said, but it came out harsher than he'd intended. More like a bark than a question.

If she noticed, she didn't let it show. She didn't even look up from the pile of clothes she was folding. "What does it look like?"

It looked like she was leaving, but for some reason he couldn't make himself say that.

This was what he wanted at first. But now it just felt so wrong.

"I figure, if I leave now, I can spend the holidays with my mother and be there for her wedding."

So she was just going home for the holidays? Then she would be back? He wished that were true, but he was sure that was merely wishful thinking.

He held up the necklace. "I found this in my room."

She finally looked up at him, her face tired and sad. "It didn't seem right, me keeping it."

"It was a gift. It's yours." He held it out. "Take it."

She took a deep, unsteady breath. "I can't. I'm sorry."

His hand fell to his side. "I'll hold it for you, until you come back."

"I'm not coming back."

The finality of her words jabbed him like a spear, directly through his heart.

"We can do this as quietly as possible," she said, folding as she talked. Probably so she didn't have to look at him. "I know there will be a certain amount of scandal, but I'll do what I can to keep it out of the press. I'll fade out of sight for a while. Until things settle down. And you can blame it on me. Say I was at fault."

She had it all figured out. And after everything,

she seemed to be more worried how her leaving would impact the royal family, than how it would affect her own life.

He wished she would stop being so bloody reasonable. Why didn't she fight this? Fight him?

"You're talking about a divorce."

"I can't do this anymore. I thought I was strong enough…." She shrugged. "I guess I was wrong."

Not strong enough? She was the strongest person he had ever known. Yet somehow he had managed to break her. He always told himself they would both be better off if she left; only now did he realize that he never really thought she would do it. And there was this feeling in his chest. This…*pain.* An ache in his heart like nothing he had ever felt before.

"Hannah…"

"Staying together would be unfair to both of us. I deserve to be with a man who loves me as much as I love him. And you deserve to have a wife who is willing to love you just the way you are."

So, by loving him, she felt she had wronged him somehow? That didn't even make sense. He was the one in the wrong here. He was the one with the problem, not her. She had done everything right.

Sophie was right. The last few months had been the happiest in his life. And the thought of his life without her in it, well, what was the point?

He closed the door, as if that alone could stop her. "You're not leaving."

"You just don't like the idea of losing."

"This has nothing to do with winning or losing. I don't want you to go."

"Why?"

"I don't want you to go because…" He struggled with the words, the right thing to say to make her understand, but all he could come up with was, "Because…*I love you.*"

They may have been the toughest three words he had ever said in his life, but the instant they were out, he knew they were true. He knew it with a certainty he'd never felt before. And he said it again, just to be sure he could. "I love you."

"These last few weeks I've been convincing myself that there was someone out there who would love you and make you happy. But I realized that I'm that someone. I've been fighting it for so long and I let my ideas of what a marriage was get in the way of my feelings for you."

Instead of looking elated, or throwing herself into his arms, Hannah just looked sad.

He took another step toward her, and when she didn't retreat, he took another, until she was close enough to touch. "Sophie was right. I am an idiot."

"You really want me to stay?"

"I don't just want you to stay. I *need* you, Hannah."

Tears welled up in her eyes, and she looked as though maybe she was starting to believe him. "You do?"

He nodded, feeling a little choked up himself. "Am I too late?"

"No." The tears spilled over onto her cheeks. "You're not too late."

He pulled her into his arms and held her tight, buried his nose in her hair. And she clung to him. It felt so good, so right that it stung. But it was the good kind of pain. And he swore that as long as he lived, he would never let go of her again.

She looked up at him, smiling through her tears. "You love me?"

He cupped her cheek, kissed her softly. "I love you."

Hannah buried her face against his chest and squeezed him so hard he could barely draw a breath. "Is this real, or am I dreaming?"

"It's real." In fact, he'd never felt anything so real in all his life. And now that he'd let himself feel, he couldn't seem to make it stop. He didn't want to. And to think that he'd almost let her go. He would live with that regret for the rest of his life.

"I'm so sorry, Hannah. I just didn't realize...I couldn't see it."

"Don't be sorry. You thought you were doing the

right thing. And like my dad used to say, nothing bad can come from telling the truth."

"But it wasn't the truth."

She shrugged. "But you didn't know that at the time. Besides, think how much more we'll appreciate each other. How much better it will be."

"I can't imagine that it gets much better than this."

She had that look, like she knew something he didn't. "It could."

"How?"

She took his hand and pressed it to her stomach, looked up at him and smiled. "We could have a baby."

"Right away."

She nodded. "I thought I might be, and when the test came back negative it made me realize how much I want children. I want us to have a baby, Phillip."

"I think that's a great idea. Maybe a little girl, just like you."

She smiled. "Or a little boy, just like his father."

If he was the type of man that cried, he would have lost it just then. As it was, he was having a hell of a time processing the overwhelming feelings of happiness.

"Think you can love us both?" she asked.

So he gave the honest answer. The only answer he could. "I already do."

* * * * *

THE ILLEGITIMATE
PRINCE'S BABY

BY
MICHELLE CELMER

To my newest great-nephew, Lucas Callum,
who couldn't be a cuter, sweeter little guy.

One

She couldn't believe she was really doing this.

Lizzy Pryce climbed the palace steps, feeling as if she was walking into a dream. Through the open, gilded double doors she could see a throng of guests milling about the foyer, dressed in sparkling gowns and tailored tuxedos. Waiters carried trays of mouth-watering hors d'oeuvres and champagne in delicate crystal flutes. From the ballroom she could hear the orchestra—the one she herself had chosen—playing a waltz. She could just imagine the couples dancing, swirling across the floor, so graceful and light they looked as though they hovered an inch above ground.

Everything in her wanted to turn around and run, but she'd come this far. She had to see this through.

Gathering her courage, she approached the guard posted at the door and handed him her invitation. Normally palace employees were strictly forbidden from attending royal parties, but this was the gala celebrating Morgan Isle's five hundredth anniversary. The party of the century. And because she held one of the highest positions—the queen's personal assistant—her name had been included on the guest list.

Her married name, that is. She didn't want people to recognize her. It was silly, but just for tonight, she wanted to feel as if she was one of them. The beautiful people. She certainly looked the part.

The golden-blond hair that she normally kept pinned back and fastened primly at the base of her neck now tumbled in loose tendrils across her shoulders and down her back. She'd ditched her glasses for contacts. And she'd abandoned her usual shapeless, dull—but proper—business suit for the formfitting, shimmering gold, Carlos Miele gown she had rented.

At the risk of sounding arrogant, she looked damn good.

The guard compared the name on the invitation to his list then motioned her through without a second glance.

As Lizzy stepped through the door into the foyer, one by one heads began to turn her way until what must have been a hundred pairs of curious eyes fixed right on her.

Don't get too excited, she told herself. They're only looking because they don't know who you are.

But she couldn't help noticing some of those looks, particularly the male ones, conveyed more appreciation than curiosity.

Head held high, she made her way through the crowd to the ballroom, nodding graciously and returning polite greetings with people she'd only read about in the papers or seen on television. Heads of state, Hollywood film stars and business moguls.

She was way out of her league. The value of the jewelry alone would probably feed an entire Third World country for a year. She hadn't even made it out of the foyer and she was a nervous wreck.

Lizzy, you have just as much right to be here as anyone else.

She swiped a glass of champagne from a passing waiter and took a generous swallow, the bubbles tickling her nose. She was only a few steps from the ballroom doors.

Just do it, walk in, her conscience taunted. So she took a deep breath and forced her feet to propel her forward.

Stepping through the doors and into the ballroom was like entering some ethereal, fairy-tale fantasyland where everything sparkled and shimmered. Handsome couples swished across the dance floor while others congregated in small groups, sipping their champagne and chatting, nibbling on decadent treats.

It was just as she had imagined. And for an instant she felt swept away.

"Excuse me," a male voice said from behind her,

and the first thing that struck her was the very distinct American accent.

Taking another fortifying sip of her champagne, she turned and nearly spit it right back out.

Not only was he American, he was the Prince of Morgan Isle. Illegitimate half brother to the king. Half brother-in-law to the queen, Lizzy's boss.

Georgeous, rich, undeniably arrogant but charming to a fault. Of all the men who could have approached her, the one who was by far the most off limits, did.

"I don't believe we've met," he said.

She thought he was toying with her, then she realized, by the look on his handsome, chiseled face and the curiosity in his charcoal-gray eyes, he honestly had no idea who she was. And why would he? The few times he had passed her in the halls of the palace, he hadn't given her more than a fleeting glance. And why would he? She was an employee.

"I don't believe we have," she said.

He offered his hand. "Ethan Rafferty."

When she took it, instead of shaking her hand, he bent at the waist and brushed a gentle, and dare she say seductive, kiss across the top. No big surprise there. She didn't know a lot about the prince, only that he was a confirmed bachelor and a shameless womanizer. She had overheard the queen countless times commenting on the rather scandalous state of his very public personal life. She had also heard the king complain of Ethan's lack of respect for their royal customs and policies. Which would explain why Ethan was dressed in a tux and not the royal uniform. The dark hair was slicked back away from his face. A face that bore an uncanny resemblance to his brother's.

Ethan's recent acceptance into the royal fold, and his new business partnership with the family, was all anyone at the palace talked about these days.

Though she couldn't deny that seeing him like this, watching the way his eyes raked over her, was the tiniest bit thrilling. He was the epitome of male perfection, and he smelled absolutely delicious. Just as a prince and a multimillionaire should, she supposed.

Her ex-husband had been gorgeous, too, and smelled just as nice, though he was lacking the millions of dollars or the motivation to earn even a fraction of that. And like the prince he was also an arrogant, womanizing, philandering dolt.

But because Ethan *was* royalty, she curtsied and replied, "It's a pleasure, Your Highness."

He actually cringed. "I'm not much into titles. I prefer just Ethan."

She was pretty sure that if he knew who she really was, he wouldn't be so gracious. And while this had been kind of fun, it was time to move on. Find a guest who wasn't quite so far out of her league. And against policy. Palace employees were strictly forbidden from intimate relationships with the royal family.

"Well, it was nice to meet you." She nodded and curtsied—force of habit—then turned and headed in the opposite direction.

"I didn't catch your name," Ethan said from behind her, and her heart sank.

Bugger. Couldn't the man take a hint? She set her empty glass on a passing waiter's tray and grabbed a fresh drink. "That's because I didn't tell you my name." She tossed the quip back over her shoulder.

"And why is that?" he asked, right beside her now.

She took a long swallow for strength. A smart person was not rude to royalty. Even though the last documented beheading had been well over two hundred years ago.

Of course, he had no idea who she was, so really, what did she have to lose? And who knew, maybe it was time someone put Mr. Wonderful in his place.

"Because you're not my type," she told him, and he had the gall to laugh.

"You're a liar."

She stopped so abruptly the contents of her glass sloshed over and dripped onto her fingers. He stopped, too. "I beg your pardon?"

"Look at me," he said, spreading his arms. "What's not to love?"

She couldn't tell if he was joking or actually had such a high opinion of himself. Could he honestly be *that* arrogant? "I have to know, does that pathetic excuse for a pickup line actually work?"

He grinned, a sexy, playful smile that made her heart flutter. "I'll let you know in a minute."

He was adorable, and he knew it. And she knew, before she opened her mouth, that telling him her name was a very bad idea. But maybe if she did, he would lose interest and leave her alone.

"Lizzy," she told him, since everyone at work knew her strictly as Elizabeth. And instead of Pryce, the name she had switched back to before the ink was dry on the divorce papers, she used her married name. "Lizzy Sinclaire."

"Would you do me the honor of a dance, Ms. Sinclaire?"

Because she so hated that name and everything it stood for, she told him, "I prefer Lizzy."

"All right, Lizzy."

"And no, I won't dance with you. Because as I said, you're not my type."

Rather than be insulted, or discouraged, his grin widened. "I'm not asking for your hand in marriage. Just a dance. Unless…" His brow wrinkled. "Oh, I see. You don't know how to dance, do you?"

Oh, please, did he really think she would fall for his pathetic attempt at reverse psychology?

The truth was, she and her ex had taken ballroom dance classes several years ago. Only later had she learned that he'd been the one giving personal lessons to the instructor.

"You've found me out," she told him. "Now, if you would please excuse me." She spared him one last dismissive nod then turned and walked back in the direction of the foyer, chanting to herself, *Please don't let him follow me. Please don't let him follow me.*

"I could teach you," she heard him say, and cursed

under her breath. He was right back beside her, matching her step for step.

"I might step on your foot and scuff your shoe," she said.

He shrugged. "It's been stepped on before."

She stopped again and turned to him. "Why is it so important you dance with a woman who has no desire to dance with you?"

He flashed her that grin again, and she swore she could feel it all the way through to her bones. "Because the woman in question is the most captivating in the room."

Oh, man, was he good. He almost had her believing he was sincere. Ethan's words could have melted her into a puddle. Which she was sure was exactly his intention. Men like him didn't see women as people. They were conquests. A notch in the bedpost, so to speak.

She drained the last of her second glass. "I just don't think it would be a good idea."

Ethan took her empty glass and set it on the tray of the waiter who magically appeared at his side. "Please, one dance."

She didn't think a man like him used the word *please*. And there was something about it that sounded so…genuine. She could feel her resolve slip the tiniest bit. And it certainly didn't help that she was feeling a little giddy from the champagne.

All she had to do was to tell him who she was, and she was sure he would lose interest, but for some reason she couldn't make herself say the words. How often in life was a girl lucky enough to be pursued by a prince? And honestly, what harm would one little dance do? Even if someone recognized her, she could claim she was simply being polite.

"Fine," she told him. "*One* dance."

He offered her his arm and led her out to the dance floor. She glanced nervously around, noting with relief that the queen, the one person who might actually recognize her, was nowhere in sight.

Ethan took her in his arms and she experienced a delicious shiver of awareness, one she blamed on the champagne. Because in her right mind she would never feel sexually attracted to an arrogant womanizing cad like him. She didn't care how many millions he possessed or hotel resorts he owned.

But one little dance never hurt anyone.

He led her in a waltz and she found him to be quite an accomplished dancer.

"So, you *are* a liar," he said, and she shot him a questioning look. "I think my shoes are safe."

"Your shoes?"

"This is definitely not the first time you've danced." Caught red-handed. "No," she admitted. "It isn't."

And it obviously wasn't his first time, either. He seemed to glide, light as the air, across the floor.

"It's not so bad, is it? Dancing with me, I mean."

Not bad at all. In fact, it was so *not* bad, that when the song ended and a new one began, she didn't pull away. And still she couldn't completely relax.

One dance could easily be explained. But two? And why hadn't she told him who she was? She really *should* tell him.

"I didn't see the queen," she said. "Is she here?"

"Why, would you like to meet her?"

"No, I was just curious."

"She's probably in the parlor resting. She's expecting soon."

"I believe I had heard that." And Lizzy was grateful to know that Queen Hannah was staying off her feet, as the doctor had advised when she began to complain of regular and intense back pain. Lizzy was constantly after her to take it easy, put her feet up and relax a little. Just as she was always after Lizzy to not work so hard, to take some time off and have fun. But ten- and twelve-hour workdays were an excellent excuse to continue to ignore the fact that she had no life.

"Are you excited to become an uncle?" she asked Ethan.

He shrugged and the planes of his face hardened almost imperceptibly. "I suppose."

He didn't look excited. "You don't like kids?"

"Kids are great. It's the child's father I'm not all that crazy about."

Lizzy knew they didn't get along, but wasn't aware that Ethan harbored such a deep animosity toward the king. And she was a sucker for juicy gossip. So, when the song ended and another began, a slower melody, she pretended not to notice that their one dance had now become three.

"Sibling rivalry?" she asked, shamelessly pumping him for information. "My sisters and I certainly had our share."

"To call him a brother is a stretch. We simply have the misfortune of sharing a few chromosomes. Any familiarity stops there." He spun her around then pulled her back in, much closer than she had been before. So close she could feel the heat of his body radiating through his clothes. Close enough to make her heart do a quick back-and-forth shimmy in her chest.

She felt like a princess, whirling across the dance floor with the world's elite, as though she actually belonged here. As if she were one of them.

But it was an illusion. A fluke.

Tell him who you are, her conscience insisted, but she blocked the annoying voice out. Just a few more minutes.

One more dance, then she would walk away.

Two

Ethan had never intended to spend the entire evening with one woman, but there was something about Lizzy, something that set her apart.

It wasn't her striking beauty, at least not entirely. At a function like this, beautiful women ran in packs. She was different in a way that he couldn't quite put his finger on.

Whatever it was, the instant he'd seen her enter the ballroom, he'd known he'd had to meet her.

Excusing himself from the Hollywood starlet that had been clamoring for his attention—his third or fourth already this evening—he'd approached her. And though she'd tried to hide it, he'd seen her initial surprise when he'd introduced himself. Not unusual these days. The fact that she'd brushed him off had only intrigued him more.

It had been an awfully long time since he'd had to pursue a woman. More often than not they were fighting each other for his attention. Anything to get close to the hotel mogul and self-made millionaire. Of course, if they knew just how close he had come to losing it all, they might not be so hot on his heels.

But Lizzy seemed to genuinely dislike him, which for some twisted reason, he'd found undeniably attractive. And when he'd taken her in his arms, his reaction had been unexpected and surprisingly intense physical attraction. Another rare occurrence these days. In the past he would never pass up a night of good company and a quick roll in the hay. But lately even the most attractive of women held little or no appeal.

Which made him all the more determined to get inside her head. Under her skin. And with any luck, get her out of her clothes.

The music set ended and everyone stopped to applaud. Now that they weren't dancing, would she try to escape?

"I don't know about you," he said, "but I could use some fresh air."

She glanced toward the foyer. "I really should go."

And he should relent, but for some reason he didn't want to let her get away. "A short stroll on the balcony is all I'm asking for."

Indecision clouded her face.

"Five minutes," he cajoled.

She hesitated, then said, "Only five."

He offered his arm and she slipped hers through it. He led her to the balcony doors and added, "Ten, tops." And before she could object, they were already out the door.

The night air was cool and damp, although unusually warm for late May. Or so he'd been told. He knew little about his native country's climate and weather patterns. And honestly, he didn't care. He cared even less about the traditions and customs the king had been all but cramming down his throat lately. If he had realized all of the hassle this partnership would cost him, he might have taken his chances and stayed on his own continent. But he was in too deep to back out now. The royal family was saving him and he had to tread lightly.

He signaled a passing waiter and stole a drink from his tray. "Champagne?" he offered.

She nodded and took it from him, sipping, he noticed, much slower than the first two. He took one for himself, and walked her over to the wrought-iron railing that overlooked acres of manicured lawn, trees of every size and shape exploding with green, and in the distance, his half sister Princess Sophie's private residence.

She let go of his arm and leaned on the railing, looking out over the estate with what could only be described as longing in her eyes. "It's beautiful at night, isn't it? All the lights in the garden."

She said it as though it wasn't her first time here, and that surprised him. "You've been to the palace before?"

She blinked rapidly, as though she just realized she'd said something she shouldn't have. Revealed too much. And she seemed to choose her next words carefully. "A time or two."

"Friend or family?"

She shrugged. "Neither, really."

He studied her profile. Her features managed to be delicate but strong at the same time. Refined, but with an element of something wild and untamed.

What was going on in her head? What was she hiding? There was obviously something. And it intrigued him. "How is it, then, that you know the royal family?"

Again she took great care in her response. "I guess you could say…through business."

He leaned on the railing beside her. "What is it you do for a living?"

"It's getting colder." She shivered and rubbed her bare arms, deliberately avoiding his question.

He wasn't quite ready to go back inside, so he shrugged out of his jacket and draped it across her shoulders. The silky ribbons of her hair brushed against him and he couldn't help wondering how it would feel to tangle his fingers through it.

All in good time, he assured himself.

He turned her to face him, adjusting the lapel. "Better?"

"Much. Thank you." She looked up at him and

smiled. An honest-to-goodness, genuine smile. Her first of the night, he realized, and the result was devastating. He thought she was beautiful before, but he could see now that it was merely the tip of the iceberg.

But as abruptly as the smile formed, it disappeared, as though it suddenly occurred to her what she'd done and it was wrong somehow.

Even more startling was the realization that he would do practically anything to see her smile again.

"What are you thinking right now?" he asked.

"That you're really not at all what I expected."

"I take it that's a good thing."

"Yes. And no."

Their eyes caught and held. Hers were bright and inquisitive. With a shadow of vulnerability that he might never have noticed, had he not been looking so hard. Normally that would be enough to send him running in the opposite direction. Instead he was that much more intrigued. Everything about her fascinated him.

He reached up to touch her face and was surprised when she let him. "What would you say if I asked to see you again?"

She thought about that for a second, then answered, "I think I would say, why me?"

"Why not you?"

"Because there are hundreds of other women here, any number of them more…acceptable. All clamoring for your attention. Why pick on me?"

He'd been asking himself that same question all

night, and damned if he could figure it out. "Honestly, I have no idea."

But he hoped she would give him the chance to find out.

Everything in Lizzy told her to get away, but she felt rooted to the floor. Not that she would get far with Ethan still clutching the lapel of his jacket.

She was outside in a dark, secluded corner of the balcony, no one else around, with a total stranger—a man whose reputation *far* preceded him—yet she didn't feel the least bit alarmed.

Instead she felt an undeniable curiosity to see what he would say next. What he would do. Although, she had a pretty good idea.

He stroked her cheek and she could feel herself starting to melt, her head going loopy. His eyes searched her face, as though something about it fascinated him. Then he said the words she both longed for and dreaded to hear. "Can I kiss you, Lizzy?"

God, yes, she wanted to shout. And the fact that he'd been polite enough to ask, made her want it that much more. Already her heart was beating faster, her lips tingling in anticipation.

But as much as she wanted him to, she knew it wouldn't be right.

Not only would it not be right, it would be bloody *crazy*. He was a multimilionaire prince.

"I would prefer you didn't."

"Because I'm not your type?"

Because you're wonderful, she wanted to say. *Because it would be so easy to let myself fall for you.* But she couldn't exactly tell him that, could she? So instead she said, "Something like that."

"I can see your pulse." He stroked her throat with the backs of his fingers, barely more than a tease, and her knees started to feel squishy. "Which means you must be excited."

"I'm just a little breathless from the dancing."

He grinned and shook his head. "Lizzy, you're telling another fib."

She liked the way he said her name. The playful tone he used. God help her, she *wanted* him to kiss her. Just to know what it would feel like. Would his lips feel different than the average man's? Better somehow?

Honestly, what would be the harm in *one* little kiss?

Her head was telling her that this was a really bad idea, but those frantic words of warning were being drowned out by the relentless thud of her own heartbeat.

"One kiss," she heard herself say.

"One kiss," he agreed, lowering his head as she rose up to meet him halfway. And the instant before his lips brushed hers, he added, "Or two."

But by then it was too late. He was kissing her and all she could comprehend was his mouth, and her mouth. The soft but firm pressure of his lips. The salty-sweet taste of champagne when his tongue touched hers. Then his arms were around her and she found herself pressed against the length of his body. Her breasts, her stomach, the tops of her thighs. The cool night air brushed her skin as the jacket slipped from her shoulders. She could feel the rapid-fire pounding of his heart keeping perfect time with her own.

She knew she should stop him, but her body, her thought process, had switched to autopilot. And all she cared about, all she wanted, was to be closer.

She'd done some reckless, ill-advised things in her twenty-nine years, but of them all, nothing this bad had ever felt so good.

He broke the kiss, pressed his forehead to hers and said in breathless whisper, "I have a room in the palace."

She knew without explanation that he wasn't giving her a geography lesson. And God help her, she would have said yes. She would have said yes to practically anything just then. But the instant she opened her mouth to say the words, she heard the distinct sound of someone clearing their throat. Then a voice, calm and controlled—but undeniably firm—said, *"Ethan."*

A voice all too familiar.

Lizzy froze with terror and Ethan cursed under his breath. He let go of her slowly, taking his time, before turning to face his half brother. The king. And Lizzy did the only thing she could—curtsied and lowered her eyes to the floor, hoping like hell he didn't figure out who she was.

Talk about a mood killer.

"Yes, Your *Highness?*" Ethan said, his tone balancing precariously on the thin line between firm and sarcastic.

"It's time for the unveiling. Your presence is required in the parlor."

The unveiling of the current family portrait. Lizzy had almost forgotten. She both cursed and thanked God for his very lousy timing.

"I'll be right there," Ethan said.

The king looked from Ethan to Lizzy, and as she glanced up through the fringe of her lashes, she could swear she saw a hint of recognition in his eyes. But it was fleeting. With any luck he would focus only on the fact that he'd caught the prince and some unidentified woman groping like two hormonally challenged adolescents. She was sure that to him, women like her were a regular routine and not worth his time or energy.

"See that you are," he finally said, then turned and walked back inside.

Lizzy breathed a quiet sigh of relief.

Ethan turned to her. "I'm sorry."

She shrugged. "It's okay."

"No. It was rude of me not to introduce you."

Is that why he was apologizing? If he only knew how completely fine it was that he hadn't. So much for the kiss being harmless.

"Well, then," she said, "I guess you have to go."

"I guess." But he didn't sound very happy about it. He leaned down and retrieved his jacket from the floor. He offered it back to her but she shook her head. So he slipped it on. "Tell me you'll stay awhile."

Now she couldn't stay. If she did, and someone

recognized her, and it got back to the king and queen, it would be all over. She had to leave. "I can't. I've stayed too long already."

"What's wrong? Will you turn into a pumpkin at midnight?"

She smiled. "Something like that."

"I have to go out of town tomorrow, but I'll be back later in the week. Can I see you again?"

Oh, how she wanted to say yes. But not only was her job at stake, she was sure that next week there would probably already be someone new and he would have forgotten about her anyway. Why put herself through that? The waiting. The wondering if he would call. It was best to end this right here, right now. "I don't think that would be a good idea."

He looked more amused than insulted by her snub. "Because I'm not your type?"

Considering what they had just done, that flimsy excuse wasn't going to work again. "Because it's just not a good idea. I had a nice time tonight, though."

He looked as though he wanted to argue, then changed his mind. "How will you get home?"

The same way she got here. "A cab."

"Let my driver take you."

Did she want to ride home in a cab or the luxury of a shiny, new Rolls-Royce?

"Please," he said. "It's the least I can do."

Something deep down told her that she shouldn't, but he had said please. And, what the heck, she could think of it as her final hurrah.

"All right," she agreed, and could see that he was pleased.

"I'll arrange it with my driver and he'll meet you out front."

"Thank you."

He turned to leave, then hesitated. "Maybe I'll see you again someday?"

"Maybe." But even if he did, he probably wouldn't know it was her. He would walk right past her with barely a glance, because to him she would be nothing but an employee. A nobody.

The thought made her both sad and relieved.

He flashed her one last adorable, sexy grin, then he was gone. And she couldn't help thinking that he knew something she didn't.

Three

"Did you go?" Maddie demanded, her call waking Lizzy from a dead sleep bright and early at eight the next morning.

She sat up and rubbed the sleep from her eyes, her first coherent thought of Ethan. "I went."

Maddie squealed with delight. "Was it as marvelous as you'd hoped?"

Beyond marvelous. "I guess."

"You *guess?*"

Maddie was her best friend. Confidants since the first day of primary school. They told each other everything. But for some reason, Lizzy couldn't bring herself to tell her about Ethan. The dancing and the kissing. Maybe she was worried that Maddie would hear in her voice, silly as they were, the feelings she had for Ethan. Feelings she was sure would be as fleeting and insignificant as the time they'd shared.

This was a secret Lizzy felt compelled to keep. "I wasn't there long."

"And I was stuck in the kitchen until the wee hours," Maddie said with an indignant snort. "We must have made a million hors d'oeuvres. Boy, can those people eat."

Having worked in the palace even longer than Lizzy, Maddie had developed a certain degree of contempt for the royal family, and the wealthy jet set in general. Lizzy worried, should Maddie let her feelings slip in front of the wrong people, it might get her into trouble one of these days.

"*Those* people pay your salary," Lizzy reminded her, not for the first time. Being stuck in the kitchen all the time, Maddie didn't have much exposure to the family. Lizzy had always been regarded with respect, and since the queen's arrival from America last fall, she had never been treated so kindly, or fairly. But no matter how many times she tried to convince Maddie, she still harbored this irrational animosity.

Maddie would have been ecstatic at the idea of Lizzy kissing the prince, infiltrating their turf.

In hindsight, it was a stupid, irresponsible thing to do. And Lizzy swore she would never put herself in that sort of dangerous situation again.

"Why didn't you stay?" Maddie asked.

"I just felt out of place."

"Well then, I guess I owe you dinner and a pint," Maddie said, then went on to talk about something that happened in the kitchen during the party, but Lizzy was only half listening.

What if someone *had* recognized her? The king had looked at her, but had she really seen recognition or mere curiosity? And if the king did recognize her, the whole kingdom would know of her late-night affair with the prince.

Lizzy spent the rest of the week trying to forget about Ethan and that wonderfully, fantastically, amazing kiss. She convinced herself that if he had known who she was, he never would have so much as talked to her. She was an outsider. Not a beggar by any means, but she was staff, far enough below his class of people to not merit a second glance. Royals did not intermingle with commoners.

So even if she had agreed to see him again, the instant he realized she worked for the queen, it would have been *hasta la vista*, baby.

That was what she had been telling herself, anyway. It helped that Ethan had been away on business all week. Or so she had overheard from the queen. By Friday evening when she left for home to get ready for that dinner and a pint Maddie owed her, she was over it. In fact, she had developed something of a renewed outlook on her love life.

Since her divorce, when it came to romance, she was convinced that part of her had died. Spending that short time with Ethan, feeling those feelings again, made her realize that maybe there was life after divorce. Maybe she could find love again.

She took a little extra care getting ready, seeing that her makeup and hair were just right. She even dressed a bit sexier than usual, thinking that maybe, just maybe, a man would catch her eye.

The doorbell rang just as she was digging through the closet for her heeled boots. She glanced at the digital clock by the bedside table and saw that Maddie was ten minutes early.

She abandoned her search and jogged through the living room in her stockinged feet to the door. She unlatched the dead bolt and pulled the door open, ready to congratulate Maddie for not being late for a change, the words dying in her throat, and her good mood fizzing, when she saw that it wasn't Maddie standing there.

"Hey, love," her ex-husband said, wearing that smarmy smile she detested.

She was so not in the mood for this. "What do you want, Roger?"

His eyes traveled up and down her body in a way that made her feel violated and unclean. "Baby, you look smashing."

She shifted so that she was partially behind the door. "If it's money you need, that well has dried up." She'd learned her lesson the first two times she'd loaned him money that, to date, he had yet to pay back. Probably because he never held down a job long enough. He was an artist. A long time ago she used to find that sexy. Before she realized he used the title as license to be a bum.

"Baby, you know I wouldn't do that."

Yes he would, but she was in no mood to argue. "Then what do you want?"

"You know that several of my pieces were on display at the gallery on Third Street?"

She shrugged impatiently. Like she even cared.

He pulled a wad of cash from the inside pocket of his jacket. "I sold two."

"Smashing. You can pay me what you owe me." She could use a bit of extra spending money. By the time she put money in savings, paid the bills, then sent some to her mum in England, there wasn't a whole lot left for splurging.

"That's why I'm here," he said.

She reached for the cash, but he snatched it from her grasp.

"Let me take you to dinner. To celebrate."

Not in this lifetime. The mere thought filled her with disgust. Not that Roger was physically repugnant. Quite the opposite. He was a blond Adonis, with a dazzling smile and a sharp wit. And she was sure the other women he had been with during the course of their marriage would agree.

"I have plans," she told him.

"A date?"

"That's none of your business. Are you going to give me the money or not?"

"That means you're going out with Maddie. Dinner and a pint, is it?"

She held out her hand. "The money."

"Only if you go to dinner with me."

"Absolutely not."

He shrugged and tucked the money back into his pocket. "No dinner, no money."

"Fine." She didn't have time for his twisted little games. "*Goodbye*, Roger."

"Lizzy," she heard him say, taking far too much satisfaction from slamming the door in his arrogant face. And knowing he would be bold enough to walk in uninvited, she snapped the dead bolt in place.

As she was heading back to her bedroom, the phone rang. It was Maddie.

"I'm leaving now. I'll be there in ten. Twenty if there's traffic."

Which would make her late, as usual. "I'll see you then."

"Oh, and it's raining, so bring a jacket."

"Call me when you get here and I'll run down." No point in both of them getting rained on. She hung up the phone and was about to resume her boot search when the bell chimed again.

Did Roger not understand the meaning of the words *absolutely not?* She ignored it, hoping he would go away, but after a minute or so, he knocked.

"Bloody hell!" She stomped to the door, tired to death of his games. She unsnapped the bolt and yanked it open. "I told you that I will not—" But it wasn't Roger at her door this time. And she was so stunned to see him, she had to blink several times to make sure her eyes weren't playing tricks on her. Then he grinned, and she knew it couldn't be an illusion.

She was so stunned, she completely forgot to curtsy. Or address him by his proper title. "Ethan?"

He leaned against the door frame, dressed in slacks and a black leather jacket dotted with rain. His hair lay in soft, loose waves around his face, and he wore that adorable sexy, teasing grin. The one she hadn't been able to get out of her head for the better part of a week.

"Not who you were expecting?" he asked.

She shook her head. "What are you doing here?"

"I told you that I wanted to see you again. So here I am."

"How did you—" Before she could complete the sentence, she knew. Bloody hell, how could she be so stupid? "Your driver. That's why you offered the ride. So you could find out where I live."

He only grinned, but she knew she was right. She should have known when he'd offered her a ride that something was up.

Who knows, maybe deep down she had known. Maybe she had unconsciously hoped he would find her. And now that he had, every emotion she'd felt for him, the desire and soul-deep longing to be close, all came back to her in a heady, molten rush.

"Can I come in?" he asked.

"I'm going out." Then she added for good measure, "On a date."

"Just for a minute."

Maybe she should. Maybe she should come clean with him. She could claim that she'd been intoxicated—which wasn't a complete lie—and that was the only reason she hadn't been honest about who she was. They could go their separate ways and with any luck he wouldn't have her fired because she kept her identity from him.

She stepped back and motioned him inside. "Only for a minute."

He stepped inside and she shut the door behind him. His presence was overwhelming in the small room, as though he was eating up all the breathable oxygen. And as a result, she instantly began to feel light-headed.

"As you can see, it's not exactly the palace," she said.

He gazed around her cozy apartment, that up until that instant never seemed inferior to her. Now it seemed small and insignificant.

"It's great," he said.

Obviously he was missing the point. "Ethan, why are you here?"

Tell him where you work. And for whom.

He slipped out of his jacket and draped it across the back of her couch. Underneath he wore an emerald-green cashmere sweater that fit him just right. "You could offer me a drink."

"Your brother—"

"*Half* brother."

"Your *half* brother, the *king*, wouldn't approve. Trust me."

He sat and made himself comfortable on her couch. "Is that why you were so secretive at the party? Did you think it would matter?"

"It *does* matter. As a member of the royal family—"

"Let's leave my family out of this, okay? Just tell me, was I imagining things, or did we connect the other night?"

"Ethan—"

"Did we connect? Or are you going to try that *you're-not-my-type* excuse again."

He was completely missing the point. And she couldn't help but suspect that he was missing it on purpose.

She took a deep breath and blew it out. "Yes, we connected."

He sat up, elbows resting on his knees. "Do you like me?"

"What?"

"You heard me. Do you like me?"

Bugger, he was direct. *Tell him who you are, and put an end to this immediately.* But she couldn't make herself say the words. Instead she said, "Your minute is up."

He rose to his feet. "Do you, Lizzy?"

There he went again, saying her name, making her go all soft and mushy inside. *Just tell him already.* "You should leave."

"Do you like me?" He walked toward her, stealing all of her precious air again. "A simple yes or no."

She retreated a step, then another, then her back collided with the door. And he was right in front of her. Blocking her way, smelling so wonderful she was practically drunk from it.

She never should have let him in.

He had to know she was toast. Now he was just toying with her. To see how long it would take to completely break her will.

Probably not long.

And what was it that she was supposed to tell him? There was something…

He flattened his palms on the door, one on either side of her, boxing her in. His mouth this close to hers, the heat of his body seeping through the weave of his sweater to smother her skin.

"There it goes again." He touched that same spot on her throat as he had the other night, stroking lightly with the backs of his fingers. "I guess it's not from the dancing this time, huh?"

Her heart was pounding like mad and her knees were absolutely useless. Why didn't he just get on with it and kiss her already?

He drew the tip of one finger across her lower lip and she was wound so tight, she actually shivered and her breath caught in her throat.

He leaned in, his mouth close to her ear, and said softly, "I think you like me, Lizzy, even if you won't admit it. And that's good, because I like you, too."

Then he nipped her earlobe with his teeth, just hard enough to startle but not to cause pain. And though she tried to stop it, a sound forced its way up from deep inside her, something resembling a moan, but more…desperate.

Why did he have to be so bloody direct? So… honest? Her first mistake was letting him in. No, her first mistake had been agreeing to dance with him. She was already on mistake three or four tonight. Maybe even more.

She held her arms at her sides, hands balled into tight fists, to stop herself from doing something monumentally stupid. But she suspected that it was already too late. She could feel herself caving. And just as she decided to give in, to wrap her arms around his neck and kiss him, the bloody phone started to ring.

It rang once, then twice, then she heard a car horn out front.

Maddie was here to pick her up. Bloody hell.

Lizzy couldn't decide if her timing was good or lousy. Or maybe a bit of both.

"Let me guess," he said, a flicker of amusement in his eyes. "Would that be your date?"

She nodded.

"Nice guy. He can't even come to the door?"

"It's my friend Maddie," she admitted. "We're supposed to go out for dinner and a pint."

"So, you lied to me."

Well, duh! "Of course I lied. I was trying to get rid of you!"

The phone went silent for several seconds, then started ringing again, and there was another beep from out front. This one longer and more impatient.

"I should get that," she said, slipping out from under his arm and dashing to the cordless on the table by the couch. "Hey, Maddie."

"Aren't you ready? Let's go before all the tables are full up."

She glanced over her shoulder at Ethan, where he leaned casually against the door, watching her. She couldn't think straight when those smoky eyes were fixed her way, so she looked at the window instead, into the rainy darkness.

"Lizzy? Are you there?"

This was it. She could leave now and put an end to this. For tonight anyway, and possibly forever. Or she could stay. With Ethan. Knowing exactly what that would mean.

This time, it wouldn't end with a kiss.

Four

"Maddie, something came up and I can't go out tonight," Lizzy told her. Ethan knew as well as she did what that meant. She could feel it. The air in the room seemed to shift, become just a little thicker. A bit harder to pull into her lungs.

"What happened?" Maddie asked, sounding alarmed. "Are you okay?"

"I'm fine." Lizzy could hear Ethan's steps against the hardwood floor as he walked to where she stood. She could feel his presence behind her. "A…friend stopped by."

"Don't tell me Roger is there."

"No, it's definitely not Roger."

Maddie absorbed that, then asked, "Is this a male friend?"

One of Ethan's hands folded over her shoulder, large and steady. "Uh, huh."

"An attractive, *available* male friend?"

His other hand settled on her hip and she shivered. "More or less."

"Which part. Attractive or available?"

His hand slid around to her stomach and he eased her back against him, pressed the long, solid length of his body to hers. And, oh, did it feel good. And it was apparent, from the ridge beneath his slacks, that he was enjoying this just as much as she was. Though she doubted it was the novelty for him that it was for her.

How long had it been since a man had touched her this way? Since she'd let one. Or, God, how long since she'd *wanted* one to? Pressed up against Ethan, absorbing his warmth, surrounded by his scent, she felt so…*alive*. As if she'd been asleep and was just now waking up and feeling things again.

She closed her eyes and let her head fall back against his wide chest. She could hear his heart beating, feel the thu-thump against her cheek as she leaned into him.

"Lizzy, are you there?" Maddie asked.

She'd almost forgotten about the phone still pressed to her ear. "Maddie, I'm going to have to call you back."

"You better," Maddie said. "And I'm going to want details."

She felt Ethan's breath on her neck, felt the hand

on her stomach slide up. Over her rib cage, around her breast…

"Bye Maddie." She pressed the disconnect button and tossed the phone onto the couch, then turned so she was facing Ethan. His lids looked heavy, his eyes shiny. "Commit this to memory, because it isn't going to happen again."

She could swear she saw disappointment flicker in his eyes, but it was gone so fast, she was sure it had been an illusion.

"I guess I'll just have to work extra hard to make it memorable," he said, then he picked her up—actually swept her off of her feet. She'd read about men doing that in books, but she didn't think it actually happened in real life. At least, not to her.

If he really was trying to make it memorable, it was working.

He carried her into her bedroom and set her down on her feet beside the bed. She took quick inventory of the dimly lit room. Clean sheets on the bed, no discarded undies on the floor. Not perfect, but presentable enough for a one-night stand.

Then he kissed her and she stopped caring about the room and started thinking about the fastest way to get him out of his clothes. It had been a long time since she'd been with a man, and now that she was so close to making that leap, she couldn't seem to get there fast enough. She had the feeling that, since the moment he'd pulled her into his arms on that dance floor, this had been inevitable.

She shoved at his sweater and he helped by tugging it up over his head. She touched him, put her hands on his chest. His skin felt hot to the touch, the muscle solid underneath. She ran her hands across his shoulders, down his biceps.

This wasn't like her. This total lack of inhibition. Not that she had ever been shy when it came to sex, but she barely knew him, nor would she ever get to know him. Maybe that in itself was reason enough to let her defenses down. Since there wouldn't be a second chance.

He tugged at the buttons on her shirt, but he was taking too long. "Tear it off."

It was his lack of hesitation that was so arousing, the swift jerking motion that had her buttons flying in all directions and landing with sharp little snaps on the hardwood floor, the rush of cool air against her hot skin. He popped the snap on her bra and the instant her breasts were exposed, he took one in his mouth. It felt so good her legs nearly gave out.

This man who was touching her intimately was wealthy beyond her wildest dreams. Not to mention a *prince*. So why did she not feel the least bit intimidated? How was it that two people so completely different could be perfectly in sync?

But then he hesitated. He cradled her face in his hands, looked her in the eye. "You're sure about this?"

She had never been so sure of anything in her life. And the idea that he cared enough to ask made her want him that much more.

"I'm sure," she said, then she wrapped her arms around his neck, pressed the length of her body against his and kissed him. After that, everything was something of a blur. A frenzied contest to see who could undress the other faster. They tore at each other's clothes, and he was so beautiful, so *perfect*.

They fell into bed naked, rolled and tumbled, the struggle for the upperhand becoming more fevered. She ran her nails along his body, and nipped him with her teeth, and the more aggressive she became, the more it seemed to turn him on. And she *liked* it. She'd spent years being proper— the proper employee, the proper wife—and she couldn't stand it another second. Just this once she wanted to feel wild and out of control. Just this one time, then she would go back to being the Lizzy everyone expected.

She let down her guard for just a second and Ethan rolled her onto her back, pinning her wrists to the mattress. But rather than feel intimidated, or trapped, she was even more excited. She wrapped her legs around his waist, arched against the long, hard length of him, milking the deep groan that pushed out from his lungs. Then he pulled back and bit out a curse.

"What's wrong?"

"I just realized, I don't have a condom."

"What?" He had to be kidding. "How can you not have a condom?"

"I didn't come here with the intention of sleeping with you."

She couldn't come this far, only to have it fall apart. She was so hot, she was half tempted to tell him to do it anyway, but that was how disasters happened. Things like diseases and unwanted pregnancies. Not that she thought for a second that he carried a STD. But the fear of getting pregnant was enough to keep her mouth shut. Then she remembered, there used to be a box in the nightstand drawer. "Check the nightstand drawer. There may be some in there."

He let go of her wrist so he could lean over, and in his haste, yanked the drawer so hard it came dislodged and crashed to the floor, its contents spilling everywhere.

"Sorry," he said.

She didn't give a damn about her furniture. "Are they there?"

He leaned over, squishing her with his weight for a second. "Aha!"

He triumphantly held up the box.

"Thank God!" She grabbed it from him and dumped the contents out on the mattress, snatched one up and ripped it open.

He tried to take it from her, and she said, "Let me."

He watched with heavy lids as she took him in her hand and very carefully, very slowly, rolled it on.

"Keep that up and you're going to set me off," he warned, and she had half a mind to do just that, but the second the condom was on, he manacled her wrists in his hands and pinned them again.

"Are you ready for me, Lizzy?"

"Yes."

He rocked his hips, sliding the length of his erection against her. The sensation was so erotic, she gasped and arched against him. "You sure?"

She answered him though gritted teeth. "Yes."

He did it again, but slower. One excruciating inch at a time. "Tell me what you want, Lizzy."

One more and he was going to set *her* off. She tugged against his grip, but he held tighter, pinning her with his weight. She groaned with frustration, but he wouldn't give in. Wouldn't give her what she wanted. Even worse, she could see from his wicked smile that he was enjoying this.

"I'm just going to torture you until you say the words." Making good on his threat, he lowered his head and nipped the swell of her breast with his teeth. Then he took the tip in his mouth and sucked hard, hard enough to make her gasp in surprise and struggle uselessly beneath him.

"Tell me," he coaxed. And because she couldn't stand it another second without going completely out of her mind, she told him, in very direct and graphic language, exactly what she wanted him to do.

He plunged inside her, so swift and deep it stole her breath. He stayed that way for several heartbeats, nestled deep inside of her, then he eased back, inch by excruciating inch. He held himself there, very still, his eyes pinned on hers, for several long seconds, then rocked into her with a force that made her cry out.

"Too much?" he asked, his voice gravely, eyes glazed.

"No," she answered, but it didn't even sound like her voice, and her vision was fuzzy, as though she was watching the scene unfold through a fogged camera lens. "Do it again."

He eased back, then plunged forward. Again. And again. And then she stopped counting. Stopped thinking about anything but how good it felt. The way their bodies moved together, hips thrust in perfect sync. She knew without a doubt that she would remember this moment for the rest of her life. The instant she found perfection. Figures she would find it with a man she could never be with. But that didn't even matter now. All she cared about was this moment. Their release came simultaneously, deep and intense, and the force of it seemed to suck every last molecule of energy from her and all she could do was lay there, limp and useless.

"You still with me?" she heard Ethan ask, but he sounded far away.

She pried her eyes open to look up at him. He was propped up on one elbow grinning down at her.

She took a long, deep breath, then blew it out. "God, did I need that."

"You say that like we're finished."

That had always been the drill with Roger. One time and he was out for the count. And only if she was lucky would she be satisfied, too. "We're not?"

His smile grew and he got this adorable, devilish gleam in his eye. "Sweetheart, I'm only getting started."

Hours later Lizzy lay draped across Ethan, their arms and legs tangled, her head resting on his chest, more sexually satisfied than she'd felt in her entire life. The man was unstoppable. If she did an Internet search on the word "stamina," Ethan's photo would pop up on the screen.

The bed was in shambles, the comforter shoved down and bunched up at the footboard and the top sheet twisted. The bottom sheet had pulled loose and was coming off one corner. Add to that the clothes strewn on the floor and the contents of her drawer spilled and it looked as though a hurricane had ripped through her bedroom.

They may have been all wrong for each other, but there was no denying they had the sexual compatibility thing to a science. Unfortunately that was all they had. And sex just wasn't enough for any kind of lasting relationship. Not that she was looking for that, and she knew for a fact that Ethan wasn't a settling-down kind of man.

As it was, though, she was in danger of falling deeply in lust with him.

"You tired?" Ethan asked, shifting against her. He slid a hand down her back and with the other started to play with her breast.

She looked up at him like he was nuts. "You have got to be kidding me."

Ethan grinned.

"You should have rolled over and gone to sleep hours ago. You're like the Energizer bunny."

"Is that what Roger does?"

"Roger?" How did he…?

"When you were on the phone you said it wasn't Roger. Is he your boyfriend?"

If she didn't know better, she might suspect that he was a little jealous. "Ex-husband. And yes, his…*performance* was less than memorable. With me anyway. I can't speak for the other women he slept with during the course of our marriage."

"Ouch."

"The first time I caught him cheating he was so miserable. He cried like a baby and begged me to forgive him. So, like a fool, I did."

"How long were you married?" he asked.

"Four years. Four years too long." She had no idea why she was telling him this. Maybe because he made her feel comfortable, she knew instinctively that he wouldn't judge her. Talking to him felt…natural. It was weird how they had breezed right past that new relationship awkwardness. Not that they had a relationship. What they did have was sex. Correction, *had*. They *had* sex—great sex—and now it was over.

She untangled herself from his limbs and sat up, covering herself with the sheet. "I have to work in the morning."

"Saturday?"

She nodded and shrugged. "Sorry."

"Sounds like you're kicking me out."

More like saving him the trouble of coming up with an excuse to leave. "I'm afraid so."

He didn't argue, didn't try to change her mind. He just sat up and started putting on his clothes. That was a good thing, so why did she feel a dash of disappointment? This was exactly what she wanted, right?

Since it was likely going to be the last time she ever saw him this way, she watched as he dressed. Bloody hell, he was beautiful. As long as she lived, she would remember this night.

He pulled on his slacks and stood to fasten them. "You know that I didn't come here to sleep with you. I just wanted a chance to get to know you."

"And you did." In the biblical sense, no less. "Now it's over."

He cast her a wounded look that was about as genuine as she was royal. "I feel so...*used*."

"I'm sure you'll recover." Not only that, but she had saved herself the necessity of trying to explain who she was and why she'd lied to him in the first place. In a week or so, he would have moved on to the next woman and wouldn't even remember her name. It probably wouldn't even take him that long.

When he was dressed, she rolled out of bed and grabbed her robe. The least she could do was see him out. They walked in silence to the door, then he turned to her.

"I had a good time tonight."

"Me, too."

"If you change your mind—"

"I won't."

"Don't be so sure. I'm pretty irresistible."

"You just keep telling yourself that."

He opened the door and leaned in the jamb. "One kiss for the road?"

She rose up on her toes and pressed a kiss to his cheek. "Goodbye, Ethan."

This was best, but as he stepped into the hall, why did she have to force herself to shut the door behind him? And why did she press her ear to the door to listen to his retreating footsteps?

To be sure that he really left. That's all. She couldn't have him loitering out in her hall. What would the neighbors think?

She locked the door and latched the chain then turned off the lights. It was when she walked back into her bedroom that she saw it lying on the floor with contents of her bedside table drawer. Ethan's watch.

She picked it up and sat on the edge of the bed. It was a Rolex, in solid platinum. It had to be worth thousands, so how could he just forget it? Or maybe he hadn't. Maybe he'd left his watch there on purpose, so she would have to see him again. Honestly, she wouldn't put it past him. He was a man who was used to getting what he wanted.

Wouldn't he be surprised when this time she wasn't so quick to succumb to his charms.

Five

Ethan met his cousin, Charles, at their health club the next morning for their weekly game of squash. And though Ethan usually slaughtered him, today he was off his game by miles.

"What's up?" Charles asked as they walked to the locker room. "You usually kick my ass all up and down the court."

"Guess it's just your lucky day." It didn't help that he'd only gotten an hour or two of sleep. Or that a certain woman had been on his mind all morning.

He opened his locker, peeled his sweaty shirt off and tossed it in.

"Jesus," he heard Charles say from behind him. "I should have known."

He turned to him. "What?"

"That it was a woman distracting you."

What was he, telepathic? "Why would you think this has anything to do with a woman?"

"I guess you haven't looked in a mirror lately."

He glanced in the mirror on the inside of his locker door, but other than appearing a bit tired, he didn't look any different than usual. He shot Charles a questioning look.

"Other side," Charles said.

Ethan turned and looked back over his shoulder, realizing instantly what Charles meant. There were scratch marks—deep ones—crisscrossed all up and down his back. That explained the sting he'd felt when he'd soaped up in the shower this morning.

Charles wore a cocky grin. "You going to try to tell me a woman didn't do that?"

"It was a woman," Ethan admitted. An amazing, spectacular woman who he hadn't been able to keep his mind off of.

"So, you got yourself some crumpet," Charles said.

"I don't even want to know what that means." Because if it was coming from Charles, it was most likely X-rated.

Charles just laughed.

Inside his locker, Ethan's phone began to ring. He looked at the display, but it was a blocked call. Something told him he should answer it. "I have to take this."

Charles grabbed a towel from his locker. "I'm going to hit the shower. I'll meet you in the bar."

"Order me my usual," Ethan said, then answered the call with a cocky, "I told you that you couldn't resist me."

There was a long pause, then Lizzy's voice, sounding suspicious. "How did you know it was me?"

Ethan laughed and admitted, "Lucky guess. Although I would love to know how you managed to get my private cell number."

"Let's just say I have connections."

"Military intelligence?"

There was a brief pause, then, "I could tell you, but then I would have to kill you."

He considered that for a second, then dismissed the possibility. She was too sweet, too feminine, to be military. The only logical explanation was that she knew someone in the royal family, or at the very least someone with connections to the royal family, and had gotten his number through them. But at this point, did it really matter?

"You left your watch here," she said.

"I know."

"So you actually *admit* it?"

"I didn't leave it on purpose, if that's what you're implying. I was halfway to my car when I realized I wasn't wearing it. I would have come back, but I had the sneaking suspicion you wouldn't let me in."

"I'm supposed to believe you didn't leave it here on purpose?"

"If I wanted to see you again, do I strike you as the kind of man who would need an excuse?"

"Honestly, could you be more arrogant?"

And could she be more brutally honest? But that was one of the things he liked most about her. She was tough. With a soft, gooey center. "I could be there around seven."

There was another pause, then, "Make it eight."

"Eight it is, then."

"Be forewarned that I'm not letting you inside. I'm not even going to unlatch the chain. I have no intention of sleeping with you again."

And he had no intention of leaving her apartment until he'd seduced her. But he didn't tell her that. "That's fine. I just want my watch."

"Fine. I'll see you at eight," she said, then the line went dead.

He grinned and tossed his phone back in his locker. She seemed pretty intent on keeping the upper hand, but what she didn't realize is that she was already as good as his.

When Lizzy looked up and saw the queen standing in her doorway, she snapped her cell phone shut. How long had she been standing there? And how much had she heard?

"I'm sorry," the queen said. Well into her eighth month of pregnancy, her rounded belly proceeded her into the room, and her gait had taken on a slight waddle. "I didn't mean to interrupt."

Lizzy wanted to ask how long she had been standing there, but she could never be so rude. She stuck her phone in the top drawer of her desk. "No, ma'am, I'm sorry. I should never have accepted a personal call at work. It was totally inappropriate of me."

"Elizabeth, it's Saturday for heaven's sake. You should be at home. I though we agreed that you would take some time off to relax."

An entire day sitting at home alone, with all the time in the world to think about Ethan? She would rather be at work. "I had a few things to do that couldn't wait."

The queen sighed and shook her head. "You're hopeless."

She had no idea how right she was about that. How pathetic was it that Lizzy had so little a life, she preferred to spend her Saturdays in the office? "Can I get you something?"

She shook her head. "Backache. I've found it helps if I walk around."

Lizzy could only imagine what it would feel like to have a little human being growing inside her. She used to think that she would have children. She'd always wanted to. Now she wasn't sure if that was in the cards for her. She didn't want to be a single mother, and since her disastrous first marriage, she had vowed never to tie the knot again.

The queen gave a little gasp and flattened a hand on her belly. "He's kicking, want to feel?"

Lizzy nodded eagerly. Because she knew the queen loved to share her experiences, and also because it made Lizzy feel a little less like a subordinate.

The queen walked around her desk, took Lizzy's hand and placed it on her belly. A second later she felt a very pronounced thump against her palm.

"The kicks are so much stronger now."

The queen smiled. "Sometimes I think he's trying to beat his way through my belly. I've enjoyed being pregnant, but I think I'll be glad when it's over." She put her hand over Lizzy's and gave it a squeeze. "You've been such a wonderful help these past few months. I probably don't thank you often enough."

Her words filled Lizzy with guilt. The truth is, the queen thanked her constantly. And how did Lizzy repay her? By going behind her back and breaking the cardinal rule of her employment. At least she would never find out. Even if Lizzy had to live with the guilt for the rest of her life.

"Well, I should let you get back to work. Don't stay too late."

Lizzy dropped her hand from her belly. "I won't, ma'am."

She half walked, half waddled to the door, then paused before stepping into the hall. "You know, Elizabeth, men do so enjoy a good chase. But don't play too hard to get."

So she *had* heard her conversation. Lizzy's cheeks blushed with embarrassment and she scrambled for something to say, but before she could, the queen was gone.

That was too close. If the queen had figured out

who Lizzy had been talking to, it would have been a disaster. But how could she?

Inside her drawer, she could hear her phone vibrate. She opened it and checked the screen. It was Maddie. And it was at least the tenth time she'd called. Lizzy could only put her off for so long.

At the risk of being caught in a personal call again, she pulled her phone from the drawer and answered it, "I'm at work."

"I know," Maddie said apologetically, "but the suspense is killing me! How did it go last night?"

She kept her voice low, in case one of the office girls was in the vicinity. "It was…enlightening."

Maddie squealed with delight. "Are you saying you actually put an end to over a year of abstinence?"

"Hard to believe, I know."

"No, that's fantastic! Who is he? Someone I know? Are you going to see him again? Tell me everything! I want details!"

Unfortunately she couldn't give her any. Considering Maddie's opinion of the royal family, she would very likely interpret Lizzy's actions as some sort of mutiny. Besides, it would be best if no one knew what she had done. "It was one night, now it's over."

"What? *Why?*" Maddie sucked in a breath and asked, "Bloody hell, did he dump you?"

Lizzy could feel her bristling through the phone line, and couldn't help but laugh. Maddie was always there, watching her back. If it hadn't been for her,

Lizzy might never have survived her divorce. "No, nothing like that. I told him I only wanted one night."

"He was that lousy?"

Lizzy laughed. "No, he was fantastic. I'm just not in the right place for a relationship."

"Who is he?"

"Just a guy. Someone very bad for me."

"Another artist?" she said with an indignant snort.

"Something like that."

"Well, I'm sorry it didn't work out, but I'm so glad you finally took the plunge, so to speak."

So was she. And tonight was it. The last time she could ever see Ethan again. She would give him his watch, then close the door on him for the last time.

When Ethan walked into the bar Charles was at their usual table near the fireplace, just below the widescreen HD television, flirting with a young, attractive waitress. Women found him charming, and his looks irresistible. He was the kind of man that other men looked at and thought, Damn I wish I looked like him.

He was with a different woman every week, and sometimes several at once. Dating was like a sport to him. And though he never led any woman to believe he would be exclusive, they all seemed to think that they would be the one to change him. And they tried. But Ethan couldn't imagine him ever settling down.

The waitress walked away and Charles followed her with his eyes.

Ethan crossed the bar and took a seat at the table, where his drink waited for him. "Cute waitress."

Charles nodded, not peeling his gaze from her shapely behind.

"She doesn't look familiar."

"She started Wednesday. Great body, don't you think?"

"Ask her out yet?"

She disappeared through the door leading to the kitchen, and Charles finally turned to look at him, grinning from ear to ear. "We're meeting for drinks tonight."

Ethan laughed and shook his head. "You don't waste any time."

He shrugged. "Don't see the point in waiting. No time like the present, right?" He took a swallow of his drink. "So, tell me about this woman. Anyone I know?"

"I don't think so. I met her at the gala."

"The woman in the gold dress?"

Ethan nodded. "You know her?"

"I remember thinking that she looked familiar. I was going to ask her to dance, but you beat me to it. Who is she? Who's her family?"

Ethan shrugged. "No one. She's a secretary. Lives in a small apartment in town."

He narrowed his eyes. "Is it serious?"

"It was just sex, and one night," he said, and when Charles raised one questioning brow, he added, "Her rules, not mine."

"Sounds like my kind of woman."

That's exactly what Ethan thought. At first. But Lizzy had gotten under his skin. "I want more."

"More sex?"

"More…something." He shrugged. "I like her, Charles."

"I don't have to tell you how that's going to go over with your brother."

"Half brother," Ethan automatically corrected. Despite their blood ties, there was nothing familial about their relationship. Phillip never missed an opportunity to remind him of his illegitimacy. Even if it was nothing more than a scathing look. Ethan always knew his place. "And since when do I give a damn what Phillip thinks."

"Maybe you should. You're in a sensitive spot with the partnership."

"If he pulled anything now, Sophie would eviscerate him."

"He's not afraid of Sophie." Maybe not afraid, but Sophie had more influence over her brother than Phillip would ever admit. On tenacity alone, Sophie always seemed to get what she wanted. "You know that Phillip is stubborn enough to make your life hell," Charles warned.

Charles would know. He and Phillip had been close friends since childhood. And though Ethan trusted Charles to a certain degree, because of his ties to the king, theirs was a complicated relationship. Ethan made it a point to be very careful what he said to him. Especially when it came to the partnership, as, among other things, Charles acted as attorney for the royal family. But like Sophie, and despite the tension it might have caused, Charles welcomed Ethan into the family and treated him as an equal. And for that Ethan was grateful.

"Speaking of business," Charles said. "I've been gathering information on the Houghton hotel, like you asked."

The Houghtons owned a hotel that had been in their family for generations, and just happened to sit adjacent to the building the royal family was renovating, not to mention on the prime resort land on the island. "Do you think they'll sell?"

"If not, we can acquire it at auction in a few months. Old man Houghton has gotten himself into something of a financial jam. He's so far behind in his taxes, the property will be seized, if the mortgage company doesn't foreclose first."

"So, it's as good as ours?" he asked, and Charles nodded. "What course of action do you recommend?"

"I think we should buy him out. Make him an offer he can't resist. And I think we should do it soon. If it goes to auction, someone could try to outbid us and we could pay even more than it's currently worth."

"Sounds good. Work up a proposal and we'll present it to the board."

"I'm already on it."

With business out of the way, Charles went on to talk about the "tasty little thing" he'd had the pleasure of acquainting himself with last night, and that got Ethan thinking about Lizzy. And how he would manage to insinuate himself into her apartment. Not that she'd been all that difficult to sweet talk.

He always got what he wanted.

Six

Lizzy was prepared when Ethan rang the bell that evening. She would hand him his watch, then say goodbye and shut the door, and if he knocked again, there was no way in hell she would answer it. She'd abandoned the idea of keeping the chain latched. After all, she wasn't so weak that she couldn't see him face to face without completely losing her cool.

But after a full day of anticipating his arrival, when she reached for the knob her heart leaped up into her throat.

He stood in the hallway looking delicious dressed head to toe in black. Delicious and dangerous. Appropriately so, considering what would happen if he learned who she really was. And she was so close to getting him out of her life forever.

"You look like a cat burglar," she said.

He grinned and leaned in the doorway. "Yeah, but you love it."

God help her, she did. *Give him the bloody watch and get rid of him.*

"Here you go," she said, holding it out, and he took it.

"You're not going to invite me in?"

"I thought we covered this on the phone."

He grinned and her legs felt a little wobbly. "I figured you were forgetting that you find me completely irresistible."

She folded her arms under her breasts. "My, don't we have a high opinion of ourselves."

He shrugged. "I just call it like I see it."

She was about to close the door on him forever when she heard footsteps on the stairs. She peered around Ethan, down the hall, and nearly had a coronary when she saw Roger round the corner. He was looking down at something he held in his hands. Money, she realized. He was counting it.

Damn, damn, damn! There was no way she could let him see Ethan. He would recognize him instantly and he knew the palace rules. She didn't doubt for a second that out of spite he would make trouble for her.

So she did the only thing she could. She grabbed Ethan by the front of his leather jacket and yanked him inside, slamming the door behind him.

When he got over the initial surprise of being manhandled, he shot her a smug grin and said, "You're not letting me in, huh?"

"Shh!" Barely ten seconds passed before there was a loud knock. "Don't say a word," she whispered to Ethan, and when he opened his mouth to speak, she pointed a stern finger his way. "I mean it. Shush."

She latched the chain and opened the door a crack. "What do you want?"

"Hey, love, you've got company?"

"No."

"Really? I could swear I just saw someone walk into your apartment."

"You must have been mistaken."

He shrugged and flashed her that smarmy smile. How could she have ever found that charming? "Well then, how about that dinner I promised you?"

"I already ate."

He produced the wad of money he'd been counting on the way up, as though it were some sort of bait. "A drink, then?"

"Honestly, I would rather remove my own skin with a cheese grater."

Behind her, Ethan chuckled quietly, and she swung blindly, connecting with what felt like his biceps.

Roger, on the other hand, wasn't amused. Something bitter and nasty flashed across his face. It was a side he rarely let show. "Same old repressed Lizzy," he said in a voice filled with pity. "No wonder you're still alone. And probably always will be."

No matter how many times she vowed not to let his words bother her, it still stung. He knew exactly where to strike to do the most damage. Maybe she had been a little cold during the last year of their marriage. Call her crazy, but after a spouse cheats, it pretty much dooms the concept of intimacy. Every time he touched her, she pictured him with someone else.

The truth was, she'd stayed with Roger after that first time, but she'd never really managed to forgive him. And maybe if she had, maybe if she had let him back into her heart, he would have been faithful.

There you go, Lizzy, blaming yourself again.

"Last chance," he said, waving the money under her nose like bait.

She wasn't that hard up for the cash he owed her. "Keep the money and just consider us even," she said, then took extreme pleasure from slamming the door in his smug face. She leaned her forehead against it, closed her eyes and sighed.

"Let me guess," Ethan said. "Roger?"

She nodded.

"Nice guy."

"Charming to a fault," she agreed.

"And for the record, you're the least repressed woman I've ever met in my life."

Did he have to be so darned nice? Why couldn't he be the arrogant, womanizing jerk she had heard so many things about?

"You know what this means, don't you?" she asked.

"What?"

She turned to face him, leaning her back against the door. "Just to prove him wrong, I'm going to have to sleep with you again."

"Revenge sex?"

"You've got a problem with that?"

He shook his head. "Just as long as you realize that you've got nothing to prove. I know how passionate you are."

It wasn't Ethan she needed to prove it to. Hell, maybe she didn't need to prove anything to anyone. Maybe she just needed an excuse to sleep with him one more time and this was as good a one as any. At this point, did it even matter why?

She would sleep with him one last time. One more night together—the entire night this time—and she would never see Ethan again.

Ethan walked Lizzy backward toward her bedroom, kissing and undressing her along the way. He flung her shirt onto the floor and unsnapped her bra with the ease of a man who had removed a bra or two in his time. He hadn't seemed to notice that she wasn't exactly voluptuous. Or maybe he did, and just didn't care. Not every man liked large breasts.

More than once Roger had not so subtly suggested she consider implants. He had excelled at finding every one of her physical imperfections. And a few others that, she realized later after she'd kicked his sorry ass out, didn't even exist.

This is not the time to be thinking about Roger, she reminded herself.

Besides, Ethan seemed perfectly content with her breasts and more concerned now with getting her jeans unbuttoned and pushed down her legs. She helped, then kicked them off and out of the way.

He slipped a hand between her legs, stroking her through her panties, lightly though, so it was more of a tease than an actual touch. And so erotic she shuddered.

"Lay down," he ordered, and she did, anticipation making her shiver. He knelt on the bed, between her legs, still fully dressed. He hooked his fingers in the waistband of her panties, eased them down and slipped them off. She was naked, and he was staring at her, his eyes black with desire. "You're amazing."

She tried to think of some snappy comeback, but her hormone-drenched brain was incapable of all but the most basic functions.

Ethan put his hands on her thighs, easing them apart. She knew instinctively, by his body language and the expression on his face, what was coming next. At least, she *hoped* she did.

Ethan lowered his head, and when she felt his mouth brush her inner thigh the sensation was so erotic she nearly vaulted off the bed.

He looked up at her. "Good or bad?"

"Good," she said, but the word came out as more of a croak.

"Are you sure?" He made a move like he might back away. "I can stop."

"No!" That time it came out loud and clear, and Ethan grinned.

He touched her inner thigh, starting at the knee, and slowly stroked his way upward. He lowered his head and took her in his mouth, and the feeling was so deeply rooted, so explosively physical, she could barely stand it. She turned her head into the pillow to muffle a moan of pleasure.

It had been so long, *too long*, since anyone had touched her this way, and she wanted it to last, but she could already feel herself unraveling. She curled her fingers into the sheets, digging her heels into the mattress as every muscle in her body coiled tight, then peaked and let go in a hot rush. Wave after wave of pleasure washed over her and she slowly sank back down, feeling limp and sated.

"You still with me?" Ethan asked.

She opened her eyes, saw that he was kneeling over her. Her eyes drifted upward, until she reached his face, a satisfied grin curling the corners of her mouth. "Oh, yeah."

He grinned. "You all right?"

"Hmm. That was…" She sighed, unable to put into words exactly how she was feeling. Maybe there were no words to describe it. So she settled for a simple, "Wow."

* * *

It was official.

Ethan had just had what was by far the best sex of his life. He and Lizzy lay side by side in her bed, naked, sweaty and breathless, and too spent to move a muscle. He could barely work up the energy to breathe.

"What time is it?" she asked.

"Why, are you going to kick me out again? Let me guess, you work Sundays, too."

"I'm not kicking you out. I can't see the clock, and I was curious as to how long we've been at it."

He craned his neck to see the digital clock on the bedside table. "It's eleven-forty."

"Three and a half hours? Wow."

And he could be expecting fresh scrapes on his back. If they kept this up, he was going to make her either cut her nails or wear gloves. But according to her, they wouldn't be doing this again. "Can I ask you a question?"

"Sure," she said.

"Why do you let what he said bother you?"

She exhaled a long sigh. "It's complicated."

"Is that code for it's none of my business?"

There was a pause, then she said, "The second time I caught Roger cheating, he said it was my own fault. I was so cold that I drove him to it."

"You're not cold."

"Maybe I was then. It's hard to be intimate with someone when you know they've been unfaithful."

"That isn't your fault."

"Maybe not, but he knows it bothers me, so when he's angry it's the first thing he pulls from his bag of tricks." She rolled over onto her stomach and propped herself up on her elbows. Her hair tumbled across her shoulders and down her back. He reached out to touch it, curling a lock around his finger.

"Have you ever been married?" she asked.

"Nope."

"Ever come close?"

"Never."

"Is it marriage in general that you're against?"

He shrugged. "Not really. I guess I just haven't met anyone I could imagine spending the rest of my life with."

"But if you did?"

He turned to look at her. "Why, are you interested in the position?"

"God no!" she said a bit too forcefully, then added, "No offense."

"None taken."

"Really, it has nothing to do with you personally. I won't ever get married again. To *anyone*. When I was with Roger I felt so…out of control."

"You like being in control."

She nodded. "I'll be the first to admit that I'm a control freak. It took me a long time to get back to feeling as though I was my own person again. I'm still not one hundred percent there."

"Well, for the record, I'm in no rush to tie the knot. I enjoy my freedom."

They were both silent for a minute, then she said, "Can I ask *you* a question?"

"Sure."

"When did you find out who you are? Or did you always know?"

"Are we talking self-awareness or genetics?"

"Genetics."

His parentage wasn't something he was ashamed of, but he also didn't feel the need to talk about it. In fact, he preferred not to. He preferred to keep his private life private. But for some reason, talking to Lizzy didn't bother him so much. Maybe because she was so damned honest with him. "I was in college."

"Your mom told you?"

"She died before she got the chance. Honestly, I'm not sure if she ever would have." And he would always wonder why. If she had done it to protect him, or to protect herself. "She told me my father was a businessman who traveled a lot and didn't have time for us."

"You grew up in the U.S.?"

"In New York. We moved there when I was a baby. But she was born here, in Morgan Isle."

"She died young?"

"Very young. She was only thirty-nine."

"Was she sick?"

"Car wreck. I was going through her things afterward and found financial documents. Apparently they had an agreement. As long as she kept her mouth shut, there would be monthly checks until I reached the age of eighteen. If she ever told anyone the truth, the funds would stop."

"I guess I can see why the king wouldn't want it to get out. They don't like scandal."

"She didn't have an agreement with the king. It was Phillip's mother, the former queen."

Her mouth fell open in surprise. "The *queen* paid her off?"

He nodded. "To be honest, I still don't know if my father even knew about me. I probably never will know. After the queen died, Sophie learned the truth, pretty much the same way I did, and contacted me. She talked me into visiting."

"If she hadn't, do you think you would have ever connected with the royal family?"

"Probably not." He rolled onto his side to face her. "But I'm glad I have Sophie in my life."

"And the king."

"We *tolerate* each other." Barely. But they were brothers—if only half—and more or less stuck with each other. And he didn't want to talk about this any longer. It was too…depressing.

He reached out and touched her hair, brushing a pale lock back from her face and draping it over her shoulder. "Let me take you out."

"Right now?"

"Tonight, tomorrow. Whenever."

She looked away. "I can't."

She puzzled him. It seemed as though every time he made a connection, she cut him off at the pass. In his experience it was usually the woman grasping for connective tissue. Lizzy was different than any woman he'd ever been with. "Sure you can. You don't want a commitment, I don't want a commitment. It's perfect."

"It wouldn't work."

He stroked his hand down her back, over the swell of her behind, and she made a purring sound deep in her throat. "If you ask me, everything works just fine."

She shot him a look. "You know what I mean. We're too different."

Most women went after him for his money. This is the first time he'd met one that was intimidated by it.

"Lizzy, I'm not asking for your hand in marriage. Just dinner. Besides, I've dated *my kind*. Maybe I'm looking for something different."

"Maybe I'm not."

"How will you know unless you give it a chance?"

She groaned and dropped her head in the pillow, then offered him a muffled, "Has anyone ever told you that you're unbelievably stubborn?"

He grinned. "All my life. And I usually get what I want." He gave her a nudge. "One date. That's all I'm asking."

She looked over at him, her eyes filled with regret. "I can't. I wish things were different. I really do. Can't we just enjoy this night together and leave it at that?"

And she called him stubborn? But this wasn't over. "If that's what you want."

"It really is."

He wasn't kidding when he said he always got

what he wanted. And he wanted her. And though it might take time, he would wear her down.

Eventually she would see things his way.

Seven

Lizzy came awake slowly, the scent of something delicious tickling her nose. Bacon, she realized. And freshly brewed coffee. For a moment she was sure it was the fringe of some wonderful dream, but when she opened her eyes, it didn't disappear. Then she heard the sound of dishes clanking together from the open doorway.

Either someone had broken into her apartment or Ethan was making her breakfast.

She had to remind herself that he wasn't always a wealthy prince. He was a self-made millionaire, rejected by the man who'd fathered him. Only recently had he connected with the royal family.

But that didn't change who he was. Someone who could potentially get her fired.

She sat up and looked at the clock. It was after nine. She never slept this late. Even on a Sunday. But that was bound to happen when one spent three-quarters of the night having sex.

To say it had been fun was the understatement of her life, but now it had to end.

She crawled out of bed and slipped into her robe. She used the bathroom then fastened her hair up into a ponytail and brushed her teeth. There was a wet towel hanging on the rack, meaning he must have showered. It was a wonder that she'd slept through it.

She found Ethan in the kitchen, his back to her, dressed in his slacks and shirt, the sleeves rolled to the elbows. His hair was wet and slicked back from his face and he was barefoot. She watched him from the doorway. She didn't know why, but there was something so intimate about a barefoot, recently showered, sexy man in her kitchen making breakfast.

She gave herself the luxury of one brief, warm fuzzy feeling, then steeled her emotions and re-minded herself that this was the first and last time she would be seeing him this way.

He startled her by saying, without even turning around, "Good morning. There's fresh coffee."

"How did you know I was standing here?"

He turned to her. His shirt was unbuttoned, show-ing off his perfectly toned chest. Forget breakfast. He looked good enough to eat.

"I can feel you thinking," he said. "Working out how you're going to get rid of me."

Was he psychic or something? "Really?"

"Honestly? No. I saw your reflection in the microwave. I just guessed about the other part. I was right, though, wasn't I?"

She figured it was best not to answer that. "You're up early," she said instead, though it was late for her.

"I don't sleep much."

She stepped closer, the scents from the stove making her mouth water. "What are you making?"

"Eggs and bacon. I hope you don't mind that I made myself at home."

Even if she did, it was a bit late to do anything about it. Besides, it was kind of nice not waking to a quiet, empty apartment. Not that she would ever admit it to him. Or even wanted to make a habit out of it. She liked being alone, living by her own schedule. Setting her own rules.

Eating when she wanted to eat, sleeping when it suited her. Sole possession of the remote control. These things were precious.

She took a seat at the table. "I never imagined you as the cooking type."

"I am more than just a pretty face. In fact, there's a lot you don't know about me." He opened the cupboard to the left of the sink and pulled two mugs out. "How do you take your coffee?"

"Cream and sugar." It was a bit unsettling, how

quickly he had acquainted himself with her kitchen. How easily he had insinuated himself into her life.

This is what she got for not booting him out last night.

He fixed her coffee and set it on the table in front of her, then went back to the stove.

She sipped, then asked, "So, why does a gazillion-aire prince need to learn to cook?"

"I didn't always have money." He used tongs to flip the bacon frying in one of the pans. "Besides, I like cooking."

"How did you wind up a hotel mogul?"

"I worked my way through college in the hotel business. I started out as a bellboy."

"Seriously?" She couldn't see him hauling luggage. Royals didn't even carry their own luggage, much less someone else's.

"I started at the bottom."

"How do you go from bellboy to owner?"

"Hard work." He turned to her and grinned. "And a rich partner."

A partner who was even richer now, since he'd embezzled and dropped off the radar. But she didn't mention that. He would wonder where she'd gotten her information, and she might have to admit that it came directly from the royal family. Information was the one advantage to being invisible. People said things in her presence that they wouldn't normally admit.

"You have me at a disadvantage," he said. "You

know quite a bit about me, but I know next to nothing about you."

And she intended to keep it that way.

She got up and walked over to the window, the hum of traffic on the street below rumbling through the panes. It was dark and dreary and spitting rain. "Not much to tell."

"You've lived here all your life?"

"I grew up in England, actually. My mom and two sisters still live there. I moved here to go to university on a scholarship."

"Are you the oldest? Youngest?"

"What difference does it make?" She turned to face him, to tell him he had to go now, and nearly collided with his chest. He was right behind her, and she hadn't even heard him cross the room. "What are you? Part cat?"

He grinned and tugged her to him by the tie of her robe. In the process, the bow came loose and her robe fell open.

He made a sound of appreciation in his throat, kind of a sexy growl. "You're naked under there."

She reached for the two sides, to yank them closed, but it was too late. His hands were already on her, touching her. And when he touched her, she lost the ability to think logically.

He lowered his head and nibbled her neck and a shiver coursed through her. "I hope you didn't have plans today."

If she had, she couldn't remember them now. Not

with his lips on her neck, his hot breath on her skin. His big, warm hands cupping her breasts.

She tried a futile, "You need to leave." But they both knew where this was going, and his leaving was no part of it. He was already walking her in the direction of the bedroom. Kissing her. Touching her.

"The food," she reminded him, but he was feasting on her skin instead, and his glassy-eyed, heavy-lidded look told her he was too far gone to think of anything else.

"Honestly," he said, flashing her that hungry grin, the one that made her go weak in the knees. "I think I'd rather have you for breakfast."

Honestly, that sounded pretty good to her, too. So she didn't put up a fight. But as soon as they'd had their *breakfast,* he was out of there.

Ethan didn't leave her apartment until after the sun set that evening. And when he told her he had to travel to the U.S. on business Monday morning, and wouldn't be back until the following Friday, it had been a relief. With any luck, he would meet someone else and she would never hear from him again.

At least, that's what she was telling herself. Until the first batch of flowers came Monday evening. A mixed bouquet. An explosion of color wrapped up in a bow. Wild and beautiful, yet delicate somehow. And there was a handwritten card that read, *These reminded me of you.* It wasn't signed, but she knew who had sent it.

A second bouquet, larger and more colorful than the last followed on Tuesday. The card on that one said simply, *Missing you*. Another came on Wednesday, and a fourth on Thursday. At which point her apartment was so stuffed with fresh flowers it was beginning to smell like a nursery.

By Friday, she sat on pins and needles, missing him terribly and anxious to see him again. She even left work a bit early to primp. She sat eagerly, watching the time tick by on the clock, waiting for that inevitable knock on her door. She turned on the television and switched through the cable channels, stopping on a film about a group of women on a road trip that looked entertaining, but it only barely held her attention.

By ten she began to suspect that he wasn't going to show. By eleven, the hollow pang of disappointment filled her stomach. At midnight she switched off the television and crawled into bed.

Something must have happened between the time he'd bought Thursday's flowers and the time he'd left the plane. She should have been relieved that it was over, instead she felt like the world's biggest fool.

She had fallen for him. Hard. She a lowly secretary in deep lust with the Prince of Morgan Isle. At least now she wouldn't have to figure out a way to explain who she really was.

On Saturday, she sat at her desk sulking most of the day, not getting much done. Trying to tell herself that it was for the best. Wallowing in self-pity.

Honestly, what had she expected? That he would sweep her off her feet and make her a princess? She didn't even *want* that. The life of a royal was so cloying and suffocating. To be under constant scrutiny from millions of people, to regularly see her own name in the papers and tabloids. She couldn't imagine anything worse. She would much rather be invisible.

Around noon, when the queen called Lizzy to her suite, she had herself thoroughly convinced it was for the best. If she never saw Ethan again, that would be a good thing.

Lizzy knocked on the door of the queen's suite and she called her inside. She stepped in and shut the door behind her. The queen was in her favorite chair with her feet up, and there was a man sitting on the sofa. It took several long seconds to register that it was Ethan. And when it did, she froze. Every instinct told her to turn around and dash back out the door. Or to take the leather binder she held and use it to cover her face, but she was too stunned to move a muscle. To even blink her eyes.

She'd heard the reference "a deer in headlights" and realized this was how the poor deer probably felt.

Ethan glanced up at her, briefly, fleetingly, then looked away, dismissing her as just another random employee. And she held her breath, hoping, *praying,* it didn't register. Then his gaze snapped back in her direction and recognition filed his eyes.

Oh, *bloody hell*.

She knew this was bound to happen. Knew it the instant he asked her to dance at the gala and she didn't tell him the truth right then. It had just been a matter of time.

"Elizabeth, what does my schedule look like on June eighteenth?" the queen asked, and for one tense, excruciating moment, Lizzy just stood there, unable to respond. Unable to move a muscle. And Ethan just stared, but she could see his mind working, see him figuring things out.

And he wasn't happy.

"Elizabeth?" the queen asked, looking concerned. "Are you all right?"

Lizzy could only imagine how her face must have looked. She pulled herself together and forced a smile. "Yes, sorry. What was it you wanted to know?"

"My schedule on the eighteenth of June. The prince has asked me to come and tour the progress on the hotel." She paused, looking back and forth between them, then asked, "Have you two met?"

At first she thought the queen had caught on to their discomfort, then realized she was only being her usual polite self.

"No, ma'am, we haven't," Lizzy said, praying that Ethan went along with it, that he wouldn't put her on the chopping block.

"Ethan," the queen said, "this is my assistant, Elizabeth Pryce."

She performed the formal curtsy, even though she knew Ethan hated that. It wasn't as if she had a choice. He was royalty. Technically, that is. When he was naked in her bed, their bodies entwined, his hands on her skin, then he was just Ethan.

But she had the feeling that he would never be *just Ethan* again.

Ethan smiled warmly and addressed her with a nod and a polite, "Miss Pryce."

"Or is it 'Mrs.'?" he asked, though he knew darned well she was divorced. Not that she could blame him for his skepticism. She should have told him who she was. The instant he approached her at the gala she should have been honest.

But then she would have missed out on those two wonderful days with him. And she wouldn't trade those for anything. He'd made her feel alive again, like a whole person, and for that she would always be grateful.

"Miss," she said, and because she couldn't bear to look at him another second, knowing what must be going through his head, the betrayal he must feel, she busied herself with opening the leather binder and checking the queen's calendar. "You have a morning meeting with the chairman of the Hausworth Children's Foundation, but you're free that afternoon."

"Perfect!" the queen said. "Could you please pen in a visit to the hotel?"

"Of course, ma'am."

The queen turned to Ethan. "Shall we say one o'clock?"

"Perfect," he agreed, then rose to his feet. "I should be going. I appreciate the advice."

He couldn't be more pleasant, but she could hear a tone in his voice, see a glimmer of something dark and unpleasant in his eyes. Underneath the good cheer, he was fuming.

And she couldn't blame him for it.

The queen smiled, blissfully unaware there was a problem. "I'm happy to help. Anytime."

He walked toward the door, his eyes on Lizzy, and she stepped out of his way, probably a bit too far, so he could pass. And she couldn't help but wonder what advice the queen had given him.

"It was a pleasure to meet you, Miss Pryce," he said. His voice was courteous, but his eyes belied his anger.

She curtsied again. "Your Highness."

Then he left and shut the door behind him, and Lizzy took her first full breath since she'd stepped into the room and seen him sitting there.

"He's very sweet," the queen said, then added, "And handsome."

Lizzy nodded and uttered a noncommittal, "Hmm."

"You don't think so?"

What was she getting at? Did she suspect something? She didn't want the queen to think she found Ethan attractive, but if Lizzy played it too casual, would she be even more suspicious?

She settled for a non-answer. "He looks very much like the king."

"Yes, he does. And they have the same stubborn

streak." She sighed and waved away the thought as if it were a pesky insect. "Oh, well, I'm sure they'll come around and start seeing each other as family."

Somehow Lizzy doubted that. "Is there anything else, ma'am?"

"No, Elizabeth, you can go. I'll call if I need you."

She curtsied, then opened the door and stepped out into the hall. The instant it was shut and she was alone, the gravity of the situation hit her hard. She leaned against the door, weak-kneed and trembling.

She had brought this on herself. She could only hope that Ethan took pity on her and didn't report what she'd done to the royal family. But honestly, she wouldn't blame him if he fed her to the wolves.

Eight

Lizzy walked back to the administrative wing where her office was located, thankful that she didn't run into anyone along the way. Since it was Saturday, only a few secretaries were working, but for the most part the entire wing was deserted.

She stepped into her office, walked to her desk and set down the leather binder. She'd been clutching it so firmly her fingers ached. In fact, she was so tense, she ached all over.

Behind her the door snapped closed and she spun around in surprise.

Ethan stood there glaring at her. "You're just a secretary, huh? Miss *Sinclaire*."

Whatever emotion he'd been hiding back in the

queen's suite, he let go now with a force that nearly knocked her physically backward. He wasn't just angry or hurt, or even disappointed. He was livid.

"Sinclaire was my married name. I wanted to tell you the truth. I *should* have told you."

"You think?"

"I'm sorry."

"Did you plan this all along," he stormed. "Did you think you could seduce your way into the family?"

Plan it? Was he kidding? Did he really have the gall to suggest that *she* had seduced *him?* "That's completely unfair," she snapped back at him, keeping her voice low so no one else would hear. "Maybe I wasn't totally honest with you, but you know bloody well that you were the one to seek me out. You asked me to dance at the gala, and you were the one to show up at my apartment."

"And at no point you felt it necessary to tell me who you really were?"

"If I told you who I was, and you got angry, sort of like you are now, I could lose my job."

"So, what you're saying is, you didn't trust me."

"I didn't *know* you. I wasn't even supposed to see you again."

"You could have told me at the gala, when we were out on the dance floor."

She lowered her eyes. "I know, and I should have, but I was…curious."

"Curious?"

She looked up at him. "Okay, sue me, but just for

one night I wanted to know how the other half lived. I wanted to feel like I belonged. I know that's a horrible offense, for a commoner to step above her station. I figured, what the hell, it's just one night. But then you kept coming back."

"You lied to me."

She couldn't deny it. She'd never actually said she *didn't* work for the palace. But lying by omission wasn't any less deceitful. "You're right. I made a mistake. And I'm sorry. If I could go back and do things differently, I would."

He just stood there, staring, his eyes boring through her like lasers. It was worse than any words he could have flung at her.

"Are you going to tell the queen?" she asked.

"Are you asking if I'm going to get you fired? Do you really think I would do that?"

She bit her lip, ashamed for even suggesting it.

"And here I thought you were different. I thought you actually saw me." He shook his head, disgusted, and even worse, disappointed. "I guess I was wrong."

"I don't know why it even matters. It was over. You got back from your trip yesterday, yet I didn't see you."

"My flight was delayed. I got back this morning." He narrowed his eyes at her. "Were you waiting for me last night?"

Why did she have to go and open her big mouth? "Of course not," she said.

He wasn't buying it. "Another lie, Lizzy?"

Did he want to completely strip her of her dignity?

Would that make him feel better? Well, fine, he could have it. "Yes, I waited for you. I wanted to see you. Even though I knew we had no future, no hope of this relationship going anywhere. Our social differences aside, I tried the marriage thing once before and I don't ever want to put myself through that again. And no offense to you personally, but I find the life of a royal suffocating and claustrophobic. I wouldn't wish it on my worst enemy."

She couldn't tell if he was insulted or disappointed or just plain angry. His face gave nothing away.

"We had good sex, Ethan."

"Great sex," he corrected. "And that's all it was ever going to be."

"And now it's over." Because as much as she cared for him, lusted after him, they had reached a dead end. There was nowhere left to go.

"Well, then," he said, his hand on the doorknob, "I guess I'll see you around."

"Maybe." But she hoped not. "And by the way, thank you for the flowers."

He paused for a moment, as though he might say something, and she realized there were so many things she wanted to say to him. Mostly she wanted to thank him. For reminding her what it was like to feel passionate and alive. That there was more to life than work and responsibility. For making her feel…happy. But she couldn't make herself say the words.

And by the time she worked up the nerve, he was already gone.

Lizzy had only been home a few minutes when her phone rang, and her heart jumped up into her throat. Then slid right back down again when she looked at the caller ID and saw that it was Maddie and not Ethan.

"A couple of us are meeting at the pub tonight," she told Lizzy. "Want to come with?"

The only thing she wanted to do was to change into her pajamas, curl up on the couch and feel sorry for herself. "I don't think so."

"Oh, come on. I've hardly seen you for weeks. And I still owe you dinner and a pint."

"I'm not feeling very good," she said, and it wasn't a lie really. She felt lousy. Heartsick and guilty. And sad. Deep-down-into-her-soul sad. And not so much because it was over, since it was bound to end eventually anyway, but because she was pretty sure that not only had she made him angry, but she'd hurt him, as well.

"I hope you didn't work today," Maddie said. "If the queen finds out you're sick and she in her fragile state catches it, they'll sack you for sure."

Sometimes Lizzy got so tired of her backhanded comments about the royal family. What had they ever done to Maddie, other than supply her with reliable employment for the past twelve years? But she bit her tongue. She had given up trying to convince Maddie that the new queen was nothing like the former. Nor was Phillip like his father. In fact, he seemed to go out of his way lately to distance himself from that distinction.

"Maybe we can go out next weekend," she said instead.

"You know what we need? A girl's weekend away. Maybe we could catch a bus and spend a few days on the other side of the island. We could shop until we drop, drink ourselves silly and meet sexy, un-available men. What do you think?"

Meeting more men was the last thing Lizzy had on her mind right now. "I really can't leave. Not with the queen so close to her due date."

"Why?"

"She might need me. What if she goes into labor early?"

"So what? It's not like you're delivering the baby."

"But I want to be there."

"*Why?* I mean, honestly, Lizzy. Why do you even care? Do you think they give a damn about you? Well, I hate to break it to you, but they don't. You're just a servant to them. A glorified slave."

Lizzy bit her tongue so hard she tasted blood. Maddie would never understand. She wouldn't even try. "I'm going to let you go, Maddie."

She sighed, probably thinking that Lizzy was hopeless. A lost cause. "Take care of yourself. Eat chicken soup. I hope you feel better soon."

"Thanks. I will."

"I'll call tomorrow to check on you."

"Bye." She hung up and set the phone back in the

cradle. Then she turned and looked around the apartment. It was the same as it had been before Ethan showed up at her door that first time, but for some reason it felt different. Empty and far too quiet. Maybe she should have taken Maddie up on her offer. Maybe she should have gone out and had fun and forgotten about Ethan.

But she had the sneaking suspicion that he was going to be hard to forget.

After leaving the palace, Ethan had gotten into his car and driven. To no place in particular. Through town, then up the coast. He drove for hours, trying to clear his head, replaying what Lizzy had said. At first he was so angry, he was sure that he would stay mad at her forever.

When she'd walked into the queen's sitting room, he hadn't recognized her right away. He'd never imagined her looking so plain and unassuming. She bore no resemblance to the feisty, passionate woman he had come to know. It was as if she were two completely different people.

And maybe she had lied to him, but she was right about one thing. He had been the one to pursue her. Accusing her of using him had been a cheap shot, and said out of anger. He'd made the first move at the gala, and he was the one to keep coming back. How many times had she said it had to end, but he hadn't listened?

And he still wasn't listening. Because he was accustomed to getting what he wanted. And despite everything that had happened, her deceit and their angry words, he wanted *her.* And why did their affair have to end? Neither wanted a relationship. It was the ideal arrangement. Now he could have his cake and eat it, too.

He got out of his car and walked to the building. He let himself inside and climbed the stairs to the second floor. The hallway was empty and quiet. From outside Lizzy's door he could hear the low hum of the television playing.

Only for an instant did he question if he was doing the right thing, then he raised his hand and knocked. A moment later he heard the unlatching of the chain, the turning of the dead bolt, then the opening of the door.

Lizzy stood there, dressed in her robe, even though it was only nine o'clock, looking exhausted. But not all that surprised to see him. Only then did he realize how much he had missed her in the week he'd been gone. And how much he didn't want this to end.

"I wondered if you were ever coming up," she said. When he regarded her questioningly, she added, "There aren't too many people in this neighborhood who drive expensive black sports cars. Back to berate me again?"

"I just want to talk."

She hesitated, then stepped back and gestured him inside. The room was dim but for the light of the television. She walked over to the end table and switched on a lamp. "What do you want to talk about?"

"Us."

"I thought we already established that there is no us."

"I want you to know that I realize the position I put you in by pursuing you, and I understand why you weren't completely honest with me. Why you handled things the way you did. And I was overly harsh. I should have been more understanding."

"You had every right to be angry."

"Would you stop that?" he snapped, and she flinched. "Stop blaming yourself. I acted like a jerk and I'm trying to tell you I'm sorry."

She bit her lip and lowered her head, and for an instant he thought she might cry. But when she looked up again, her eyes were dry. She looked relieved and conflicted.

"Can you forgive me?"

She nodded. "Can you forgive me for lying?"

"I already have." He took a step toward her. "I missed you while I was gone."

She took a step back, narrowing her eyes at him. "Don't do it."

"Do what?"

"You know exactly what I mean. Don't you dare touch me. Don't even think about it."

"Why?" he asked in the most innocent voice he could manage, though he knew damned well why. When he touched her, she lost the ability to think rationally, to tell him no. Which was exactly what he was counting on.

She held up a hand, as though that would be enough to stop him. "Just keep your distance."

"Did you miss me?"

She just stared at him.

"Lizzy?"

"Of course I did! But that doesn't make our relationship any less doomed. This will never work."

"On the contrary, I think it's perfect. Neither of us wants a commitment, and you can't say the sex isn't fantastic. I mean, honestly, what more could we possibly ask for? It's the perfect situation. We get to indulge without the strings."

"There's one thing that you're forgetting. I still work at the palace, and you're still a prince."

"What I do in my personal life is no one else's business."

"This isn't just about you. I happen to enjoy being employed. I can't throw away a career I've spent years building for a night in bed."

"No one has to know."

"So, what, we're going to sneak around? Hope no one recognizes us? You're a prince, for God's sake. People know who you are."

He took another step toward her and this time she stood her ground. She was trying to be brave, to be strong, but she was no match for the attraction they felt for each other. It grew and pulsed around them, like a living, breathing thing. "You can't deny that you want this as much as I do."

"Wanting something doesn't mean it's good for you," she said, but he could see the conflict in her eyes. She was so close to cracking. All he had to do was to touch her and she would melt.

He moved closer. "Admit it, Lizzy. Tell me you want me."

Her throat worked as she swallowed. "You know I do. But that doesn't change anything. This still isn't going to work."

He reached out and curled a hand around her waist, tugged her closer to him. So she would be forced to meet him halfway. And she didn't fight it. She went willingly, melting against him, pressing her cheek to his chest.

"This is a mistake," she said as she wrapped her arms around him, inside his jacket, her body warm and soft, squeezing as though she never wanted to let go. She breathed in deeply and exhaled hot breath against his shirt. It soaked through to his skin, warming him all over.

He stroked her hair back and tucked his fingers under her chin, lifting her face so she would look him in the eye. "Tell me, Lizzy."

She gazed up at him with sleepy eyes, her cheeks rosy with arousal. Her pulse pounding a frantic rhythm through the veins in her throat. "I want you, Ethan."

Before she had the opportunity to change her mind, he lowered his head and kissed her. She tasted warm and sweet and familiar. She wrapped her arms around his neck, pressed herself against him, as though she couldn't get close enough. It was almost eerie how perfect it felt, the depth of his affection for her. The undeniable and intense connection, as though some invisible grip kept them emotionally linked.

He could tell himself a million times that it was only sex, but he knew it was more than that. He also knew that these feelings, as intense as they might be, were only temporary.

He'd been passionate about women in the past, but it never lasted very long. A month maybe, three or four at most. He would begin to make excuses, reasons he couldn't see her. They would begin to drift, spending less and less time together. Then he would meet someone else, someone he found too fascinating to ignore, and he would end it with Lizzy for good.

That was his MO, after all. Have his fun, then get out of Dodge.

Nine

Ethan had showed up at her door Saturday night at nine, and didn't leave again until late Sunday night. And most of that time they spent in bed, crawling out only occasionally to seek nourishment to rebuild their strength. Monday, when she got home from work, he was already there, parked in the street outside her building, waiting for her. And when they stepped inside the foyer, where no one could see, he pulled her to him and planted a toe-curling, knee-weakening kiss on her.

She smiled up at him, feeling all warm and fuzzy. It was nice to have someone to come home to. Someone to share the events of her day with.

Ethan made her feel special, and it was a welcome

change. Roger certainly never had. To boost his own ego, he had always focused on her faults. And even knowing that, recognizing the behavior, it still tore down her self-esteem. And she'd stuck around too long. Maybe because she believed no one else would want her. He had *made* her believe that.

This thing with Ethan was temporary, yet he managed to make her feel more loved and accepted than Roger ever had. And she couldn't help wondering how long they would last. How long would it take for them to tire of each other? A month? Maybe two. Or would it be longer? There was no reason to put a limit on it. At least, not yet.

For the first time in her life she was going to live in the present and not worry about the future.

"If you haven't had dinner yet, I can cook for us," she said as they walked upstairs, his arm looped around her waist, hand curled around her hip. And it felt right. It was…comfortable.

He shot her a simmering smile. "There's only one thing I'm hungry for right now."

And his appetite seemed insatiable. They stepped into her apartment and she barely had time to close the door before he began ravaging her. He slipped the pins from her hair and watched it tumble down over her shoulders, then started undoing the buttons on her suit jacket.

She decided dinner would have to wait, and dragged him by the lapels of his jacket to the bedroom, where they all but tore at each other's clothes, then tossed and tumbled for the next hour and a half. Afterward, since it was late to start cooking, they ordered delivery Thai from a restaurant around the corner and ate in, talking about each other's day. It was a nice change, being able to talk about her work, not having to appease him with half truths and non-answers.

"You really love what you do," Ethan said, and since she was in midchew, she nodded. "That's good. Too many people hate their jobs."

She swallowed and wiped the corners of her mouth with a napkin. "It's been especially rewarding since the queen arrived. She's been wonderful to me. Never once disrespectful or unkind. And working in the palace for as long as I have, I've run into my share of unkind people."

"I like Hannah," he said, draining his wineglass. "But for the life of me I don't know what she sees in Phillip. They seem very happy though."

"Their marriage seemed a bit rocky at first. He wasn't around much. I could tell she was unhappy, even though she tried to hide it. I'm not exactly sure what happened, but a month or so before she announced she was pregnant, everything seemed to change. Now the two are practically inseparable. Sometimes the king will look at her and his eyes are so filled with love. It makes me think, if anyone ever looked at me that way, I would be the happiest, luckiest woman alive."

He grabbed the wine bottle from the bedside table

and emptied it into their glasses. "Except, you don't want a commitment."

She nodded. "Yes, that would be a problem. But maybe, if someone loved me that much, I would have to make an exception."

"As long as he wasn't a royal," he said with a grin. "Because that would be too suffocating and claustrophobic."

She returned his smile. "Exactly."

"Have you ever been in love like that?"

"I thought I was, with Roger, but looking back, I can see that I was just fooling myself. I wanted it so badly, to be loved and accepted, I convinced myself the relationship was something that it wasn't." She took a sip of her wine. "How about you? Have you ever been in love?"

He leaned back on his elbows. "Yep. Madly in love."

Was that a twinge of jealousy she just felt? Of course not, because that would just be ridiculous. People didn't get jealous in casual relationships. There was no point. "Who was she?"

"Allison Williams. I met her in school."

"High school or college?"

"Kindergarten," he said with a grin. "She moved away halfway through the year. I was devastated."

She laughed. "Cute. And since Allison?"

He shook his head. "No one."

For some reason that surprised her. He was so... passionate. "Why not?"

He shrugged. "No time. I have a business to

maintain and no woman can get in the way of that. I prefer a no-strings-attached lifestyle."

She set her plate on the floor beside the bed, set her glass down, then scooted close to Ethan and snuggled up beside him.

He wrapped an arm around her and pulled her close, kissed the top of her head. "I guess we don't have to worry then."

"About what?"

"Falling in love. Since neither of us is looking for that."

"Exactly," she agreed. And he was right, so why did the idea make her feel sad? The truth of it was, even if Ethan was that man, the one to look at her with that deep, unconditional love, she could never be the woman he needed. They were too different. They may have started out life on level ground, but now they were miles apart.

Who was she kidding? They had never been on level ground.

"Phillip would love nothing more," Ethan said. "He's pushing for me to settle down. He says it will be good for the family. As if I plan to live my life by their rules."

And they did have lots of rules. Hundreds of them. Working for the family was one thing, but she couldn't ever imagine wanting to be one of them. She was too independent.

Ethan lazily stroked her hip with one large, warm hand. "Can I ask you a question?"

"Sure."

"You knew the king? My father, I mean."

She nodded. "Somewhat."

"What was he like?"

She looked up at him. "You never met him?"

He shook his head. He looked so sad it nearly broke her heart.

She wished she could tell him that his father was a wonderful, noble man, but that would be a lie. "He was…complicated."

"Sophie told me that he was a coldhearted, overbearing, pompous ass."

"Yeah, that sounds about right." She'd always had the feeling that Princess Sophie and her brother resented their father, but it wasn't as though they shared that kind of thing with the staff. And if they ever did, no one was talking. "And unfortunately, the queen wasn't much better. I always felt sorry for them, having a mother and father so cold."

"He cheated openly. Or so Sophie has said."

"He could be charming when he wanted to be." Lizzy had friends, other employees at the palace, who had succumbed to those charms. Even though it meant immediate dismissal afterward. No mistress ever lasted long.

Ethan narrowed his eyes at her. "How charming?"

She laughed. "Not *that* charming. I won't say that he didn't notice me at first. But I made it damned clear that I wasn't interested."

"That explains it."

"Explains what?"

"Why you dress the way you do for work. Why you look so plain."

"Being invisible is always easier."

He sighed. "At times I wish I'd had the chance to meet him, but I get the feeling I would only be disappointed. I think my mom knew that. It's probably why she never told me. Although I can't help resenting that she kept it from me."

"I'm sure she did what she thought was best. Just like my mom, although she failed miserably."

"How's that?"

"My father left us just after my baby sister was born. I was six. My mom tried to find a replacement, a father figure for us, but she had horrible taste in men. Most of them drank, and a few hit her. When I won a scholarship to attend school in Morgan Isle, I couldn't pack fast enough. I didn't even wait until fall, when courses began. I left right after graduation."

"Do you ever go back to visit?"

She shook her head. "Too many hard feelings, and my sisters resent me for leaving them. And sadly, they haven't fared much better in love. They attract losers. Men who drain them then move on. Not that I've been all that lucky in love myself. Roger was a leach, sucking me dry of my dignity and my money. Sometimes I think the women in my family are cursed."

"Or just unlucky?"

"Maybe. I send my mom money every month, though, to help make things a bit easier."

"Even though you resent her?"

She shrugged. "She's still my mom, still family. Despite all of her faults, I love her. You would do the same for your mom if she were alive."

"You're right. I would."

She rose up on her elbow to look at him. "I think we're both too kind for our own good."

"That would explain a lot."

"Maybe that's why this thing we have feels so nice. It's selfish. And it's bad for me. I've spent my entire life playing by the rules. It's liberating to do something just because it feels good."

"I'll bet…" Ethan rolled her over onto her back and settled himself between her thighs, grinning. "I can make you feel really good."

She didn't doubt that for an instant. No man had ever made her feel as good as Ethan did. She arched up, rubbing herself against him where she was still slick and warm from the last time they made love. She felt him pulse, growing hard and long. "I think I'm going to need proof."

He leaned down, brushed his lips against hers, soft and teasing. "And what will I get in return?"

"Anything you want."

"All I want is you," he said, and with a shift of his hips sank deep inside her. And it was just so… perfect. And so wrong. It was going to have to end, and when it did, she hoped it wasn't badly.

* * *

"Elizabeth, are you all right?" the queen asked her later that week, after, for about the third time that day, Lizzy had completely blanked out and hadn't heard the queen talking to her.

They were in the queen's sitting room, she on the sofa with her feet up and Lizzy beside her, looking at baby announcements. But Lizzy was having a terrible time concentrating. It was Ethan's fault, keeping her up way past her bedtime last night. Business meetings had kept them apart Tuesday and Wednesday, so Thursday they had spent quality time together. He hadn't left her place until after one and she was paying the price this morning.

"Fine, ma'am. I apologize. I didn't sleep well last night."

"You can go home early if you like."

She was so nice, it filled Lizzy with guilt. Lizzy was slacking off because she was having a forbidden, lurid affair with the queen's brother-in-law. "I'm fine, ma'am."

The queen held up an announcement with pastel ducks and bunnies on it. "What do you think of this one? Too feminine for a boy?"

The truth was, they had looked at so many, they were all beginning to look the same. "The one with the blue blocks is still my favorite, I think."

The queen sighed. "This shouldn't be so hard."

"You want it to be perfect," Lizzy said. She imagined she would be the same way if she ever had children. She was still young enough. And maybe, if she met the right man…

But that would be a few years down the road. Or maybe not so far. It was amazing how quickly things could change. Her entire outlook on life had changed in just a few weeks. She had let down her guard and trusted a man. If someone had told her a year ago that she would be where she is today, she would have called them crazy. But now, she could honestly say she was happy.

She wondered what kind of a father Ethan would be. Not that she thought she would ever find out. Not firsthand anyway. Did he even want children? Having a family wasn't something couples discussed in a relationship that was deemed temporary. There was no point.

"Elizabeth?"

She looked over at the queen and realized she'd been talking, and once again Lizzy had completely zoned out on her. "Sorry, ma'am."

"Is it a man? The one you were talking to the other day. Is that why you're so distracted?"

Though Lizzy tried to hide it, her cheeks burned with embarrassment. The weird thing was, she wanted to tell the queen about it. She wanted to tell *someone.* But she was the last person Lizzy should be spilling her guts to. Not only would it be totally inappropriate to discuss personal matters with her employer, but it would mean certain termination. She bit her lip, unsure of what to say.

"I'm sorry," the queen said. "I'm being nosy."

"No, it's okay. I just…" She took a deep breath and blew it out. "It's complicated."

"Are you in love?"

God, no, she would never be that foolish.

"You can tell me to mind my own business," the queen said.

"No," Lizzy said. "I just…I guess I'm not really sure how I feel about him. He's too…" She shrugged.

A hopeless romantic, the queen persisted. "Too what?"

"Too…*perfect*." If it wasn't for the fact that he didn't want a relationship, that this was strictly sex, she reminded herself.

The queen just laughed. "That's the silliest thing I've ever heard. How can a man be *too* perfect?"

"I guess what I'm trying to say is, it's so right, it must be wrong." Her own words surprised her. What she and Ethan had was as *right* as good sex could be. It wasn't anything more than that. It never would be. "We're too different."

"Sometimes different works. Look at me and Phillip. We couldn't be more different. We're from different countries, came from completely different backgrounds. Yet, we're happy."

She and the king weren't so different. They both came from money, and unlike Lizzy, the queen had royal blood in her veins. And if the queen had a clue who the man in question was, she wouldn't be so supportive.

"As I said, it's complicated."

The queen just smiled. "Whether you want to admit it or not, I can see that you really care about him."

The queen was mistaking lust and infatuation for love. But Lizzy wasn't about to admit that she would rather have a brief, no-strings-attached affair than be in a committed relationship. Even if she had a choice. Not yet anyway.

"I'm sure you noticed, but when I first moved here, things with Phillip were, shall we say…bumpy."

Lizzy nodded. "I noticed. And I'm so pleased that everything worked out."

"It just takes time." She touched Lizzy's arm. "Maybe you should give this man a chance."

She could see that it was a losing argument, so she just smiled and promised she would, and that seemed to appease her. Then Lizzy changed the subject back to birth announcements.

But she had the sinking feeling that she hadn't heard the last of this.

Ten

Ethan had missed his last two games with Charles, so Saturday morning he crawled quietly from Lizzy's bed, so he wouldn't wake her, then dressed and headed to the club. Charles was already in the locker room changing when he got there.

"I wasn't sure if I was going to see you this week," Charles said. "I tried to call you at home last night, but no one answered."

"That's because I didn't go home." He hadn't been home much at all lately. Almost all of his free time he'd spent with Lizzy.

Out of fear of being spotted, she refused to go to his penthouse apartment. Or out to dinner, or the theater. She'd never even so much as ridden in his car. So they hung out at her place, but they always managed to find something to do to keep them occupied.

"Who is it this time?" Charles asked. "Anyone I know?"

He shrugged out of his jacket and hung it in his locker. "I told you about her."

"You did?" He looked puzzled for a second, then asked, "The secretary?"

He nodded.

"*Still?* I thought that was only supposed to be one night." He paused then added. "Her rules, not yours. Remember?"

"If I want something, I go after it." He was half-tempted to tell Charles who she was. Ethan knew of at least half a dozen palace staff members who Charles had dated, and was pretty sure he could trust him. But he'd promised Lizzy he wouldn't tell anyone, and he always kept his word.

"You see her often?"

"Almost every night."

His eyes went wide with alarm. "Seriously."

Ethan nodded.

"Bloody hell. You're not worried she'll get too attached?"

"I like her, Charles. She…gets me. I can be myself when I'm with her. Besides, we've agreed to keep it casual."

Charles looked wary. "Women say that all the time. To hook us in. And before you know it they're expecting a ring and a happily ever after."

"Lizzy isn't like that. She's divorced and not looking to remarry."

"I hope you're right. It's scandalous enough to marry a nonroyal, but a *divorced* nonroyal? I think that's considered a cardinal sin."

"It's never going to be an issue. I have no interest in marrying anyone."

Charles shook his head, as though he couldn't believe it, or he felt sorry for Ethan. "I hope you know what you're doing."

"I have the best of both worlds. All the fantastic sex a man could ask for, and none of the hassle."

Ethan slaughtered Charles at squash, then, after a shower and a quick drink, decided to pay a visit to the palace. To see Lizzy, of course, since she insisted working Saturday, even though Phillip and Hannah were out for the day at some charity function. Which got him thinking about what Charles had said.

It was true that he and Lizzy were spending an awful lot of time together. Even if it was only an hour or two in the evenings. He couldn't help but wonder if he was pushing his luck, if he should take a step back.

But as quickly as the idea formed, he dismissed it as paranoia. Lizzy didn't want a commitment any more than he did. They were on borrowed time, so why not take advantage of what time they did have together?

The palace was quiet with only a skeleton staff in the administrative offices. When he entered, one of the office girls rose from her seat. She was young, probably an intern still in school. She curtsied and asked, "Can I help you, sir?"

God, did he hate being addressed that way, but he turned on the charm and flashed her a flirting smile. "I sure hope so." He looked around, as though what he had to say was a secret, and lowered his voice to a whisper. "I'd like to get a gift for my brother and his wife, to celebrate the birth of their first child, but I'm pretty clueless when it comes to things like that."

The intern nodded sympathetically.

"Would there be a way to find out what they need? Maybe someone who would know and could be discreet. I'd like it to be a surprise."

"The person you want is Miss Pryce, the queen's assistant," she said in a hushed voice.

She had no idea just how right she was about that. "I don't suppose she would be in today."

"She is, actually. She could tell you exactly what they need."

"And she'll be discreet?"

"Of course, sir. Her office is just down the corridor. Third on the left."

"Perfect. Thanks." He started to walk down the hall, then turned back to her. "Let's keep this between us." He flashed her a grin. "If anyone asks, I was never here."

"Absolutely, sir." She smiled and made a motion across her lips as though she was turning a lock and throwing away the key.

He gave a quick knock on the door and heard Lizzy call, "Come in."

He opened the door and stepped inside and she looked up from her computer. If she was surprised to see him she didn't let it show. She sat primly behind her desk, glasses perched on her nose, looking very professional. Conservative blue suit, no make-up, hair pinned sternly back in a knot.

"Miss Pryce, is it?"

She regarded him coolly, as though his being here was an everyday occurrence. "Your Highness?"

"I was hoping you could help me." He closed the door behind him. Then he locked it.

That got her attention. Her eyes went wide and she rasped under her breath, "What are you doing?"

He grinned and walked toward her desk. "What do you think I'm doing?"

It took her a moment to process what he meant, then her mouth fell open with surprise. "*Here?* You can't be serious."

"I told the girl out there that I need help picking out a baby gift for my brother. She sent me to you." He walked around her desk, then he swiveled her chair so she was facing him. "Convenient, huh?"

"Are you nuts?"

"Probably." He lifted her up and deposited her on the desktop then sat in her chair. "But you love it."

She wouldn't admit it, but she didn't have to. He could see it in her face. Her rosy cheeks and shiny eyes. She was turned on.

"We could get caught," she said, but didn't stop him when he slipped her shoes off.

He grinned up at her. "I know. That's what makes it so hot."

"Ethan, no. We can't."

"You don't mean that." He eased her skirt up, past her thighs and up around her waist, and she helped him by lifting her hips. She had on thigh-high stockings underneath and he growled with appreciation. His favorite part of the day lately had been peeling those stockings from her legs, but that would have to wait until later.

"What if someone hears?" she said, but she wasn't putting up much of a resistance.

He shrugged. "Don't make any noise."

"Easy for you to say."

He touched her through her underwear and she sucked in a breath.

"Feel good?"

She bit her lip and nodded.

"How about this?" He slipped his fingers underneath, stroked her bare skin, and she trembled. He leaned forward and kissed one thigh, then the other, and she slid closer to his face, right to the edge of the desk, her eyes glossy and half-closed. She wasn't behaving like a woman who wanted him to stop. He worked his way upward, kissing and stroking, until she all but melted into a puddle. Then he stopped and pulled away and she groaned with disappointment.

"Still want me to stop?" he asked.

She didn't answer, but her expression said it all. She was burning up. And if they had more time, he might have made her say the words out loud. But having a quick romp was one thing, taking too long would look suspicious and he didn't want to put her job in danger.

His eyes glued on hers, he hooked his fingers on the waistband of her panties and dragged them down her legs.

He had barely touched her, just one sweep of his tongue, and her entire body shuddered with release. She threw her head back, sinking her fingers in his hair, and rode it out. The intensity of it left her shaky and out of breath. And it seemed to cure her of her fear of being discovered. She gazed down at him, lips damp and red, then slipped off the desk to unfasten his belt. "No noises, remember."

Ethan was in and out of Lizzy's office in under twenty minutes, with the promise that he would see her later that evening back at her place. When he left, the girl from the outer office looked up and smiled.

"Did you get what you came for?"

"Yes, I did." That, and then some. "Thanks for your help."

He made a quick stop in the public washroom, then headed downstairs, running into Sophie on his way out. Literally. She rounded the same corner at the exact same time from the opposite direction and they collided into one another. She was so willowy and light, if he hadn't grabbed hold of her arm, he might have knocked her clear over. Which wasn't to say she was a pushover. Sophie might have appeared soft and gentle, and undeniably feminine in her gauzy dresses and silk outfits, but on the inside she was tough.

"Ethan! What are you doing here!" She threw her arms around his neck and planted a firm kiss on his cheek.

"Business," he said, and hoped she didn't press for specifics.

But Sophie being Sophie, she did. "What business?"

"I came to talk to Phillip. But he and Hannah are gone for the day."

Her brow wrinkled. "He hasn't been giving you a hard time?"

"No. No more than usual." He changed the subject, hoping he could bait her away from the topic of their brother. "Has Charles told you about the Houghton hotel deal?"

"Yes!" she said excitedly. It was Sophie who had pushed for the addition of a spa and advanced fitness center, complete with state-of-the-art equipment and staff trained in all of the latest beauty and exercise trends, not to mention two Olympic-size pools, one indoor and one out. "I'm already working with the designer I told you about. And I've ordered the appliances for the kitchen."

"Top of the line, I hope."

She grinned. "Of course. I've been busy testing new recipes for the menu. Want to come over and be my guinea pig?"

"I wish I could, but I have plans tonight."

"What kind of plans? Like a date?"

"Something like that."

She had a sparkle of curiosity in her eyes. She was forever trying to set him up with her available friends. Although, unlike Phillip, she wasn't pushing him to the altar. She just wanted him to be happy. "Really? Anyone I know?"

"I don't think so."

One brow perked slightly higher than the other. "From around here?"

"She lives in town."

"Is this a first date?"

He folded his arms across his chest. "Is this twenty questions?"

"What?" She shrugged innocently. "I can't help that I have a curious nature. You're my big brother. I like to know what's going on in your life."

He sighed. "No it's not a first date, and before you ask, no, it isn't serious. Nor will it ever be."

"So, you're having an affair?"

The term *affair* made it sound cheap or immoral, and it wasn't either. But they were engaged in a temporary sexual relationship, which he supposed, by definition, *was* an affair. "I guess you could call it that."

"Is she married?"

"Of course not!"

"Engaged?"

"Not engaged, either." What kind of man did she think him to be?

She shrugged. "Just asking."

"She's single. Divorced actually."

"I would love to meet her. Maybe we can all go out?"

That was not going to happen. "She wouldn't. She's a little intimidated by the whole royal thing. She would be…uncomfortable."

The irony of that particular lie was that in all honesty, Lizzy was probably more comfortable and more accustomed to dealing with royalty than he was. Professionally, that is.

"She would be uncomfortable, or *you* would?" Sophie asked.

Now she was fishing, and he had things to do before Lizzy got out of work. "I have to go, Soph. I'll see you soon."

"Okay, but I want you to reserve a night for me next week. I miss you."

"I will," he promised, then he gave her a quick peck on the cheek. "See you soon."

He could feel her eyes on him as he walked out the door and reminded himself that this was not an affair. So why did he feel the slightest bit of regret that he would never go public with their relationship?

Eleven

As good as this thing with her and Ethan turned out to be, Lizzy couldn't help wondering how long it would take the element of newness to wear off. When the sneaking around would become more annoying than exciting.

As it turned out, not long. Barely three weeks.

"Let me take you out to dinner," Ethan said to her that third week when they met at her place on Friday after work. "Anywhere you want to go."

She wanted to. Since that was what normal couples did on a Friday night. They saw films or shows, dined in restaurants. Alone or with friends. She wanted them to have a normal relationship. But the fact was, they didn't. And they never would. He was always dropping hints, reminding her that this was just sex. Just for fun.

"I like staying in," she told him, but it was a lie. She felt just as bored and confined as he did.

"We can go somewhere quiet and out of the way," he said.

Unfortunately there was no place they could go where he wouldn't be recognized. "I want to, but I can't."

He let it drop and they ordered in, like they usually did. The next morning he left for the U.S. to attend a college friend's birthday party.

She'd missed him terribly and could hardly wait to see him when he returned. His flight arrived too late Tuesday night to come see her, so she sat at work all day Wednesday on pins and needles, edgy with anticipation. Thankfully the queen was too excited with her own news to notice. Her physician had been by yesterday and she was already dilated to two centimeters.

"He said it could still be a few weeks," she told Lizzy. "And the cramps I've been feeling are probably Braxton Hicks, but it seems so real all of the sudden. So close."

They sat together in her suite, going through piles and piles of baby clothes, burp cloths and blankets. Sorting and folding them neatly in preparation for the big day.

When the queen's phone rang, Lizzy got up from the sofa to answer it. It was the king. But he didn't want to speak to his wife. He wanted Lizzy.

"Please come down to my office," he said, then hung up the phone. She tried not to feel alarm, but something in his voice told her she should be worried.

Even if something was wrong, that didn't mean it had anything to do with her, she assured herself. It could be anything.

But why didn't he have his secretary summon her? Why make the call himself?

Lizzy, stop it! She was probably reading way more into this than was actually there.

"The king needs me in his office," she told the queen.

If she had any idea what this was about, she didn't let on. She didn't look the least bit concerned. She was too busy folding onesies and sorting them by color and size. "All right. Tell him not to keep you too long, though. We have organizing to do."

She left the queen's suite and walked down the hall to the king's private office, a feeling of dread building in her belly.

She greeted his secretary with a cheery smile, one she didn't return. Not that she'd ever been the warm and fuzzy type. But it wasn't a good sign.

"Go on in," she said. "They're waiting for you."

They? There was someone else in there?

The feeling of dread multiplied and she had the sudden urge to turn and run. Her hand trembled as she turned the knob and opened the door. The king sat at his desk, looking stern and regal, and when she stepped inside, she saw the other person the secretary had been referring to and her heart sank so low she could swear she felt it slither down into her pelvis. Sitting across the room, slouched in a chair, his legs crossed, was Ethan. His body language said he was relaxed and without care. Bored even.

What the heck was going on?

When she spoke, she struggled to keep her voice even, in case this was some kind of test. On the off chance it had nothing to do with her and Ethan and their affair. "You wanted to see me, sir?"

"Close the door, Miss Pryce."

She closed it quietly, trying to read the expression on Ethan's face, and it was obvious, the way he looked her directly in the eye, almost apologetically, that they had been discovered. Despite how careful they had been, somehow the king found out.

"I guess I don't have to tell you why I called you here," the king said sternly.

Lizzy shook her head, feeling sick to her stomach. So nauseous in fact that she was afraid she might lose her lunch right there on his office carpet.

"I also don't have to tell you how this looks for the family. The prince marrying a secretary."

"No, Your Highness, I—" Wait a minute, did he say *marrying?* Did Ethan actually tell him they were getting *married?*

She glanced over at Ethan and he was wearing this look, one that said just go along with it.

"I…I'm sorry," she finished.

"Don't apologize," Ethan said sharply. "You didn't do anything wrong."

The king shot Ethan a stern look, then turned his attention to Lizzy. "The prince tells me that he approached you at the gala, and despite your objections continued to pursue you afterward. Is that true?"

She could barely breathe much less form words, so she nodded. She was still stuck on the word *married*. Ethan couldn't have actually told him they were planning to wed.

"And you let it go on," the king asked. "Despite knowing that it is grounds for dismissal?"

She lowered her eyes to her feet and nodded.

"Like I told you, Phillip," Ethan said. "You can't fight true love."

True love? Did he love her?

"Ethan tells me that he proposed and you are to be married next spring."

Just the thought made her woozy. Though she had no choice but to go along with it. "Yes, sir, next spring."

"At which time you will no longer continue your employment with the royal family?"

Wait a minute. Was he saying that he *wasn't* going to fire her on the spot? That until this so-called wedding she could keep her job? A glimmer of hope sparked a dim light at the end of the very long, dark tunnel she'd gotten herself trapped in.

She swallowed hard and shook her head. "No, sir."

"Ethan tells me that after the wedding you plan to work in the resort. Although I have to say that I don't approve of a member of the royal family being employed anywhere."

A member of the royal family.

Now she was sure she really would be sick. It was like her nightmare coming true. She didn't want to be a member of the royal family. She didn't even want to be engaged! And the weirdest part about all of this was the king's attitude. She would have expected him to rant and protest and insist they end their relationship. Instead he was acting almost as though he *approved*.

Ethan rose to his feet, casual as you please, while she was on the verge of a panic attack. He turned to his brother. "So, are you satisfied now?"

The king nodded. "However, I would have appreciated a bit of warning."

"I think I've made it pretty clear that my life is none of your business," Ethan replied haughtily.

Lizzy could see the king stewing behind dark, brooding eyes. "I'll see that an announcement is made."

Ethan shrugged. "Fine."

Wait, what? *Announcement?* Ethan was going to let him announce an engagement that never happened?

"If we're finished here, I'd like a private word with my fiancée."

The king nodded. "And I'll talk to my wife."

"Let's go, sweetheart," Ethan said, but Lizzy felt rooted to the floor.

When she didn't budge, he took her upper arm and led her out of the king's office and into the hall. She opened her mouth to speak and he whispered sharply, "Not a word until we're alone."

He all but dragged her to the opposite end of the

wing where he kept an office. Once they were inside he shut the door and locked it. Then he turned to her and said firmly, "You need to calm down and let me explain."

Only then did she realize that she was breathing so hard she was practically hyperventilating, and she was shaking all over. "What the bloody hell did you do?"

"Saved your job, that's what." He led her to a chair and she collapsed into it, her legs shaky and weak.

"By telling the king that we're *engaged?*"

"He found out about us. I'm not sure how, but he confronted me today."

"So you told him we're *engaged?*"

"I didn't have a choice, Lizzy."

"What about the truth? That was a choice."

"You think so? What sounds better to you, that we're madly in love and planning to get married, or that we're having a brief, torrid affair?"

She bit her lip. He had a point.

"I figured it was your best shot at keeping your job. After all, how would it look if the king fired his future sister-in-law? His brother's mistress, on the other hand, would be expendable. The scandal would cause too much damage to the family's image."

He was right. If he had told the king the truth, she definitely would have been sacked. Here Ethan was doing everything he could to save her job, at the risk of his already rocky relationship with his brother, and she was acting selfish and ungrateful.

"I'm sorry, Ethan. I should be thanking you, not complaining. I was just caught off guard."

He smiled. "It's okay. I know you like to be in control. I'd have given you advance warning, but there was no time."

"So what do we do now?" she asked. "We can't actually get married."

"Of course not." She should have been relieved, so why did she feel a tinge of disappointment instead? "We'll pretend to be engaged for a while, a couple of months, tops, then we'll amicably split. You get to keep your job, and everyone is happy."

It made sense. And if it meant keeping her job, how could she argue? "That might actually work. Unless, after we split, they fire me anyway. Then what?"

"Then you come to work for me at the resort. Either way, I'll see to it that you come out of this gainfully employed. I promise."

He looked so earnest, so apologetic, she couldn't be angry with him. Everything he'd done, all the lies he'd told his brother, had been for her. And besides, she had gotten herself into this mess. He may of pursued her, but she'd had a thousand opportunities to tell him no. And she didn't. She had wanted this as much as he did.

"I guess this means we don't have to sneak around any longer," she said.

"On the contrary. We need to make this as public as possible. We have to convince everyone that we really are engaged."

She couldn't help thinking that this was fun for him. Not that she believed for an instant that he had done this on purpose. She had been both arrogant and foolish to believe that they could keep their relationship a secret.

And maybe, for a short while at least, being engaged to a gazillionaire prince might be a little bit exciting. To be on the inside, instead of the outside looking in. Maybe she should just let herself enjoy it.

"So, what's our next move?" she asked.

He sat on the edge of his desk. "Well, first we have to see about a ring."

"A *ring?*"

He shrugged. "Can't be engaged without a ring."

"You don't mean a real ring."

"I could get one out of a Cracker Jack box."

"A what?"

He chuckled. "Never mind. But yes, it will be a real one."

"Won't that be expensive?"

He gave her this look, like, *Yeah, so?* She had to remind herself that he was loaded. But that didn't mean she expected him to spend a lot of money on her. "I'll give it back. After we call it off."

"You don't have to. Consider it…a parting gift."

"I don't think I would feel comfortable doing that."

"Tell you what. Why don't we worry about that when the time comes, okay?"

She was a planner. She liked to know what would happen when, and how she would handle it. Indecision made her nuts. But this time she was just going to have to play it by ear. She nodded reluctantly and asked, "Anything else?"

"An engagement party."

Oh, God, she hadn't even thought of that. But the family would be expecting it. They would probably insist. The idea of all those rich and famous people gathered together in her honor made her knees knock. How could they lie to all of those people?

"Don't worry." He slid off the desk, propped his hands on the arms of her chair, leaned in and kissed her. Then he looked her in the eye and said, "It'll be okay. It's all for show. Nothing in our relationship will change."

Maybe that was part of the problem. "What if the family is angry with me?"

"They'll get over it."

"And the other staff. They're going to hate me."

"It doesn't matter what they think."

To him maybe, but these were people she had to work with every day. People who could potentially make her life a waking nightmare if they wanted to. She'd seen other employees ostracized for less. And the queen, what was she going to think? Lizzy could hardly stand the idea of disappointing her. And all for a relationship that was pretend.

"I should get back to work. I wonder if the king talked to the queen yet."

"You know, you're going to have to start calling them by name."

"I don't know that I could ever do that." Especially since this whole engagement was a sham.

"When do you want to go ring shopping?" he asked. "How about if I pick you up at your place around seven?"

"Okay."

"And I'll take you out to dinner."

She nodded numbly.

Ethan walked her back to the queen's suite, kissed her—actually kissed her in the hallway where anyone could see—then left. Left her to fend for herself. She stood in the hall for a moment, trying to work up the nerve to open the door. If the queen was angry or upset, she wasn't sure what she would do.

And there wasn't a damned thing she could do about it, so she might as well just get it over with.

She forced herself to open the door and step inside. The queen was standing at the window, looking out over the gardens, her back to Lizzy. Lizzy's hands shook as she shut the door and said, "Ma'am?"

She turned to Lizzy, her face unreadable. "I just had an interesting talk with Phillip. Is it true?"

Lizzy bit her lip and nodded.

The queen walked slowly toward her. "So, the mystery man you've been seeing is Ethan?"

She felt sick to her stomach again. "I'm sorry I didn't tell you. I understand if you're angry, or you want me to transfer to a different position."

She stopped in front of Lizzy. "There won't be any transfer. But you know what this means, don't you?"

She was afraid to ask.

It happened so fast, it made her head spin. But one second the queen was standing in front of her, and the next she had pulled Lizzy into a bone-crushing hug.

"It means we're going to be sisters!"

Twelve

Lizzy didn't think anything could be worse than disappointing the queen, but she was wrong. The queen's excitement, as she gushed on about planning the engagement party and wedding preparations, was more scathing than any angry words she could have spoken. Guilt burned a hole in Lizzy's gut and made her ears ring. Because it was all a big lie.

And it kept getting worse.

"You have to call me Hannah now," the queen said, but Lizzy just couldn't see herself being comfortable doing that. Maybe if they were really going to be in-laws, but they weren't.

"Ma'am," she started, but the queen shushed her.

"I *insist*. You're family now."

"Only socially. Until the wedding," she forced herself to say. "I just wouldn't feel comfortable addressing you by your name in a professional context."

She thought about that for a second, then said, "I guess that would be all right. For now. But after it's official, you aren't ever allowed to call me *ma'am* or *Your Highness* again. Agreed?"

Lizzy nodded. And feeling it would only be fair to make an effort, said, "And you can call me Lizzy. All my friends and family do."

"Okay, Lizzy." She beamed with happiness. "I am so excited for you! I can't wait to start planning everything. We're going to have so much fun!"

Lizzy forced a smile. "But it should wait until after the baby is born. You don't need any extra stress right now. In fact, we should postpone the engagement party until the baby is at least a few months old, so you've had proper time to heal." At which time she and Ethan would have already called it quits, saving them all a lot of unnecessary trouble.

But the queen quashed that idea. "Nonsense. I'll need maybe a week to recover. And you know how much I love planning parties. In fact, I have a book of invitation samples in my bedroom. I'll go get it, and we can decide which ones you like best."

She dashed excitedly off to the bedroom, as fast as her protruding belly would allow, leaving Lizzy standing helplessly by herself. With any luck, the baby would be born a few weeks late, and by then she and Ethan would be over.

This was all happening so fast, her head was spinning. And she had a blazing headache forming in her temples.

Probably the stress of lying to royalty.

To kill time, she sat on the couch and tackled the basket of baby clothes still sitting there, fluffing and folding the tiny outfits and fuzzy blankets. Preparing for the baby's arrival was the only real thing in her life right now. Everything else felt like a fabrication. And lies were work. They seemed to have a way of snowballing out of control. Of course, besides the engagement, everything Ethan told the king had been true. He had approached her at the gala, and he had been the one to pursue her.

That didn't make her feel any less guilty though.

She was beginning to wonder what was taking the queen so long, when she heard her call, "Eliza— I mean, Lizzy, could you come here, please?" There was a frantic note to her voice that filled Lizzy with alarm. Tossing the blanket she'd been folding aside, she jumped up and sprinted to the bedroom. But she wasn't there. "Ma'am?"

"I'm in the bathroom," she called.

Lizzy walked over and peeked inside. The queen stood at the counter, gripping the edge, a pained look on her face. "Are you okay?"

She looked at Lizzy, then nodded toward the floor, and Lizzy realized she was standing in a puddle. "Oh, my gosh. Is that what I think it is?"

"My water broke. And there is no way that the

contraction I just felt is a Braxton Hicks." She looked over at Lizzy and smiled. "I think I'm in labor!"

The king wanted to go directly to the hospital but the queen, *Hannah,* as Lizzy had been forcing herself to call her all afternoon, wanted to spend the long, painful hours ahead at home. The doctor came by to check her, and suggested she keep moving to get the labor progressing more rapidly, so Lizzy, the king and Princess Sophie all took turns walking the grounds with her, and as the sun began to set, and her contractions grew stronger, they moved the party inside and walked up and down the halls of the residence.

Lizzy had taken off her suit jacket hours ago, and with her feet beginning to throb, she kicked her shoes off and paced in her stocking feet. Something she never could have imagined herself doing under *any* circumstances. She even plucked the pins from her hair and let it tumble down loose. And the weirdest thing about it all? It didn't feel uncomfortable or strange.

It was funny how quickly things could change.

She was so busy helping out that until her cell phone rang at seven, she had completely forgotten that she was supposed to meet Ethan to go ring shopping and out to dinner. She stepped into the queen—Hannah's—bedroom to answer it.

"You stood me up," he said, and joked, "You sick of me *already?*"

"I'm sorry. I meant to call. But it's been a little crazy around her. The queen—Hannah, I mean, is in labor."

"Really? Are you at the hospital?"

"Not yet. She wants to stay home as long as possible."

"Is there anything I can do?"

"Not right now. I'll call you and let you know when we go to the hospital."

"So I guess ring shopping will have to wait."

"Why don't you go without me?"

"Isn't this something we should do together? What if I pick out a ring that you hate?"

"I trust you. Besides, I like surprises."

"No, you don't. You like predictability and order."

He was right. It was creepy that he knew her that well. But comforting in a way, because he didn't use it to exploit her. "I'm sure whatever you get will be perfect."

"If that's what you want," he said, and she could swear she detected a note of disappointment in his voice. But it was better this way. Picking out a ring together would feel too…real. She didn't want to get too swept up in this charade and do something dumb, like fall in love with him.

And even if she did, it would never work. They were too different. Besides, he didn't have time for her.

"What size?" he asked.

"Size?"

"Ring. I want it to fit."

"Oh, a five and a half."

"Five and a half it is. Call me later and I'll meet you at the hospital. I'd like to be there when my first nephew is born."

"I will. I promise. Talk to you later." She disconnected, and turned, startled to see Princess Sophie leaning in the doorway.

"Talking to Ethan?" she asked, then added, "Your fiancé?"

Was she angry? According to the queen—Hannah—Sophie was very protective of Ethan.

Lizzy nodded, wringing her hands. This was turning into the most stressful, topsy-turvy day of her entire life.

"My brother told me. Congratulations."

"Thank you."

Sophie's face split into a grin. "Relax. I don't bite."

"Sorry," she said, her cheeks burning with embarrassment. "I wasn't sure how everyone would take the news. When you thought of Ethan getting married, I'm probably not what you imagined."

"Why would you say that?"

"Not only am I an employee, but as far as I know, I don't have a drop of royal blood in me."

She waved away the notion with a flip of her hand. "That's my brother talking. Phillip, I mean. Personally I think it's great. I've never seen Ethan so happy."

Sophie's words surprised her. "Really?"

"When he first came to us, Ethan was…lost, I guess. He didn't have anyone. Lot's of business associates and friends, and lots of women but no one special. It took quite some time to trust that what he had here was real. Phillip hasn't helped, being so overbearing and judgmental. He means well, but he has the unfortunate tendency to alienate anyone who doesn't see things exactly his way. But lately, Ethan seems to have accepted his position in the family, and the responsibilities of that position."

"I noticed that, too," Lizzy said. It had been weeks since Ethan had had anything negative to say about Phillip.

"The real test," Sophie said, "is going to be if *you* can."

"I'm going to try." At least until this charade was over.

Sophie smiled. "All that really matters is that you love each other."

Oh, God. More guilt to add to the heaping, festering pile.

"And by the way, I really like your hair down," Sophie said. "It's very sexy. You should wear it like that all the time."

Maybe she would.

Philip appeared behind them. "The doctor just checked Hannah again. She's dilated to six centimeters. He said if we keep her moving, it might only be a few more hours."

"I'll go next," Lizzy said, because walking the halls, uttering soothing words, kept her from thinking about the mess she was currently in and the idea that she may be falling in love with Ethan.

She just had to keep telling herself that Ethan knew what he was doing, and everything would eventually turn out all right.

Ethan never realized how long it took for a woman to have a baby. He met Lizzy and Sophie in the royal family's private wing of the hospital around ten, and despite that Hannah had gone into labor nearly nine hours earlier, at midnight they were still sitting there waiting.

When he'd first walked in, Lizzy wasn't there, but Sophie grabbed him and hugged him fiercely. She smelled like apples.

"Congratulations, you big jerk." But it was said with affection. "I can't believe you kept it from me."

Ethan smiled and shrugged. "You know me. I like to keep you on your toes. Where is she?"

"In the loo, I think." She leaned close and whispered, "Between us, of all our staff, Elizabeth has always been one of my favorites. You'll never find one more loyal. I know she'll be a fantastic wife."

"Me, too." He only felt a little guilty for lying.

"I did notice, however, that she isn't wearing a ring."

"Funny you should mention that." He pulled the ring box from the pocket of his slacks and opened it. "The engagement happened a bit abruptly, and I only now got around to it."

Sophie took it from him and examined the sparkling diamond. "What you lacked in timing, you certainly made up for in size. How many karats?"

"Six. The setting is platinum, since the only jewelry I ever see her wear is silver."

She snapped it closed and handed it back. "It's lovely."

"You think she'll like it?"

"I think she'll love it."

He hoped so, since he wouldn't be accepting it back when this was over. He wanted to do something nice for her, since he was the one who had set out to seduce her and now had them engaged. His selfishness had almost cost her a career she'd spent almost ten years building. He could easily relate to that feeling of dread. He experienced it after his partner's embezzling, when he saw everything he'd worked so hard for slipping away before his eyes.

Besides, he was in no rush to end this. He was actually looking forward to the truth being out, the opportunity to have a somewhat normal relationship. And that certainly surprised him.

Lizzy had walked into the room after that, and though he wanted to give her the ring right away, he figured it would be best if he waited until they were alone.

At one-fifteen Phillip stepped through the door to the waiting room, beaming with the smile of a proud new father.

"Eight pounds, eleven ounces, and twenty-three inches long," he bragged. "He and Hannah are both doing great."

"Congratulations!" Sophie squealed, giving him a big hug.

Ethan put their differences aside and gave him a firm handshake. "What's the big guy's name?"

"Frederick," Phillip said. "After our father."

Ethan realized it was the first time Phillip had referred to Ethan as a part of their family. And he was surprised to find that he liked it. Maybe this rift between them was beginning to heal.

"That's a good name," he said.

"Can we see him?" Sophie asked excitedly.

"Of course. Hannah is tired, but excited to show him off."

Sophie turned to Ethan and Lizzy. "Are you coming?"

"Why don't you go first, get some time alone," Ethan told her. "We'll wait out here."

"Are you sure?"

Lizzy smiled. "Go ahead."

When they were gone, Ethan told Lizzy, "I hope you don't mind that I spoke for us both."

She smiled. "That's okay. They should have some family time. But really, you should be in there with them."

He shrugged. "They're not going anywhere. Besides, I'd rather be out here with you."

They reclaimed their seats on the sofa and he pulled her close to him. He wrapped his arms around her and she leaned her head back against his shoulder. They were a good fit. It was comfortable.

"That was really amazing," she said. "Being there to help her through her labor. It was a little scary. She was in a lot of pain. But I guess we all have to go through it eventually, and it's better to know what's coming than to be surprised."

He wondered if she meant that she wanted kids. He'd never asked, and she'd never brought it up. "You want them? Kids, I mean."

"Someday."

He couldn't see her face, but her voice sounded a little wistful.

"How about you?" she asked.

"I don't know. I never really thought about it. I can't see that I would ever have time to be a father."

He wondered, if he and Lizzy were to have children, what they would look like. Would they have her fair coloring or his darker features? Would they have her petite stature, or take after his side of the family and be tall? Would they have boys or girls, or a few of each? God, where did those thoughts come from? He didn't want kids. Not with Lizzy or anyone else.

They sat in silence for several minutes, and Lizzy's breathing had become slow and even. She'd looked utterly exhausted when he'd arrived at ten. She had to be beyond tired now. "You still with me?"

"Sort of," she said in a sleepy voice.

"Do you want me to take you home?"

She sighed and curled against him, snuggling herself up to his chest. "Not until I see the baby."

"I have something for you."

She yawned. "Oh, yeah?"

"I went shopping tonight."

That seemed to wake her. She sat up and said, "You did?"

She looked so excited, it made him smile. This might not have been real, but that didn't mean they couldn't enjoy it. "You want to see?"

She nodded eagerly.

He pulled the box from his pocket and handed it to her. But for a second she just held it. "Aren't you going to open it?"

"Before I look, I wanted to thank you again for everything you did today. For saving my job."

"It's okay." It wasn't a hardship. "Open it."

She took a deep breath and flipped the lid open. Her eyes settled on the ring and her breath caught. For what felt like a full minute she just sat there staring at it, not uttering a word.

"Well?" he asked.

"It's amazing," she said, finally peeling her eyes from the stone to look at him. "It's the most beautiful thing I've ever seen."

He grinned. "You don't think it's too small?"

"Small?" she asked incredulously. "What is this, fifteen karats?"

"Only six."

"Only six. The ring that Roger got me had a stone so tiny it couldn't even be measured in karats. It was a fleck of dust compared to this."

"Let's see if it fits." He took the box from her and

lifted the ring from its velvet bed. She held out her hand and he slipped it on. Perfect.

She shifted her hand in the light, making the stone shimmer. "It's so beautiful. But it's too much, Ethan."

"Lizzy, I can afford it. And I'm probably going to be spending a fair amount of money on you in the next few weeks, so you'd better get used to it."

She opened her mouth to object—at least he assumed it was going to be an objection—but the door opened and Sophie poked her head out.

"She's asking for you."

Thirteen

Lizzy thought that Hannah looked like an angel, sitting up in bed, the baby swaddled in blue and cradled in her arms. She had never seen her look more beautiful or content. Or happy.

She smiled brightly when Lizzy and Ethan walked in the room. "Come see him."

Lizzy walked to her bedside, Ethan behind her, and Hannah held him out so they could see. He was round and pink with a shock of jet-black hair. His eyes were open and alert, and a deep, clear blue. He looked just like his daddy.

"He's beautiful," Lizzy said.

"Do you want to hold him?"

She nodded eagerly, and Hannah set him in her

arms. He smelled of baby powder and soap. She touched his tiny fingers and they curled around hers.

She had this sudden sensation, this intense feeling of longing deep down inside her.

She wanted this. She wanted what Hannah had. Marriage to a man who adored her. A family. She wanted it so much she ached. She wanted this with Ethan.

You're just caught up in the moment, she told herself. And loopy from lack of sleep. What she wasn't thinking about was the midnight feedings and sleepless nights. The spitting up and dirty diapers. The *responsibility.* She liked her freedom and she wasn't ready to give that up. Not for anyone. "He's perfect," she said.

"And already stubborn," Hannah joked. "I had to push for almost two hours."

"I think he gets that from you," Phillip teased.

The king was so quiet and serious all of the time. It was strange to see him so relaxed and personable. But Lizzy liked it. Even though at some point she would go back to being just another employee, and he would go back to being her employer and any friendliness between them would cease.

She turned to Ethan. "You want to hold him?"

He put out his arms and she set the baby in them. He looked a little awkward, like someone who wasn't accustomed to holding a baby.

"He's so tiny," Ethan said.

"He didn't feel tiny on the way out," Hannah said.

"I can't imagine how much bigger he would have been if I'd carried him to term."

Ethan touched his little fingers and his lips and his button nose, and something in Lizzy's heart shifted almost imperceptibly. If they had a baby, that would be the way Ethan looked at it and held it.

Stop it, Lizzy!

What the heck was wrong with her? It was one thing to get sentimental, but this was over the top.

Hannah yawned deeply and Phillip said, "We should let you get some sleep."

"You both must be exhausted." Ethan handed the baby to him, and it was the closest Lizzy had ever seen them. They looked so similar it gave her chills. And she hoped after this they might start acting like real brothers.

Phillip handed the baby back to Hannah and said, "I'll walk you out."

He walked with them to the waiting room and stood with Lizzy while Ethan stopped in the restroom.

"Long day," he said, and she nodded. "I expect you to take tomorrow off." He looked at his watch. "Or should I say today."

"I will." For once she didn't mind the idea of missing work. News would get around of their engagement, and God only knows how the other palace employees were going to take it.

He touched her arm, and she was so surprised, she almost flinched. "I wanted to thank you for all your help today."

"Of course, sir."

"It meant a lot to my wife," he said, then added, "And to me."

"It was a pleasure."

"And I'm sorry if I was harsh yesterday afternoon. I'm sure Ethan has told you that we don't see eye to eye on everything."

That was an understatement. "He may have mentioned that."

"I'm hardheaded, I'll admit it, but I try to be fair."

"I know, sir."

"Ethan is different since he met you."

Was he? "Different how?"

"He's less belligerent. He seems…settled. He's ready for this."

Was he trying to convince himself, or her? If she didn't know any better, she might suspect that Phillip knew the truth about this so-called engagement. But how could he?

He gave her arm a squeeze, then let go. "I should get back. If I don't kick Sophie out she'll stay all night. Get some sleep."

"You, too, sir."

He started to walk away, then turned back. "When we're not at work, you can call me Phillip."

"Okay," she said, and forced herself to say, "Phillip." It was very…odd.

He smiled. "Good night, Lizzy."

He disappeared through the door, and she realized

she was smiling, too. This had been a really good day. A weird, confusing day. But a good one.

"What was that about?" Ethan asked from behind her.

She turned to him, half-tempted to tell him what Phillip said, but decided against it. "Nothing. We were just talking."

"Ready to go?"

"Am I ever. I'm exhausted."

"Am I just dropping you off, or would you like company?"

Considering her state of mind, it would be much better if she went to bed alone, but she didn't want to be alone. Knowing she was asking for trouble, she smiled and said, "I would love some company."

Ethan spent the night, and they slept in late, then they showered and he took her out to lunch. Out of her apartment, in a real restaurant, where there were other people. And it was so nice not having to worry about being seen. Due to the headlines in the local morning papers—the birth of the king's first son and the prince's engagement—everyone seemed to notice them. They must have heard a dozen congratulations and well wishes.

She wasn't used to being the center of attention. To being noticed at all. And it wasn't as bad as she anticipated. A little strange, but she had the feeling her entire life would be strange for quite some time.

When they pulled onto her street later, it was clear just how strange.

Outside her building was a crowd of reporters and news vans so vast the entire street was blocked and the police had been called to direct traffic.

"Oh, my God." She stared with her mouth hanging open.

"I thought this might happen," Ethan said.

"How did they even know where I live?"

"They're the press." As though that were reason enough. And he was probably right. The press in Morgan Isle was only slightly less aggressive and vicious than in England.

"I can't believe this."

"Does your building have a back entrance?"

She shook her head. The only way in was through them.

When he got to the intersection just before her building he swung a sharp left and zipped down the road in the opposite direction.

"Where are we going?"

"My place. You can stay there until this dies down."

"How long?"

"Just a day or two."

"I don't have any clothes with me. And what about work?"

"Do you really feel like dealing with that mob?"

She sighed. "No, not really."

"I can send one of my people over to get some clothes for you."

That would be too weird. Some stranger rooting around in her things. "I can have my friend Maddie do it. She has a key."

She pulled out her cell phone and tried calling Maddie but she didn't answer. She was sure she had probably already heard the news. And knowing Maddie's opinion of the royal family, she might be upset with Lizzy. She left her a message asking her to call as soon as she got in, then used her cell phone to call her voice mail. There were a couple dozen messages. From reporters mostly. Everyone wanted an exclusive on her rags-to-riches story. She deleted them all. There was also a message from her mother, and one from each of her sisters. She saved those to listen to them later. The only time they ever called was when they wanted or needed something. And when they got what they wanted, they would cut all ties again.

No doubt they were seeing this as their ticket out of the public housing project.

It took the entire fifteen-minute drive across town to Ethan's building on the coast to wade through all the messages, and she had half a mind to call the phone company and have her number changed.

Ethan pulled up to the underground garage, punched in a code, and the door raised. The spots were filled with sports cars and other expensive luxury imports. He parked in a spot right by the elevator and they climbed out. Inside the elevator he pressed the button for the top floor. It rose without stopping and opened into a hallway outside a set of double doors.

He opened the door, stepping aside so she could enter. Her first impression was the sheer size of the apartment, and the fact that it was painfully modern. The kitchen, dining area and living room were one large open space with a cathedral ceiling and it was all decorated in a pallet of black, white, chrome, glass and stainless steel. It desperately needed a woman's touch.

"This is it," he said. "Home sweet home."

"It's…nice."

He shut the door behind them. "It's cold and impersonal, but I'm only leasing until I find something more permanent."

She set her purse down on the glass entry table next to the door. "It's very clean."

"I'm not here much. And I have a housekeeper who comes in Monday, Wednesday and Friday. You want a tour?"

"There's more?"

He grinned. "Four bedrooms, my office and four baths."

"Well, let's see it then."

The rest of the rooms were decorated very much the same way. And his bedroom alone was larger than her entire apartment. What could one person need with all of this space? Of course, if she had money to burn, and could hire a housekeeper to keep it up, who's to say she wouldn't live somewhere like this.

They had just finished the tour and were still

standing in his bedroom when her cell phone rang. It was Maddie.

"I have to take this," she said.

"You want some privacy?"

"Is that all right?"

"Of course. Make yourself at home. I'll go open us a couple of beers."

"Sounds good."

He left, shutting the bedroom door behind him, and she answered her phone. "Hey, Maddie. I'll bet you're wondering what's going on."

"How could you, Lizzy? How could you go sneaking around behind everyone's backs. And with a man like that? Don't you have any pride?"

She could hear by her voice that she was just as hurt as she was angry. "It's not what you think. And besides, I wanted to tell you, but I couldn't."

"Are you pregnant?"

"No, of course not!"

"Then why would you marry someone like him? You know that he's using you."

"It's not like that."

"You think he actually loves you? Well, he doesn't."

Maddie was right about that. And it pained Lizzy to know that. Lizzy owed her the truth. She trusted her not to tell anyone. "It's not about love. And we're not really getting married."

"What do you mean? It's all over the papers."

Starting from the night of the gala, all the way to yesterday afternoon, Lizzy told her the entire story.

"So he did it to save your job?" Maddie asked incredulously, as though she couldn't believe someone like Ethan could have a decent bone in his body.

"And he's letting me stay at his place until the media swamping my apartment goes away. Unfortunately, I don't have any clothes with me."

"Just tell me what you need. I'll bring it to you."

She gave her a list of clothes and toiletries she would need. "Thank you so much, Maddie. And I'm sorry I didn't tell you the truth. The whole thing just sort of snowballed out of control."

"I shouldn't have been so harsh."

"It's okay."

"No, it isn't. I guess you could say my opinion of the royal family is somewhat jaded."

"Why, Maddie? What has anyone ever done to you?" The instant the words were out of her mouth, she knew. Before Maddie even said a word.

"You know how the former king used to be with new female employees," Maddie said.

"Oh, Maddie."

"Everyone warned me about him. But I thought I was different. I though I meant something to him. But he used me. I never told anyone what happened. I was too ashamed."

"Maddie, I'm so sorry."

"It was my own fault, Lizzy. And I didn't want to see you make the same mistake."

"Phillip and Ethan are nothing like their father. They're good people."

"It was a long time ago, and I should let it go. I'm going to try."

That was all Lizzy could ask. And maybe finally talking about it would help her move on.

"Just do me a favor," Maddie said.

"What? Anything."

"Whatever you do, don't fall in love with him."

"I won't," she promised, but she couldn't deny it even if she tried. She had fallen in love with Ethan. Now she had to figure out a way to fall back out again.

Fourteen

Work Monday morning was a strange experience for Lizzy. Reactions from the other employees were varied. Some of the older, more experienced people gave her scathing looks or the cold shoulder, while some of the younger office girls regarded her with envy. But she was so busy in the following weeks, she really didn't have time to concern herself with it.

A week after the announcement, the mob outside her building still hadn't cleared, then one of her neighbors came in late one night and caught a stranger hanging around Lizzy's apartment door. He was scared off, but when the police arrived, they found that the lock had been tampered with. Because her building had no security, Phillip and Hannah insisted she find a safer place to live. Unfortunately that sort of place wasn't exactly in her budget. They offered her a room at the palace, but Ethan surprised her by saying that she would be staying with him.

"Are you sure?" she asked him when they were alone.

"It's fine," Ethan assured her, and surprisingly, he seemed to mean it. Even weirder, she *liked* living with him and they slipped easily into a routine. She didn't even mind having someone else doing her laundry or cleaning up after her, and Ethan's housekeeper was a fantastic cook. Even the attention from the public was getting easier, though she didn't think she would ever get completely used to it. Not that she would have to. She knew Ethan wasn't in love with her and this wasn't going to last. But she could enjoy her new life.

As the days turned to weeks, and the weeks into almost two months, Ethan made no mention of when this fake engagement would come to an end. Just yesterday he informed her that he'd purchased tickets for the opera in late September, almost two months away, and he brought up the idea of them taking a trip to the States together for the holidays.

"I don't know what I'll do when you leave," Hannah had begun telling her. "My life will fall apart."

And for the first time she began to wonder if maybe her days as a palace employee were numbered. Maybe she would be taking that job in the resort

Ethan had mentioned. Since she couldn't imagine ever not working.

"I can train a replacement."

"I'm just being selfish," Hannah said. "I think it's wonderful about you and Ethan. I've never seen him so content. And you're positively glowing."

Lizzy's heart flipped over in her chest. "Glowing?"

Hannah nodded. "You look radiant. And that's a definite sign of a woman in love."

According to Lizzy's mom, it was the sign of something else, too. Hadn't her mom told her the story a million times of how, when she was pregnant with Lizzy, everyone used to comment on how her skin glowed. She said it was the best she'd ever looked in her life.

But that was ridiculous. Her period was a few days late, but that wasn't unusual for her, and she was sure they used protection every time. Didn't they? Of course they did. Although she had been feeling especially tired the last few days…

No, it wasn't possible. It couldn't be.

"Lizzy, are you okay?" Hannah asked, concern in her eyes. "All the color just drained from your face."

Lizzy forced a smile. "I'm fine. Just feeling a little woozy all of a sudden."

"Sit down."

Her legs were feeling a little shaky, so she sank down onto the sofa. She was being silly. There was no way she was pregnant. It was impossible.

"Can I get you anything?" Hannah asked.

She shook her head. The wooziness was subsiding, but there was a feeling of dread building inside her. She knew she wouldn't be able to relax until she knew for sure. "I'm feeling better."

"Even so, maybe you should take the rest of the day off."

In the nine years she had worked in the palace she had never left early for any reason. Not even when she was going through her divorce and it felt as though her entire world was crashing down around her.

Not until today.

"You know, I think I will."

Though she knew it was a waste of money, Lizzy stopped at the pharmacy on the way home from work. She wasn't pregnant. She *knew* she wasn't.

When she got to Ethan's, she set her purchase on the table. Thankfully he wouldn't be home for several hours, and it was the housekeeper's day off. Deliberately taking her time, she put water on for tea and checked her voice mail for messages. She wasn't in a rush, because the test was really only a formality.

She waited for the water to boil and fixed her tea just the way she liked it, with plenty of cream and sugar, and took a few sips.

No rush. Just taking her time.

Using the master bath, she took the test, following the directions to the letter, then sat the convenient little wand on the counter facedown and waited for the results. The directions said two minutes, but she waited four just to be sure. She turned it over, assuring herself it was going to be negative, and looked at the convenient little indicator window where it would say *Pregnant* or *Not Pregnant*. For several long seconds she stared at it, to be sure it wasn't a trick of the light.

She was pregnant with Ethan's baby.

For a moment she was too stunned to think straight, to even breathe. Then she started to get this feeling. It began as a tingle in her belly, then it slowly worked it's way outward. To her arms and legs, then her fingers and toes, and though it took a moment to register, she realized finally that what she was feeling was excitement.

She was pregnant, and she was…happy. But how would Ethan feel?

Surprised at first, she was sure, but considering how close they had become, and how well they got along, he couldn't possibly see this as anything but a blessing. Could he? He'd been talking less and less about the temporary nature of their relationship. Not that he'd come right out and said he wanted a commitment, or that he loved her, but all the signs were there. Weren't they?

She would just have to figure out a way to break it to him gently.

It shouldn't take more than a day. Two tops. Then she would definitely tell him. And when she did, she knew that everything would be okay.

* * *

Something was up with Lizzy.

The past couple of weeks she had been acting… different. Ethan couldn't quite put his finger on the change, and when he'd asked if something was wrong, she swore that everything was fine. But he wasn't buying it.

He was beginning to suspect that this relationship had become more than just sex—for both of them. Which meant things would start to get complicated, to interfere with his work—hell, they already were— and that was a luxury he could not afford. He had just got his professional life back on track.

Which had him thinking that maybe it was time to end this charade and go their separate ways. But it never seemed like the right time, and every time he tried, something stopped him. He just didn't feel ready to let her go. And the longer he waited, the harder it would be. Every day he thought, tomorrow, then tomorrow would come, and she would do or say something to endear her to him even more, and he would completely lose his nerve.

His biggest mistake had been letting her stay at his flat. He should have encouraged her to accept Phillip and Hannah's offer to stay at the palace. It had been a knee-jerk decision. One that he was sure would come back to bite him in the behind. And the following morning, the depth of that wound became all too clear.

Lizzy had already left for work. Ethan was on his way out the door when he heard her cell phone ring, and realized she'd left it on the table by the door. When he checked the display, it was a palace number.

"You forgot your phone," he said, in lieu of a hello, and heard her groan.

"Bugger. I'd forget my head if it wasn't attached. I don't suppose you'll be at the palace today."

He hadn't planned on it, but he could make the time. Since it was very likely that their time was limited. "I might be able to drop it off later this afternoon."

He could feel her smile through the phone line. "If you do, it just might earn you something extra special tonight."

Which meant he was definitely in for a treat. Meaning that talk they were going to have to have would be postponed at least another day. "I have a meeting at eleven. How about one-thirty?"

"Perfect. We could have lunch together."

"Sure," he said, before he could think better of it. The more time they spent together, the harder it was going to be to let go. But what harm could one lunch do? "I'll see you then."

"See you then," she said, then disconnected.

He slipped her phone into his jacket pocket and let himself out of the flat. He punched the button for the elevator, and while he waited, Lizzy's phone rang a second time. The number on the display was unfamiliar, but in case it was something important, he answered.

"I'm calling from Pearson's pharmacy to let Ms.

Pryce know that her physician's office phoned in her prescription."

Prescription? Was Lizzy sick? The swift feeling of alarm caught him by surprise. If there was something wrong, she would have told him, wouldn't she?

He knew it was none of his business, but he asked anyway. "Which prescription is that?"

"Her prenatal vitamins."

It took a moment for her words to register, and when they did, their meaning hit him like a sucker punch. Then he realized it had to be a mistake. A mix-up at the pharmacy. "Are you sure?"

"Quite sure, sir. They're ready to be picked up."

"I…I'll tell her, thank you." He disconnected, too stunned to think straight, to process the information. There was only one reason he knew of that a woman would take prenatal vitamins.

Lizzy was pregnant.

It was barely nine-thirty when Lizzy's office door opened and Ethan stepped inside. She greeted him with a smile and said, "You're early." And when he didn't return the smile, her heart dropped. "What's wrong?"

He closed the door and turned to her. "You don't know?"

Oh, my gosh, had someone died? Was something wrong with Frederick? A million possibilities raced through her mind in the instant it took her to rise from her chair. "Tell me."

"The pharmacy called this morning," he said. "Your prescription is ready."

Uh-oh.

Her heart sank even deeper in her chest. *Don't panic just yet,* she told herself. It was entirely possible that he didn't know what the prescription was for. *Maybe he's just worried that you might be sick.*

Then he tossed a small white bag onto her desk. "I took the liberty of picking it up for you."

Oh, God.

"Is there something you neglected to tell me?" he asked.

Once again, she'd waited so long to tell him the truth that he'd found out for himself. And she had to try to explain why she had essentially lied to him. Her mouth was suddenly so dry she could barely peel her tongue from the roof of her mouth to speak. And when she did, her voice came out as a croak. "I was going to tell you."

"So it's true," he said, and it was clear that he was upset with her. Not that she blamed him. She only hoped that he was upset that she'd lied, not that she was pregnant. She wanted him to be happy about becoming a father.

She nodded and said, "I'm pregnant."

"How long have you known?"

"Just a couple of weeks." But it might as well have been a lifetime. She should have told him right away. The day she took the test. "I should have told you. I'm sorry. I did try. I just…" She shrugged. "I just didn't know what to say."

"How did this happen?" he asked. His voice was calm and even. *Too* patient.

"I don't know. We've always been careful."

Ethan cursed under his breath, a really bad sign.

"I know that neither of us was expecting this, and at first I was pretty freaked out, too. I love my career, and my freedom, but the more time I've had to think about it, the more I see it as a blessing."

Something in Ethan's face said he didn't see it as a blessing.

He just needed time, she told herself. A day or two to let it sink in, then everything would be fine. Then he would be just as happy as she was.

"I need to ask you something, and I want the truth," he said.

"Okay."

He looked her directly in the eye and asked, "Did you do this on purpose?"

She was so stunned by his words, she couldn't speak. That he would even suggest such a thing was so far out of her realm of comprehension, she could only stare at him with her mouth hanging open.

"The truth, Lizzy."

She'd never seen his eyes so cold, or heard his voice so devoid of emotion. And when she finally found her own voice, it came out unusually high-pitched. "Are you serious?"

"Just tell me. Yes or no."

Only then did everything become crystal clear. He didn't want the baby. And even worse, he didn't want her. It was all a charade to him. Their engagement. All the time they had been spending together. He was only playing a role.

She had never felt so cheap, so *used* in her entire life. Maddie had been right. Despite his claims to be different, Ethan was a royal through and through. And no different than his father.

"What did you expect?" he asked. "Did you really think I would be happy about this?"

Foolishly, she had. "Get out."

He just stared at her.

"I mean it, Ethan." Her voice rose in pitch. She didn't even care that anyone in the main office might hear. She just needed to be alone to think. "Leave, right now."

And he did, without saying another word. She even managed to wait until the door closed behind him before she completely fell apart.

Fifteen

Ethan got in his car and drove. For hours, going nowhere in particular. And the longer he drove, the more painfully aware he became of the fact that he was a jerk.

He had dragged Lizzy into this relationship, wheedled his way into her life, then had the gall to be mad at her for wanting to protect her feelings.

What the hell was wrong with him?

That was easy. The intensity and depth of his feelings for Lizzy scared the hell out of him. When they were keeping things casual, when he knew she wasn't interested in a commitment, he'd had no trouble. Even the ribbing he'd been getting from

Charles about the engagement hadn't bothered him. Because in his mind, it still wasn't real.

The look on Lizzy's face when he'd asked her if she'd done it on purpose. He'd never seen her look like that. So devastated and hurt. And disappointed. But how was he supposed to act? She'd been keeping this child from him. Even after he'd moved her into his penthouse, into his *life*.

So she wasn't perfect. Well, neither was he. And like it or not, they were going to have to work this out.

Instead of driving home, where he would have to face Lizzy, he found himself back at the palace. It was late, the palace dark and quiet. He roamed the halls for a while, studying the portraits of his ancestors. His family. Though he always saw a resemblance in looks, he never really felt as though he belonged. Maybe he felt as though, if he accepted his role in the family, his *proper* place, the person he had been—his mother's son—would cease to exist.

But lately, since he'd met Lizzy, he'd let his guard down. He had started to feel more accepted. He'd let it happen. And the truth was, he liked himself now more than he ever had before.

As Ethan walked back down the stairs, he noticed a light on in the study. Curious, he walked over to the door and looked in, surprised to find Phillip there, reading a book, his son asleep on his shoulder.

He knocked lightly on the door and Phillip looked up, surprised to see him, too. "Ethan. Is something wrong?"

"Am I disturbing you?"

"No. I'm trying to let Hannah get some sleep." He set his book down. "Frederick has been fussy the last few nights. He prefers to be held."

"Don't you have a nanny for this sort of thing?"

A nerve in his jaw ticked. "I was raised by a nanny. My children will know their father loves them."

His honesty threw Ethan for a second. "Are you saying our father didn't love you?"

"If he did, he never showed it." Phillip gestured to the sofa and Ethan sat down. "I assume there's a reason you're here and not with Lizzy?"

He almost told Phillip to mind his own business. A knee-jerk reaction. Then it registered that Phillip was asking not to control or manipulate him, but because he cared. "We had a fight," he admitted.

"Your first?"

"Actually, yeah." Up until tonight, they'd barely had so much as a difference of opinion. That had to say something, didn't it?

"She's pregnant?" Phillip asked, surprising Ethan once again.

For an instant he wondered if Phillip had planted listening devices in his apartment, but that would be over the top even for him. This wasn't a covert operation. This was just family. Ethan's family. "How did you know?"

"Hannah guessed. She mentioned something about Lizzy glowing, and Lizzy went white as a sheet."

"Glowing?"

Phillip shrugged. "Don't ask me. But apparently Lizzy knew what she meant."

"It must be one of those female things us guys aren't meant to understand."

"One of many." The baby shifted and made a soft noise of protest, so Phillip shifted him to the opposite shoulder and patted his back gently.

In seven months or so, Ethan would be doing the same thing. And at the moment instead of freaking him out, the idea of being a father felt settling somehow.

"So," Phillip asked, "are you going to ask her to marry you?"

He opened his mouth to answer him, then the meaning of his words sunk in. As far as Phillip knew, he had already asked. At least, that's what Ethan thought. Apparently he'd been wrong about that, too. "You knew that the engagement was a sham?"

Phillip nodded, and though he could have been smug about it, he wasn't.

"How long did you know? About me and Lizzy, I mean."

"I recognized her that night at the gala."

So he knew the entire time? And never said a word? Ethan shook his head in disbelief. And all the while Ethan had strut around, foolishly believing that he had gotten the best of his brother. How could he have been so blindly arrogant? So childish?

He chose Lizzy, at least in part, because he believed Phillip would disapprove. But the joke was on Ethan. Not only did Phillip approve, but somewhere along the way Ethan had gone and fallen in love.

Yes, he realized, he loved her.

"Did you really think I wouldn't be keeping close tabs on my investment?" Phillip asked.

Ethan wanted to be offended, but in all honesty, put in his brother's position, he probably would have done the same thing. "I figured you would disapprove."

"Call me sentimental, but I thought she might be good for you."

"So why confront me?"

"It was beginning to look as though things were getting serious. I was going to tell you that you either needed to end the affair or make a commitment. But then you claimed to be engaged, and I thought it might be fun to let you hang yourself with your own rope. It was a noble act, though. Sacrificing yourself to save her job. I gained a great amount of respect for you that day."

Ethan felt like an idiot. "I'm sorry, Phillip, for the way I've acted. I haven't shown you the respect you deserve."

"No, you haven't, but I haven't exactly made your life easy, either. I had to know that I could trust you. And I supposed I unfairly blamed your mother for our father's infidelity. But it's not as if she was the first. Or the last. Just convenient, I suppose."

"Can we call a truce?"

"I think that would be good idea."

It was more of a relief than Ethan could have imagined. And if not for Lizzy, he might still be the same pigheaded man who seemed to think the world owed him. Maybe it was just that he'd been jealous of Phillip for having a father. Something Ethan had always wanted. He had hated and resented the queen for taking that from him, and transferred that hate to her son. But now it seemed as though Ethan may have been better off never knowing him.

"Do you think there could be others?" Ethan asked.

"Others?"

"Illegitimate heirs."

Phillip shrugged. "It's possible, I suppose. But unless they come forward, we may never know."

"I'd like to look."

"Why?"

Ethan shrugged. He didn't know why it was suddenly important to him to know. It just was. "I guess, lately, the idea of family has taken on new meaning."

"It could mean more scandal for the family. More bad press."

"It could also mean getting to know a brother or sister we didn't know we had. But I won't do it without your blessing."

Phillip considered that for a moment, then said, "Do it."

"You're sure?"

He nodded. "You have my blessing. Just keep me apprised of what you find before you make any contacts."

"I will."

"You know, Ethan, I learned the hard way that when you find something good, you hang on to it."

"You mean Lizzy?"

Phillip nodded. "Do you love her?"

He did. He knew it all along, he just wouldn't let himself see it. "Yes, I do."

"And she loves you?"

"Yeah, she does. At least I think she does."

"Then you should probably try groveling. It worked for me."

The idea of Phillip groveling to win Hannah was a humbling thought, and it made Ethan feel at least a little less inept. And if groveling was what it was going to take, that was what he would do.

Ethan half expected Lizzy to be gone when he pulled into the garage, but her car was there. At least she hadn't bailed on him. Not that he would have blamed her if she had.

But as he stepped inside the flat, he almost tripped over the bags piled there. It looked as though she was completely packed. He should have expected as much, but for some reason the reality of it still stung. Because he honestly didn't want her to go. He could scarcely imagine his life without her in it.

He shut the door quietly behind him and went looking for her.

He found her in the master bath, her makeup and

toiletries in a pile on the vanity. Her eyes looked red, as though she had been crying, but her face was somber. Determined even.

She must have heard him come in, because the sound of his voice when he spoke didn't startle her. "You're leaving?"

She didn't look at him. She just piled everything into a small case and zipped it shut. "That shouldn't surprise you."

"What if I said that I don't want you to go?"

She stared at her hands, which he noticed were trembling. "I'd tell you that it's too late."

She didn't mean that, even though she wanted him to think she did. Apparently this was the part where he did the groveling.

He took a step closer. "Suppose I told you that I love you."

He waited for a reply, instead she grabbed her case and brushed past him. She wasn't going to cut him any slack.

He followed her into the living room. "You can't tell me you don't love me."

"What difference does it make?" She tucked the makeup bag into the front pocket of one of the suit-cases. "Nothing about this relationship makes sense."

"When do relationships ever make sense?"

She turned to him, her eyes full of confusion. "I keep thinking about this thing we have. Going over and over it in my head. Trying to figure out how we got here. To this place."

"What place?"

"*Together.* We may have both gone into this not wanting a commitment, but somewhere along the way, it just happened."

"I guess we just never talked about it."

"Not talking about the future doesn't stop it from coming."

She was right. Their future had happened. And it had been such a gradual, smooth transition, he had never noticed.

"You know, I used to think you were the perfect woman for me. Beautiful, funny, fantastic in bed. And as relationship-phobic as I am."

She frowned. "And now you think I'm not the perfect woman for you?"

"Now I *know* you are. It's just that my reasons for thinking so were off. At least, one of them was." He took a step toward her, then another, and when he touched her, she didn't try to stop him. Then he pulled her to him and she practically melted in his arms, then he knew, the bravado was just for show. "I love you, Lizzy, and I want to make this work."

She clung to him, burying her face against his shirt, so that her voice came out muffled when she said, "I do, too."

"Which part?"

She looked up at him and smiled. "Both. I love you Ethan. I didn't mean for it to happen, but it did anyway."

"But there is one problem," he said.

A crease formed in her brow. "What problem?"

"I won't let my son or daughter grow up feeling like I did."

"Like what?"

"Illegitimate. Incomplete. Which means I'm going to have to figure out a way to get you to marry me. For real this time."

The hint of a smile curled the corners of her mouth. "You could ask. I mean, how hard could it be?" She held up her hand. "I've already got the ring."

"You must be forgetting, you told me you would never marry a royal. Too suffocating and claustrophobic, I believe were your exact words. And I'm a royal. Even if I only just realized it."

She took a deep breath and blew it out, as though giving the matter intense consideration, but there was a smile in her eyes. "Well, I suppose, since you're technically only *half*-royal, just this one time I could make an exception."

"You *suppose?*"

She grinned. "Why don't you just ask already and find out?"

He knelt down in front of her. Properly, on one knee. May as well give her the full treatment. She'd more than earned it.

He reached for her, and when she slipped her hand in his he realized she was trembling. He wasn't sure if she was scared, or excited or maybe a bit of both. The only thing he did know for sure was that this was right.

"This is good," he said, and she smiled down at him. "This is really good."

"Yes, it is."

"Lizzy, will you marry me?"

She let loose everything she'd been holding back, threw her arms around his neck and hugged him. "Of course I will!"

He scooped her up and kissed her, never so sure of anything in his life, and amazed that since the day he'd met her, his life hadn't been the same.

"I have an idea," she said, nibbling his lower lip and threading her fingers through his hair. "Since we're getting married eventually anyway, why don't we start the honeymoon right now?"

He laughed and carried her in the direction of the bedroom, because honestly, he was thinking the same thing. "The sooner the better."

* * * * *

AN AFFAIR
WITH THE PRINCESS

BY
MICHELLE CELMER

To my granddaughter Hannah.

One

Since she had been born into the royal family of Morgan Isle, there had been days when Princess Sophie Renee Agustus Mead felt restrained by her title.

Today was one of those days.

King Phillip sat behind his desk, in the palace office. She loved her brother to death, but there were times when the similarities between him and their late father were uncanny. The same jet-black hair and smoky gray eyes. The same towering height and lean, muscular build. The same *stubborn* streak.

Sophie on the other hand had inherited their father's quick and sometimes volatile temper. She took a deep breath and forced herself to remain calm, because she had learned years ago that blowing her top and pitching a fit only made Phillip dig his heels in deeper. "When you said I would be involved in the hotel project, Phillip, I had no idea my duties would include babysitting."

"No one knows this island like you do, Sophie. And if the architect is going to design a structure that complements the unique characteristics of our country, he's going to have to see it first."

She had wanted, had *hoped* that for the first time in her life the family would set aside their archaic traditions and allow her to take on a bit more than the royal responsibilities she sometimes grew so tired of. Something slightly more challenging than planning parties, attending charity functions and playing goodwill ambassador.

Both Phillip and their half brother, Prince Ethan, had assured her that if she stuck to the royal program without complaint, she would be involved in the business of the hotel chain the family had recently purchased. And in light of her current *assignment,* she couldn't help but feel she was getting, as the Americans liked to say, the raw end of the deal.

But if she refused, she wouldn't put it past Phillip to cut her out of the project completely. What he really wanted was to see Sophie settle down and start squeezing out royal heirs. With the recent birth of his son, Frederick, and the pregnancy of Ethan's wife, Lizzy, suddenly everyone was looking at her as though to say, *okay, now it's your turn.* But she wasn't ready. She wasn't sure if she *ever* would be.

"Fine," she said with a smile. "I'll do it. Although I'm not crazy about the idea of spending two weeks with a stranger."

Phillip relaxed back in his chair, satisfied now that he had gotten what he wanted. "Well then, you'll be relieved to know that he's not."

"I don't recall ever meeting any American architect."

"It was years ago, and when you met him, he wasn't an architect yet. He came home with me from university and spent the holidays."

Sophie's heart dropped so hard and fast that she could swear she felt it split in two and hit the balls of her feet. He couldn't possibly mean...

"I seem to recall," Phillip continued, "the two of you getting along somewhat famously."

If he was referring to the man she suspected he was, famously didn't begin to describe those two weeks. But there was no way Phillip could have known about that. Only her mother, who unbeknownst to Sophie had been listening in on her phone conversations, knew the extent of Alex's and her "friendship."

Behind her the office door opened and she turned to see her half brother, Prince Ethan, enter the room. Behind him appeared a man who, despite ten years apart, was still strikingly familiar. In fact, he hadn't changed much at all. He wore his pale brown hair in the same short, meticulous style and his deep-set eyes were the same piercing, hypnotizing blue. Eyes she had once hoped to spend an entire lifetime gazing into.

Alexander Rutledge, the only man she had ever loved.

Typically reserved, Phillip rose from his chair to greet his friend with an enthusiastic, "Alex, welcome back to Morgan Isle!"

Alex stepped forward, a smile breaking out across his handsome, chiseled features. He was dressed just like her brothers, in an expensive-looking suit and shoes polished to a gleaming shine. And he was standing so close that Sophie could reach out and touch him, yet he didn't even seem to notice her there. Had he forgotten about her?

Something that felt like a boulder settled in the pit of her stomach. As if it mattered after all this time. He was nothing to her.

Alex gripped the king's hand and gave it a firm shake. "Phillip. It's been far too long. How have you been?"

"Busy. I'm a family man now."

"I've heard. I'm anxious to meet your wife and son."

"You must remember my sister," Phillip said, gesturing her way. "Princess Sophie."

Sophie's heart soared up to lodge in her throat. This was it. The first time they would share words in over ten years. Ten years in which barely a day passed when she hadn't thought of him.

Alex turned in her direction, greeting her with a perfunctory nod, wearing a polite smile that didn't quite reach his eyes. "Your Highness. It's good to see you again."

That was it? That was all she got? *Good to see you again?*

She was appalled to feel the beginnings of tears sting the corners of her eyes. She bit down hard on the inside of her cheek and forced herself to smile. "Alex," she said, her voice surprisingly even considering she was trembling from the inside out.

"I understand you're to be my guide for the duration of my stay," he said, and she honestly couldn't tell how he felt about that. Nary a trace of any discernible emotion showed on his face. Had he forgotten about her? About those two amazing weeks?

"Yes, I am. However, I was just now informed, and haven't had time to create an itinerary. You won't mind if the tour doesn't officially begin until tomorrow morning."

"Of course not." He wasn't rude or unpleasant or even cold. Just…indifferent. But how had she expected him to react? Did she think he would sweep her up in his arms and declare his undying love for her? As far as she knew, he was a happily married family man, like Phillip.

"Sophie," Phillip said, "could you please show Alex to the guest suite?"

"Of course." As if she had a choice. "The garden suite?" she asked, and Phillip nodded.

"Take some time to settle in," Phillip told Alex. "I'll take you on a tour of the palace later this afternoon. Oh, and, Sophie, I'd like to see the itinerary when you're done."

"Of course. I'll fax it to you later this evening."

"Why don't you just bring it with you to dinner tonight?"

She'd had no idea that she was expected to have dinner at the palace. She usually ate at her own residence on the palace grounds.

"Is that an invitation?" she asked her brother, smiling sweetly, because she knew, Phillip didn't invite. He demanded.

"I thought it would be nice that we all be here to welcome our guest." He worded it as a suggestion, but what he really meant was be there or else.

"The usual time?" she asked.

He nodded.

"Fine, I'll see you then." She turned to their *guest*. "If you'll follow me, I'll show you to your suite."

He gestured to the door. "After you. Your Highness."

She wasn't a self-conscious person. Not even when it came to her physical appearance. She had been blessed with good genes, and at thirty was still tall and very slim and nothing had yet begun to sag. But for some reason knowing that Alex was behind her was making her incredibly self-conscious. And as they walked to the stairs the lack of conversation stretched like a mile-wide void between them. But if there was one thing she had learned in all of her years as goodwill ambassador, it was the art of small talk.

"How was your trip?" she asked him as they climbed the stairs to the second floor, where the guest suites were located.

"Tiring," he said. "I'd forgotten what a long flight it is from the U.S. to Morgan Isle."

He stayed to the side and one step behind her. Which was proper, but it still annoyed her. She wanted to see his face. Relearn his features. Not that she'd ever really forgotten. In fact, it was probably better that she not let herself get caught up in what they used to have. That was a long time ago. Although it was a wonder he wasn't bitter for the way things had ended. Of course, for all she knew, the instant they were alone he might read her the riot act. And could she blame him? It was she who had ended things without an explanation. She who refused his calls and sent his letters back unopened.

But what choice did she have? The decision had been taken out of her hands.

"The palace hasn't changed much since I was here last," Alex noted.

"Nothing much around here ever changes."

"I see that," he said, and something in his tone made the surface of her skin tingle. "You're still as beautiful as you were ten years ago."

She waited for the qualifier to that statement, something like, *and still as coldhearted.* But when she realized he was sincere, her stubborn heart jumped back up in her throat.

"You look the same, too," she conceded, disconcerted by how vulnerable it made her feel. Uncomfortable. And she rarely felt uncomfortable around *anyone.*

As they passed the doorway to the residence she

nodded to the guard on duty, then took Alex in the opposite direction, into the guest wing to the first door on the left.

"I believe this is the same suite you stayed in the last time you were here." In fact, she knew it was. She'd spent enough time there with him in those two weeks to remember quite precisely.

She opened the door and gestured him inside, following a few steps behind. "As you probably remember, this is the sitting room, and there's also a sleeping chamber and bath."

"I remember," he said, sounding almost wistful. Was he thinking the same thing that she was? Was he remembering the way they stood on the balcony overlooking the gardens and talked for hours? The first time he drew her to him and kissed her.

Did he remember the first time they made love?

Never before or since had another man made her feel more loved and accepted. More special. But that was a long time ago and so much had changed since then. *She* had changed.

"I remember this," he said, gazing around the room. "You know what else I remember?"

"What?"

He turned to her, reached out to touch her arm. "This…"

It happened so quickly that she barely had a chance to process it. One second she was standing beside Alex, and the next she was in his arms, the only place in the world that she'd ever felt she truly belonged. Her first instinct was to push him away, but instead she went weak all over. Then his lips were touching hers, as naturally as if they had never spent a day apart.

She knew this was wrong in more ways than she could count, not the least of which that he was married, but as the kiss deepened, as she tasted the familiar flavor of his mouth, breathed in the scent of his skin and hair, there wasn't a thing she could do, or would even *want* to do, to stop him.

Well, that was easy, Alex mused as Sophie all but dissolved in his arms. He tunneled his fingers through the soft black ribbons of hair that fell loose around her face. She tasted sweet and exciting and sexy. He nibbled her lower lip lightly wondering if that still drove her nuts, and was answered with a shiver and a soft moan of pleasure.

And here he thought seducing her was going to be a time-consuming, tedious task. And why wouldn't he? After she vowed her eternal love for him, then dumped him with no explanation.

As though reading his mind, she tensed. He felt her hands flatten against his chest. And because he didn't want to push too far to soon, he didn't try to stop her when she backed away from him.

She stared at him with eyes the color of a storm blowing inland off the Atlantic Ocean. Deep, turbulent gray. Her cheeks were pink and he could see the flutter of her pulse at the base of her long, graceful throat. And to be honest he was feeling a bit breathless himself. Despite everything that had happened, the way she had used him, she still turned him on.

Which would make using *her* that much more satisfying.

"Why did you do that?" she asked, her voice shaky.

"Sophie, I've been wanting to do that for ten years."

She took another step away, pressing the backs of her fingers to her lips, as though his touch had seared her. "I could call a guard and have you detained for assault."

He just smiled, because he knew she would never do that. She may have been self-centered, spoiled and manipulative, but she wasn't vindictive. At least, not back then. "But you won't, because that would be a lie. You wanted it as much as I did."

He could see from her reaction that he was right, but he also knew that she wouldn't let him off the hook that easily.

"I'm not sure what kind of woman you think I am, but I don't involve myself with married men."

Is that why she looked so scandalized? Not that she was in any position to be questioning his character. Or morals.

He folded his arms across his chest. "I guess you haven't heard. I've just been through the nastiest divorce in recorded history."

That information seemed to sober her. "No, I hadn't. I'm sorry to hear that."

The odd thing was that she looked truly sorry.

And here he thought the only person she cared about was herself. But he didn't believe for a second that she had made some startling transformation over the past ten years. He didn't doubt that sooner or later the real Sophie would make a grand entrance. And when she did, he would be ready.

"I suppose that's what happens when you marry someone you don't love," he said. "I guess you had the right idea."

She looked confused.

"You didn't love your fiancé, and you didn't marry him. In fact, Phillip tells me that you've never been married."

"No, I haven't." She glanced toward the door, then back to him. "I should leave you to unpack."

"Running away again, Sophie?"

A frown furrowed the space between her brows. "I have to ask you from now on to please keep your hands to yourself. Next time I *will* alert security."

No, she wouldn't, but for now he would play along. Let her think that she had the upper hand. It was all a part of the game. "Of course, Your Highness. I apologize for my…inappropriate behavior."

"Dinner is in the main dining room at seven sharp. Do you remember where that is?"

"I'm sure I can find my way."

She nodded. "If you have any questions or need anything, there's a directory beside the phone. The kitchen is open twenty-four hours. You also have a full wet bar."

"Thank you."

She nodded, then turned and left, closing the door firmly behind her.

Maybe this wouldn't be quite as easy as he thought, but he'd always enjoyed a challenge. The harder he worked for something, the more satisfying the payoff when he finally got it.

He was taking a risk, putting his personal and professional relationship with Phillip on the line. The family firm, Rutledge Design, was unrivaled in North America, but they needed this credit to their portfolio if they were going to take the company international. Just as his father had always dreamed of doing but never accomplished himself.

And hadn't Alex always done what his father expected of him? He'd been dead and buried for three years now and Alex was *still* trying to please him.

Which in part was to blame for the mother of all divorces that Alex had just endured. An inevitability, he supposed, when a man married for convenience instead of love. To please his family instead of himself. In his entire life he'd met only one woman who had ever understood the pressures of living up to the expectations of others.

That woman was Sophie. When Alex had come to stay at the palace during a college break, he and Sophie had immediately connected. When he was with her, Alex had felt as though he could let down his guard and just be himself.

Little had he known it was just a game to her.

Seeing her again brought it all back—the confusion and humiliation. So what better time than now to get a little revenge? Give her a taste of her own medicine.

Seduce her, make her fall in love with him, then dump her, just as she'd done to him.

Two

Sophie was still trembling as she descended the stairs and headed for the back entrance. What she needed right now was to be alone. She needed time to process what had just happened, and figure out why it had scared her half to death.

But as she was rounding the corner just before the outer door, she ran into Ethan, who was also on his way out.

"Heading home?" he asked, holding the door for her.

She forced a smile. "I have an itinerary to plan." Since leaving Alex's suite, she had felt chilled to the bone, and the bright afternoon sunshine and warm breeze felt soothing on her face and arms.

They walked together toward his black, convertible Porsche.

"You realize you'll never get a car seat in that thing," she teased.

"Don't remind me," he said, pulling his keys from his pants pocket. Although everyone in the family had their own custom Rolls-Royce and driver, Ethan still preferred to drive himself most days. And he rarely used the services of a bodyguard.

They stopped by the driver's-side door. "Our guest all settled in?" he asked.

"Yes, all settled in."

"He seems like a nice guy."

"Yes, very nice." A little *too* nice, actually. Far too…*friendly*. And she didn't trust him.

Ethan narrowed his eyes at her, looking so much like Phillip that it was almost eerie. "Is something wrong?"

It amazed her that, despite having only learned of each other's existence last year, he could read her so well. Must have been some sort of paternal bond that linked them despite being only half siblings. And at a time like now, it was incredibly inconvenient.

"I'm fine," she told him, but could tell he didn't believe her. She prayed silently that he would drop it. He didn't of course.

"I know what's going on here, Sophie."

She swallowed hard. How could he possibly know about her relationship with Alex? Unless Alex had told him. Which he had *no* right doing. It was between him and Sophie.

He put a hand on her arm. "I understand how you feel."

"You do?"

"I felt the same way when I started in the hotel business. I wanted to be the one in control. The one calling the shots. But it was easier for me in the sense that I didn't have a well-meaning family trying to hold me back."

He was talking about the business, not her and Alex's complicated past. She was so relieved she felt faint. Although, if there was anyone in the world she would feel comfortable confiding in, other than her sister-in-law, Hannah, it would be Ethan. But as was her way, she preferred to figure out things on her own.

"You want more responsibility," Ethan continued. "More than shuttling guests around the island."

She shrugged. "But that just isn't the way things are done in this family. I'm a princess and my royal duties must come first."

He gave her arm an affectionate squeeze. "Although I don't have a lot of influence with Phillip, I am working on it. But honestly, between the hotel and the baby coming, I barely have a free minute."

"Is Lizzy feeling better? She has to be close to her fourth month now."

"She still has terrible morning sickness. She had hoped to keep working until her eighth month. You know how restless she gets when she's not busy, but she can barely crawl out of bed in the morning. She tries to eat but can't keep anything down and the doctor is concerned that she's losing a dangerous amount of weight. I hate to leave her alone all the time while I'm working, so I'm considering moving us into the palace for a while. At least until she's feeling better. Or gives birth. Whichever comes first I guess."

"I think that would be a good idea, and I'm sure Phillip will be thrilled. You know how he feels about keeping the family close. Although I have to say I'm a bit surprised. This coming from the man who swore he would *never* live in the palace?"

He grinned and shrugged. "I guess I never expected to feel at home here. Or to think of Phillip as family. It's amazing how quickly things change."

Wasn't that the truth. Just this morning it had been business as usual, and now it felt as though her entire life had just been turned upside down.

He unlocked his car. "Guess I should go. Can I give you a lift home?"

"No, thanks. It's such a beautiful day." And it was only a brisk five-minute walk if she followed the stone path. "Give Lizzy my best. And tell her if she needs help with anything, all she has to do is ask."

"I will." He gave her a quick hug and a peck on the cheek, then climbed into his car. Sophie started down the path toward home, watching as he zipped out of the lot and drove away.

It seemed as though lately everyone she knew was settling down and starting a family. People who, like her, swore they would never give up their freedom. Ethan was right, things did change quickly. But for her, certain things, things like wanting a husband and family, would never change. She'd spent her entire life struggling for her freedom, and she wasn't going to give that up.

Not for anyone.

Referencing files of itineraries she had created in the past few years, Sophie was able to whip up a suitable plan for the next two weeks well before dinner. It was something of a challenge considering the average guest stayed several days. Thankfully, though, several of those afternoons Alex would spend with Phillip doing the usual guy things, like fishing and golfing. But for the remainder of the trip, he was basically all hers.

She was printing off copies for herself, Phillip and the social secretary when her butler knocked on her office door. "Yes, Wilson."

He bowed his head. "Sorry to interrupt, Miss, but you have a visitor."

A visitor? She wasn't expecting anyone today. How would they even get past the guards at the main gate without her consent? "Who?"

"A Mr. Rutledge."

Just as it had in Phillip's office earlier that day, her heart took a deep dive downward. Bloody hell, why did it keep doing that? And what was Alex doing here? At *her* house? He had no right to just barge in on her.

She considered ordering Wilson to tell Alex that she was busy and didn't have time for guests, but if she refused to see him, he would realize how much his stunt back in the palace had rattled her. And if she had to spend the next two weeks carting him around the island, showing vulnerability was not an option.

She would *have* to see him.

"Show him to the study. I'll be down in just a minute."

Wilson nodded and disappeared into the hall. Sophie took a long, deep breath and rose from her chair. She had no reason to be nervous, but as she crossed the room her legs felt weak and trembly. *Get a grip, Sophie.*

If she had this reaction every time she saw him, this was going to be a very long and exhausting two weeks.

She stopped in front of the mirror in the upstairs hallway and checked her reflection. She looked as pale as death. She smoothed her hair and pinched a little color back into her cheeks, reminding herself once again that Alex was no longer a man of consequence. That part of her life was over. Now he was merely a business associate.

She descended the stairs slowly, her heart creeping further up her throat with every step. Alex was in the study by the window, gazing out across the pristinely manicured lawn. He seemed lost in thought, a million miles away, and it struck her again how handsome he was. How familiar. And for a moment she gave herself permission to just look at him. And remember.

"Thanks for seeing me," he said, nearly startling her out of her skin.

Bloody hell! No matter how collected she tried to be, he always managed to throw her off kilter. "I thought you understood that the tour would begin tomorrow."

"I know, but I wanted to see you." He turned to her, looking humbled. "So I could apologize."

Well, this was unexpected. "There's really no need."

"Yes, there is. What I did was wrong. I guess..." He shrugged. "I guess I just got caught up in the past. And I assumed, or maybe *hoped,* that you felt the same way. That you missed me as much as I've missed you."

He looked sincere, but something in his words didn't ring true. In her world, men did not offer up their feelings like a neatly wrapped gift. So naturally, she couldn't escape the suspicion that he was saying what he *thought* she wanted to hear.

Or had thirty years living in the midst of nothing but emotionally vacant men left her jaded?

"And since you obviously don't feel that way," he continued. "I just wanted to say that I was sorry, and assure you that it won't happen again."

Was that disappointment she just felt? Surely she didn't *want* it to happen again.

But the memory of his lips pressed to hers, his hands cupping her face, fingers tangling in her hair, made her scalp tingle and her knees even weaker than they already felt. But that was just physical. Emotionally she had no place for a man like him in her life. Not even temporarily. "Apology accepted."

"I'm not usually so impulsive. Or reckless. It's a

lousy excuse, but going through this divorce really has me off my game."

She stepped a little farther into the room. "I'm sorry to hear that."

"If you're not busy, I was hoping we could take a while to talk, get reacquainted. Because it seems we're stuck with each other."

With the itinerary completed, there was really nothing pressing on her schedule, and it was still several hours until dinner. Besides, it might make things a bit less awkward. It wouldn't kill her to give him the benefit of the doubt and grant him the concession of a simple conversation. If only she could shake the feeling that he had ulterior motives.

For now she would give him what he wanted, but she would tread lightly, and at the first sign of trouble she would put him in his place.

"Would you like a drink?" Sophie asked, and Alex knew she was as good as his. It might take a bit longer than he expected to break down the barriers, but it was only a matter of time now. She looked and acted tough, but he knew what it took to make a woman melt. His ability to accurately read the subtle emotional cues of the opposite sex and respond accordingly was something of a gift. It was the only reason his marriage had lasted as long as it had. Although in retrospect, that hadn't been one of his brightest moves. He should have left her a long time ago. Or even better, never married her in the first place.

"Mineral water, if you have it," he said.

"With lime?"

"Please."

He expected her to call her butler, instead she walked to the bar and poured the drinks herself. A mineral water for him, and a glass of white wine for herself. She carried the glass to him, and when he took it, she gestured to the couch.

"Please, sit."

She waited until he was seated then took a place on an adjacent chair. She wore a gauzy, cotton dress that accentuated her long, willowy form. She had always struck him as more of an earthy, free spirit than a royal. Back then she had felt stifled and suffocated by her title, yet now she seemed to embrace it.

He wondered if she was still as self-centered and spoiled.

"Nice house," he said. "I'm surprised you don't still live in the palace with the rest of the family."

"I like my privacy."

"Have you lived here long?"

"I moved in after my mother passed away."

Which made sense. He couldn't see her parents allowing her to live in her own place. He remembered her parents to be very strict and controlling. Which probably part of the thrill of their affair. That element of danger. Had she been discovered sneaking into his suite every night, he'd have been booted out on his ear and most likely banished from the country for life.

She sipped her wine and asked, "How was it that you and my brother reconnected?"

She was asking polite, benign questions. Holding him at arm's length. But that was fine. He had two weeks to work his way under her skin. For now he would play along.

"We've kept in touch occasionally over the years, and he remembered that I was interested in taking my firm international. So when he needed someone to design the fitness center, I was the first one he called. He and Ethan looked at my portfolio and liked what they saw. When Phillip learned of my less-than-amicable divorce, he suggested I take a few weeks off and come visit. And I have to admit, this is the most relaxed I've been in months."

"You own the architectural firm?"

He nodded. "Since my father passed three years ago."

"I'm so sorry to hear that. How is your mother?"

"Good. She lives in upstate New York now, near my sister."

"And you're still based in Manhattan?"

"I got the apartment in the settlement. She got the mansion upstate." Then he added, "If I sound bitter, it's because I am."

She nodded sympathetically. It couldn't hurt to play the pity card, even though the truth of the matter was, the monstrosity his ex had insisted on buying had never felt like home to him. He spent the majority of his time in the city, commuting upstate on the weekends to see her. However, over the past year he'd been making the trip less and less. At times only once a month.

When he'd learned of her infidelity, he'd been more relieved than angry. Finally he had an out.

That, however, hadn't stopped her from trying to bleed him dry.

He took a sip of his drink and set it on the table beside him. "So, I take it from your reaction in Phillip's office that you had no idea I was coming to visit."

"No, I didn't."

"I remember how much you hated being left out of the loop. You used to say that you felt like window dressing."

"I'm surprised you remember that."

He leaned forward slightly. "I remember lots of things, Princess."

He could see her working that one through, but before she had the opportunity to reply, her butler appeared in the open doorway. "The King to see you, Miss."

Alex and Sophie both rose from their seats as Phillip stepped into the room. When Phillip saw him there, he smiled. "There you are, Alex."

"I'm sorry," Alex said. "I didn't realize you were looking for me."

"Nothing urgent," Phillip assured him. "I just wanted to be sure that you were all settled in."

"I am. I have everything I could possibly need."

"Alex thought it would be a good idea for us to get

acquainted," Sophie said, with no hint of the nature of her and Alex's true relationship. Or, *ex*-relationship.

"I'm actually here because I need to have a word with my sister," Phillip said. "If you'll excuse us for a moment, Alex."

"Of course. I should get back to the palace anyway. I have a few phone calls to make before dinner. It was nice talking to you, Sophie."

"You, too," she said, with one of those smiles that was a little too indifferent to be genuine. Was that for his benefit or her brother's?

She turned to her butler. "Please show our guest out."

"I guess I'll see you at dinner," Alex said, nodding to both Sophie and Phillip, then he followed the butler to the door.

Why, he wondered, would Phillip come all the way to her residence instead of just picking up the phone?

He had the distinct feeling he would eventually find out.

Three

Alex's cell phone rang as he was walking back to the palace. He checked the display and saw that it was his attorney, Jonah Livingston, who also happened to be his best friend. Over the years that had proved to be both a good and a bad thing. There wasn't much about his life Jonah didn't know. And he'd been known to give Alex hell when he thought he was acting in a manner contrary to his best interests. Professional *and* personal. And he was usually right. Like the day of Alex's wedding, when Jonah implored him to take a step back and think about what he was doing. He tried to convince Alex that marrying someone he didn't love was far worse than not getting married at all. And eventually Alex's father would give him his job back and write him back into the will.

Now Alex wished he had listened.

He almost dreaded answering the call. When he left for Morgan Isle, everything pertaining to the divorce had been settled, or so they believed, but his ex hadn't actually signed on the dotted line yet. It wouldn't be the first time she'd agreed to the terms, then changed her mind at the last minute and lashed out with more demands.

They had been going back and forth with this for more than a year now. A long, tedious year he would have much rather spent forgetting he was ever married and starting with a clean slate. He just wanted it to be over. And now he needed to know if it was.

Just before the call went to voice mail he flipped open the phone. "This better be good news."

Jonah chuckled. "Hello, to you, too. I trust you're having a good time."

"I'd be having a better time if you had some good news. Did you hear from the divorce attorney?"

"I just got off the phone with her."

"And?"

"You want to know what she said?"

He closed his eyes and sighed heavily. "This is so not the time to mess with me, Jonah."

Jonah laughed. "You can relax, buddy. This time it's definitely good news."

"She signed?"

"In her lawyer's office yesterday, with plenty of

witnesses to make it binding. As of this morning the papers are officially signed and filed and you, my friend, are a free man."

He should have felt some level of regret or even sadness, but all he could manage to feel was relieved. "That is *very* good news."

"She's going by the apartment tomorrow to pick up the rest of her things."

"And you'll be there?"

"Me and three of my associates, just to be safe. We won't take our eyes off her for a second. She won't take anything that she isn't supposed to. And if she tries, I won't hesitate to get the police involved."

He was just glad Jonah was handling this, so he didn't have to. If he never saw her again, that would be fine with him. In fact, he preferred it that way. "You think it will come to that?"

"She may be manipulative and greedy, but she's not stupid. And honestly, I think she's as ready for this to be over as you are."

"Guess I should have listened all those years ago when you warned me not to marry her."

"Yeah, but when do you ever listen to me? Which reminds me, how are things going with your princess?"

"She's not my princess," he said, then added with a grin, "Not yet anyway."

"I hope you know what you're doing."

"Don't I always?"

He laughed. "Honestly, *no*. That's why you have me. To keep you out of trouble."

"Well, this time I'm in total control."

"Like I haven't heard that before."

"Don't worry," he told Jonah. "This time it's different. I know *exactly* what I'm doing."

"Sophie, this behavior is completely inappropriate," Phillip said after Alex left and they were alone.

There he went with the stern look again. Sophie had to make an effort not to roll her eyes. Would he never learn? "What is it that you find inappropriate, Phillip?"

"Don't play dumb."

"Let's pretend for a second that I am dumb. Because, frankly, I have no clue why you're in such a snit."

"Your being alone in *your* residence with *my* guest."

"You can't be serious." Where in bloody hell did he get off telling her who she could and couldn't invite into her home? She was sick to death of everyone thinking they had the right to tell her how to live her own life. "Are you forgetting that *you're* the one who stuck me with him for two weeks? Not to mention that who I choose to invite into *my* house is none of your damned business."

"He's not one of your disposable distractions. This is business, Sophie. If you expect to be treated like an equal, you have to act the part."

She couldn't deny that his words stung. Wasn't it just like her brother to assume the worst. "He was at my home, so you just assume I'm sleeping with him? He was here, what, *ten* minutes? I certainly don't waste any time, do I?"

"I'm just making sure you understand my feelings on this."

If she didn't know any better, she would think that Phillip knew about her complicated past with Alex. But if he did, he surely would have said something about it years ago. He'd never held back before when he disapproved of her conduct.

And she was tired of feeling as though she was living her life under a microscope.

She had half a mind to sleep with Alex just to spite him. But what would that prove other than the fact that he was right about her?

She walked toward the door. "I have to dress for dinner now."

Her way of saying, "Get the hell out," without actually saying it. And wonder of all wonders, he actually acquiesced. He walked to the door, then stopped and turned back to her. "You know that I only do things that I feel are in your best interest."

"I know that, Phillip."

And that was the problem. Everyone thinking they knew what was better for her than she did.

Thankfully, Alex was seated at the opposite end of the table from Sophie during dinner. And although the entire family was there—Phillip and his wife, Queen Hannah, Ethan and Lizzy, who was looking decidedly green, and their cousin Charles, the family attorney—the tone of conversation was more business than personal. They talked mainly of the hotel and the plans for the new fitness center Alex's firm would be designing, and when the purchase of the property would be final.

"It's as good as ours," Charles assured them. "Old man Houghton has no choice but to sell. Considering the financial ruin he's facing, what we're offering is a gift. He would be a fool not to take it."

"The existing building will have to come down immediately," Phillip said.

"Demolition has already been scheduled," Ethan told him.

"But it's such a beautiful old building," Hannah said wistfully. "Isn't there a way to salvage it?"

"Although it may be aesthetically pleasing," Alex explained. "The building is so old and structurally unsound that it would be more cost-effective to tear it down and put a new building in its place."

"What about all of the employees who will be out of work when it shuts down?" Lizzy asked, though it was obvious, despite her attempts to join the conversation, that she felt awful. She only picked at her food and often reached over to clutch Ethan's hand for support.

"We'll hire as many as we can," Ethan said. "A deal is already in the works to have Houghton's daughter, Victoria, brought in as a manager. It's the one thing he's insisted on."

"But is she trustworthy?" Charles asked, because protecting the family was his duly appointed task. "Despite the generous nature of our offer, Houghton hasn't been shy about his negative feelings toward the family. What if he wants his daughter involved so she can make trouble?"

"We thought of that," Ethan said. "Until we know we can trust her, we're going to have her work in your office, so you can keep an eye on her. Once it's determined that her loyalties lie with us, she'll be transferred to the hotel. You can find a spot for her, can't you?"

Charles nodded. "No problem."

As the dessert plates were being cleared, Lizzy, now as pale as a ghost, excused herself to go lie down and Ethan left with her to be both moral and, apparently, physical support.

Hannah watched with concern, and when they were gone, said to Phillip, "She's not looking well. I was sick in my first few months, but never that bad."

"I'm concerned, too," Phillip admitted. "But according to Ethan, there isn't anything the doctor can do for her. She just has to ride it out. I told Ethan they didn't have to be here for dinner, but he said Lizzy insisted." He glanced over to Sophie. "She's strong-willed."

She flashed him a wry smile. "To survive in this family you have to be."

Hannah shot them both a look that seemed to say, *behave, you two,* then said, "If you'll all excuse me, I have to go check on Fredrick."

As she stood, so did the men at the table.

"I'll go with you," Phillip said.

Charles looked at his watch. "I should push off, as well. Hot date tonight."

Sophie rolled her eyes. "Is there ever a night when you don't have a hot date?"

Charles just grinned.

"Sophie," Phillip said, "why don't you take Alex on a walk through the gardens?"

"Oh, yes!" Hannah agreed. "It's lovely at sunset."

Either it was a show of faith on Phillip's part or he was sending some insanely mixed messages. But it wasn't as though she had anything better to do.

Ethan had Lizzy to care for, Phillip and Hannah were off to spend time with their infant son and Charles was going on a date. Sophie couldn't help feeling she'd just been handed the booby prize.

But because she was the goodwill ambassador, and God knows she had played this game a million times before, she turned to Alex and smiled. "Would you care to take a walk in the gardens, Alex?"

He returned the smile, and she could swear she saw the spark of a twinkle in his eye. "I would love to, Your Highness."

They all went their separate ways, and Sophie led Alex outside, with the undeniable sneaking suspicion that this was some sort of test. That Phillip would be watching. She wondered what he would do if he saw her plant a wet one on Alex right there amid the rose and hydrangea bushes.

The light was just beginning to fade and the sun sat like a shimmering orange globe just above the tree line in the cloudless evening sky. The heat of the day had begun to fade and a cool breeze blew from the north, rustling the leaves and spreading the faint aroma of moss. Sophie led Alex down the flagstone path that wound its way carelessly through a long stretch of flower gardens that had become the pride of the royal family. Every year it grew and expanded as new species of plants and flowers were added. Hybrids mostly, and many that had been bred by the palace gardener himself.

She pointed out the different varieties, giving both their common and scientific names, but Alex seemed distant.

"Am I boring you?" she finally asked.

He grinned. "No, sorry. I guess I'm still processing everything that I've seen this evening."

"What do you mean?"

"It's been so long, I'd nearly forgotten what it was like to have a family dinner."

"Well, the topic usually doesn't revolve around business. Typically it's everyone sticking their noses into everyone else's business. But in sort of a good way, I guess."

"Even so, it was remarkably…cohesive."

She supposed that it was. They were a close family. Now, anyway. They didn't used to be. The only family dinners she and Phillip ever shared with their parents was during holidays or royal functions. Their mother and father led very separate lives. From not just each other, but their children, as well. Child rearing in their opinion was better left to the nannies. Sophie often used to feel that it was her and Phillip against the world.

"I take it you and your wife didn't share dinner," she said, realizing immediately the personal nature of the question, but it was too late to take it back. And she was at least a little curious about his life.

He shook his head. "Not for a long time."

He looked so sad, she couldn't help but feel sorry for him. And she found herself asking, "Do you have children?"

He shook his head. "That was a major sore spot. She wanted them, I didn't."

That surprised her. Ten years ago he had seemed eager to start a family, but then, so had she. If the family she would have been starting was his, that is. Now, there didn't seem much point. She couldn't imagine finding a man she could care enough about to bear his children. She no longer had the energy to look. The men she passed the time with these days were, as Phillip had pointed out, nothing more than a temporary distraction.

"But I wasn't being entirely honest," he admitted. "I wanted kids. Just not with her."

So why did he marry her?

"I know what you're thinking," he said. "Why marry a woman I didn't want to start a family with?"

Whoa, that was weird. And she couldn't stop herself from asking, "Why did you?"

"Pressure from my family. I was young and naive and thought that in time I would learn to love her. By the time I realized that you have to like someone before you can learn to love them, it was too late."

That was the difference between them, she supposed. She knew that she would never fall in love with the man her parents had chosen for her. That only happened in fairy tales. Her parents' arranged marriage had been riddled with problems, the least of which was their father's seeming inability to keep his fly zipped. And because of it her mother, despite all the money and power, had been a lonely, incomplete, miserable woman.

As far as Sophie was concerned, life was too short to spend it with a spouse she could only barely tolerate. She would rather be alone.

"So I'm guessing you didn't," she said. "Learn to love her, I mean."

"It would have been tough, seeing as how I was in love with someone else."

That admission nearly floored her, because she suspected the someone else he was referring to was her. She glanced up at him and could see from the look in his eyes, the way they cut through her, that she was. It was both disturbing and a little exciting to know that a man had loved her so much no other woman could make him happy. It also made her feel guilty, as though she had ruined his life somehow. Which was ridiculous. She hadn't forced him to marry a woman he didn't love. Just like her, he'd had choices. Any mistakes he'd made were his own.

So why wasn't that much of a consolation?

"But," he continued, "she didn't love me, either. So I guess you could say we were even. She was just in it for the name. And society rank. Beyond that, she had few real ambitions." He tucked his hands into the pockets of his slacks. "Why is it that you never married?"

"I suppose I never met a man I would want to marry."

He laughed and shook his head.

"You find that amusing?"

"In fact, I do. You claimed that you wanted to marry me. Or is that your M.O.? Seduce men, make them believe you want to marry them, then dump them with no explanation." He sounded more curious than angry, but there was an undeniable undercurrent of tension in his voice.

"It wasn't like that, Alex."

He laughed, a sharp and ironic sound. "It was exactly like that."

She shook her head. "What difference does it make now?"

"Just tell me this much—did you care at all, or were you just bored?"

"Of course I cared," she said softly. She had been weak, unable to stand up for herself. For their love. It's not something she was proud of, but there was no changing the past, and rehashing it all now wasn't going to solve anything. "I did what I had to."

That should have been the end of it, but Alex wouldn't let it drop. "So what that means is your parents disapproved, and you didn't have the guts to fight for us. Or maybe you just didn't care."

"I did care, but it's...*complicated*."

"I'm a marginally intelligent man, Princess. Why don't you try explaining it to me?"

Nothing good would come from this, but maybe after all this time he deserved the truth. "When my parents found out about our plans to elope, they were against it, of course. But I told them I loved you, and I was going to marry you, and there was nothing they could do to stop me."

"At which point they forced you to break it off?"

She shook her head. "They started...*planning.*"

He looked confused. "Planning what?"

"Our life together, Alex."

"Are you saying that they approved? That they were going to let us get married?"

She bit her lip and nodded, and she could see he was clearly confused.

"I don't understand. If they were okay with it, why did you stop taking my calls? Answering my letters?"

"I wanted to escape, Alex. I wanted...*freedom.* To live my life and make my own decisions. And there I was, right back in the very situation I was trying to avoid. My parents controlling my every move."

He digested that for a moment, then said in a very calm voice, "So what you're saying is you didn't really love me. You were just using me. You needed a ticket out, and I was convenient."

She shook her head. "No, I didn't mean it to sound like that. I loved you."

"As long as I served some sort of purpose," he said. She could see that he was angry. Angry and hurt.

"No! Letting go of you was the hardest thing I've ever done. But I had to. You had so many dreams. So many plans. You would have had to give them all up. By letting you go, I was giving you a chance to live your life."

"But that's a decision I should have made for myself."

"You would have had no idea what you were getting yourself into. Eventually you would have hated me for it, and I just couldn't bear the thought of that."

"And if you could go back and do it over?" he asked.

Had it not been for Alex, she wouldn't have known how true love, true passion and yearning felt. She may have even married the man her parents had chosen for her and spent her life lonely and miserable. Simply because that was the way things were done. In a way, Alex had saved her life.

He reached up, brushed his fingers softly against her cheek. The gesture was so sweet and tender, she wanted to cry. And she wanted to kiss him again. She wanted to feel him hold her. But Phillip's words about business and what was proper ran like a ticker tape through her head.

She turned away. "Please, Alex. Don't."

A strong breeze whipped through the gardens, chilling her to the bone. She rubbed her arms, realized how late it was getting. The sun had dipped below the trees and the outdoor lights had switched on. "It's getting dark. We should get back inside."

He shook his head, looking so...disappointed. But he let it drop.

She started in the direction of the door, but Alex just stood there. "Aren't you coming?"

"I'd like to walk for a little while longer. I'll find my way back inside."

She nodded. "I'll see you in the morning."

"What time does the tour begin?"

"Why don't we meet in the foyer at nine? Dress casually."

"Fine. I'll see you then."

Alex watched Sophie walk away, until she was swallowed up into the night, then he turned and walked in the opposite direction down the path.

Just when he thought he couldn't resent her more, she proved him wrong. He didn't buy her sob story about breaking it off for him. Sophie did things with only one person in mind. Herself.

Which made his recent plan all the more satisfying. Things were going exactly as he'd intended, and though he wasn't one to gloat, he had to admit he'd given an Oscar-worthy performance. Although it hadn't all been an act.

What he'd told her was true. He hadn't spent time with his family in ages—not since before the divorce. His mother and sister had been disappointed that he hadn't been willing to try to work things out with his wife. God only knows what Cynthia, his ex, had told them. And even if they knew about her affair, it might not have made a difference. Like most women, they stuck together.

That was one thing he'd liked about Sophie. she'd been autonomous. She claimed that most women were intimidated by her title, and those who weren't usually had some sort of agenda.

But these days he had issues with the entire female gender. And he supposed that Sophie was simply a convenient target.

She was playing right into his hand, making this almost too easy, and tomorrow the real fun would begin. And he knew without a doubt now that she deserved everything he could dish out.

Four

Alex was waiting in the foyer for her the following morning at nine sharp, just as they had agreed, and Sophie felt caught in a tug-of-war between anticipation and disappointment. So much for her silent prayer that he would be called away on business or some pressing personal matter in the wee hours of the night. It looked as though, for today at least, she was stuck with him.

But heavens, he was one attractive-looking inconvenience. He wore casual, charcoal gray slacks and a black, silk button-up shirt with the sleeves rolled to the elbows. The top two buttons were unfastened at the neck and she could see just a hint of his chest. Was it still smooth and well-defined? Would his skin still feel warm and solid under her palms?

She mentally shook away the thought. She didn't *want* to know.

"Did you sleep well?" she asked, just to be polite.

"Best sleep I've had in months," he said, and he did in fact look well-rested and chipper. She on the other hand had slept fitfully, and hopefully didn't look half as groggy and out of sorts as she felt.

"I seem to recall the last night I spent in that bed, I barely slept at all," he said, and that twinkle was back in his eye. "Of course, I had company."

She recalled that, as well. In painfully crisp detail. The way he touched her, the feel of his hands on her. And when they *had* slept, their naked bodies lay closely entwined. Arms and legs tangled in a lover's embrace. The memory made her head feel light and her skin tingle.

Is that the way it would be? Two weeks of him turning everything she said into a sexual innuendo? Well, she wouldn't give him the satisfaction of a re-action.

She fixed a bored look on her face. "It was so long ago, I guess I'd forgotten."

He just grinned, as though he could see right through her facade.

"Are you ready to go?" she asked.

The weight of his gaze burned into her skin like a hot flame. "I was born ready, Princess."

Bugger. Did he have to keep doing that? Toying with her? At this rate, it was going to be an exhausting and tedious day.

She led him through the palace to the back entrance, where the car waited. Her bodyguard held the door while they got in, then slipped into the front seat with the driver.

"What's on the schedule for today?" Alex asked as the car pulled down the driveway.

"First a tour of the Royal Inn. Some parts of the hotel are still under construction, but the majority of the renovations have already been completed. We'll have lunch in the hotel restaurant, then continue on to a tour of the area surrounding the hotel. Then we're back at the palace for dinner."

"And tomorrow?"

"A tour of the natural history museum and the science center, then if there's time, a drive up the coast."

"I don't suppose you scheduled any time to just kick back and relax in the next fourteen days."

"You and Phillip tee off at 7:00 a.m. Wednesday morning, and Thursday, Phillip plans to take you to the hunting cabin on the other side of the island for target practice. Saturday, you'll spend the day with Phillip and Hannah on the yacht."

"And my nights?" he asked, a spark of something warm and feral gleaming in his eyes.

Oh, please. Could he be any *less* subtle?

She spared him a polite smile. "Oh, I'm sure you'll figure out a way to amuse yourself."

Rather than be insulted, he laughed. "Phillip mentioned something about a black-tie charity event."

"That would be Friday night."

"You'll be there, too?"

"Of course."

"Then plan to save a dance for me."

She nodded politely, thinking, when hell froze over.

He leaned back and folded one leg over the other. "So, Princess, what is it that you normally do?"

"What do you mean?"

"I mean, if you weren't here with me, where would you be?"

She shrugged. "This *is* what I do. I'm a goodwill ambassador."

"So, you cart people around the island?"

"Among other things. I also attend and host charity functions, plan any parties or dinners. Basically, any and all public relations."

He nodded slowly. "Sounds…exciting."

She didn't miss the less-than-subtle sarcasm. Who was he to pass judgment on her? He was making it very difficult for her to be diplomatic. And she couldn't help but suspect that was exactly his intention.

And she refused to give him the satisfaction. "You disapprove?" she asked. Casually, as though it didn't matter either way.

"I guess I just imagined you doing something… *bigger.* Ten years ago, you had vast aspirations."

Normally she would be the first to admit her duties left much to be desired, but to Alex she found herself defending her position. Her composure slipping. "What I do is both important and necessary. And it's not nearly as small as you like to believe."

Rather than look offended, he grinned. "I know that, Sophie. I just wondered if you did."

What?

For the first time since…well…*ever,* someone had stunned her into total silence.

But it didn't take her long to recover.

"What the hell was that for?" she asked, then immediately regretted her sharp tone. What was wrong with her? It wasn't at all like her to let a man under her skin this way.

Of course, no man, or woman, for that matter, dared to speak to her so frankly. In an odd sense, it was almost…refreshing. A relief even to be in the presence of someone outside the family who didn't cater to her every whim.

"I get the distinct impression that you don't know how important you are," Alex said. "Do you know that Phillip has more than once referred to you as the glue that holds the family together."

And here she'd been under the impression Phillip considered her a nuisance. But what surprised her most wasn't that Phillip had those feelings, but that he'd actually voiced them.

"Well," she said, "he certainly has an interesting way of showing it."

"Brothers usually do. Particularly *older* brothers. Just ask my baby sister. More than once she's accused me of sticking my nose in where it doesn't belong. But we do it out of love. Honestly."

She found herself smiling, and immediately wiped

the expression from her face. This was all wrong. He was breaking down her defenses, getting under her skin. Inside her head.

She turned from him and gazed out the window, at the passing landscape. They were leaving the rural setting and entering the outskirts of the city.

"Something wrong?" he asked.

"No, I just…I don't want to talk about this. It isn't proper."

"Okay. What do you want to talk about?"

Nothing. She just wanted to sit quietly and brood. But those would not be the actions of a good hostess. She was supposed to be composed and polite, and at times even cheerful depending on the guest. She was like a chameleon, becoming whoever the situation required. But with Alex she wasn't sure *who* she was supposed to be.

Thank heavens they only had another few minutes before they reached the hotel. Already she could see snippets of deep blue ocean between the buildings dotting the shore line. Located in the Irish Sea, between England, Scotland, Ireland and Wales, their island was a small one, but that was its charm. Two hundred and twenty-seven square miles of pure bliss.

"I'd forgotten how beautiful the bay is," Alex said, gazing out the window. "A true paradise."

Finally, a topic of conversation that didn't revolve around her personal life. How refreshing. "We like to think so," she said.

"It's been built up quite a bit since I was last here, hasn't it?"

"The bay area has, but more than forty percent of the island is devoted to national parks and nature conservation."

"Phillip told me that tourism has nearly doubled in the past few years."

"It has." And it was no coincidence the changes began to happen after their father died, and Phillip had taken over, although unofficially at first because their mother was still the reigning queen. But unbeknownst to everyone, including her children, she had been hiding the fact that she was ill.

As a brother Phillip may have been a complete pain in the behind, but he was one hell of a fine leader. And it occurred to her that she'd never told him that. Or how proud she was of him.

"Our economy is thriving and property values are at an all-time high," she said.

"And the cost of living?"

"Higher on the coast, of course, but fairly reasonable inland."

"Decent tax incentives for local business owners?"

"Of course. Why do you ask?"

He shrugged. "Just curious."

He wasn't actually thinking of relocating there, was he? He did mention something about taking his company international. But would he go so far as to open an office here? And would that mean she would be seeing a lot more of him?

She honestly wasn't sure how she felt about that. It shouldn't have mattered at all. He was nothing to her now. At least, that's what she wanted to believe. And there was no point making assumptions.

"There it is," she told him gesturing out the window on her side as the hotel came into view, towering like a grand sentinel over the surrounding buildings.

He leaned over to see out her window, his body so close to hers she could feel heat emanating from him, smell the subtle yet familiar scent of his aftershave. And it took all of her restraint not to tense and shift away. And even more willpower not to reach out and touch him. Press her hand to his smooth jaw line. Bury her nose in the crook of his neck and breathe him in, the way she used to.

Instead she sat stock-still, hoping he couldn't feel the tension rolling off her like a turbulent ocean.

"I've seen photos," he said. "But they really don't do it justice, do they?"

"You can't truly appreciate it until you see it with your own eyes." The car pulled into the driveway at the hotel, and Sophie watched Alex's face. This was her favorite part of the tour. Watching the expressions of guests the first time they laid eyes on the structure and the scenic view. Set on the coast, mere steps from a pristine stretch of private beach, it was indeed like paradise. And she could see that Alex was genuinely impressed.

He finally sat back, and she felt as though she could breathe for the first time in minutes.

"The architecture is classic, but with the perfect balance of modern elements," he said. "I'm envious. I wish I had designed it."

"We were fortunate to find such a beautiful pre-existing building in the ideal location. Although renovations on the decor were extensive." She leaned forward and told her driver, "Take us to the service entrance in the back." She turned to Alex. "From there you can see the Houghton, and the land for the fitness center and spa."

The car pulled around the back and parked just outside the service door. As they climbed out, Alex slipped on a pair of Oakley sunglasses and followed her across the lot to the crumbling stone wall delineating their property from the Houghtons'. He moved with the grace and confidence of a man who knew exactly how good he looked and embraced it, without the vibe of arrogance she found common in men so physically appealing.

He seemed very comfortable in his own skin. But he always had.

"As you can see, we have a lot to work with as far as location," she said. "This was one of the first resort hotels to be built here. The Houghtons have owned this land for generations. Their ancestors can be traced back almost as far as the royal family."

He nodded, surveying the land, and she could practically see his mind working. He took off his sunglasses, shading his eyes from the sun with one hand as he gazed up at the structure that would soon be bulldozed to the ground. "It is a beautiful building. In the past few years, more than half of my business involves restoration, and if the Houghtons had taken better care of it, the structure might have been salvageable. But in its present condition…" He shook his head, a look of genuine regret on his face. "It's just not a cost-effective option."

"For many years now local businesses with qualifying historical buildings in the bay area have been offered grants to participate in a rejuvenation project. Unfortunately the Houghtons never applied."

"I guess you can't help people who don't want to be helped." He slipped his sunglasses back on and turned to her. "Why don't we head inside the Royal Inn."

"Of course." They walked to the back service entrance that led to the main kitchen. Although breakfast was over, and lunch still a few hours away, it was bustling with activity and teeming with delicious scents.

"Nice," Alex said. "Very modern."

"Only the best."

"Phillip tells me you're responsible for the kitchen renovations."

"Partially, yes."

"He also said that you're an accomplished chef."

Did he also mention that he disapproved? She wouldn't be at all surprised. "It's my one true passion. I studied in France."

"I remember that you used to be very passionate," he said, with that sizzling grin. Why was he so intent on trying to knock her off base? "That must have been after I met you. Culinary school, I mean."

She nodded. Although not long after. One more thing she could thank him for, in a roundabout way.

"I never would have imagined that your parents would just let you leave."

Normally they wouldn't have. But for the first time in her life, she'd had leverage. "Let's just say we bartered a deal."

"That must have been some deal."

For all the good it did her. After she came home, it was back to her royal duties. She should have known her parents would never let her have an actual career. And leave it to Phillip, despite his animosity toward their parents, to cling to the same archaic ideas.

"It's always been my dream to own a restaurant and run the kitchen." She looked around, at the interior that was almost solely her design, the appliances she had ordered. The menu she herself had supplied.

She may never get the opportunity to use it, but this was *her* kitchen. "I guess this is the closest I'll ever get."

Someone dropped a pan in the kitchen, and at the loud clang that vibrated through the room, her bodyguard was instantly at her side. She waved him away, and he immediately backed off.

Alex looked as apprehensive as he was impressed. "How many bodyguards normally escort you?"

"Depending on the occasion, members of the royal family never leave the palace without at least one armed escort. Except Ethan, but he's the only exception." She nodded toward the bodyguard who now trailed them by a watchful ten paces. "And Maurice is one of our most lethal. Isn't that right, Maurice?"

Maurice cracked just the hint of a dangerous-looking grin.

"You don't find it unnerving to have someone constantly following you?" Alex asked.

"I'm so used to it, I barely notice him there. And it's a necessity."

"Have there been threats against you?"

She was surprised to see a look of genuine concern on his face. Did he honestly still care about her after all these years?

"Not me personally," she assured him. "Or Phillip. But you can never be too careful. There was an attempted assassination on our father's father many years ago. And our father, King Frederick, had his share of disgruntled citizens. He was a very arrogant and, I'm sorry to say, self-serving leader."

Sadly, her father's methods and ideals had turned Sophie against the entire idea of a monarchy. Only since Phillip had taken over had her feelings begun to change, and it had been a gradual transformation.

"Let's move on," she said, gesturing to the kitchen door.

They walked through the service hallway out into the main wing, and while her appearances in public often caused something of a spectacle, as they toured the lobby with it's elegant decor and grand water display, she noticed that many eyes were instead focused on Alex. And why wouldn't they be? He was the type of man that other men viewed with envy and women eyed with appreciation. She wasn't the jealous type, but under different circumstances…

Circumstances that would never happen in a million years, she reminded herself.

Five

After a walkthrough of the guest rooms and facilities, and lunch at *Les Régals du Rois,* the hotel's newly acclaimed French restaurant, Alex was thoroughly impressed by the Royal Inn. It was both elegant and elite, but tailored to the common traveler, as well as the privileged, businesspeople and vacationers alike.

In terms of size, this project wasn't what he would consider significant; but in terms of notoriety, he'd hit pay dirt.

"So, what do you think of our hotel?" Sophie asked, when they were in the car and on their way back to the palace.

"I think the royal family has one hell of a sound investment."

She actually smiled. And here he'd been wondering if she'd forgotten how. And it was evident that she was quite proud of what the royal family had accomplished.

"I'm no hotel expert, but there is one thing I would consider," he said.

"Yes, please." She sat forward, looking genuinely interested. "You probably know far more than I do."

Her reaction made him smile. The women in his life, especially lately, seemed to think they knew everything, it was refreshing to meet one who wasn't afraid to admit her weaknesses.

"In researching the bay area, I noticed that there are no hotels equipped to handle a conference of any significant size. You may want to look into expanding your facilities."

"And you think that would bring more business?"

"It's an untapped market, so I think it would be worth looking into."

"I'll mention it to Phillip and Ethan."

Finally, he'd said something that hadn't elicited a frown or a disapproving look. But when it came to business, he didn't mess around. But now maybe it was time to shake things up a bit.

"So, what are we doing next?" he asked. "A ride up the coast?"

"That will have to wait. Phillip set aside time this afternoon so you and he can catch up."

Although he looked forward to spending time with his friend, Alex couldn't deny feeling a little disappointed. He'd made progress with Sophie today, managed to chip away at her resolve. She wasn't so tense around him. So quick to distrust. At this rate, in a few days he would have her right where he wanted her.

But there was no rush, he reminded himself. He had two weeks. Plenty of time to get what he wanted. And honestly, this vacation was exactly what he needed. He couldn't recall the last time he'd felt so relaxed, a morning when he woke not dreading the day.

"Thanks for taking the time to shuttle me around," he told Sophie.

She shrugged. "It's what I do."

"And you do it well, Your Highness."

Her brow furrowed and she studied him for several seconds, then she shook her head.

"What?" he asked.

"Nothing."

"It's obviously not nothing," he said, playing dumb. "Why did you look at me like that?"

"Just drop it."

"You need to learn how to take a compliment, Princess."

Her jaw tensed almost imperceptibly and there was an edge to her tone. "Maybe you should word your compliments so they're not so…"

"So what?"

"Suggestive."

He laughed. "Telling you that you're good at your job? How is that suggestive?"

He could see her struggling with her composure. She wanted to explode, but he knew she wouldn't give him the satisfaction. What she didn't realize is that he felt more satisfaction watching her struggle than if she'd blown up in his face.

"Okay," he admitted. "Maybe it was a little suggestive, but, Princess, you are awfully fun to tease. I take it you don't get that very often."

"No, I don't"

He grinned. "Well, you'll just have to get used to it, I guess."

She made a quiet huffing noise. "It's not as if I have a choice."

She had no idea. "You shouldn't take life so seriously, Your Highness."

Her expression darkened. "You know nothing about me, Alex."

He knew she was spoiled and arrogant. And let's not forget entitled. And although she was obviously used to getting her way, she had no idea who she was up against.

And he was having far too much fun breaking her spirit.

It was barely three in the afternoon, but when Sophie returned to her residence, she felt as though she had just endured one of the longest days of her life.

She didn't blame Alex for feeling bitter about their past, but the man was sending so many mixed signals that she was getting whiplash.

The car dropped her at her front door, and Wilson met her in the vestibule.

"Prince Ethan rang while you were gone, Miss. He asked that you contact him immediately upon your return home. He said it's urgent."

She sighed quietly. The last thing she needed was more undue drama in her day, but Ethan wasn't one to exaggerate. If he said it was important, it most likely was.

"Thank you, Wilson. I'll ring him right now."

Using the phone in the study, she dialed his number and he answered on the first ring.

"Could I come by and speak with you?" he asked, and he did indeed sound rattled. Which wasn't at all like him.

Her first thought was that Lizzy had taken a turn for the worse.

"Of course. Is something wrong?"

"Not exactly. I'm at the palace, so I'll be there in a few minutes."

She barely had time to use the powder room and freshen her makeup before she heard the throaty growl of his engine out front, then the sound of the bell announcing his presence.

Rather than wait for Wilson, she opened the door herself. "That was quick."

He tagged her with a quick peck on the cheek on his way in. In his hand he clutched a manila envelope. "I could use a drink."

Although Ethan was one of the most laid-back

men she'd ever known, he was visibly agitated. "Well then, let's go to the study," she said.

He followed her there and watched while she poured him two fingers of her best scotch straight up, then poured herself a glass of white wine.

She handed him his drink. "What's so urgent that it couldn't wait?"

He took a long swallow, then asked, "Does the name Richard Thornsby ring a bell?"

"If you're referring to the Richard Thornsby who was prime minister of Morgan Isle when our father's reign began, then yes, of course I know who he is." But the question was, why did Ethan know? Thornsby had been dead for years. And what did it matter?

"The way I understand it, he and our father didn't exactly see eye to eye," Ethan said.

"That's putting it mildly. They were mortal enemies."

"Did he ever tell you why?"

"I would never dare ask. We weren't even permitted to so much as utter his name in the palace. Even after his death he was never mentioned. I just assumed it was because they had vast differences of opinion."

"I read that our father had him ousted from his position, which more or less ruined him politically."

"King Frederick was ruthless. He had no tolerance for anyone who didn't see things his way." She couldn't help wondering where he was going with this. "Why are you suddenly so interested in our father's political dealings?"

"I'm getting to that." He took another swallow of his drink and set the empty glass down on the table. "Thornsby and his wife were killed a couple of years later."

"Yes. A car accident."

"But there was one survivor of the crash."

"That's right. Their ten-year-old daughter. I believe her name is Melissa."

"It is. Melissa Angelica Thornsby. When her parents died, she was sent to live with relatives in the States."

"If you say so. Like I told you, their names weren't spoken in our home. And I mean, *never.*"

"I think I know why. And it has nothing to do with political diversity."

"I'm not following you." And the curiosity of what could possibly be in the envelope was gnawing away at her patience.

"I think their differences were more…*personal* in nature."

All this ambiguity was getting on her nerves. "Ethan, would you please just say what you have to say?"

"Our father's reputation as a womanizer is no secret, so it stands to reason that there could be more of us out there."

"Us?"

"Royal heirs. Illegitimate ones, like me. With Phillip's permission I've been looking into it. Yesterday I was in the attic going through our father's things and I found these." He finally handed her the envelope.

She opened it up and dumped the contents out on the table. It was mostly magazine articles and newspaper clippings. And it didn't take long to determine their theme. They were all about Thornsby's daughter, Melissa. "I don't get it."

"Think about it, Sophie. Why would our father collect a bunch of articles about the daughter of his most despised rival?"

He couldn't possibly mean what she thought he meant. "Ethan, that's ridiculous."

He picked out one of the articles that had a snapshot of Melissa. "Look at her, Sophie. The dark hair, the shape of her face."

She couldn't deny there were striking similarities. "You honestly think she's our sister?"

"I think it's a definite possibility."

If their father had an affair with the Prime Minister's wife, that would certainly explain their ill will toward each other. And sadly, given their father's reputation, it was not only very possible, but altogether likely.

"And if she is family?" Sophie asked.

"If she is, we might have a huge problem."

"Well, yes, more scandal that the royal family really doesn't need."

"It's worse than that."

"How much worse?"

"She was born the same year as Phillip. One month *before* him. And as I'm sure you well know that the king's firstborn, male or female, inherits the crown."

Oh, yeah, that was pretty bad.

Sophie's heart fisted into a knot. "So if she is our sister, then she would be the rightful leader. Not Phillip."

"It seems that way."

She couldn't even imagine what that would do to Phillip, or what it would mean for their country. "Does Phillip know?"

Ethan shook his head. "I wanted to talk to you first, get your take on this."

Her first instinct was to burn what proof Ethan had already gathered and sweep the charred remains under the nearest rug. But what if it was true and Melissa Thornsby really was their sister? Had Sophie denied Ethan as her brother, she would have lost out on what had become one of her closest and dearest relationships. How could they deny a member of their family?

But there was so much at stake.

"So, do we tell Phillip?" Ethan asked.

"I think for now we should keep this quiet and not say anything to Phillip until we have some proof. There's no reason to upset him over nothing."

"I'd like to talk with Charles and ask him to find out what he can about her."

"I think that's a good idea. We can trust him to be discreet. We should also have him look into what can be done if she *is* an heir and decides she wants to question Phillip's reign."

"If Phillip finds out that we went behind his back on this, he'll be furious."

"When the time comes, I'll deal with Phillip. You just worry about finding out if she's an heir."

"This could be a real mess, Sophie. Especially if she harbors any ill will against the royal family."

Which was entirely possible. "We'll worry about that when we know a bit more about who she is. If she is the rightful heir, with any luck she'll have no interest in the crown."

She wanted to believe that, but lately, it seemed as though nothing was ever that simple.

Pleading a headache, which, after her conversation with Ethan was the wholehearted truth, Sophie was spared dinner that night with their "guest." Unfortunately she had no choice but to spend the entire next day with Alex, touring the science center and natural history museum. And even though this was usually her favorite part of any tour, she had so many other things on her mind that she was distracted. She found herself rushing through the exhibits. Or trying to at least. Alex seemed content to take his time. She'd seen snails in the garden move faster.

And why did he have to stand so close all the time? It seemed he was always right there. *Touching* her. Not any kind of overt groping. Even he was more subtle than that. Just a brush of his arm or the bump of his shoulder. Did he have no concept of personal space?

And if it was so awful, why did her skin break out in goose bumps every time he made contact? Why did she shiver with awareness?

And God help her did he smell good. The familiar, ideal blend of his aftershave, shampoo and his unique scent. Every time he was close, she had to fight the urge to bury her face against his neck and breathe him in. How could she loathe someone so, yet lust after him like a hormonally challenged adolescent?

All day he seemed intent on testing her patience, and it was working. She felt as if she were being pulled in ten different directions at once.

By the time they reached the palace gate, she was so edgy and out of sorts that her left eye had begun to twitch. She asked the driver to please drop her at home first, and when they pulled up to her residence, she was so desperate to be free of the cloying confines of the backseat that she had to sit on her hands to keep herself from clawing the car door open, and instead waited for her bodyguard.

"Well," she said, turning to Alex. "It was a pleasant day. I'll see you Thursday."

She was almost home free, with one foot out the door, when Alex asked, "Aren't you going to invite me in for a drink?"

She closed her eyes and sighed quietly. *Don't let him see you squirm.*

The most disturbing thing about his request is that she actually wanted him to come in, which was precisely why she couldn't allow it.

She turned to him. "Today isn't convenient."

He studied her for a moment, then smiled and said, "Oh, I get it."

Every fiber of her being was screaming that he was baiting her. Despite that, she couldn't stop herself from saying, "You get what?"

"I see the way you react when I'm around. The way you look at me, the way you shudder when we touch."

Shudder? Shiver a little, maybe, and not *every* time.

But to deny it would only give him exactly what he wanted. An argument.

Gathering the last strands of her patience, she fixed a bored look on her face. "And your point is…?"

"Simple. You want me, and you don't trust yourself to be alone with me."

He was clever. No matter what she did now, invite him in or tell him to get lost, she would be giving Alex what he wanted. A reaction. And whether he actually believed that or was just baiting her, she had the uneasy suspicion that he might be right. She was still attracted to Alex on a deep, visceral level. If he kissed her again, against her will or not, she was afraid this time she might not stop him.

She sat there with one foot still in the car and the other on the driveway, unsure of what to do.

"Well," he asked, looking more amused than impatient.

"There's no winning this one, is there?" she said. "I'm damned if I do and damned if I don't."

"You seem to believe that I have some evil ulterior motives, Your Highness. But has it occurred to you that maybe I'd just like a little time to get to know you? So you could maybe get to know me? I'm not a bad guy. Honestly."

She couldn't decide which was worse. Men with ulterior motives she could handle. They were refreshingly predictable and easy to deconstruct. It was the sincere ones she had trouble with.

Probably because they were such a rare anomaly.

"We just spent two days together," she reminded him. "How much time do you need?"

"Maybe I'd like a little time *without* the bodyguard hanging on our every word."

There lies the problem, she mused. She *needed* her bodyguard around hanging on their every word. And not just to protect her from Alex. That would be too easy.

She needed someone to protect her from herself.

Six

For the first time since he'd arrived, Alex saw a brief but very real flash of vulnerability in Sophie's face. And he almost felt guilty for manipulating her.

Almost.

He hadn't gotten this far in life by being soft. Unfortunately, neither had she. Which is why he figured a few drinks would probably take the edge off. Loosen her up a little.

But he had the distinct feeling he was one step away from pushing too far, so he tried a different angle. The pity card. When all else failed, women could never resist a man who shared his feelings.

"I happen to know for a fact that Phillip is away

today," he told her. "And the truth is, I don't feel like spending the rest of the afternoon alone."

He could see the arrow hit its mark. Her eyes warmed and the hard edges of her expression softened almost imperceptibly.

She considered that for a moment, then sighed quietly, and he knew he had her.

"I had planned to take a walk on the grounds," she finally said. "You could join me, I suppose. But then afterward I really have things to do."

He should have known she would suggest a compromise. That way she was giving in without actually relinquishing control.

She was good, no doubt about it. But he was better.

He grinned and said, "You've got yourself a deal, Princess."

She got out of the car and he climbed out behind her. The sun was high in the cloudless blue, its rays relentlessly intense. It seemed like a better day to lay around in the shade than take a walk, but he wasn't in any position to argue.

The bodyguard looked from Alex to Sophie and asked, "Will you be needing me, Your Highness?"

What did he think Alex was going to do? Kidnap her? Drag her off the grounds on foot?

He looked over at Sophie, and when he saw her expression, thought for a second that she just might tell him to join them. But after a slight pause she shook her head and said, "You can go."

Alex followed her to the door, mesmerized by

the liquid grace that propelled her forward. The hypnotizing sway of her hips. She was wearing one of those sheer, gauzy numbers that conformed to her figure. Hugged her in all the right places. The sharp tug of arousal low in his gut was undeniable and intense.

They reached the threshold and the door swung open.

"Miss," Wilson said, bowing his head as they stepped inside. Alex could swear the man shot him a disapproving look. Her staff was obviously protective of her, and he had the feeling their concern was as much personal as it was professional. Which had him wondering, if she was as spoiled and manipulative as she used to be, why would they hold her in such high regard?

Or maybe she reserved that behavior for her lovers.

"Wilson, will you show our guest into the study and pour him a drink?"

"Of course," Wilson said.

She turned to Alex. "I just need to change. I'll only be a minute or two."

"Take your time," he said, watching her climb the steps, the way she seemed to almost float, as light as air. Damn she was sexy, and he was looking forward to getting his hands on her again, to see just how much she'd changed over the past ten years.

"Mr. Rutledge," Wilson said with a distinct note of disapproval in his voice. And when Alex turned to him, he gestured toward the study door. "After you."

When they were in the study Wilson asked, "What can I get you, sir?"

"Mineral water with lemon, if it's not too much trouble."

Wilson crossed the room to the bar, and Alex made himself comfortable on the sofa. "Have you worked for Princess Sophie very long?" he asked.

"I've been with the royal family for more than forty years."

"That's a long time."

"Yes, sir."

"You take care of Sophie."

"Yes, sir, I do. And it's not a task I take lightly."

Alex couldn't escape the feeling that he was being judged not by an employee, but a father considering the motives of a potential son-in-law.

And because Alex had always been one to face his adversaries head-on, he asked very bluntly. "You don't trust me, do you?"

Wilson walked over to the couch and handed him his drink. "I've found, sir, that paranoia is often the result when one has something to hide."

Oh, ouch. A direct hit. Were he a weaker man, he might have retreated. And while some considered him reckless for it, Jonah in particular, he never backed down from a challenge. Even when the odds weren't necessarily in his favor. "And what is it that you think I'm hiding?"

"I couldn't say, but it's quite obvious you have some sort of agenda."

"And you feel the need to protect her from me?"

Wilson smiled and there was an undeniable twinkle of amusement in his eyes. "Oh, no, sir. Her Highness doesn't need protecting. Not from you or anyone else. And if you believe she does, that will be your downfall."

They would just see about that, wouldn't they?

Before he could manufacture a snappy comeback, Sophie appeared in the doorway. She had changed into jogging shorts, a tank top and athletic shoes, and her hair was pulled back in a ponytail.

And she still managed to look superior and elegant.

"Heading to the gym?" Alex asked.

"Going on a walk," she said. "I walk briskly for an hour every day."

"I was thinking more along the lines of a casual stroll."

She shrugged. "So don't go with me."

It was pushing eighty-five degrees outside, and dressed the way he was, he risked heat stroke. Not to mention ruining his four-hundred-dollar Brazilian leather loafers. But he couldn't exactly back out now, could he? And he didn't bother to ask for time to change, since he already knew what the answer would be.

Wilson cleared his throat. "If there's nothing else you need, Your Highness, I should check on dinner."

"Of course," Sophie said, dismissing him with a nod and a smile.

On his way out, Wilson wore a polite smile, but

as he glanced Alex's way, his eyes clearly said, *I told you so.*

Sophie stepped behind the bar and grabbed two bottles of water from the refrigerator, then looked Alex up and down, said, "I don't think one is going to cut it," and grabbed one more.

She was probably right.

"Are you ready?" she asked.

At this point he didn't have much choice. And damned if Wilson wasn't right. He had underestimated her.

But that wasn't a mistake he would be making again.

Despite the heat, and his inappropriate clothing, Sophie had to admit that Alex did a pretty good job keeping up with her. Not that he wasn't feeling the heat. Sweat poured from his face and soaked the back of his silk shirt. He had already guzzled one bottle of water and was a third of the way through his second.

That's what he got for messing with her. As she'd heard Wilson say, he shouldn't underestimate her. He was clever, but she had a few tricks up her sleeve, too.

She led him along the lawn paths, even though typically, on a day as hot as this one, she would have taken refuge on the paths in the woods under the dense canopy of leaves. Someone up there must have been looking out for him though, because a line of dark clouds rolled in shortly after they began walking, dampening the sun's relentless afternoon glare.

"Looks like rain," he said, gazing up at the sky.

Then he looked back at her residence, a good quarter mile from their current location. "Maybe we should head back."

Nice try. "Afraid you'll melt?"

"I'm already melting," he said wryly. "I just don't want to get stuck out here during a storm."

"This is the dry season. It hardly ever rains. The clouds will most likely blow right over us." Although they did look rather dark and ominous and the wind was picking up.

"It doesn't look like it's going to roll over us," he pressed.

She rolled her eyes. "Don't be such a baby."

"I don't know about you, but I don't relish the idea of getting struck by lightning."

"Even if it does rain, these storms blow over quickly. I'm sure we're perfectly safe." Just in case, she altered her direction so they were walking in the direction of the woods.

They barely made it another ten paces when a fat, cold drop of rain landed on her cheek. Then another splashed on her forearm.

"See," Alex said, holding a hand out to catch a drop in his palm. "Those are raindrops."

"A little rain isn't going to kill us. In fact, you look as if you could use some cooling off."

He opened his mouth to reply just as a bolt of lightning streaked across the sky and a deafening crack of thunder drowned out whatever sarcastic snipe he'd been about to fling her way.

She screeched in surprise and they both instinctively ducked. In the next instant, the heavens seemed to open like a floodgate and rain came down in a waterfall. Big, fat, cold drops, soaking her to the skin in a matter of seconds.

"Head for the woods!" she yelled, and they both took off running in that direction. Probably not the best place to be in a thunderstorm, but if they didn't find cover, they risked drowning.

In the thirty seconds it took to reach the marginal cover of the trees, she felt, and probably looked, like a drowned rat.

"I'm officially cooled off," he said, slicking back his hair. It was drenched and leaking water down his face and his clothes were plastered to his body like a second skin.

And, *oh,* what a body it was. She could see every sculpted ridge of muscle in his chest and arms, his slim waist and muscular thighs. He was bigger than he'd been in college. Even more perfect, if that was possible.

Suddenly she wasn't feeling cold anymore. There was a delicious warmth building inside her that had absolutely nothing to do with the weather and everything to do with the man standing in front of her.

Fight it, Sophie.

"So much for it just *blowing over*," Alex said.

"Yeah. Oops." She shivered and pulled the band from her drooping ponytail, twisting the rain from her hair. "You're the one who insisted on going with me."

He squeezed the excess rain from his shirt. "Yet I can't help but think you did this on purpose."

"You think I can control the weather? I'm good, Alex, but I'm not that good."

Only after the words were out, when Alex's eyes locked on hers, deep and piercing and full of lust, did she realize how that sounded. But it was too late to take it back. She wasn't even sure if she wanted to.

"That's not the way I remember it," he said, his voice husky. His eyes slipped lower, to her lips, then her throat, then lower still, and she knew without looking that her nipples were two hard points poking through the wet fabric of her sports bra and tank. She couldn't help noticing that he, too, was looking a bit chilly. On top anyway. Down below, she could swear that things were looking rather…lofty.

He lifted his eyes to hers, blue and piercing, and she practically shuddered with awareness. He took a step closer and every cell in her body went on high alert.

A drop of rain leaked out of her hair and rolled down her cheek. Alex reached up, almost absently, and wiped it away with the pad of his thumb. He might as well have brushed that thumb between her thighs because that's where the sensation seemed to settle.

She had no doubt that the end result of this situation was going to be a kiss. It was inevitable. And the only thing worse than kissing him would be letting him make the first move, allowing him to take control. So she didn't give him the chance. She grabbed the front of his shirt, curling her fingers in the sodden fabric, tugged him to her, and pressed her lips to his.

If he was surprised by her advances, it didn't take him long to collect himself. He groaned and wove a hand through her wet and tangled hair, pulled her against him. She parted her lips for him, invited him, and when his tongue touched hers, she went weak all over.

They feasted on...no, *devoured* each other. But it wasn't enough. She wanted him closer, *deeper.* She felt as though she were starving, that she'd been slowly withering away the past ten years and the only thing that could nourish her back to life was his touch. His hands on her skin. And that need seemed to cancel out whatever was left of her rational side.

She tore at the front of his shirt, wanting, no *needing,* bare skin to touch, to run her hands over. She felt buttons give way and heard the fabric tear. His skin was warm and wet and she could feel his heart hammering wildly in his chest.

Alex backed her against the nearest tree, pinning her to the rough bark with the full length of his body. Sophie gasped at the sharp sting, but it was both pain and pleasure. For the first time in God knows how long, she felt whole again, and it frightened her half to death. This was just like the first time. Passionate to the point of feeling almost desperate. A deep yearning to connect.

It was just starting to get good when he tore his

mouth from hers, his breath rasping out in harsh bursts, and said, "Listen."

Did he hear someone coming? She stopped to listen, but she didn't hear a thing other than the quiet sounds of the forest. "What?"

"It stopped raining," he said.

Yeah, so?

He eased away from her. "We should head back."

Head back? Was he *serious?*

For a moment she was too stunned to reply. He obviously wanted this just as much as she did. He'd been leading up to this for days. So why the sudden change of heart?

Then she realized exactly what was happening. This was just a game to him. He'd planned this all along. She should have known. He obviously got some kind of warped satisfaction from getting her all worked up then shooting her down.

And shame on her for falling for it. For letting him get the best of her.

And he could be damned sure it wouldn't happen again.

Seven

In the blink of an eye, Sophie's expression went from one of confusion to barely contained rage. And all Alex could do was follow her as she turned and walked purposely back in the direction they'd come, toward her house.

He'd had Sophie right where he wanted her, but when the time came to seal the deal, he couldn't go through with it. It wasn't supposed to happen this way. She wasn't supposed to make the first move. And he wasn't supposed to feel this deep sense of…something. An emotion so foreign he couldn't identify it. Something more than desire or lust. He felt…whole.

Complete.

And that was just sentimental bull. She'd caught him off guard, that was all.

Sophie was moving so fast she was practically jogging, and any second he expected her to break into full run.

"You want to slow down?" he asked, his feet squishing in shoes swimming with at least an inch of water.

She didn't answer. She just kept chugging along, and damn, she was fast. But he was faster.

He caught up and clamped a hand around her upper arm. "Slow down, Sophie."

She jerked free. "Why should I? I'm do exactly as you suggested. Heading back."

"Jesus, you're stubborn," he muttered.

She stopped so abruptly, swinging around to face him, that he nearly plowed right into her.

"I'm *stubborn,*" she ground out through clenched teeth, unleashing the full wrath of her anger.

He knew she had a temper, but damn.

He took a step back, for fear that if he got too close, she might take a swing at him. "I just want to talk to you."

"What for? You already won."

"Won what?"

"This juvenile little game you've been playing with me."

She was right. It was a game. And he should be enjoying this, basking in the glow of defeat. Instead he felt like a slime.

It would seem that the joke was on him.

He just needed a chance to regroup, to get things back on track. To shake off these feelings of guilt.

And to perform a bit of damage control.

"Do you feel better now that you've gotten your revenge?" she asked. "Do you feel vindicated?"

"Sophie, listen to yourself," he said calmly. "I kiss you and you threaten to have me arrested for assault, then you kiss me, and you get mad when I put on the brakes? And you accuse *me* of playing games?"

"You're absolutely right," she said, even though it was obvious she was just agreeing with him to shut him up. "Case closed."

He opened his mouth to argue, but she held up a hand to shush him. "I'm going home now. *Do not* follow me."

Even though he was tempted to follow her anyway, push her just a little further, instinct told him to back off. He changed direction and headed toward the palace instead.

Sophie charged into Phillip's outer office, stunning his secretary into silence before she could even try to stop her from flinging open Phillip's office door. And Phillip was there, sitting behind his desk, despite the fact that Alex said he was away this afternoon.

Another lie. No big surprise.

Phillip looked her up and down, taking in her dripping, tangled hair and soaked clothes. "What the hell happened to you?"

She held up the agenda for Alex's visit and flung

it onto his desk. "Find someone else to babysit your friend. I'm finished."

He calmly folded his hands, looking almost amused. "I could swear we already had this discussion."

"Well, we're having it *again*."

He sat back in his chair and for a long moment only studied her. Then he shook his head. "No, you're going to do it, as planned."

She struggled to maintain an iota of control. "*No*, I'm not."

"You're sure about that?"

She parked her hands on her hips and glared at him. "Don't I *sound* sure?"

"Fine. Then from this moment forward you'll be cut out of the business. The only duties you'll have will be your royal ones."

Her mouth fell open. "Are you joking?"

"Do I look like I'm joking?"

She was so angry and frustrated that she felt like stomping her feet.

"You can see that I'm miserable. Are you *trying* to torture me?"

"What I'm trying to do is teach you that this is a business and you can't pick and choose what you will or won't do on a whim. Because what that says to me is that you cannot be counted on."

"This is different."

"*How* is it different? Give me one good reason why I should grant your request."

She couldn't tell him the real reason. And the best she could come up with was, "He makes me… uncomfortable."

One of Phillip's eyebrows rose a notch. "He's behaved inappropriately?"

Alex *had* kissed her his first day here, but to be fair, she'd been the one to make the first move today in the woods, so they were kind of even in the inappropriate-behavior department. "Not exactly."

Phillip sat up a little straighter in his chair. "If he has, friend or not, I'll fire him from the project immediately and send him back to the U.S. on the first available flight. Just say the word."

She may have been furious with Alex, but she also didn't want to come between him and Phillip. Not personally or professionally. "He hasn't done anything inappropriate. I just…I don't like him."

"So, what, he doesn't kiss your royal behind, and therefore you can't tolerate him?"

"Phillip!"

"That's what I figured." He relaxed back into his chair, a wry grin curling his mouth. "Sophie, do you think I like everyone I have to work with? That's just business. Get used to it."

She was no stranger to the concept. Had he forgotten the countless "guests" she had catered to and shuttled all over the island? They ranged from polite and friendly to odd and unusual and some who were just downright creepy. And she'd never complained. At least, not *too* much. And she always did what was expected of her. She would think that just this once he could cut her a little slack.

But then he wouldn't be Phillip if he did that.

"Fine," she said, smoothing back her knotted hair as best she could. She must have looked positively dreadful. She could have at least taken the time to change into dry clothes and run a brush through her hair. Of course, if she'd been at all rational, she never would have come to see him in the first place.

"You might want to rethink the new look," he said, amusement dancing in his eyes. He did that a lot now. Smiling, laughing. Before Hannah came into his life he was a much darker person. She was glad he was happy. She only wished he weren't so determined to make her miserable instead.

She looked down at her ensemble. "What, you don't like it?"

"Got caught in the rain during your walk?"

"How'd you guess?"

"I was on my way in from a meeting a few minutes before you barged in here, and I ran into Alex who was in pretty much the same condition."

So, Phillip *had* been away at a meeting. At least Alex hadn't lied about that. She wondered if Phillip had noticed that Alex's shirt had been suspiciously divested of its buttons. "I guess he got caught in the rain, too."

"I figured you would know that since, according to Alex, you were walking together."

She couldn't help but wonder what else Alex had told him. And rather than try to come up with a plausible explanation for her sudden memory loss, she didn't say anything at all. And he let it slide.

"So, we're in agreement?" he asked.

"We're in agreement."

"You're not going to barge in here in a day or two with the same demands."

"You won't hear another word out of me about it." And at the very least, she had tomorrow to herself. A full day to recover before having to play babysitter again.

"Good."

"I should go change."

"Please do."

"I'll see you later."

She was almost to the door when he called out to her. "By the way, I forgot to mention, I had to cancel our golf trip tomorrow morning. Urgent business. So Alex is in your capable hands for the day. With any luck I can squeeze in an evening round."

So much for her day off. Would she ever catch a break?

"Is that a problem?"

She forced a smile, when what she really felt like doing was groaning, and said, "No, no problem."

"Good. I've already told Alex, and he said he'll meet you in the foyer tomorrow morning. The usual time."

"Very well. It's short notice, but I'm sure I can come up with something for us to do."

"He said he would like a relaxing day, so I took

the liberty of suggesting a day out on the yacht. He's quite looking forward to it."

Hours stuck together on a boat. She could hardly wait. "Even better. I'll call the marina and have everything prepared."

"It's already been done."

"Good."

"Also, we're taking Alex to the country club for dinner and wondered if you could watch Frederick. Maybe until eleven or so?"

"Of course." That at least wouldn't be a hardship. She adored her nephew.

"Hannah will call and let you know what time we plan to leave."

"Anything else?" she asked.

"No, I believe that's it."

"You know, I'm proud of you, Phillip."

"I beg your pardon."

"I said, I'm proud of you."

He narrowed his eyes at her. "What do you want?"

She smiled. "Nothing at all."

He looked skeptical, as though he wasn't sure he could believe her.

"Really," she assured him. "I just wanted you to know."

"Well then…thank you."

She turned to leave, but he called to her just before she reached the door.

"You know that the things I say and do are because I care."

"I know."

"Have fun tomorrow." He turned to his computer and started tapping away at the keyboard, his less-than-subtle way to dismiss her.

But as she was closing the door behind her she glanced back and saw that he had an amused, almost quirky grin and she couldn't shake the feeling that Phillip knew more than he was letting on.

All the way back to her residence Sophie mulled over in her head how she planned to handle the rest of Alex's visit. They simply couldn't go on with the way things had been these first two days. She would be loony by week's end. There had to be some way to fix this, some sort of compromise in which she would maintain control, of course.

Despite knowing what a pest Alex could be, she was still surprised to see him sitting on her porch step when she returned to her residence. And even though the idea of another argument was utterly exhausting, leaving this unresolved to ferment and fester wasn't high on her list of fun options, either. So, rather than storm past him into the house, she took a seat next to him.

He had changed into dry clothes—and a shirt with buttons—and sat slightly hunched with his arms draped over his knees. He looked unassuming and maybe a little tired. And he was so handsome, so physically perfect in every way that a hollow ache settled in her heart.

For several minutes they sat together in silence, then he finally said, "I feel as though I owe you an apology, but I'm not really sure what I'm apologizing for."

That was probably the most honest thing he'd said since this nightmare of a week had begun. Clueless, but honest nonetheless.

They had spent a total of two days together, yet she felt that she *knew* him. And she felt she barely knew him at all. Nothing about this made any sense.

"If it's any consolation," she said. "I feel the same way."

He shot her a grin. "Then technically, our feelings should just what, cancel out each other?"

"If only life worked that way, the world would be a much simpler place."

"Amen to that."

She sighed and hugged her legs, resting her chin on her knees. "It's not my fault, you know."

He looked over at her. "What isn't your fault?"

"Your marriage. The fact that it was so bad."

"Did I say it was?"

"Not in so many words, but it's obvious you blame me. Or you're just bitter at the entire gender and I'm an easy target."

A frown furrowed the space between his brows. "I'd considered that as a definite possibility."

Again, very honest. Maybe that was the key to solving their problem. Maybe, rather than ignoring this undercurrent of tension, this unfinished business between them, it would be more productive to just lay all their cards on the table and settle this once and for all.

Easier said than done. Baring her soul had never been one of her strengths. She had been groomed since birth to hold her feelings inside. To never show weakness. And right now, she'd never felt more vulnerable in her life.

But she had to at least try.

She took a deep breath and blew it out. Here goes nothing.

"I did love you, Alex, and I wanted to marry you. But believe me when I say I did you a favor by ending it. It was too…big. Bigger than either of us was prepared for. The sacrifices we would have had to make…" She shook her head. "We just would have ended up resenting each other."

He shrugged. "I guess we'll never know."

That was just the thing. She *did* know. She'd seen it time and time again. "I'm sorry for hurting you. But I honestly felt as though I didn't have a choice."

"You did what you felt was right. I can't really fault you for that, can I? I just would have liked the opportunity to make the choice myself."

He could fault her if he wanted to. If he wanted to hold a grudge. But she hoped he wouldn't. She would like them to be able to get past this. To be friends.

"As far as my marriage goes," he said, "I'm the only one to blame. I may have been pressured by my family, but no one held a gun to my head. The truth is, I took the easy way out. Or at least, at the time it seemed easy."

In a way, she was guilty of the same thing. Ending things with Alex had been so much easier than sticking around and trying to make it work. Surely they would have had a few good years before it all fell apart. At the time she'd felt that by ending it sooner rather than later, she had been giving each of them a chance to find happiness with someone else. How could she have known neither of them would take it?

"I ended it badly," she said. "I should have called or written, given you some explanation. I was just so afraid."

"Afraid of what?"

"That if I heard your voice, I would change my mind. Or that you would talk me out of it."

"I guess you did what you had to."

"Think we'll ever get past it?"

He looked over at her, the hint of a grin tugging at the corner of his mouth. "I think it's a definite possibility."

"There's that other problem, too."

"Which problem is that?"

She hugged her legs tighter. "The sexual tension."

He shrugged. "I don't have a problem with that."

"Come on, Alex. You have to admit it's getting… *tedious*."

"Okay," he conceded. "A little, maybe."

"We're basically stuck together, and quite frankly I'm tired of feeling so…edgy all the time. It would be nice if we could enjoy our time together." The instant the words left her mouth, she had a sudden and brilliant idea. It was absolutely ingenious!

"Uh-oh," he said, narrowing his eyes at her. "You look as though you've just had a lightbulb moment."

"I did. I don't know why I didn't think of it before."

"Why do I get the feeling I'm not going to like this?"

"On the contrary, I think you'll agree it's the only logical course of action."

"Okay," he said, looking skeptical. "Let's have it."

"I think, Alex, that I should sleep with you."

Eight

Alex's brows rose with surprise. "Say again?"

"Think about it," Sophie said. "After all this time, we're both wondering what it would be like."

"I am?"

She pinned him with a disbelieving look.

"Okay," he admitted. "I am."

"So maybe we should find out."

"And you think if we make love—"

"Sex, Alex, not love." Love had nothing, and would never have, anything to do with sex. "This is just…*chemistry.*"

"My apologies. You think if we have *sex,* we won't be tense around each other anymore?"

"Exactly." In fact, the more she thought about it, the more logical the idea seemed.

"What if it doesn't?" he asked.

"Why wouldn't it? It's not as if our feelings toward each other are anything other than…"

"Chemistry?"

"Sexual *curiosity.*"

"So, if I had just had sex with you today in the woods, we wouldn't even be having this conversation?"

He folded his arms across his chest and studied her, brow furrowed. "I don't know about this."

"What do you mean, you don't know?" It was completely logical. What sane man would pass up an offer like that?

He shrugged. "It just sounds a little too easy."

"No, it doesn't. It's the perfect plan."

"You say that now, but I can't help thinking that something is bound to go wrong."

"What could possibly go wrong?"

"You could fall in love with me."

She bit her lip to hold in a laugh. "No offense, but I don't think we have to worry about that *ever* happening."

"Wow. I'm not sure if should feel relieved or insulted."

She shot him an exasperated look. Now he was just being obtuse. What man wouldn't jump at the chance for a night of no-strings-attached sex?

None she had ever known.

"What if once doesn't do the trick?" he asked.

"What if we have sex and we still feel this tension? Do we get to do it again?"

She couldn't really see that being a problem, not if they approached this logically. Not for her anyway. But for the sake of argument, she would humor him. "Let's just say that I'm open to the possibility."

"Fair enough."

"Well," she asked, anxious to settle this once and for all. "Are you in or out?"

He grinned. "What you're asking for would necessitate a bit of both, don't you think?"

She rolled her eyes. "Would you please be serious?"

He gave it a moment's thought, then said, "I'm trying to imagine a potential problem with this scenario, and honestly, I'm drawing a blank. No matter how I look at it, it's a win-win situation."

"So?"

He shrugged. "Yeah, sure, what the hell. I'm in."

"Splendid." It stunned her a little to realize what a huge weight this was off her shoulders. This was a *good* idea. A good plan. "Needless to say, we have to be discreet about this."

"Of course."

"*Especially* where Phillip is concerned."

"I agree." He rubbed his palms together and wiggled his brows at her. "So, Princess, when do we get started?"

She looked at her watch. "Tonight I have a charity function that I simply can't miss, and I won't be in until late this evening. Probably after midnight." To do this properly, she should at least be awake.

"Tomorrow, then?"

"Well, we'll be on the yacht with a full staff, so that won't work, then you have golf with Phillip and he mentioned taking you for dinner at the country club afterward. He's asked me to babysit Frederick until eleven."

He was beginning to look exasperated. "How about Thursday?"

"Thursday, you'll be at the hunting cabin and not back until Friday afternoon."

"And Friday is the black-tie charity deal, which I'm assuming will be another late one."

"At least midnight."

"How about Friday afternoon after we get back from the cabin?"

"Afternoons are difficult. Too many people around. Besides, I need a few hours to prepare for the evening."

"This is shaping up to be one stressful week, Your Highness."

He was right. This was a great idea, if they could just find the time to make it happen.

"You said you're watching Frederick until eleven tomorrow night?"

"That's right."

He grinned. "Eleven isn't too late. And I couldn't call myself a gentleman if I didn't offer to walk you home afterward."

That might work. "I suppose you couldn't."

"So, tomorrow at eleven?"

"Eleven it is." They could get this over and done with, then maybe they could actually enjoy each other's company for the remainder of his stay. And even better, they could walk away from this as friends.

In fact, the more she thought about it, the more convinced she was that this was exactly what they both needed.

She rose from the step, and he stood, too. "Now that we have that settled, I really need to get ready."

"You know, Princess, I think you're right. This is a good idea."

Of course it was. What man, especially one newly divorced and admittedly angry with all women, wouldn't see gratuitous sex as a good thing? And God knows that she hadn't been with a man in far too long. And contrary to what men seemed to think, women had needs, too. This would undoubtedly be a mutually beneficial arrangement.

Enough rationalizing, she told herself. She was doing the right thing.

"We'll leave for the yacht at nine," she told him. "So let's plan to meet in the foyer at our usual time."

"I'll be ready."

"The sun is quite intense this time of year, so make sure you bring sunscreen."

"Gotcha."

"Well then, I'll see you in the morning."

She turned toward the door, but he caught her forearm in his hand. "Hey, Princess."

She turned, and although she should have expected it, once again he caught her completely off guard. He cupped the back of her head, drew her to him and kissed her. But not a deep desperate joining like the last time. This was sweet and soft and maybe even a little tentative, his tongue barely sweeping the seam of her lips before he drew it back. Then he lingered for just another second or two before he finally pulled away.

"What was that for?" she asked, her words coming out soft and breathy. Her lips tingled and her legs were suddenly so wobbly that she almost had to sit back down.

He smiled and shrugged. "Consider it a sneak peek at what you have to look forward to tomorrow night."

He turned and started down the path toward the palace.

If that was what she had to look forward to, eleven o'clock tomorrow night couldn't come fast enough.

Sophie thought she had him. Thought she had gotten the best of him this time, but it was all part of the game.

He watched her until she reached her front door. She turned to flash him one last suggestive smile, then stepped inside and closed the door behind her.

He lingered for a moment, then turned and walked back to the palace. The dark clouds had blown over and the sun burned hot in the afternoon sky, but there was a cool breeze blowing in from the coast. A perfect afternoon for a walk. He needed the time to clear his head, get his priorities straight. Get himself back on track.

Sophie was good—he would give her that. For a second there, he had actually believed her seemingly heartfelt apology, had let himself think that she had changed. But that was the way women, especially women like her, operated. They said and did nothing without ulterior motives, every word and action carefully measured and executed to get exactly what they wanted.

That was why, when she'd first suggested they sleep together, he'd been convinced she was up to something. That she would lead him on briefly, then inevitably change her mind. But something in her eyes told him that wasn't the case. She wanted him. His seduction had been a success. And by making the first move, being the one to suggest they sleep together, she was operating under the delusion that she was the one in control, the one calling the shots.

And by the time she figured it out, it would be too late.

Eyes closed behind her darkest sunglasses, Sophie drifted in and out of consciousness, lulled by the gentle sway of the Irish Sea and the warm glow of the sun against her skin, hearing the occasional hum of a boat engine or the squawk of a gull. The spray of the wake against the hull.

Despite having been exhausted when she finally arrived home last night, sleep had evaded her. She had lain awake, her mind racing, the anticipation of her night with Alex teasing her like a gift under the tree at Christmastime. And he was one gift she couldn't wait to unwrap.

What would he feel like and how would he taste? Would it be as exciting as it had been ten years ago, or had youth been part of the magic back then? The element of danger?

Well, regardless of quality, she realized now that sleeping with Alex had been an inevitability. With her ingenious plan they would get it neatly out of the way and she would manage to retain complete control of the situation, which was really all she had wanted in the first place.

Speaking of Alex, she hadn't seen him in some time now. As soon as they'd boarded the boat, he had wandered off with the captain to get a look at the engine room. And because he seemed suitably amused, she had changed into her bathing suit, grabbed a deck chair and all but melted into it. Considering the current intensity of the sun, that had to have been at least two hours ago, but she was too relaxed to open her eyes, much less move a muscle to roll over and look through her bag for her watch.

The sun dipped behind a cloud and the gentle breeze cooled her sun-drenched skin. She waited patiently for the cloud to pass, but instead felt several drops of ice-cold liquid on her calves. Still mostly asleep, she crinkled her brow. Another series of drops landed on her left thigh, then a few more on her right.

The weather authority hadn't predicted rain for the rest of the week. And she found it awfully peculiar that this particular rain cloud had centered itself over her legs. Another icy splash hit her stomach and her eyes shot open. It wasn't a cloud blocking the sun—it was a person. A very tall person with wide shoulders.

With the sun behind him, his face was hidden in shadow, but there was only one man on board rude enough to wake her this way.

Alex stood over her chair, dipping his fingers in her iced tea and flicking it at her. "Wake up."

She groaned and closed her eyes. "Go away."

A few more icy drops hit her right arm.

"That is unbelievably juvenile," she mumbled.

"I'm bored."

She flung an arm across her face. "And how is that my problem?"

"You're my guide."

"I got you on the yacht—what more do you want?"

Freezing-cold tea landed with a sploosh on her stomach and she moved her arm to glare up at him. "*Stop* that!"

He was holding the glass over her, poised to dump the entire thing. She couldn't see his face, but she didn't doubt he was wearing the devilish grin that was becoming so familiar. In fact, he'd been wearing it this morning when they met in the foyer. He'd flashed her that smile, wiggled his brows at her and mouthed the words *you, me, eleven.*

As though she could forget.

"Is a little peace too much to ask for?" she asked.

"You've been out for almost three hours."

Three hours? Had it really been that long? She must have been more tired than she realized.

"Not that I haven't been enjoying the view," he said. There was a warm and sexy note to his voice and she had the distinct impression he wasn't talking about the landscape outside the yacht.

He shook the glass, rattling the ice. "You know I'll do it."

He probably would, and because it was obvious he wasn't going to go away, she had no choice but to humor him. "Fine. I'm awake."

He stepped out of the sun, and when she got a good look at him, her heart did a backflip with a triple twist.

When they'd met in the foyer he'd been wearing a polo shirt and canvas shorts. Now he was wearing a pair of Hawaiian-patterned swim trunks.

And nothing else.

Her blood instantly ran hot, pumping faster through her veins, and her eyes felt virtually glued to his body.

With his wet clothes sticking to him yesterday, she hadn't really gotten a good look at him. His chest was even more magnificent than she remembered. Strong and smooth, with just a dusting of hair on his pecks. And he had abs to die for. Well-defined and solid. She wondered absently how many hours a day he had to work to look this good, or if he just grew all these muscles naturally.

Come on, Soph, get a grip. So he wasn't wearing a shirt. Big deal. It was just a chest, for pity's sake. Nothing to lose her head over. It's not as if she'd never seen one before. Or this one in particular.

And she realized suddenly that she was openly staring. She swiftly peeled her gaze from his small, pink nipples and dragged her eyes upward, to his face, only to find that he was watching her watch him.

A quirky grin played at the corner of his mouth. "Something wrong?"

She blinked innocently. "Wrong?"

"You kind of zoned out there for a minute."

"I'm still half asleep," she snapped.

"You want to go for a swim? Wake up. *Cool off* a bit."

She glared at him. "Not particularly."

He shrugged, drawing her gaze to his strong, wide shoulders. They were looking a little pink. She peered over the top of her sunglasses and realized that they were more than a little pink. He was well on his way to a nasty-looking burn.

"Are you wearing sunblock?"

He shook his head. "Nope."

"How long have you had your shirt off?"

He shrugged. "A couple of hours, I guess. Why?"

If he was sunburned, he might not be able to… *perform* later. "I told you yesterday to wear sunblock. Let me guess—you didn't even bring any."

"I forgot."

She blew out an exasperated breath and sat up. She

had some in her bag, but it was only SPF 8, which would never suffice. "I'm sure there must be some belowdecks in the bedroom. Wait here. I'll go look."

She dragged herself up from the chair, adjusting her suit top. She could feel his eyes burning into her bare skin as she crossed the deck to the stairs. She wasn't wearing her skimpiest bikini; still, it didn't leave a heck of a lot to the imagination. She knew for a fact that he was getting quite an eyeful.

He could consider it—how did he phrase it?—as his own *sneak preview*. A glimpse of what he would be enjoying later tonight. And he would be enjoying it.

She didn't doubt that if Phillip were on board, he would cite anything more revealing than a modest one-piece inappropriate. But Phillip wasn't here. Besides, it felt good to be a little rebellious for a change.

She padded down the stairs and across the plush bedroom carpet to the private head. She found what she was looking for in the cabinet below the sink. SPF 30 lotion. Just to be safe.

She turned to leave, startled to find the bedroom door now closed, and Alex standing in front of it.

"Nice bedroom," he said, but he wasn't looking around the room. His eyes were glued to her body.

"What are you doing in here?" she said in a loud whisper. Was he trying to get them caught?

He started walking slowly toward her. "Helping you look for the sunblock."

"I already found it." She noticed that not only had

he closed the door, but he'd locked it, too. "Is this your idea of being discreet?"

"What do you expect? That bathing suit is… *wow*." He looked her up and down as he moved closer, devouring her with his eyes. "Look me in the eye and tell me you didn't wear it just to tease me."

That was exactly what she'd done. She just hadn't anticipated it being quite so effective. "We can't be in here together."

"Yet here we are," he said, moving closer still, and other than vaulting over the bed to get to the door, she had no way to escape. And she had never been terribly athletic.

"We said eleven tonight," she reminded him.

"Eleven tonight is the main course." A grin quirked up one corner of his mouth. "Consider this an appetizer."

And what a delicious treat he would be, but she really couldn't allow him to do this. Not here, where, for all she knew, Phillip had the employees spying on her. A skimpy bikini was one thing, but a tryst be-lowdecks with a client was pushing it. "I appreciate the thought, but it's really going to have to wait."

His eyes raked over her, dilated and intense, like an animal anticipating the kill. Then he reached out for her and the instant his fingers brushed her hip, when her skin tingled with awareness and her knees went weak, she knew it was pointless to try and fight it. She didn't *want* to fight it anymore. It felt too bloody good.

"Still want me to leave?"

"You have five minutes."

He reached for the opposite hip, cupping it in his palm, his skin so hot to the touch she nearly gasped. "This is going to take a lot longer than five minutes."

He pulled her to him, her breasts brushing against the solid, unyielding wall of his chest. Her nipples tingled and stiffened into two painfully erect, yearning buds.

He dipped his head and nuzzled the side of her throat, just below her ear, then he nipped her lobe lightly and the bottle she'd been holding slipped from her fingers and landed with a muffled thump on the carpet.

"You know," he said, his breath hot on her neck, his lips brushing her skin as he spoke, "you're even more beautiful than you were ten years ago."

"Coincidentally," she told him, her voice coming out breathy and soft, "so are you."

His hands slipped lower, sliding around to cup her behind. A purr of pleasure worked its way up from deep inside of her. She leaned into him, resting her face against his smooth cheek, savoring the sensations of skin against skin. It had been so long since someone—anyone—had touched her like this, so tenderly. Every second that passed felt like an eternity. She waited for his next move, for him to slip his hands inside her bikini bottoms. The thought of him touching her that way made her dizzy and light-headed, as though she would pass out from the anticipation of his next move.

Was this her idea of maintaining control of the situation? It was obvious that, right now anyway, Alex was calling the shots. And even worse, she didn't care.

She actually liked it, even though the concept went against everything she ever believed or was taught.

With barely more than gentle tug she was pressed against the length of Alex's body. His skin felt smooth and hot, and she could feel his heart thumping the wall of his chest.

"Still want me to stop?" he asked.

"I want you to kiss me."

A slow smile curled his lips. "I can do that."

He lowered his head nuzzled her cheek. His skin smelled warm and salty from the sea air and faintly of coconut.

Wait a minute. *Coconut?*

She leaned in and sniffed his shoulder. He *did*. He smelled like sunblock!

She looked up at him.

His brow furrowed. "What?"

She sniffed him again and asked, "Are you wearing sunblock?"

The smile went from sexy to devious in the blink of an eye. *"Maybe."*

"You are, aren't you? Why did you tell me you weren't?"

"What sane man would pass up the chance to have you rub sunblock all over him? Although I never imagined it would get us alone in the bedroom together. That was just dumb luck."

She gave him a playful shove. "You're a creep."

He just smiled. He was a creep, but an adorable one. "We need to get back up on deck before someone—"

There was a loud rap on the bedroom door and she nearly jumped out of her skin.

A voice called, "Lunch is served, Your Highness."

So much for not being caught in a compromising position. They had to have figured out by now that Alex was in there with her.

She called back, "I'll be up in a minute."

Alex exhaled an exasperated breath. "So much for an appetizer."

"I told you this wasn't the time." She pushed lightly against his chest and he let go of her.

"Maybe, but you weren't putting up much of a fight."

In all fairness, she hadn't been. In fact, her actions could have easily been interpreted as encouragement. "We should leave the room one at a time."

He folded his arms across his chest. "That won't look suspicious."

She straightened her bikini bottoms and checked her reflection in the mirror on the bedroom door. Her cheeks were flushed, but that could easily be explained away by her three-hour nap in the sun. "You have a better idea?"

It was obvious, by his lack of response, that he didn't.

"Besides, it looks as though you could use a min-

ute or two to—" she nodded at the recent and con-
spicuously tight fit of his swim trunks "—*cool off.*"

"I was thinking more along the lines of a cold
shower."

"Well, that's what you get for bending the rules,"
she said, crossing the room to the door.

"What rules are those?" he asked.

"The rules of nutrition."

A grin quirked up the corners of his lips. *"Nutrition."*

She opened the door and grinned back at him.
"No snacking between meals."

Nine

Alex had no time to be alone with Sophie after lunch, although not for lack of trying, but the staff always seemed to be around. Just before three they docked in the marina and were driven back to the palace. He barely had time to change before he and Phillip were off to the golf course.

Under normal circumstances Alex enjoyed golf, but today he was distracted. And even though they hadn't played together in years, Phillip noticed.

"Off your game today?" he said, when they got back to the clubhouse. "I remember you being slightly better at this."

"Normally I am. I'm a bit sunburned from sail-ing." It wasn't a total lie. His shoulders were a bit tender, despite the sunblock he'd put on not long after they'd left the marina—which Sophie would have known if she hadn't passed out in a deck chair the minute they boarded. And honestly, he doubted she was as scandalized as she wanted him to believe. She'd wanted him in that bedroom just as much as he wanted to be there.

And as much as he was enjoying all the teasing and foreplay, he was ready for the main event tonight. It seemed to be all he could think about, which was the real reason he'd shot such a pathetic nine holes today. But he couldn't exactly tell Phillip that.

"Would you like the palace physician to take a look at it?" Phillip asked.

"No, thanks. I'm sure I'll be fine by tomorrow."

They dropped off their gear and headed to the lounge to wait for Hannah. An attractive young waitress took their drink order, but Phillip barely seemed to notice her. He was polite, but distant. The complete opposite of the Phillip from college. Back then if he found a woman attractive, he wasn't shy about letting her know. Now it would seem that he had eyes only for his wife.

Alex wondered what it would be like to love someone so much that he didn't even look at other women. What Phillip and Hannah had must have been very special.

"You had a good time on the yacht today?" Phillip asked.

"I did." An exceptionally good time.

"I seem to recall you mentioned having a yacht, too."

"I used to. My ex got that in the divorce." She would have tried to get the family jewels if they weren't attached. And he wasn't talking about his grandmother's diamonds. "It was good to get back out on the water."

"How are you and Sophie getting on?"

"Good. Sophie is…" He struggled for the words to describe her. But all he could come up with was sexy and smart and stubborn as hell, but somehow he didn't think that was what Phillip would want to hear. So instead he said, "An excellent hostess."

If Phillip noticed the pause, he let it slide. "Sophie knows more of this island, of the country, than anyone."

"I have learned a lot the last few days."

"I'll bet you have," Phillip said, and Alex had the distinct impression he knew more than he was letting on. But Hannah walked in just then and they stood to greet her. From there they moved on to the royal family's private dining room. The waitress had just left with their food order when Phillip's cell phone rang.

He reached to answer and Hannah shot him a stern look.

He checked the display and said, "I know we have a no-phone rule at dinner, but I really need to take this."

"Fine." She waved him away with a grudging smile. "Go answer it."

He rose from his chair. "If you'll excuse me for a moment."

Hannah sighed and watched him walk away, phone to her ear. "That's what I get for marrying a king, I suppose." She turned to Alex, laying a hand on his forearm. "At least this will give us a moment to chat. Are you enjoying your stay with us?"

"Very much. It's exactly what I needed."

She gave his arm a sympathetic pat. "Phillip said it's been rough for you."

She was so sweet, so kind. There was something refreshingly...*simple* about her. Elegant and refined, yet amazingly down-to-earth. A stranger on the street would never guess she was royalty, and several years Phillip's junior, they might have a tough time buying that she was a wife and mother. Of course, there probably wasn't anyone in the country, in much of the world even, who wouldn't recognize Queen Hannah. She was regarded around the globe as a compassionate royal and tireless philanthropist.

"No divorce is ever fun," he said with a shrug. "I am glad it's over though."

"If you need anything at all you be sure to let us know." She gave his arm a quick squeeze, then drew her hand back. "Have you and Sophie had time to get reacquainted?"

He could swear there was a suggestive lilt to her tone. "Yes. She's very much like I remember her."

She sipped her water, peering at him over the rim of her glass, and asked, "Does she know how you feel about her?"

And here he thought he'd done a pretty good job of

hiding his feelings. Either he was far more transparent than he thought or Her Highness was quite perceptive. "What makes you think I have feelings for her?"

She shrugged. "Something about that first night at dinner. A subtle vibe I was getting."

The only vibe he'd been giving off then had been derision. Maybe she was mistaking contempt for attraction.

Maybe he was, too.

"Sophie may be tough on the outside," Hannah said, "but don't let her fool you. She has a soft center. But I have the feeling you already know that. In fact, I think you've known that for a very long time."

She obviously suspected they had some sort of history, but did she know just how personal?

"Me and Sophie," Alex said. "It's…complicated."

"Relationships usually are, Alex. Even more so when you're dealing with royalty."

Wasn't that the truth.

He wondered if Phillip had the same suspicions. If he and Hannah had discussed it. And if so, why hadn't he ever said anything to Alex?

Hannah seemed to read his mind. "Phillip doesn't know. At least, he's never said anything to me about it."

And considering the nature of Alex and Sophie's relationship, hopefully Phillip wouldn't figure it out. Even though this sexual liaison had been her idea, he doubted that argument would hold much water with Phillip.

"So, being newly divorced and all, I suppose your

relationship with Sophie will most likely be... *fleeting,*" Hannah said.

"I would imagine so." That was a polite and diplomatic way to say they were having an affair. And he wouldn't lie to her by denying it. It's not as if it had been his idea.

All right, maybe it had been. But his plan had been to seduce her against her will, not ask her permission. But either way, he was getting what he wanted. She may have thought she wouldn't fall in love with him, but she had no idea who she was dealing with.

Although he had to admit that this was feeling less and less like a plot for revenge and more like... Well, honestly, he wasn't sure *what* it felt like.

"That's a shame," Hannah said. "I get the feeling you two would be very good for each other."

There had been a time when he would have agreed with her. But this time he wouldn't be sticking around long enough to find out.

"I would imagine you'd prefer I didn't say anything to Phillip about this."

"I would never ask you to keep secrets from your husband," he said.

"But you would really appreciate it if I didn't. I don't tell Phillip every little thing. Besides, Sophie is one of my dearest friends, and if you hurt her, Phillip's wrath would pale in comparison to what I would do to you."

"I'll consider myself warned," he said.

She smiled. "Good."

Phillip reappeared at that moment and reclaimed his chair. "Good news! The meeting I had planned for first thing tomorrow has been cancelled."

Alex wasn't sure why that was such good news, and his confusion must have shown, because Phillip added, "No meeting in the morning means we can get an early start on our trip."

"Oh, great," he said, even though leaving earlier meant less time tonight with Sophie.

"In fact, I see no reason why we should wait until tomorrow," Phillip said. "The cabin is only an hour away. We should leave tonight."

Normally Sophie loved babysitting her nephew, but tonight she'd been edgy. She'd put him to bed at eight, and hadn't stopped pacing past the window, watching for Phillip and Hannah's car. By nine-thirty, when it pulled up the driveway, an hour and a half early, *thank God,* she'd practically worn a path in the carpet. She forced herself to take a seat on the sofa and crack open the book she'd brought with her. It seemed to take them forever to get up the stairs to their suite.

"How is my little angel?" Hannah asked the instant they were through the door.

"Sleeping," Sophie said, rising from her seat, expecting Alex to follow them inside. She waited, thinking maybe he was just a few steps behind, but Phillip closed the door behind him.

How was Alex going to offer to walk her home if he wasn't there?

"How was he?" Phillip asked.

"He?"

"Frederick."

"Oh, right. He was good. Perfect, as usual."

"I'm so glad," Hannah said. "He's cutting his bottom teeth, so I was afraid he might be cranky."

"How was dinner?" Sophie asked, when what she really wanted to know was where the heck was Alex?

"Pleasant," Phillip said, then he tagged her with a kiss on the cheek on his way to the bedroom. "I'm going to go pack."

Pack? "Are you going somewhere?"

Hannah dropped her purse on the coffee table and collapsed onto the sofa. "Phillip and Alex have decided to leave for the cabin tonight instead of waiting until morning."

They were leaving *tonight?*

No, no, no! They couldn't leave tonight. She and Alex had plans. They were going to have sex, dammit. "It's kind of late, isn't it?"

Hannah shrugged. "You know men and their insatiable desire to bear arms."

She bit the inside of her cheek so hard she drew blood. "You don't care that he's going to leave you and Frederick alone all night?"

"It's not a big deal. I'll probably just go straight to bed anyway. I'm exhausted."

There had to be a way to stop this. She had to talk

to Alex. "Well, if you don't need me for anything else, I'll be heading home."

"Sure, Sophie," Hannah said, her voice already heavy with sleep and her lids drooping. "Thanks so much for watching the munchkin."

"Tell my brother I said to have a good time."

She let herself out of their suite, then left the family residence, but rather than take the stairs down, she crossed to the guest wing and rapped on Alex's door.

He opened it, looking apologetic, and said, "I know you're probably upset."

She stepped inside and shut the door behind her. "You're going *tonight?*"

"This is so not my fault."

"Alex!"

"What was I supposed to do? He said he wanted to go early. What reason could I give him to wait until the morning?"

"You could have come up with *something*."

He looked at his watch. "I have to pack. I'm meeting him downstairs in fifteen minutes."

He walked to the bedroom and she followed him.

Fifteen minutes wasn't very long, but they could probably pull it off. But if they were only going to do this once, she didn't want to rush.

"By the way, Hannah knows," Alex said.

"Knows what?"

He stepped into the closet and pulled down a small travel case from the shelf. "About us."

"What?" Sophie stopped in her tracks. "What did you say to her?"

"Nothing." He tossed the case on the bed and began shoving clothes in it. "She approached me about it, said she picked up on a vibe that first night at dinner."

Oh, not good. "Did she say it in front of Phillip?"

He shook his head. "He was away from the table taking a call. She told me she wouldn't say anything to him. And she more or less threatened to do me bodily harm if I hurt you."

"*Hannah* did?"

"Yeah, it was weird. She seems so sweet and unassuming." He stepped into the bathroom and she followed him.

"Does she know the extent of it?"

"If she does, she came to that conclusion on her own. We didn't talk specifics." He gathered his toiletries and dropped them into a case. "Although we did determine that it's temporary."

"And she's not going to tell Phillip?"

"That's what she said."

That was good at least.

He zipped his case and brushed past her to the bedroom, and goodness did he smell good. Like fresh air and sunshine.

She followed him, watching as he stuffed the case into his bag and zipped it closed. It wasn't fair. This was supposed to be *their* night. This wouldn't be so bad if she had at least gotten to enjoy that appetizer this afternoon. Or who knows, maybe that would have been worse.

He checked his watch and grabbed the bag from the bed. "I have to go."

She didn't want him to go, but what could she do? Beg him not to leave? Implore him to fabricate some excuse to leave the following morning instead? She wouldn't give him the satisfaction of knowing just how important this had become to her. After all, she didn't want to give him false hope. Because if anyone was going to be doing any falling in love, it would most likely be him.

It had happened before.

"Well, have a good time shooting things," she said.

"I'll try to talk Phillip into coming home Thursday," he said.

"If you do, and I'm free, perhaps we can spend the evening together."

He grinned. "If you're free, huh?" Then he hooked his free arm around her waist, tugged her against him and planted a kiss on her that curled her toes and melted her bones. When he abruptly let go, she nearly sank to the floor. "Think about that while I'm gone, and tell me you won't be free."

She opened her mouth to reply, but by the time her brain cleared and she formulated a snappy comeback, he was already gone.

Ten

Alex had a good time at the hunting cabin. It was his and Phillip's first chance to really catch up and speak frankly about what they had been up to since college. And it made him realize how much he missed their friendship since they had drifted apart. Jonah would always be Alex's best friend, his brother, but it was a nice change to hang out with someone who didn't know him so well. Someone not so quick to judge Alex, but instead observe his life with an unbiased opinion.

But late Thursday evening Hannah called to say that Frederick had a fever, and even though the doctor said it was nothing to worry about, Phillip insisted on coming home.

"I hope you don't mind," Phillip said as they loaded their bags into the car.

"Of course not," Alex told him. "Family comes first."

"The physician said it could be a reaction to his teething, and there's nothing to be done, but I feel better if I'm there with them."

If Alex had kids, he was sure he would feel the same way. And had he and his ex produced children together, they would have been pawns in the divorce. One more weapon for her to use against him. And he didn't doubt that she would have. She'd had no problem lying to his family and twisting the truth. And even worse, they seemed to trust her over their own flesh and blood.

His ex spent years spinning her web of lies, and by the time he realized what she'd been up to, it was too late. She had everyone snowed.

And yes, he admitted to himself as he and Phillip climbed in the car, he had unfairly transferred some of that pent up animosity on to Sophie. If his only motivation for sleeping with her had been revenge, would he have missed her company this past day? And would her face be the first thing he wanted to see when they got back to the palace? Which seemed to take an immeasurably long time for some reason. The hour drive felt more like two, but his watch confirmed that it was indeed only ten forty-five.

He wondered if Sophie was *available*. Or if she might have already gone to bed.

When they walked inside, Hannah was in the foyer pacing, a sleeping Frederick sprawled limply in her arms.

"I just got him to sleep," she whispered as Phillip leaned in to kiss her. He pressed a cheek to his son's forehead. Checking for a temperature, Alex supposed. He recalled seeing his sister do that with his niece and nephew. It was a reminder of what a devoted family man Phillip had become. And for the first time, Alex wondered if he had missed out on something special by refusing to have children.

Not that he couldn't still have them with someone else.

"He still feels warm," Phillip whispered back, caressing his son's flushed cheek.

"Every time I try to lay him down he has a fit. My arms ache from carrying him all day."

"Give him to me and I'll try to lay him down."

She transferred Frederick into his arms.

It still struck Alex to see Phillip so settled. And content to be that way. "See you tomorrow," he told Alex, then carried the baby up the stairs.

"I'm sorry to make you come home early," Hannah told him. "I would have been fine alone for another night, but Phillip is very devoted to his son. More than most fathers I think, because his own parents were so absent from his life. He and Sophie were raised by nannies and housekeepers. I think it left deep scars in them both."

"Speaking of Sophie," he said, glancing at his watch, "do you think it's too late to call her?"

He didn't say why, and he hoped Hannah wouldn't ask.

"She's not home. She helped me with Fredrick for while, but when she heard Phillip was on his way home, she left. She said something about having a date."

A date? She knew for a fact that he was coming back to the palace, but rather than wait, she'd found someone else to occupy her time? Not that he cared either way.

And if he didn't care, why did he feel as though he'd just been kicked in the gut?

"I hope it was all right to tell you that. I mean…I don't want to cause any hurt feelings. But since what you and she have is casual, I just figured…" She shrugged.

"It's fine," Alex told her, because it should have been. He had no expectation of fidelity from a woman he wasn't technically seeing. "I just had a question about the fund-raiser tomorrow night."

"Do you have her cell number?" Hannah asked. "I'm sure you can reach her."

"It's not important. I can talk to her tomorrow."

"Well, I should get upstairs and help Phillip."

"I'll walk you up," he said.

They walked up together, then parted ways at the top of the stairs. She disappeared into the residence, and he walked to the guest wing. Once inside his room he fixed himself a drink and walked over to the window, looking out across the dark yard to Sophie's residence. The exterior was brightly lit, and several of the upstairs lights were burning. It looked as though she was home. It was possible she wasn't really on a date. She may have only told Hannah that to take the focus off her and Alex.

And if that was true, he should at least let her know that he was back.

He walked to the phone and dialed the number she'd left him on the itinerary. Wilson answered, and when Alex asked for Sophie, he was curtly informed him that the princess was out for the evening.

Alex thanked him and hung up, feeling like an ass for calling in the first place. And even more of an ass for caring where Sophie was or who she might be with. And the last thing he felt like doing was sitting around sulking about it.

He carried his drink to the bedroom and switched on the light beside the bed, and felt, for the second time that day, as if he'd been poleaxed. Lying on top of the covers, curled in a ball and sleeping soundly, was Sophie.

He had no idea what she was doing there when she was supposed to be out on a date, but he couldn't deny he was happy to see her. So happy that it was more than a little disconcerting. It wasn't supposed to feel this good. Just seeing her, knowing she was there.

By being here, she was in her own way telling him just how much she wanted to be with him. And he didn't think he would ever look at her quite the same way again. Or for that matter, himself.

He set down his drink and sat on the edge of the bed to take off his shoes and socks, then lay down and rolled on his side, facing her. She didn't budge. And although he wanted to wake her, he liked her this way. Quiet and vulnerable. And peaceful. For a few minutes he lay there just looking at her, memorizing her face, wondering what the hell he was doing. What he was getting himself into.

Just to see what she would do, he leaned closer and brushed his lips against her cheek, the tip of her nose. She wrinkled her nose and mumbled something in her sleep.

He brushed his lips against hers, whispered, "Wake up, Sleeping Beauty."

Her eyes fluttered open, hazy and unfocused at first, but when she saw him lying there, she smiled. "You're back."

"Boring date?"

She looked confused, then she laughed softly. "Oh, yeah. I just told Hannah that to throw her off. Then I sneaked in here to wait for you." She yawned and stretched out beside him. "I guess I was tired."

She was dressed in a pair of white cropped pants and a pink silk tank that rode up to expose a sliver of soft, deeply tanned stomach, and her hair was pulled back in a ponytail. She looked young and sassy. And completely irresistible. He reached up to brush a wisp of dark hair back from her face. Any excuse to touch her.

"So, here we are," she said.

"Here we are." And she had come to him.

She touched his face, stroking his cheek with her fingers. "I'm sorry that Frederick isn't feeling well. But the kid has great timing."

He wrapped an arm around her and tugged her against him. "How are we on time, by the way?"

She folded her arms around his neck, shifted closer, winding her legs around his. Her body felt long and soft, and warm from sleep. "You mean, when do I have to leave?"

"Exactly."

"Phillip and Hannah have no idea that I'm here, and I told Wilson that I would be staying at the palace tonight."

That was just the answer he was hoping for, because it was going to take the entire night to do all the things to her that he'd been imagining.

She burrowed closer, nuzzling her face against his neck. "Do you remember the first night I came to your room? The last time you stayed here? The way we just kissed and touched and talked all night and didn't make love until the sun was coming up?"

He slipped his hand under her top, stroking her back. "I remember."

She tunneled her fingers through his hair and nibbled on his throat, her breath hot on his skin. "I'd like to do that again."

"Except we're not making love," he reminded her. "We're having sex."

"There is that," she said, and smiled up at him, a look of pure mischief in her eyes. "And I could probably do without all the talking."

He brushed his lips against hers. "So that leaves kissing and touching."

"And sex. Although I'm not sure I want to wait all night for that." She arched against him, nipping his lower lip with her teeth.

He cupped her breast, trapping her nipple between his thumb and forefinger. It was high and firm and fit perfectly in his palm. "How's that?"

She gazed up at him, lids heavy with desire. "On second thought, why don't we just forget about that first night and make some new memories instead." Then she grabbed his head, pulled his face to hers and kissed him. Slow and deep and long. And she was already working on the buttons of his shirt, undressing him.

If they were only doing this once and they had all night, he'd be damned if he was going to let her rush him. He grabbed her wrists, tried to put her arms back up around his neck, but she wiggled free. "Slow down."

She was back at his buttons. "I don't want to slow down. I want you naked."

He made a move to grab her arm and she nipped at his hand. He yanked away, and didn't doubt for a second that she would have actually bitten him. Just for that, she wouldn't be seeing him naked for a very long time.

When she had his shirt unbuttoned and reached for his fly, he grabbed both of her wrists. He pinned her arms over her head and rolled on top of her, stilling her with his weight.

"That isn't fair," she said, struggling to free herself. But she wasn't struggling so hard that he thought she really wanted to get away. He could see that if he didn't let her know who was calling the shots, this night was going to be long, unending power struggle.

He grinned down at her. "No one ever said anything about playing fair."

He kissed her again, just as slow and deep as she'd kissed him, and it wasn't long before she stopped struggling, before she melted into the mattress beneath him. He let go of her arms and she wrapped them around his neck, digging her fingers through his hair, feeding off his mouth. She was even more fiery and passionate than he remembered.

He pulled her shirt up and over her head, and tossed it onto the floor. She was wearing a pink push-up bra constructed entirely of lace that left nothing to the imagination. Her nipples were small and dark and tightly puckered. He'd never seen anything so beautiful.

He lowered his head and nipped at one with his teeth. Sophie gasped and arched up against him. And when he tried to lift his head, she forced it back down again. And this time he decided he would humor her. He yanked one side of her bra down, baring her breast, and took her into his mouth. She moaned and arched up closer to his mouth, and because he liked the reaction he got, he did the same to the opposite side. He licked and nipped at her skin, until Sophie was writhing underneath him.

She tried to guide his mouth to hers, struggling for control again, so instead he slipped down her body, nuzzling his face against her rib cage and her stomach. He got up on his knees to unfasten her pants. She reached for him, trying to get to his zipper again, and he shot her a stern look. "Don't make me tie you down."

A sexy smile curled her mouth and her eyes were an inferno. "You say that like it's a bad thing."

Maybe later, but right now he had other things planned.

Instead she reached back to unsnap her bra and tossed it somewhere in the vicinity of her shirt. Her breasts were perfect. Small and firm but soft.

He leaned forward, gave each one another kiss, then worked his way lower, across her stomach as he eased her pants down her legs, until all that was left was one tiny scrap of pink lace that could barely pass for a pair of panties. And underneath it was nothing but bare, smooth, golden tan skin.

He nuzzled her stomach, just above the top edge of the lace. She let her head fall back against the pillow. She had the most amazing throat, long and slender and graceful. He kissed her through the lace, blowing hot air against her skin and she made a soft mewling sound deep in her throat. Her scent was light and fresh and feminine.

He hooked his thumbs under the edge of the waistband, sliding the lace down her legs and off her feet, and tossed it over his shoulder. Then he sat back on his heels and just looked at her.

She gazed up at him, her eyes glassy and confused. "What?"

"Nothing."

"Why are you staring at me like that?"

"I just want to look at you."

"Oh. Okay."

He sat there for a minute, taking in every inch of her perfect body. Her feet were small for a woman of her height and surprisingly petite, her ankles slender and delicate-looking. And damn, her legs were long. He couldn't wait to feel them locked around him.

He leaned forward, kissed the inside of one knee.

"Why am I the only one naked?" she asked.

"Because it's not my turn yet."

"Says who?"

"Me."

"Oh, I get it. You're shy and you're afraid to admit it."

He pressed his lips to the opposite knee. "If that didn't work on you, Princess, do you really think it would work on me?"

She looked only slightly defeated, like she'd known it was a long shot but had to try anyway. "I don't suppose you could drop the 'Princess' and 'Your Highness' thing, and just call me Sophie."

"I'll think about it…" He ran his tongue up her

inner thigh, making her shudder, then looked down at her and grinned. "...Your Highness."

She might have balked, were she not so turned on, but her body didn't lie. He could see how slick and ready she was for him. And God knows he was ready, too. It had been too damned long. Too long since he felt so connected to a woman. Since sex had been this...fun.

And he didn't want to rush things, but Sophie seemed to think he was taking things a bit too slow.

"Touch me, Alex," she said in a pleading voice, so he brushed her lightly with his fingers, where she was slippery and warm. She whimpered softly, biting her lip. He went one step further, sliding one finger inside her.

She sucked in a breath and her hips rocked up toward his hand, forcing him in deeper.

"You want more?"

"Yes," she hissed, her eyes bleary and unfocused, and he loved that he was making her feel good, that it was so damned easy.

He gave her one more, then a third, but he could see it still wasn't enough. He lowered his head and touched her with his tongue and was rewarded with a low, throaty moan. Then he took her in his mouth and she nearly vaulted off the bed. She tasted sweeter and more delicious than his favorite dessert, and was a hell of a lot more satisfying. Then he felt those amazing legs hooking over his shoulders, locking him in, as if he'd actually stop. It didn't get any better than this.

He kept his touch light, just a flick of his tongue or tug with his mouth, to make it last, because he didn't want it to be over too fast and it was obvious she was almost there already. Her fingers were tangled in his hair, her head thrown back and her eyes closed, her heels digging into his back.

Careful as he was though, he could feel her slipping, coming closer, then she tensed and arched up, crushing his head between her thighs. Her body coiled and locked, and a deep shudder rocked through her. But damn, he didn't want it to be over so soon. He wanted to see just how far he could take her. So instead of stopping, he increased the pressure of his mouth, of his tongue. She made a sound of protest and tried to push his head away, press her legs together, but he held her down. And after a minute of that, she was no longer pushing him away, and instead pulling him closer. Making soft, desperate, pleading sounds. And she shattered almost instantly.

He kissed his way up her stomach. Her skin was warm and flushed and he could feel her heart thumping, the blood rushing through her veins.

She sighed, sprawling limply across the comforter. "That felt *so* good."

He kissed and nipped his way upward, through the valley between her perfect breasts. To her throat and chin, and when he got to her face, he grinned down at her. "Lucky for you, Your Highness, I'm just getting warmed up."

Eleven

So much for his using her name. But she felt so damned good that right now, she didn't care what he called her. She was too limp to move, to even open her eyes. "That's never happened to me before."

"Which part?" Alex asked.

"The multiple part."

"Really?" There was a note of both disbelief and pride in his voice.

"As a rule, I try to limit my orgasms one at a time."

"Why is that?"

"It's never good to set the bar too high. You only end up disappointed." In fact, he had probably just ruined her for other men.

She was so relaxed and sated, she could lay there

like that for hours, but she realized, she was being terribly selfish. She had been *thoroughly* satisfied, and he hadn't even taken off his clothes yet.

She looped her arms around his neck and pulled him down for a kiss, and told him, "It's your turn to get undressed."

He grinned down at her. "Says who?"

"Me." Then she added firmly, "*Now.*"

Without argument he sat up and she sat up beside him, legs curled under her, to watch. He shrugged out of his shirt and dropped it beside the bed. He fished his wallet from his pants pocket and set it on the night table, then unfastened them and kicked them off. His boxers were the last to go, and when he slid them off, she sighed with satisfaction. She thought she'd recalled everything about him, but her memory didn't do him justice.

"Lie down," she said, pushing him onto his back. "It's my turn to look at you."

He'd been so determined to overpower her, she was a little surprised when he let her straddle his thighs, pinning him to the mattress. And for a moment she just let her eyes wander over him, taking it all in, burning it in her memory. So this time, after he was gone, she wouldn't forget. She would always remember that, no matter how short a period of time, just how good this had been.

His body was just so…perfect. So beautiful. More so because of the man on the inside. And just for tonight, he was all hers. Inside and out.

She was almost sorry it couldn't be longer, even though she knew it was better this way.

When simply looking at him wasn't enough, she put her hands on him, following the path her eyes had just taken. She touched his arms and his chest and his stomach. And when she'd made her way down to his erection, she paused for a moment, just looking, then she took him in her hand, squeezing gently. He sighed and shifted under her, his eyes slipped closed. His skin felt hot and smooth and alive with sensation.

"You're beautiful," she said. "Is it okay to call a man beautiful? I mean, I don't want to give you a complex."

"Keep touching me like that and you can call it anything you want."

She closed her hand around him and stroked, up the entire length of him, then back down again. "Like this?"

He answered her with a soft groan, gazing up at her through eyes half closed with arousal. There was nothing she loved more than experimenting with the male body, learning every trick and fetish. Exactly what to do to make him feel good. And for a while that's what she did. Touched and teased him, using her hands and mouth. But after a bit of that he caught her face between his hands and kissed her, then whispered in her ear, "As good as this feels, I really want to be inside you."

"You have protection, I hope." It would be a bloody shame if they came this far, only to have to stop.

"In my wallet," he said, nodding toward the table. She did love a man who came prepared. She grabbed his wallet and opened it. There was a thick wad of cash inside, and half a dozen credit cards. And a condom. Several in fact.

She recognized the packaging as American, meaning he'd brought them with him. Which didn't necessarily mean he'd been planning this. What single man in this day and age didn't carry prophylactics?

She plucked one out, then grabbed a second, just in case, and tossed his wallet back onto the table. She tore one of the wrappers open with her teeth and asked, "May I do the honors?"

He grinned up at her, a devilishly hungry smile. "Knock yourself out, Princess."

She rolled it on, *very* slowly, knowing by the look on his face that she was driving him crazy. Which was exactly the point of course. And when she was finished, he said, "Make love to me."

She didn't want him to know how real this was for her. How it felt like so much more than just sex. Just as it had ten years ago, when she still felt as though she had her entire life ahead of her.

He wrapped both hands around her hips, guiding her, and she lowered herself over him, slowly taking him inside her, savoring the sensation of being filled. She was still hot and slick and her muscles hugged him firmly as she rose up, then sank back down again.

Alex ran his hands up her sides to her breasts, cupping them in his palms, pinching her nipples lightly, making her shiver. He pulled her down so he could reach them with his mouth, flicking his tongue against the pebble hard peak of one nipple, then the other. Then he pulled her mouth to his and kissed her, one of those deep, soul-searching kisses that curled her toes and make her head spin. Then she realized, it wasn't just her head spinning. Alex was rolling her over without missing a beat or interrupting their rhythm, and the next thing she knew, she was on her back, pinned by his weight, and he was grinning down at her.

To hell with making love. She wanted this. She wanted it rough and desperate. And she could feel herself letting go, losing what little control she had left, arching against him, legs twined around his hips. Digging her nails into his back. Moaning and writhing. And she couldn't do a thing to stop it. She was a puppet and Alex pulled the strings.

She lost track of time after that, lost track of herself. Everything she smelled and felt and heard, every taste and touch, all melted together and became a blur. It built and climbed, higher and higher. And when she thought she couldn't stand it anymore, when it was unbearable, she went higher still.

Then Alex said her name. "Sophie, look at me."

The instant their eyes locked, she blew apart, taking him along with her. Her release welled up from a place deep inside her, grabbed hold and didn't let go.

Her body was still quaking with tiny aftershocks when Alex rolled over beside her. They were both breathing heavy, hearts thumping wildly.

"I don't know about you," Alex said, "but I'm not tense anymore."

Nope, she was as limp as a wet noodle. "I guess it worked."

"I guess."

And if they were to do this only once, they had certainly gone down in a blaze of glory. Only now, doing it just once wasn't sounding like such a hot idea anymore. The idea of touching him, making love to him again, had her heart beating faster.

Maybe instead of one time, they should limit it to one *night*. Since neither had anything better to do anyway.

She rolled on her side and curled up to him, draping one leg over both of his, playing with the soft hair on his chest. "Alex?"

"Hmm?"

"I have a problem."

He looked down at her, brow furrowed. "What kind of problem?"

"I'm feeling tense again."

The hint of a grin tipped up one corner of his mouth. "Well, then, Princess. We'll just have to do something about that.

At 5:00 a.m., before any of the family were up, and running on barely an hour of sleep, Sophie slipped out of Alex's bed, threw on her clothes and tiptoed down the stairs. She was only a dozen steps from the door and almost home free when Hannah walked out of the kitchen, Frederick awake and gurgling happily on her shoulder, and caught her red-handed sneaking out.

"My, you're up early," Hannah said, flashing Sophie a wry smile.

"You, too. The munchkin seems to be feeling better."

"His fever is gone and it looks as though his teeth are beginning to break through." She patted his back. "You know, you're lucky."

"Lucky?"

"Phillip usually does the morning feeding."

"Oh?"

"If you don't want him to know about you and Alex, you probably shouldn't spend the night."

Probably not. "Well, I should get home, then."

"I like Alex, Sophie. And I know you try to act tough, but I worry about you. That you'll get hurt."

It was early, and she'd had far too little sleep to listen to a lecture. Not to mention that she was a little worried herself. Something happened last night. Something…special. What was supposed to be just sex, felt like a heck of a lot more. To her at least. But what had Alex been thinking? And did she want to find out?

No way. They'd had one really good night together, and they would leave it at that, just as they had planned.

"There's really no need to worry," she told Hannah, then she gave both her and Frederick a kiss on the cheek. "I'll see you later tonight, at the ball."

"I just hope you know what you're doing," Hannah called after her.

So did she. She could not risk doing the one thing she swore she wouldn't.

Fall in love with him.

Alex watched Sophie from across the Royal Inn ballroom. She was dressed in a clingy, shimmering, floor-length gown suspended by two micro-thin spaghetti straps, and her hair was done up in a complicated-looking twist that showcased her long, graceful throat and narrow, deeply tanned shoulders. She glided from person to person, moving as eloquently as the orchestra that played in the background.

She managed to look elegant and refined, and sexy as hell at the same time.

Apparently she had been just what he needed, because he couldn't remember the last time he'd slept so soundly, when he hadn't woken with a dark cloud hanging over his head, a feeling of impending dread in his chest. He felt…at peace.

What he should have been feeling was some sort of satisfaction or triumph. He'd come here intending to seduce Sophie and he had. And even better, she had come to him. All he had to do now was leave her. And he knew he had her heart. He could see it in her eyes last night that she still loved him.

But there was a major kink in his plans. Now that he'd gotten to know her again, it was clear that she wasn't the woman he'd expected her to be. And the genius of his revenge plot now seemed petty and juvenile.

They had shared a car with Phillip and Hannah to the hotel, and Sophie did a damned fine job of pretending she and Alex hadn't spent the previous night in bed together. She was polite and as friendly as one might be with a colleague or business associate.

When they arrived at the Royal Inn, where the charity was being held, it was instantly clear to him the burden that the royal title could be for every member of the family. They were accosted by the press the instant they stepped from the car, then once inside, a flood of staff and guests monopolized them for what was going on two hours now.

Alex was content to sit at the bar and watch her. Every so often he would catch her eye and something would pass between them. A hungry look or a shared, secret smile, and he would know exactly what she was thinking. He couldn't escape the feeling that she was keeping her distance on purpose though.

"I don't believe we've met."

Alex turned to find a very attractive brunette sitting on the stool beside his. She wore a painted on, siren-red dress with a plunging neckline that she filled to capacity.

"Alexander Rutledge," he said, offering his hand.

"Madeline Grenaugh." Her handshake was soft and suggestive, and when she let go, she grazed his palm with nails that looked like blood-red claws. "You're an American."

"Guilty."

"East coast?" she asked.

"New York. You're good."

"Mr. Rutledge, you have no idea." She flashed him an overtly sensual smile. Man was she laying it on thick. Why not just drop a room key in front of him, or MapQuest directions to her house?

"What brings you to our fair country?" she asked.

"I'm a guest of the royal family, actually. I went to college with King Phillip."

"Then we have something in common. My family has been close friends with the royal family for years."

"Alex, there you are!"

He turned to see Sophie gliding toward him, her dress shimmering in the light of the chandeliers. The warm glow playing off all of those dips and curves he found so enticing.

"I'm sorry I haven't been much of a hostess," Sophie apologized, then glanced toward Madeline and with a polite smile said, "Oh, hello, Madeline, I didn't see you sitting there."

Alex had the feeling that Madeline was precisely the reason Sophie had taken the time to walk all the way across the room.

Madeline bowed her head and said, "Hello, Sophie."

She didn't address her by her title, which Alex suspected was an intentional slight. The tension they were giving off practically knocked him over.

"I see you've met our guest," Sophie said, laying a hand on Alex's arm. It was a territorial move. Her way of saying, *Back off, he's mine,* which was pretty funny coming from a woman who had made it very clear, on more than one occasion, that he *wasn't* hers.

"I have," Madeline said, reaching out to touch the hand he'd been resting on the bar, shooting him one of those inviting smiles. "We're finding that we have a lot in common. And I believe that he was just about to ask me to dance."

He was? And give her a chance to sink her claws in? Not in this lifetime. Sexy or not, the last thing he needed in his life was another manipulative female. Even if it was only for a five-minute twirl on the dance floor.

"I'm sorry, Madeline," he said, pulling his hand from under hers. "But I promised Princess Sophie the first dance." He rose from the bar stool. "It was nice to meet you, though."

If looks could kill. Her smile went from sizzling to arctic cold in the span of a heartbeat.

He offered Sophie his arm, and she slipped hers through it. Then she nodded and smiled to Madeline, twisting the knife. And obviously relishing it.

"You seemed to enjoy that," Alex said as he led her to the dance floor.

She put on her innocent face. "What do you mean?"

"Don't give me that. You looked as though you wanted to scratch each other's eyes out."

She cracked a smile. "Maybe I enjoyed it a little."

"You don't like her?"

"She's a vampire. And she's had her heart set on the

crown since we were children. She went after Phillip with a vengeance. When she realized that wasn't going to happen, she slept and manipulated her way through all of upper society. No intelligent man will go near her. She must have seen you and smelled fresh blood."

They stepped onto the dance floor, weaving through a throng of other formally dressed guests to an unoccupied spot in the center. He pulled her into his arms, and although he had expected her to put up at least a little resistance, she came willingly. A perfect fit against his arms, as though she belonged there.

Temporarily, of course.

"And I guess it had nothing to do with jealousy," he said.

She leveled her gaze on him. In heels, she stood nearly eye to eye. "And who would be the jealous one in this scenario?"

"You would."

She snorted indignantly. "You wish."

"I don't have to wish. I *know*. You were jealous."

She turned her nose up at him. "Your arrogance never ceases to amaze me."

He slid his hand from her waist, grazing the bare skin of her back with his fingertips, felt her shiver. With the slightest tug he drew her in just a little bit closer.

"Stop that!" she hissed. And even though her lips said no, her eyes were telling him to go for it.

He leaned forward, close to her ear, and whispered, "Admit it, Princess. You want me."

"I already *had* you," she whispered back.

"Yeah, but we both knew one night would never be enough." He nipped at the shell of her ear and a soft moan slipped from her lips. "Why fight it?"

"You're absolutely right, there must be an unoccupied closet around here somewhere. Or maybe we should just grab a room key and head upstairs."

He just grinned, because, joking or not, it might come to that. He stroked his thumb against her bare back. God, he wanted her. He wanted to put his hands on her. Peel that gown from her body and kiss every inch of her skin. "One more night, Princess. I'll make it worth your while."

"I fail to see how."

"Think multiples. Lots of them."

Her eyes warmed and a subtle grin curled the corners of her lips, and he knew she was his.

"I don't know about you, Your Highness, but I'm feeling *tense* again."

She tipped her head and gazed up at him through a curtain of dark lashes. "Are you really?"

"Yep."

"Well then, you know what that means." She glanced around to see if anyone was looking, then leaned forward, her lips brushing his ear, her breath hot on his skin, and whispered in a sultry voice. "You're going to have a really long night."

Twelve

Sophie hadn't been kidding when she said it would be a long night. And she'd made sure of it, by basically torturing him. Rubbing up against him on the dance floor when no one was looking, sliding her leg against his under the table during dinner or slipping her hand under the tablecloth to lay it on his thigh. And all with the rest of the family sitting at the table.

She was ruthless and she was good at it. By the time the second course was served he was so turned on he felt ready to crawl out of his own skin.

After dinner she excused herself to the ladies room and Alex headed straight to the bar for a drink. A strong one. With lots of ice that he may or may not dump down the front of his pants.

It was only eight, and according to Sophie they wouldn't be getting out of there any sooner than midnight. Possibly later. And then there was the problem of getting over to her residence unnoticed. Or maybe she would come to him again.

The bartender set his double scotch on the bar and Alex took a deep swallow.

"Can I have this dance?"

He turned to find Sophie standing behind him, that devilish look in her eyes.

"So you can torture me?"

She smiled. "You started it."

Yes, he had. And he was probably getting exactly what he deserved. And quite frankly loving the hell out of it. Not only was it sexually arousing, but he was having…fun. "Can you keep your hands to yourself? Miss We-Have-to-Be-Discreet."

She held out a hand to him. "I promise to behave."

He took her hand and let her lead him out to the dance floor. He seriously questioned her promise to behave, but if she had planned not to, she never got the chance. In the beginning of the first song, she slipped, and if he hadn't been holding on to her, she would have probably gone down hard on the dance floor. She let out a cry of pain, clutching his arms and holding one foot off the ground.

He steadied her, so she didn't fall over. "What happened?"

"My ankle. I think I twisted it."

"Are you all right?"

She winced and nodded. "I think so. My shoe fell off. Do you see it?"

He looked down and found it lying about a foot away. He leaned over and grabbed it for her, and saw immediately what had happened. The heel had partially snapped off. "It's broken."

"What?"

He handed it to her. "The heel busted."

Around them couples were beginning to stop and look and murmur words of sympathy. This had to be embarrassing for her, almost taking a dive on the dance floor. Not that he felt she had any reason to be embarrassed. Accidents happen. But Sophie liked to be in control, to be self-sufficient. This was the sort of thing that would really chap her pride.

"Can you put weight on it?" Alex asked, wanting to get her out of the crowd and back to the table before people started making a scene.

"I don't know." She put her foot flat on the floor and sucked in a surprised breath, her eyes welling with moisture. "Ouch."

That was a big *no.* "Let's get you back to the table."

She winced in pain. "I don't think I can walk."

He hadn't planned on making her walk, or hobble back on one foot. He scooped her up off her feet—or in this case, her *foot*—and into his arms. She gasped and looped her arms around his neck.

He carried her across the dance floor, the crowd parting like the Red Sea to allow them through. When

Hannah and Phillip saw them coming, they both flew to their feet.

"What happened?" Hannah rushed to Sophie's side as Alex set her down in her chair. "Are you okay?"

"I'm fine." She showed Hannah her shoe. "I twisted my ankle when my heel broke."

"Do you need a doctor?" Phillip asked.

Sophie rolled her eyes. "It's just twisted."

"It was probably that slippery dance floor," Hannah said. "I almost fell once, too."

"Then we should sue the owners for negligence," Sophie said. "Oh wait, that's *us*."

Hannah knelt down and examined the ankle, and when she touched it, Sophie winced. "It's swelling," she told Phillip. "She needs to ice this. And probably have the physician look at it to be on the safe side."

"I'll escort her home," Phillip said.

"Phillip, this is your benefit," Sophie told him. "You can't just *leave*. Get me to the car and I'll be fine alone."

"I'm not sending you home in a car alone."

If there was a better time to jump in, Alex couldn't think of one. "You stay," he told Phillip. "I'll see her home."

"Are you sure?" Phillip asked.

Oh, yeah, he was sure. Sophie would definitely be needing some pampering, and he was the man for the job. Not that he believed it would go any further than that with her being in obvious pain.

He was seeing a very long, cold shower in his immediate future.

"Should we call for a wheelchair?" Hannah asked, looking worried.

"I can carry her," Alex said.

Sophie shot him a wry smile. "Are you sure? I wouldn't want you to hurt yourself."

"I'll manage."

Hannah said something to one of the bodyguards, then turned back to them. "They're pulling up a car around back, so this doesn't become a press spectacle. Or we'll be reading in the papers tomorrow that she has a compound fracture or her leg was severed."

With no effort at all, Alex scooped Sophie out of the chair and followed Hannah, trailed by Phillip and two stoic bodyguards, out the back door and through the kitchen to the service entrance. As promised there was a car waiting just outside the door. As well as a small crowd of photographers. So much for avoiding the press.

Under a shower of flashes, Alex set Sophie on the seat in the back and got her settled in, then turned to Phillip and Hannah.

"Make sure she takes something for the swelling," Hannah said. "And see that she keeps the ankle elevated."

"Thanks for taking care of her, Alex," Phillip said, shaking his hand. "We'll try not to be too late."

"No need to rush. I'm sure she'll probably take something for the pain and go right to bed."

"Well then, we'll see you tomorrow when we leave for the yacht."

The bodyguards escorted them back inside and Alex climbed in beside Sophie. "Well, that was exciting."

"You know me. Never a dull moment." She removed the unbroken shoe and tossed it, along with the broken one, on the seat beside her, and told the driver. "To the palace."

"Don't you want to go back to your residence?"

"I think it's better if we go to your suite."

Was she suggesting that she still wanted to spend the night together?

She pulled the pins from her hair and it tumbled down across her shoulders in a dark and silky cascade, and he felt mesmerized watching her.

"I figured you would want to go right to bed," he said.

She flashed him a sexy smile. "Oh, I do."

"Your *own* bed," he said. "To rest."

She shrugged. "I'm not tired."

"What about your ankle?"

"What about it?"

What about it? "Doesn't it hurt?"

She twisted it back and forth a few times, then rotated it in a circle. Then she stomped it down hard on the car floor. "Well, would you look at that. It seems to be all better."

All better? Wait a minute… "Your Highness, were you *faking* it?"

"How else were we supposed to get out of there?"

"What did you do? Go in the ladies' room and break off your heel?"

She just smiled.

He should have known. He should have figured that a broken heel was too damned convenient. So much for her worrying about her pride.

He folded his arms across his chest. "That's devious, even for you."

"I've done worse, believe me. And I would have told you, but I needed it to be convincing." She laid her hand on his thigh, gazing up at him with wide, innocent eyes. "Are you angry with me?"

He eyed her sternly. "Very."

She gave him a pout. "Really?"

"Oh, yeah." He caught her behind the neck and kissed her, long and slow and deep, nipping her lip before he let go. "In fact, the minute we're alone, I plan to punish you severely."

If a punishment to Alex meant satisfying a woman until she was limp and defenseless, then he'd made good on his threat.

She lay in bed beside him, their arms and legs entwined, her head resting on his chest. And she knew already that any further *one-more-night* talk was just pointless. She wanted a hundred nights with Alex. A thousand even.

But she would settle for the little time he had left.

She stroked his chest, playing with the fine, silky hair. "Can I ask you a question?"

"I guess that depends on the question."

"What was your wife like?"

"Oh, *that* kind of question. And here I was having such a good time."

"Come on, Alex, she couldn't have been *that* bad."

"She was…" He struggled with it for a moment, then finally said, "Ambitious."

"She worked?"

"Oh, no. She was very content to spend my money. When I say ambitious, I'm talking socially. She was friends with the right people and chair of all the right clubs. She drove the right car and lived in the right neighborhood. She was even having an affair with her personal trainer. Talk about socially acceptable."

"I didn't know that. I'm sorry."

"I wasn't. That was a sobering moment for me. Learning my wife was cheating on me and not giving a damn."

Sobering and sad. "You didn't care at all?"

"I know it sounds odd. I kept waiting to feel rage or revulsion or even hurt. But the only thing I managed to feel was relieved. I felt as though I finally had an excuse to leave."

"Why did you need an excuse?"

"When I figure that out, I'll let you know."

She was so much better off not having married anyone. What a terrible way to live. Just like her parents, and probably their parents before them. And here she had believed that that only happened among the royal crowd.

Alex deserved better than that.

"It must have been lonely, being married to a woman you didn't love."

He shrugged. "We led very separate lives. Those last few months I hardly ever saw her and we barely spoke."

She rose up on her elbow, so she could see his face. "Did you ever cheat on her?"

The question seemed to surprise him. "I'm not going to lie and say I wasn't tempted, but my attorney firmly advised me to not give her any ammunition. I was faithful until we were legally separated."

Put in the same situation, she wasn't sure if she would have had the patience to be faithful. Of course, she would have never married a man she didn't love.

"You know," he said, reaching up to trace her lips with his finger. "I've always found your accent incredibly sexy."

She smiled. "Not to be obtuse, but in this country you're the one with the accent."

"You're beautiful." He cupped her cheek, searching her face. She closed her eyes and leaned into his hand.

"This feels good," she said. "You and me."

"It does. I imagine that while I'm working on the fitness center I'll be visiting here rather often."

She cuddled back down against his chest. "I imagine you will."

"It would give us the chance to spend more time together."

Her heart caught in her throat. She wanted that more than he could ever imagine. She felt good when she was with him. She felt…normal. He was the only man she'd ever known who really seemed to get her. Who didn't take any of her crap. And even more important, he didn't try to overpower or smother her. He respected her independence. And it was right then she realized that despite swearing it would never happen, she loved him.

What the bloody hell had she done?

"Casually?" she asked, heart in her throat.

"Of course. I don't think either of us is looking for a commitment."

The string of disappointment was sharp and stinging, but what did she expect?

She shook her head. "I've come to the conclusion that I'm just too independent to be tied down." At least, she tried to tell herself that. Alex would be an automatic safety net.

She couldn't get herself caught up with a man who didn't want to be caught.

Thirteen

Alex stepped out of the shower and toweled off, then walked into the bedroom to check the time. He was supposed to meet Sophie downstairs in ten minutes for a walk in the gardens, and if he didn't hurry, he was going to be late.

He would be flying home in two days, back to the U.S., to his new life, the freedom he'd been dreaming of since the day he'd said *I do*—when what he should have been saying was *hell, no*. So why was it that the thought of leaving Morgan Isle left him with a hollow feeling in his gut?

The thought of spending more time here, opening an office in the bay area, held far more appeal than going back to New York. With all the renovation projects available, he wouldn't be short on work. And taking the company international had been his father's goal. Not that Alex would be doing it for anyone but himself.

Leaving in two days meant something else, too. It was nearly time to end things with Sophie. As far as he could tell, he'd done a pretty thorough job of making her fall for him. All that was left to do was dump her and break her heart. It sounded simple enough, but whenever he considered it, it never seemed to be the right time. He wasn't even sure what he would do or say.

But he was sure that eventually an opportunity would present itself.

His cell phone rang and he grabbed it off the bed and checked the display. It was Jonah. He felt as though he hadn't talked with him in months, instead of days.

"Sorry I haven't been in touch," Jonah said. "Crazy week. I just wanted to let you know that we got through moving day."

Funny, but Alex had completely forgotten about that. A week ago he'd been dreading the very idea of it, and now it just didn't seem all that important. He felt…removed from his old life.

Alex put the phone on speaker and set it on the nightstand so he could get dressed. "Did she try to pull anything?"

"Nothing that we weren't prepared for."

"Meaning what?" he asked, tugging on his pants.

"She didn't take anything that wasn't hers. And even better, you never have to so much as talk to her again."

His family wouldn't be happy about that. They were still holding out the hope that he would change his mind and reconcile with her, despite how many times he'd told them that wasn't going to happen.

Up until then, everything he'd done, every decision he'd made had been with someone else's needs and desires above his own. From now on he was doing what *he* wanted to do. Whether he had his family's blessing or not.

"Sounds like you've been having quite the time over there," Jonah said.

"What do you mean?"

"You're a celebrity."

Celebrity? "I'm not following you."

He laughed. "You really don't know, do you?"

He grabbed his shirt and tugged it on. "Know what?"

"Photos of you carrying the wounded princess are all over the media here."

"Seriously?" He'd been too busy lately to turn on the television or pick up a newspaper.

"Everyone is speculating whether or not you'll be the newest addition to the royal family."

Fat chance. Although the speculation would make his inevitable betrayal sting that much more. Which should have been a source of great satisfaction.

"I guess I don't have to ask how the revenge plot is panning out for you. It looks as though you have her eating out of the palm of your hand."

"Just as I planned," Alex said. So why did the thought leave him feeling...*hollow?*

"Well then, you must be feeling pretty good about yourself."

He should have been. He was getting exactly what he wanted.

He heard a sound from behind him and turned to see Sophie standing in the bedroom doorway. And he could see from her expression that she'd been there awhile.

He'd been looking for the right time and here it had found him.

"Jonah, I have to call you back." He grabbed the phone and snapped it shut, and Sophie just stared at him, her expression unreadable. He kept waiting for the feeling of satisfaction to sink in. To feel vindicated. He knew he should say something—this was his *big moment*—but his mind had gone blank.

Not Sophie's. She was never at a loss for the appropriate words.

"Don't bother trying to deny it," she told him. He couldn't tell if she was angry or hurt. She just sounded...cold.

"I wasn't going to." Why wasn't he rubbing this in her face? Twisting the knife?

"I guess it explains this," she said, holding out the tabloid newspaper he hadn't even noticed in her hand. On the cover was a black-and-white photo of Alex gallantly carrying Sophie from the ballroom, and above it in ridiculously large, bold type screamed the headline The Princess Stole My Husband!

"You neglected to mention that you and your wife were planning to reconcile."

When hell froze over. More likely, it was his ex's way of trying to screw with his life. Little did she know that by spreading her lies, she was actually helping him. Or she would be if he would only stick to the program.

What the hell was wrong with him?

"You're not going to deny that, either?" she asked.

He shrugged. "If it's in the tabloid, it must be true."

She let the paper slip from her grasp. It fluttered and separated, landing in sections on the carpet between them. If she was angry, or upset, she wasn't letting it show. She would never give him the satisfaction.

"You've been an entertaining distraction," she said, nose in the air. "Just as you were ten years ago. Although back then, you served a bit more of a purpose."

He'd heard this one before. "Your ticket to freedom?"

"My ticket to culinary school. It was simple, really. I dump you, my parents let me go."

That shouldn't have stung, but it did. Maybe because deep down he had wanted to believe her when she said she'd loved him, and that she had ended it for his sake. All this time he'd been forcing himself to see her as spoiled, self-centered. And now that she was proving him right, living up to his expectations, it just felt...*wrong*. This wasn't the Sophie he knew. This arrogant, entitled persona was just a defense.

"What's the matter, Alex? You look troubled." Her words dripped with icy disdain. "Was this not the reaction you'd expected? I told you, it was just sex. It's tough to get revenge on someone who doesn't care." She flashed him a look of pity. "Oh, Alex, you didn't honestly think I'd fallen for you again?" She cocked her head to one side. "Or is it that you've fallen for me?"

He didn't believe in hitting below the belt, but what he said next just slipped out. A swift, decisive jab where he knew it would sting the most. "You once told me that your parents were so cold, they made you believe that you were unlovable."

She lifted her nose in the air. "So?"

"Well, Princess, they were right."

Her expression didn't waver, but all the color leached from her face. She stood there for another few seconds, just staring at him, then without another word turned and walked from the room. In that instant he knew he'd won.

Only problem was, he was no longer sure what he was fighting for.

Sophie walked briskly down the stairs, a wash of unshed tears blurring her vision. If Alex had reached into her chest and ripped out her heart, it couldn't have hurt more. She'd let her guard down and trusted him. She'd been foolish enough to believe that he cared about her, too. These past eleven days she had been happy. She'd felt complete. But it had all been an act. A plot.

And she would die before she let him know how much he had hurt her.

As her foot hit the bottom step, she heard clapping from behind her. She snapped around to see Phillip descending the stairs behind her.

"Bravo," he said, his hands coming together in slow, sharp snaps that made her want to cringe. "That was some performance back there."

He'd obviously been eavesdropping. She had hoped he wouldn't find out about her and Alex, but there was little point in denying it now. "Mind your own business, Phillip."

He stopped on the step above her. "You are my business."

Again, why deny it, or bother to argue? Because he was right. He was the head of the family, and as such he would always have his nose in her business. She would think after thirty years she'd have accepted that. Maybe it was time.

"Are you angry?" she asked.

"I should be, what with you sneaking in and out of the palace at all hours. And that ridiculous fake twisted ankle."

He knew about that? And here she thought she had everyone, including him, fooled. She obviously didn't give Phillip nearly enough credit.

"But why would I be angry," he continued, "after working so bloody hard to get you two back together?"

Get them *back* together. She was so stunned by

his words her mouth fell open. "You knew about me and Alex?"

"I'd have had to be blind not to. When I brought him home from university, you two couldn't keep your eyes off each other. Then there were all the shared smiles and sneaking around."

"I thought I had everyone fooled."

"After he went back to America you were inconsolable, and honestly, Sophie, you haven't been the same since. It was like something died inside you. You just...gave up."

He was right. She had given up. The part of her that was capable of love and companionship had just shut down. And since then, no matter what she did, she never felt satisfied. She'd been searching for...*something*. Be it more responsibility or more respect. But maybe what had really been missing all this time was Alex.

He was the only man she'd ever loved. Maybe the only one she *could* love. Even if he could never love her back.

"So all that stuff you said about this being business, and my behavior being inappropriate. What was that?"

"The most effective way to make you go after something is to tell you that you can't have it."

Oh, that stung. Probably because he was right. Knowing he disapproved had given her that extra little shove she needed to set things in motion. Had he pushed Alex on her, she might have—probably would have—shunned him on principle.

Honestly, how did he put up with her?

"So all this time you've been playing me?" she asked.

He just smiled.

"What about Hannah? Was she in on it, too?"

"Of course."

They'd all had her fooled. Here she thought she had been in total control, but it was all just an illusion. They had been pulling the strings.

She should have been furious, but honestly, she was tired of fighting it. Tired of pushing so hard against the people who loved her most. A life that had been good to her, despite her constant complaining and moaning that she needed more.

She shook her head. "I can't believe that all this time you knew, but you never said anything."

He shrugged. "You're so bloody stubborn, I figured what's the point."

"And now?"

"Now I'm going to help keep you from making the second biggest mistake of your life." He took her hands and squeezed them. "Not so long ago I almost let the love of my life slip away, and you didn't hesitate to give it to me straight. In fact, I believe your exact words were 'You're an idiot, Phillip.' Well, now I'm going to return the favor." He took her by the shoulders and said firmly, "Sophie, you're being an idiot. And if you don't do something, you're going to lose him again. Tell him how you feel."

"What does it matter? You heard him. He was just using me."

"Do you honestly believe that?"

She no longer knew what to believe.

He might have started out using her, but something had changed. *He* had changed. At least, she'd thought so.

And if that was true, why hadn't he told her that? Why didn't he tell her that he'd made a mistake?

Because he didn't think that he had. And even so, what difference did it make? He would never be happy here with her, stuck in the royal lifestyle. It might be good for a while, but he would grow tired of her. People always did. He would see that she really was difficult and temperamental, and he would bail.

Phillip cradled her chin in his hand. "Do you love him, Soph?"

She shrugged. "What difference does it make?"

"It might make a difference to him."

She wished she could believe that. That she could take the chance. But one more direct hit to her pride might be more than she could bear.

"Sometimes getting what you want means taking risks," he said. "You taught me that."

But what if she wasn't sure *what* she wanted?

She did something then that she hadn't done in ages. She wrapped her arms around her brother and hugged him fiercely. "Thank you."

He squeezed her hard, resting his head atop hers.

"I love you, Sophie. I know I don't say it enough, and maybe I don't always show it. But I do."

"I love you, too, Phillip." She gave him one last squeeze, then let go.

He studied her for a moment, then said, "You're not going to talk to him, are you?"

She shrugged. "It was good advice. It's just not who I am." In fact, she wasn't even sure who she was these days. She wasn't sure if she had ever known. All she did know was, charade or not, when she was with Alex, she was happy. And when he was gone, she wasn't. And despite that, it wasn't meant to be.

That pretty much said it all.

Phillip gave his head an exasperated shake. "And you call me stubborn."

"Do me a favor? Don't say anything to him about this. Don't even let on that you know. And please don't let this affect your relationship with him. Business or personal. Promise me."

He hesitated, then nodded. "I promise."

"Thank you."

She turned to leave, and he called after her. "Stubborn as you are, I hope Alex has the good sense to try to work this out."

Honestly, so did she. But she wasn't counting on it.

Fourteen

Sophie barely slept that night, and spent the entire next day indoors to avoid any chance encounters with Alex. All the while praying that he would show up on her doorstep, ready to profess his undying love for her. She was both praying for it and dreading it with all her heart. Because like before, she would have to tell him no.

But Sunday evening, just as dusk fell, she watched from her office window as the car pulled around to the back of the palace and his bags were loaded into the trunk for the trip to the airport. She knew then, without a doubt, that it was over.

She felt heartsick clear through to the marrow of her bones, but relieved, too. It was easier this way. At least, that was what she would keep telling herself.

"I see that he's leaving," Wilson said from behind her.

Thankful for the distraction, she turned away from the window. To see Alex climb into the car and watch it drive away, knowing it was her own fault, would be more than she could take right now. "I guess he is."

"Are you sure, Your Highness, that it's for the best?"

Oh, God, not him, too. She sighed deeply and rubbed at the ache that had begun to throb in her temples. Couldn't anyone stay out of her business? "Wilson, you don't even like him."

"Perhaps I was a bit hasty when I drew that conclusion. And regardless of how I feel about him, he makes you happy."

But for how long? How long would it be before he broke her heart again?

Besides, she didn't have the energy for another argument about her love life. "I'm going to take a shower, then crawl in bed and sleep for a month. It would be fabulous if you'd not disturb me."

One brow tipped up. "For a month?"

She shrugged. "At least a solid ten or twelve hours."

He nodded, then backed out of the room. "As you wish, Your Highness."

He disapproved. He would never say it, of course, but she could tell. Why couldn't everyone trust that she knew what she was doing?

Sophie locked herself in the bathroom, stripped to

the skin, turned the shower on as hot as she could stand and stood there until the water ran cold. It was meant to relax her, but as she stepped out and toweled off, she felt just as tense and miserable as before. It felt as if something was missing, as though someone had reached deep inside her, grabbed hold of whatever it was that made her a whole person and snatched it away.

It was a sensation she remembered all too well. The same thing she'd felt the first time Alex had walked out of her life.

But to be fair, he hadn't walked so much as been shoved.

She wrapped herself up in a towel and stepped into her bedroom. The sun had set and the room was dark, so she switched on the lamp beside her bed. And nearly jumped out of her own skin when she noticed the dark figure standing across the room by the window.

In the instant it took to realize it was Alex, her heart had bottomed out all the way to the balls of her feet, then slammed upward to catch in her throat.

He turned to her, looking…actually, she couldn't say for sure how he looked. His face was expressionless.

"I was beginning to think you were never coming out," he said. "I guess you royals have no concept of water conservation."

She clutched the towel to her chest. This was odd to the point of being surreal. "I'm sure you didn't come here to discuss the environment. In fact, I'm curious as to how you managed to get past Wilson."

He tucked his hands into the pockets of his slacks and took a step toward her. "Gunpoint. He's tied up in the pantry."

She shot him a disbelieving look.

"Okay," he admitted with a shrug. "He let me in."

She might have been in the shower a long time, but certainly not the ten to twelve uninterrupted hours she had requested. Meaning she and Wilson were going to have to have a talk about following instructions, and him keeping his nose out of her business.

She glanced at the clock on the bedside table. "You're going to miss your flight."

"I'm not going to miss my flight, because I'm not planning on leaving."

Surely he didn't mean to say that he was staying for her. She lifted her chin, giving him the coldest look she could manage, when on the inside she was falling to pieces.

"Aren't you going to ask me why?"

She was afraid to. And whatever the reason, it didn't really make a difference.

He sighed. "You're not going to make this easy, are you?"

She raised her chin another notch and struggled to keep her voice even. "What do you want from me, Alex?"

"I came here to apologize."

Her heart did a swift backward flip. "For?"

"For calling you unlovable. Because you're not." He took a step toward her. "Ask me how I know that." When she didn't say anything he said, "Go ahead, ask me."

"How do you know?"

"Because *I* love you." He stepped closer, until he was right in front of her, and it took everything in her not to launch herself into his arms. "And I'm not going to let you run away from me again.

"Ten years ago I should have come after you, but I let my pride get in the way. And that's a mistake I'm not going to make again."

He reached out, touched her face, and that was all it took. Her heart slammed the wall of her chest and her knees turned to mush. And when he tugged her to him, she melted into his arms. She buried her face against his shirt, breathed him in. Clinging as if she never wanted to let go.

How could something so wrong feel so…perfect?

"You used me," she reminded him.

"And you used me. But at this point, does it really matter?"

No, not really. She looked up at him, into his eyes. "I hurt you, Alex, and I never once said I was sorry. And I am. I'm so, so sorry."

He smiled. "You're forgiven."

She laid her head on his chest, felt his heart beating against her cheek. "What if it doesn't work?"

He held her tight, stroked her damp hair. "How will we know if we don't try?"

"I'm stubborn and incorrigible. I drive everyone crazy."

He cupped her chin and tipped her face up to his. "Yeah, but all the things you do that drive me crazy are the things I love most about you." He lowered his head and kissed her. A sweet brush of his lips that was filled with affection and love. "You're perfect just the way you are."

She had waited all her life to hear someone say that. And she believed that he meant it. "I love you, Alex. I've never loved anyone but you."

He grinned down at her. "I know."

She laughed. "And you call *me* self-centered."

"Well," he said with a shrug, "you can't say we don't have anything in common."

"You know that this relationship could be a logistical nightmare. Transcontinental dating?"

"Then I'll have to move here."

"Oh, Alex, I can't ask you to make a sacrifice like that."

"You didn't ask. And it's not a sacrifice. In fact, I've been considering it ever since I got here. And for the record, I have no interest in dating you."

She frowned. "You don't?"

"For ten years, deep down I've known you're the one for me. And with all that time to make up, I think we should skip the dating altogether, and move right on to living together."

"Where?"

"Here, the palace. It's up to you."

"I'm not sure how the family will take that. It wouldn't be considered proper."

He sighed. "All right, then I guess you'll just have to marry me instead."

She was so stunned, her jaw nearly fell out of joint. "But you just got *un*married."

"I was never really married to her. Not in my heart. Unless you don't *want* to marry me."

Despite everything she'd said in recent years about never tying herself down to one person, about not wanting to sacrifice her freedom, being with Alex forever was no sacrifice. In fact, she couldn't think of a more perfect way to spend the rest of her life.

She smiled up at him. "Why don't you ask me and find out?"

He actually dropped on one knee, right there on her bedroom carpet, and took her hand in his. "Sophia Renee Agustus Mead, would you do me the honor of becoming my wife?"

"Yes," she said, with more joy than she ever thought possible filling her heart. "I will."

He smiled up at her. "Well, it's about damn time."

* * * * *

A sneaky peek at next month…

By Request

BACK BY POPULAR DEMAND!

My wish list for next month's titles…

In stores from 20th June 2014:

❏ Hot Bed of Scandal – Anne Oliver, Kate Hardy & Robyn Grady

❏ Taming the Rebel Tycoon – Lee Wilkinson, Ally Blake & Crystal Green

In stores from 4th July 2014:

❏ The Dante Legacy: Blackmail – Day Leclaire

❏ The Baby Surprise – Jessica Hart, Barbara McMahon & Jackie Braun

3 stories in each book - only **£5.99!**

Available at WHSmith, Tesco, Asda, Eason, Amazon and Apple

Just can't wait?

Visit us Online

You can buy our books online a month before they hit the shops! **www.millsandboon.co.uk**

0614/05

Special Offers

Every month we put together collections and longer reads written by your favourite authors.

Here are some of next month's highlights— and don't miss our fabulous discount online!

On sale 20th June

On sale 4th July

On sale 4th July

Save 20%
on all Special Releases

Find out more at
www.millsandboon.co.uk/specialreleases

Visit us Online

0714/ST/MB477

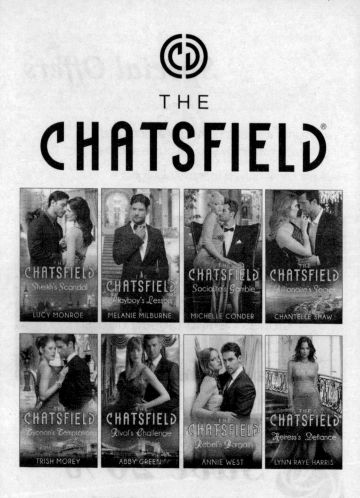

THE
CHATSFIELD®

Enter the intriguing online world of
The Chatsfield and discover secret
stories behind closed doors…

www.thechatsfield.com

Check in online now for your exclusive
welcome pack!

CHATSFIELD_WEB

Join our *EXCLUSIVE* eBook club

FROM JUST £1.99 A MONTH!

Never miss a book again with our hassle-free eBook subscription.

★ Pick how many titles you want from each series with our flexible subscription

★ Your titles are delivered to your device on the first of every month

★ Zero risk, zero obligation!

There really is nothing standing in the way of you and your favourite books!

**Start your eBook subscription today at
www.millsandboon.co.uk/subscribe**

Discover more romance at

www.millsandboon.co.uk

- ❤ WIN great prizes in our exclusive competitions
- ❤ BUY new titles before they hit the shops
- ❤ BROWSE new books and REVIEW your favourites
- ❤ SAVE on new books with the Mills & Boon® Bookclub™
- ❤ DISCOVER new authors

PLUS, to chat about your favourite reads, get the latest news and find special offers:

- 🔲 Find us on facebook.com/millsandboon
- 🐦 Follow us on twitter.com/millsandboonuk
- ❤ Sign up to our newsletter at millsandboon.co.uk

The World of Mills & Boon

There's a Mills & Boon® series that's perfect for you. There are ten different series to choose from and new titles every month, so whether you're looking for glamorous seduction, Regency rakes, homespun heroes or sizzling erotica, we'll give you plenty of inspiration for your next read.

By Request

Back by popular demand!
12 stories every month

Cherish™

Experience the ultimate rush of falling in love.
12 new stories every month

INTRIGUE...

A seductive combination of danger and desire...
7 new stories every month

Desire™

Passionate and dramatic love stories
6 new stories every month

nocturne™

An exhilarating underworld of dark desires
3 new stories every month

For exclusive member offers go to
millsandboon.co.uk/subscribe

Which series will you try next?

HEARTWARMING

Wholesome, heartfelt relationships
4 new stories every month
Only available online

Awaken the romance of the past…
6 new stories every month

Medical Romance

The ultimate in romantic medical drama
6 new stories every month

MODERN™

Power, passion and irresistible temptation
8 new stories every month

MODERN tempted™

True love and temptation!
4 new stories every month

You can also buy Mills & Boon® eBooks at
www.millsandboon.co.uk

Welcome to your new-look
By Request series!

RELIVE THE ROMANCE WITH
THE BEST OF THE BEST

This series features stories from your favourite
authors that are back by popular demand—
and, now with brand new covers, they
look even better than before!

See the new covers now at:
www.millsandboon.co.uk/byrequest